Tanis Half-Elven, leader of the companions. A skilled fighter who detests fighting, he is tormented by love for two women—the tempestuous swordswoman, Kitiara, and the enchanting elfmaiden, Laurana.

Sturm Brightblade, Knight of Solamnia. Once revered in the days before the cataclysm, the knights have since fallen into disgrace. Sturm's goal—more important to him than life itself—is to restore the honor of the knighthood.

Goldmoon, Chieftain's Daughter. Bearer of the blue crystal staff, her love for a tribal outcast, Riverwind, leads them both on a dangerous quest in search of the truth.

Riverwind, Grandson of Wanderer. Given the blue crystal staff in a city where death flew on black wings, he barely escaped with his life. And that was only the beginning. . . .

Raistlin, Caramon's twin brother, magic-user. Though his health is shattered, Raistlin possesses great powers beyond his young age. But dark mysteries are concealed behind his strange eyes.

Caramon, Raistlin's twin brother, warrior. A genial giant of a man, Caramon is the exact opposite of his twin. Raistlin in the one person he cares for—and the one person he fears.

Flint Fireforge, dwarf, fighter. Tanis's oldest friend, the ancient dwarf regards these youngsters as his "children."

Tasslehoff Burrfoot, kender, "handler." Kender—the nuisance race of Krynn—are immune to fear. Consequently, trouble just seems to follow them home.

THE EIGHT ARE GIVEN THE POWER TO SAVE THE WORLD. BUT FIRST THEY MUST LEARN TO UNDERSTAND THEMSELVES—AND EACH OTHER.

The Lands of Abanasinia

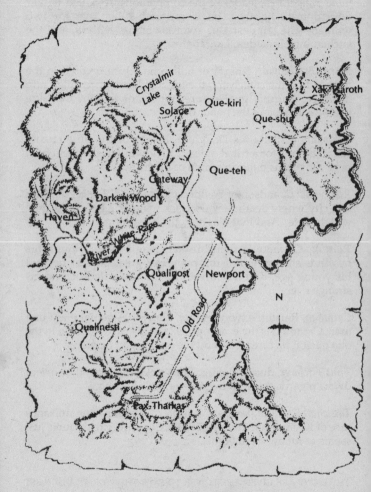

DRAGONLANCE®

CHRONICLES

VOLUME ONE

DRAGONS OF AUTUMNTWILIGHT

Margaret Weis and Tracy Hickman

Poetry by Michael Williams
Cover Art by Matt Stawicki
Interior Art by Valerie Valusek

To Laura, the true Laurana—Tracy Raye Hickman

To my children, David and Elizabeth Baldwin, for their
courage and support—Margaret Weis

DRAGONLANCE CHRONICLES
Volume one
DRAGONS OF AUTUMN TWILIGHT

©1984 Wizards of the Coast, Inc.
Cover Copyright ©2000 Wizards of the Coast, Inc.
All Rights Reserved.

Distributed in the United States by St. Martin's Press. Distributed in Canada by Fenn, Ltd.

Distributed to the hobby, toy, and comic trade in the United States and Canada by regional distributors.

Distributed worldwide by Wizards of the Coast, Inc. and regional distributors.

Cover art by Matt Stawicki
First Printing: April 1984
Library of Congress Catalog Card Number: 84-51122

9 8 7 6 5 4 3 2 1

ISBN: 0-7869-1574-9
T21574-620

U.S., CANADA,	EUROPEAN HEADQUARTERS
ASIA, PACIFIC, & LATIN AMERICA	Wizards of the Coast, Belgium
Wizards of the Coast, Inc.	P.B. 2031
P.O. Box 707	2600 BERCHEM
Renton, WA 98057-0707	Belgium
+1-800-324-6496	+32-70-23-32-77

Visit our web site at **www.wizards.com**

Canticle of the Dragon

Hear the sage as his song descends
like heaven's rain or tears,
and washes the years, the dust of the many stories
from the High Tale of the Dragonlance.
For in ages deep, past memory and word,
in the first blush of the world
when the three moons rose from the lap of the forest,
dragons, terrible and great,
made war on this world of Krynn.

Yet out of the darkness of dragons,
out of our cries for light
in the blank face of the black moon soaring,
a banked light flared in Solamnia,
a knight of truth and of power,
who called down the gods themselves
and forged the mighty Dragonlance, piercing the soul
of dragonkind, driving the shade of their wings
from the brightening shores of Krynn.

Thus Huma, Knight of Solamnia,
Lightbringer; First Lancer;
followed his light to the foot of the Khalkist Mountains,
to the stone feet of the gods,
to the crouched silence of their temple.
He called down the Lancemakers, he took on
their unspeakable power to crush the unspeakable evil,
to thrust the coiling darkness
back down the tunnel of the dragon's throat.

Paladine, the Great God of Good,
shone at the side of Huma,

1

strengthening the lance of his strong right arm,
and Huma, ablaze in a thousand moons,
banished the Queen of Darkness,
banished the swarm of her shrieking hosts
back to the senseless kingdom of death, where their curses
swooped upon nothing and nothing
deep below the brightening land.

Thus ended in thunder the Age of Dreams
and began the Age of Might,
When Istar, kingdom of light and truth, arose in the east,
where minarets of white and gold
spired to the sun and to the sun's glory,
announcing the passing of evil,
and Istar, who mothered and cradled
the long summers of good,
shone like a meteor
in the white skies of the just.

Yet in the fullness of sunlight
the Kingpriest of Istar saw shadows:
At night he saw the trees as things with daggers,
the streams
blackened and thickened under the silent moon.
He searched books for the paths of Huma,
for scrolls, signs, and spells
so that he, too, might summon the gods, might find
their aid in his holy aims,
might purge the world of sin.

Then came the time of dark and death
as the gods turned from the world.
A mountain of fire crashed like a comet through Istar,
the city split like a skull in the flames,
mountains burst from once-fertile valleys,
seas poured into the graves of mountains,
the deserts sighed on abandoned floors of the seas,
the highways of Krynn erupted
and became the paths of the dead.

Thus began the Age of Despair.
The roads were tangled.
The winds and the sandstorms dwelt in the husks of cities.
The plains and mountains became our home.
As the old gods lost their power,
we called to the blank sky
into the cold, dividing gray to the ears of new gods.
The sky is calm, silent, unmoving.
We have yet to hear their answer.

The Old Man

ika Waylan straightened her back with a sigh, flexing her shoulders to ease her cramped muscles. She tossed the soapy bar rag into the water pail and glanced around the empty room.

It was getting harder to keep up the old inn. There was a lot of love rubbed into the warm finish of the wood, but even love and tallow couldn't hide the cracks and splits in the well-used tables or prevent a customer from sitting on an occasional splinter. The Inn of the Last Home was not fancy, not like some she'd heard about in Haven. It was comfortable. The living tree in which it was built wrapped its ancient arms around it lovingly, while the walls and fixtures were crafted around the boughs of the tree with such care as to make it impossible to tell where nature's work left off and man's began. The bar seemed to ebb and flow like a polished wave around the living wood that supported it. The stained glass in the window panes cast welcoming flashes of vibrant color across the room.

Shadows were dwindling as noon approached. The Inn of the Last Home would soon be open for business. Tika looked around and smiled in satisfaction. The tables were clean and polished. All she had left to do was sweep the floor. She began to shove aside the heavy wooden benches, as Otik emerged from the kitchen, enveloped in fragrant steam.

"Should be another brisk day—for both the weather and business," he said, squeezing his stout body behind the bar. He began to set out mugs, whistling cheerfully.

"I'd like the business cooler and the weather warmer," said Tika, tugging at a bench. "I walked my feet off yesterday and got little thanks and less tips! Such a gloomy crowd! Everybody nervous, jumping at every sound. I dropped a mug last night and—I swear—Retark drew his sword!"

"Pah!" Otik snorted. "Retark's a Solace Seeker Guard. They're always nervous. You would be too if you had to work for Hederick, that faint—"

"Watch it," Tika warned.

Otik shrugged. "Unless the High Theocrat can fly now, he won't be listening to us. I'd hear his boots on the stairs before

4

he could hear me." But Tika noticed he lowered his voice as he continued. "The residents of Solace won't put up with much more, mark my words. People disappearing, being dragged off to who knows where. It's a sad time." He shook his head. Then he brightened. "But it's good for business."

"Until he closes us down," Tika said gloomily. She grabbed the broom and began sweeping briskly.

"Even theocrats need to fill their bellies and wash the fire and brimstone from their throats." Otik chuckled. "It must be thirsty work, haranguing people about the New Gods day in and day out—he's in here every night."

Tika stopped her sweeping and leaned against the bar.

"Otik," she said seriously, her voice subdued. "There's other talk, too—talk of war. Armies massing in the north. And there are these strange, hooded men in town, hanging around with the High Theocrat, asking questions."

Otik looked at the nineteen-year-old girl fondly, reached out, and patted her cheek. He'd been father to her, ever since her own had vanished so mysteriously. He tweaked her red curls.

"War. Pooh." He sniffed. "There's been talk of war ever since the Cataclysm. It's just talk, girl. Maybe the Theocrat makes it up just to keep people in line."

"I don't know," Tika frowned. "I—"

The door opened.

Both Tika and Otik started in alarm and turned to the door. They had not heard footsteps on the stairs, and that was uncanny! The Inn of the Last Home was built high in the branches of a mighty vallenwood tree, as was every other building in Solace, with the exception of the blacksmith shop. The townspeople had decided to take to the trees during the terror and chaos following the Cataclysm. And thus Solace became a tree town, one of the few truly beautiful wonders left on Krynn. Sturdy wooden bridge-walks connected the houses and businesses perched high above the ground where five hundred people went about their daily lives. The Inn of the Last Home was the largest building in Solace and stood forty feet off the ground. Stairs ran around the ancient vallenwood's gnarled trunk. As Otik had said, any visitor to the Inn would be heard approaching long before he was seen.

But neither Tika nor Otik had heard the old man.

He stood in the doorway, leaning on a worn oak staff, and peered around the Inn. The tattered hood of his plain, gray robe was drawn over his head, its shadow obscuring the features of his face except for his hawkish, shining eyes.

"Can I help you, Old One?" Tika asked the stranger, exchanging worried glances with Otik. Was this old man a Seeker spy?

"Eh?" The old man blinked. "You open?"

"Well . . ." Tika hesitated.

"Certainly," Otik said, smiling broadly. "Come in, Graybeard. Tika, find our guest a chair. He must be tired after that long climb."

"Climb?" Scratching his head, the old man glanced around the porch, then looked down to the ground below. "Oh, yes. Climb. A great many stairs . . ." He hobbled inside, then made a playful swipe at Tika with his staff. "Get along with your work, girl. I'm capable of finding my own chair."

Tika shrugged, reached for her broom, and began sweeping, keeping her eyes on the old man.

He stood in the center of the Inn, peering around as though confirming the location and position of each table and chair in the room. The common room was large and bean-shaped, wrapping around the trunk of the vallenwood. The tree's smaller limbs supported the floor and ceiling. He looked with particular interest at the fireplace, which stood about three-quarters of the way back into the room. The only stonework in the Inn, it was obviously crafted by dwarven hands to appear to be part of the tree, winding naturally through the branches above. A bin next to the side of the firepit was stacked high with cordwood and pine logs brought down from the high mountains. No resident of Solace would consider burning the wood of their own great trees. There was a back route out the kitchen; it was a forty-foot drop, but a few of Otik's customers found this setup very convenient. So did the old man.

He muttered satisfied comments to himself as his eyes went from one area to another. Then, to Tika's astonishment, he suddenly dropped his staff, hitched up the sleeves of his robes, and began rearranging the furniture!

Tika stopped sweeping and leaned on her broom. "What are you doing? That table's always been there!"

A long, narrow table stood in the center of the common room. The old man dragged it across the floor and shoved it up against the trunk of the huge vallenwood, right across from the firepit, then stepped back to admire his work.

"There," he grunted. "S'posed to be closer to the firepit. Now bring over two more chairs. Need six around here."

Tika turned to Otik. He seemed about to protest, but, at that moment, there was a flaring light from the kitchen. A scream from the cook indicated that the grease had caught fire again. Otik hurried toward the swinging kitchen doors.

"He's harmless," he puffed as he passed Tika. "Let him do what he wants—within reason. Maybe he's throwing a party."

Tika sighed and took two chairs over to the old man as requested. She set them where he indicated.

"Now," the old man said, glancing around sharply. "Bring two more chairs—comfortable ones, mind you—over here. Put them next to the firepit, in this shadowy corner."

" 'Tisn't shadowy," Tika protested. "It's sitting in full sunlight!"

"Ah"—the old man's eyes narrowed—"but it will be shadowy tonight, won't it? When the fire's lit . . ."

"I—I suppose so . . ." Tika faltered.

"Bring the chairs. That's a good girl. And I want one, right here." The old man gestured at a spot in front of the firepit. "For me."

"Are you giving a party, Old One?" Tika asked as she carried over the most comfortable, well-worn chair in the Inn.

"A party?" The thought seemed to strike the old man as funny. He chuckled. "Yes, girl. It will be a party such as the world of Krynn has not seen since before the Cataclysm! Be ready, Tika Waylan. Be ready!"

He patted her shoulder, tousled her hair, then turned and lowered himself, bones creaking, into the chair.

"A mug of ale," he ordered.

Tika went to pour the ale. It wasn't until she had brought the old man his drink and gone back to her sweeping that she stopped, wondering how he knew her name.

BOOK 1

I

Old Friends Meet.
A Rude Interruption.

lint Fireforge collapsed on a moss-covered boulder. His old dwarven bones had supported him long enough and were unwilling to continue without complaint.

"I should never have left." Flint grumbled, looking down into the valley below. He spoke aloud, though there was no sign of another living person about. Long years of solitary wandering had forced the dwarf into the habit of talking to himself. He slapped both hands on his knees. "And I'll be damned if I'm ever leaving again!" he announced vehemently.

Warmed by the afternoon sun, the boulder felt comfortable to the ancient dwarf, who had been walking all day in the chill autumn air. Flint relaxed and let the warmth seep into his bones—the warmth of the sun and the warmth of his thoughts. Because he was home.

He looked around him, his eyes lingering fondly over the familiar landscape. The mountainside below him formed one side of a high mountain bowl carpeted in autumn splendor. The vallenwood trees in the valley were ablaze in the season's colors, the brilliant reds and golds fading into the purple of the Kharolis peaks beyond. The flawless, azure sky among the trees was repeated in the waters of Crystalmir Lake. Thin columns of smoke curled among the treetops, the only sign of the presence of Solace. A soft, spreading haze blanketed the vale with the sweet aroma of home fires burning.

As Flint sat and rested, he pulled a block of wood and a gleaming dagger from his pack, his hands moving without conscious thought. Since time uncounted, his people had always had the need to shape the shapeless to their liking. He himself had been a metalsmith of some renown before his retirement some years earlier. He put the knife to the wood, then, his attention caught, Flint's hands remained idle as he watched the smoke drift up from the hidden chimneys below.

"My own home fire's gone out," Flint said softly. He shook himself, angry at feeling sentimental, and began slicing at the wood with a vengeance. He grumbled loudly, "My house has been sitting empty. Roof probably leaked, ruined the furniture. Stupid quest. Silliest thing I ever did. After one hundred and forty-eight years, I ought to have learned!"

"You'll never learn, dwarf," a distant voice answered him. "Not if you live to be *two* hundred and forty-eight!"

Dropping the wood, the dwarf's hand moved with calm assurance from the dagger to the handle of his axe as he peered down the path. The voice sounded familiar, the first familiar voice he'd heard in a long time. But he couldn't place it.

Flint squinted into the setting sun. He thought he saw the figure of a man striding up the path. Standing, Flint drew back into the shadow of a tall pine to see better. The man's walk was marked by an easy grace—an elvish grace, Flint would have said; yet the man's body had the thickness and tight muscles of a human, while the facial hair was definitely humankind's. All the dwarf could see of the man's face beneath a green hood was tan skin and a brownish-red beard. A longbow was slung over one shoulder and a sword hung at his left side. He was dressed in soft leather, carefully tooled in the intricate designs the elves loved. But no elf in the world of Krynn could grow a beard . . . no elf, but . . .

"Tanis?" said Flint hesitantly as the man neared.

"The same." The newcomer's bearded face split in a wide grin. He held open his arms and, before the dwarf could stop him, engulfed Flint in a hug that lifted him off the ground. The dwarf clasped his old friend close for a brief instant, then, re-membering his dignity, squirmed and freed himself from the half-elf's embrace.

"Well, you've learned no manners in five years," the dwarf grumbled. "Still no respect for my age or my station. Hoisting me around like a sack of potatoes." Flint peered down the road. "I hope no one who knows us saw us."

"I doubt there are many who'd remember us," Tanis said, his eyes studying his stocky friend fondly. "Time doesn't pass for you and me, old dwarf, as it does for humans. Five years is a long time for them, a few moments for us." Then he smiled. "You haven't changed."

"The same can't be said of others." Flint sat back down on the stone and began to carve once more. He scowled up at Tanis. "Why the beard? You were ugly enough."

Tanis scratched his chin. "I have been in lands that were not friendly to those of elven blood. The beard—a gift from my human father," he said with bitter irony, "did much to hide my heritage."

Flint grunted. He knew that wasn't the complete truth. Al-though the half-elf abhorred killing, Tanis would not be one to hide from a fight behind a beard. Wood chips flew.

"I have been in lands that were not friendly to anyone of any kind of blood." Flint turned the wood in his hand, exam-ining it. "But we're home now. All that's behind us."

"Not from what I've heard," Tanis said, drawing his hood up over his face again to keep the sun out of his eyes. "The Highseekers in Haven appointed a man named Hederick to govern as High Theocrat in Solace, and he's turned the town into a hotbed of fanaticism with his new religion."

Tanis and the dwarf both turned and looked down into the quiet valley. Lights began to wink on, making the homes in the trees visible among the vallenwood. The night air was still and calm and sweet, tinged with the smell of wood smoke from the home fires. Now and again they could hear the faint sound of a mother calling her children to dinner.

"I've heard of no evil in Solace," Flint said quietly.

"Religious persecution . . . inquisitions . . ." Tanis's voice sounded ominous coming from the depths of his hood. It was deeper, more somber than Flint remembered. The dwarf frowned. His friend had changed in five years. And elves never change! But then Tanis was only half-elven, a child of violence, his mother having been raped by a human warrior during one of the many wars that had divided the different races of Krynn in the chaotic years following the Cataclysm.

"Inquisitions! That's only for those who defy the new High Theocrat, according to rumor." Flint snorted. "I don't believe in the Seeker gods—never did—but I don't parade my beliefs in the street. Keep quiet and they'll let you alone, that's my motto. The Highseekers in Haven are still wise and virtuous men. It's just this one rotten apple in Solace that's spoiling the whole barrel. By the way, did you find what you sought?"

"Some sign of the ancient, true gods?" Tanis asked. "Or peace of mind? I went seeking both. Which did you mean?"

"Well, I assume one would go with the other," Flint growled. He turned the piece of wood in his hands, still not satisfied with its proportions. "Are we going to stand here all night, smelling the cooking fires? Or are we going to go into town and get some dinner?"

"Go." Tanis waved. The two started down the path together, Tanis's long strides forcing the dwarf to take two steps to his one. Though it had been many years since they had journeyed together, Tanis unconsciously slowed his pace, while Flint unconsciously quickened his.

"So you found nothing?" Flint pursued.

"Nothing," Tanis replied. "As we discovered long ago, the only clerics and priests in this world serve false gods. I heard tales of healing, but it was all trickery and magic. Fortunately, our friend Raistlin taught me what to watch—"

"Raistlin!" Flint puffed. "That pasty-faced, skinny magician. He's more than half charlatan himself. Always sniveling and whining and poking his nose where it doesn't belong. If it weren't for his twin brother looking after him, someone would've put an end to his magic long ago."

13

Tanis was glad his beard hid his smile. "I think the young man was a better magician than you give him credit for," he said. "And, you must admit, he worked long and tirelessly to help those who were taken in by the fake clerics—as I did." He sighed.

"For which you got little thanks, no doubt," the dwarf muttered.

"Very little," Tanis said. "People want to believe in something—even if, deep inside, they know it is false. But what of you? How was your journey to your homelands?"

Flint stumped along without answering, his face grim. Finally he muttered, "I should never have gone," and glanced up at Tanis, his eyes, barely visible through the thick, overhanging, white eyebrows—informing the half-elf that this turn of the conversation was not welcome. Tanis saw the look but asked his questions anyhow.

"What of the dwarven clerics? The stories we heard?"

"Not true. The clerics vanished three hundred years ago during the Cataclysm. So say the elders."

"Much like the elves," Tanis mused.

"I saw—"

"Hsst!" Tanis held out a warning hand.

Flint came to a dead stop. "What?" he whispered.

Tanis motioned. "Over in that grove."

Flint peered toward the trees, at the same time reaching for the battle-axe that was strapped behind his back.

The red rays of the setting sun glistened briefly on a piece of metal flashing among the trees. Tanis saw it once, lost it, then saw it again. At that moment, though, the sun sank, leaving the sky glowing a rich violet, and causing night's shadows to creep through the forest trees.

Flint squinted into the gloom. "I don't see anything."

"I did," Tanis said. He kept staring at the place where he'd seen the metal, and gradually his elvensight began to detect the warm red aura cast by all living beings but visible only to the elves. "Who goes there?" Tanis called.

The only answer for long moments was an eerie sound that made the hair rise on the half-elf's neck. It was a hollow, whirring sound that started out low, then grew higher and higher and eventually attained a high-pitched, screaming whine. Soaring with it, came a voice.

14

"Elven wanderer, turn from your course and leave the dwarf behind. We are the spirits of those poor souls Flint Fireforge left on the barroom floor. Did we die in combat?"

The spirit voice soared to new heights, as did the whining, whirring sound accompanying it.

"No! We died of shame, cursed by the ghost of the grape for not being able to outdrink a hill dwarf."

Flint's beard was quivering with rage, and Tanis, bursting out laughing, was forced to grab the angry dwarf's shoulder to keep him from charging headlong into the brush.

"Damn the eyes of the elves!" The spectral voice turned merry. "And damn the beards of the dwarves!"

"Wouldn't you know it?" Flint groaned. "Tasslehoff Burrfoot!"

There was a faint rustle in the underbrush, then a small figure stood on the path. It was a kender, one of a race of people considered by many on Krynn to be as much a nuisance as mosquitoes. Small-boned, the kender rarely grew over four feet tall. This particular kender was about Flint's height, but his slight build and perpetually childlike face made him seem smaller. He wore bright blue leggings that stood out in sharp contrast to his furred vest and plain, homespun tunic. His brown eyes glinted with mischief and fun; his smile seemed to reach to the tips of his pointed ears. He dipped his head in a mock bow, allowing a long tassel of brown hair—his pride and joy—to flip forward over his nose. Then he straightened up, laughing. The metallic gleam Tanis's quick eyes had spotted came from the buckle of one of the numerous packs strapped around his shoulders and waist.

Tas grinned up at them, leaning on his hoopak staff. It was this staff that had created the eerie noise. Tanis should have recognized it at once, having seen the kender scare off many would-be attackers by whirling his staff in the air, producing that screaming whine. A kender invention, the hoopak's bottom end was copper-clad and sharply pointed; the top end was forked and held a leather sling. The staff itself was made out of a single piece of supple willow wood. Although scorned by every other race on Krynn, the hoopak was more than a useful tool or weapon to a kender—it was his symbol. "New roads demand a hoopak," was a popular saying among kenderkind. It was always followed immediately by another of their sayings: "No road is ever old."

Tasslehoff suddenly ran forward, his arms open wide.

"Flint!" The kender threw his arms around the dwarf and hugged him. Flint, embarrassed, returned the embrace reluctantly, then quickly stepped back. Tasslehoff grinned, then looked up at the half-elf.

"Who's this?" He gasped. "Tanis! I didn't recognize you with a beard!" He held out his short arms.

"No, thanks," said Tanis, grinning. He waved the kender away. "I want to keep my money pouch."

With a sudden look of alarm, Flint felt under his tunic. "You rascal!" He roared and leaped at the kender, who was doubled over, laughing. The two went down in the dust.

Tanis, chuckling, started to pull Flint off the kender. Then he stopped and turned in alarm. Too late, he heard the silvery jingle of harness and bridle and the whinny of a horse. The half-elf put his hand on the hilt of his sword, but he had already lost any advantage he might have gained through alertness.

Swearing under his breath, Tanis could do nothing but stand and stare at the figure emerging from the shadows. It was seated on a small, furry-legged pony that walked with its head down as if it were ashamed of its rider. Gray, mottled skin sagged into folds about the rider's face. Two pig-pink eyes stared out at them from beneath a military-looking helmet. Its fat, flabby body leaked out between pieces of flashy, pretentious armor.

A peculiar odor hit Tanis, and he wrinkled his nose in disgust. "Hobgoblin!" his brain registered. He loosened his sword and kicked at Flint, but at that moment the dwarf gave a tremendous sneeze and sat up on the kender.

"Horse!" said Flint, sneezing again.

"Behind you," Tanis replied quietly.

Flint, hearing the warning note in his friend's voice, scrambled to his feet. Tasslehoff quickly did the same.

The hobgoblin sat astride the pony, watching them with a sneering, supercilious look on his flat face. His pink eyes reflected the last lingering traces of sunlight.

"You see, boys," the hobgoblin stated, speaking the Common

16

tongue with a thick accent, "what fools we are dealing with here in Solace."

There was gritty laughter from the trees behind the hobgoblin. Five goblin guards, dressed in crude uniforms, came out on foot. They took up positions on either side of their leader's horse.

"Now . . ." The hobgoblin leaned over his saddle. Tanis watched with a kind of horrible fascination as the creature's huge belly completely engulfed the pommel. "I am Fewmaster Toede, leader of the forces that are keeping Solace protected from undesirable elements. You have no right to be walking in the city limits after dark. You are under arrest." Fewmaster Toede leaned down to speak to a goblin near him. "Bring me the blue crystal staff, if you find it on them," he said in the croaking goblin tongue. Tanis, Flint, and Tasslehoff all looked at each other questioningly. Each of them could speak some goblin, Tas better than the others. Had they heard right? A blue crystal staff?

"If they resist," added Fewmaster Toede, switching back to Common for grand effect, "kill them."

With that, he yanked on the reins, flicked his mount with a riding crop, and galloped off down the path toward town.

"Goblins! In Solace! This new Theocrat has much to answer for!" Flint spat. Reaching up, he swung his battle-axe from its holder on his back and planted his feet firmly on the path, rocking back and forth until he felt himself balanced. "Very well," he announced. "Come on."

"I advise you to retreat," Tanis said, throwing his cloak over one shoulder and drawing his sword. "We have had a long journey. We are hungry and tired and late for a meeting with friends we have not seen in a long time. We have no intention of being arrested."

"Or of being killed," added Tasslehoff. He had drawn no weapon but stood staring at the goblins with interest.

A bit taken aback, the goblins glanced at each other nervously. One cast a baleful look down the road where his leader had vanished. The goblins were accustomed to bullying peddlers and farmers traveling to the small town, not to challenging armed and obviously skilled fighters. But their hatred of the other races of Krynn was long-standing. They drew their long, curved blades.

Flint strode forward, his hands getting a firm grip on the axe handle. "There's only one creature I hate worse than a gully dwarf," he muttered, "and that's a goblin!"

The goblin dove at Flint, hoping to knock him down. Flint swung his axe with deadly accuracy and timing. A goblin head rolled into the dust, the body crashing to the ground.

"What are you slime doing in Solace?" Tanis asked, meeting the clumsy stab of another goblin skillfully. Their swords crossed and held for a moment, then Tanis shoved the goblin backward. "Do you work for the High Theocrat?"

"Theocrat? "The goblin gurgled with laughter. Swinging its weapon wildly, it ran at Tanis. "That fool? Our Fewmaster works for the—ugh!" The creature impaled itself on Tanis's sword. It groaned, then slid off onto the ground.

"Damn!" Tanis swore and stared at the dead goblin in frustration. "The clumsy idiot! I didn't want to kill it, just find out who hired it."

"You'll find out who hired us, sooner than you'd like!" snarled another goblin, rushing at the distracted half-elf. Tanis turned quickly and disarmed the creature. He kicked it in its stomach and the goblin crumpled over.

Another goblin sprang at Flint before the dwarf had time to recover from his lethal swing. He staggered backward, trying to regain his balance.

Then Tasslehoff's shrill voice rang out. "These scum will fight for anyone, Tanis. Throw them some dog meat once in a while and they're yours forev—"

"Dog meat!" The goblin croaked and turned from Flint in a rage. "How about kender meat, you little squeaker!" The goblin flapped toward the apparently unarmed kender, its purplish red hands grasping for his neck. Tas, without ever losing the innocent, childlike expression on his face, reached into his fleecy vest, whipped out a dagger, and threw it—all in one motion. The goblin clutched his chest and fell with a groan. There was a sound of flapping feet as the remaining goblin fled. The battle was over.

Tanis sheathed his sword, grimacing in disgust at the stinking bodies; the smell reminded him of rotting fish. Flint wiped black goblin blood from his axe blade. Tas stared mournfully at the body of the goblin he killed. It had fallen facedown, his dagger buried underneath.

"I'll get it for you," Tanis offered, preparing to roll the body over.

"No." Tas made a face. "I don't want it back. You can never get rid of the smell, you know."

Tanis nodded. Flint fastened his axe in its carrier again, and the three continued on down the path.

The lights of Solace grew brighter as darkness deepened. The smell of the wood smoke on the chill night air brought thoughts of food and warmth—and safety. The companions hurried their steps. They did not speak for a long time, each hearing Flint's words echo in his mind: Goblins. In Solace.

Finally, however, the irrepressible kender giggled.

"Besides," he said, "that dagger was Flint's!"

2

Return to the Inn.
A shock. The oath is broken.

early everyone in Solace managed to drop into the
Inn of the Last Home sometime during the evening
hours these days. People felt safer in crowds.

Solace had long been a crossroads for travelers. They came
northeast from Haven, the Seeker capital. They came from the
elven kingdom of Qualinesti to the south. Sometimes they
came from the east, across the barren Plains of Abanasinia.
Throughout the civilized world, the Inn of the Last Home was
known as a traveler's refuge and center for news. It was to the
Inn that the three friends turned their steps.

The huge, convoluted trunk rose through the surrounding
trees. Against the shadow of the vallenwood, the colored panes
of the Inn's stained-glass windows glittered brightly, and
sounds of life drifted down from the windows. Lanterns, hanging from the tree limbs, lit the winding stairway. Though the

autumn night was settling chill amid the vallenwoods of Solace, the travelers felt the companionship and memories warm the soul and wash away the aches and sorrows of the road.

The Inn was so crowded on this night that the three were continually forced to stand aside on the stairs to let men, women, and children pass them. Tanis noticed that people glanced at him and his companions with suspicion—not with the welcoming looks they would have given five years ago.

Tanis's face grew grim. This was not the homecoming he had dreamed about. Never in the fifty years he had lived in Solace had he felt such tension. The rumors he had heard about the malignant corruption of the Seekers must be true.

Five years ago, the men calling themselves "seekers" ("we seek the new gods") had been a loose-knit organization of clerics practicing their new religion in the towns of Haven, Solace, and Gateway. These clerics had been misguided, Tanis believed, but at least they had been honest and sincere. In the intervening years, however, the clerics had gained more and more status as their religion flourished. Soon they became concerned not so much with glory in the afterlife as with power on Krynn. They took over the governing of the towns with the people's blessing.

A touch on Tanis's arm interrupted his thoughts. He turned and saw Flint silently pointing below. Looking down, Tanis saw guards marching past, walking in parties of four. Armed to the teeth, they strutted with an air of self-importance.

"At least they're human—not goblin," Tas said.

"That goblin sneered when I mentioned the High Theocrat," Tanis mused. "As if they were working for someone else. I wonder what's going on."

"Maybe our friends will know," Flint said.

"If they're here," Tasslehoff added. "A lot could have happened in five years."

"They'll be here—if they're alive," Flint added in an undertone. "It was a sacred oath we took—to meet again after five years had passed and report what we had found out about the evil spreading in the world. To think we should come home and find evil on our very doorsteps!"

"Hush! Shhh!" Several passersby looked so alarmed at the dwarf's words that Tanis shook his head.

"Better not talk about it here," the half-elf advised.

Reaching the top of the stairs, Tas flung the door open wide. A wave of light, noise, heat, and the familiar smell of Otik's spicy potatoes hit them full in the face. It engulfed them and washed over them soothingly. Otik, standing behind the bar as they always remembered him, hadn't changed, except maybe to grow stouter. The Inn didn't appear to have changed either, except to grow more comfortable.

Tasslehoff, his quick kender eyes sweeping the crowd, gave a yell and pointed across the room. Something else hadn't changed either—the firelight gleaming on a brightly polished, winged dragon helm.

"Who is it?" asked Flint, straining to see.

"Caramon," Tanis replied.

"Then Raistlin'll be here, too," Flint said without a great deal of warmth in his voice.

Tasslehoff was already sliding through the muttering knots of people, his small, lithe body barely noticed by those he passed. Tanis hoped fervently the kender wasn't "acquiring" any objects from the Inn's customers. Not that he stole things—Tasslehoff would have been deeply hurt if anyone had accused him of theft. But the kender had an insatiable curiosity, and various interesting items belonging to other people had a way of falling into Tas's possession. The last thing Tanis wanted tonight was trouble. He made a mental note to have a private word with the kender.

The half-elf and the dwarf made their way through the crowd with less ease than their little friend. Nearly every chair was taken, every table filled. Those who could not find room to sit down were standing, talking in low voices. People looked at Tanis and Flint darkly, suspiciously, or curiously. No one greeted Flint, although there were several who had been long-standing customers of the dwarven metalsmith. The people of Solace had their own problems, and it was apparent that Tanis and Flint were now considered outsiders.

A roar sounded from across the room, from the table where the dragon helm lay reflecting light from the firepit. Tanis's grim face relaxed into a smile as he saw the giant Caramon lift little Tas off the floor in a bear hug.

Flint, wading through a sea of belt buckles, could only

imagine the sight as he listened to Caramon's booming voice answering Tasslehoff's piping greeting. "Caramon better look to his purse," Flint grumbled. "Or count his teeth."

The dwarf and the half-elf finally broke through the press of people in front of the long bar. The table where Caramon sat was shoved back against the tree trunk. In fact, it was sitting in an odd position. Tanis wondered why Otik had moved it when everything else remained exactly the same. But the thought was crushed out of him, for it was his turn to receive the big warrior's affectionate greeting. Tanis hastily removed the longbow and quiver of arrows from his back before Caramon hugged them into kindling.

"My friend!" Caramon's eyes were wet. He seemed about to say more but was overcome by emotion. Tanis was also momentarily unable to talk, but this was because he'd had his breath squeezed out of him by Caramon's muscular arms.

"Where's Raistlin?" he asked when he could talk. The twins were never far apart.

"There." Caramon nodded toward the end of the table. Then he frowned. "He's changed," the warrior warned Tanis.

The half-elf looked into a corner formed by an irregularity of the vallenwood tree. The corner was shrouded in shadow, and for a moment he couldn't see anything after the glare of the firelight. Then he saw a slight figure sitting huddled in red robes, even in the heat of the nearby fire. The figure had a hood cast over its face.

Tanis felt a sudden reluctance to speak to the young mage alone, but Tasslehoff had flitted away to find the barmaid and Flint was being lifted off his feet by Caramon. Tanis moved to the end of the table.

"Raistlin?" he said, feeling a strange sense of foreboding.

The robed figure looked up. "Tanis?" the man whispered as he slowly pulled the hood off his head.

The half-elf sucked in his breath and fell back a pace. He stared in horror.

The face that turned toward him from the shadows was a face out of a nightmare. Changed, Caramon had said! Tanis shuddered. "Changed" wasn't the word! The mage's white skin had turned a golden color. It glistened in the firelight with a faintly metallic quality, looking like a gruesome mask.

23

The flesh had melted from the face, leaving the cheekbones outlined in dreadful shadows. The lips were pulled tight in a dark straight line. But it was the man's eyes that arrested Tanis and held him pinned in their terrible gaze. For the eyes were no longer the eyes of any living human Tanis had ever seen. The black pupils were now the shape of hourglasses! The pale blue irises Tanis remembered now glittered gold!

"I see my appearance startles you," Raistlin whispered. There was a faint suggestion of a smile on his thin lips.

Sitting down across from the young man, Tanis swallowed. "In the name of the true gods, Raistlin—"

Flint plopped into a seat next to Tanis. "I've been hoisted into the air more times today than—*Reorx!*" Flint's eyes widened. "What evil's at work here? Are you cursed?" The dwarf gasped, staring at Raistlin.

Caramon took a seat next to his brother. He picked up his mug of ale and glanced at Raistlin. "Will you tell them, Raist?" he said in a low voice.

"Yes," Raistlin said, drawing the word out into a hiss that made Tanis shiver. The young man spoke in a soft, wheezing voice, barely above a whisper, as if it were all he could do to force the words out of his body. His long, nervous hands, which were the same golden color as his face, toyed absently with uneaten food on a plate before him.

"Do you remember when we parted five years ago?" Raistlin began. "My brother and I planned a journey so secret I could not even tell you, my dear friends, where we were going."

There was a faint note of sarcasm in the gentle voice. Tanis bit his lip. Raistlin had never, in his entire life, had any "dear friends."

"I had been selected by Par-Salian, the head of my order, to take the Test," Raistlin continued.

"The Test!" Tanis repeated, stunned. "But you were too young. What, twenty? The Test is given only to mages who have studied years and years—"

"You can imagine my pride," Raistlin said coldly, irritated at the interruption—"My brother and I traveled to the secret place, the fabled Towers of High Sorcery. And there I passed the Test." The mage's voice sank. "And there I nearly died!"

Caramon choked, obviously in the grip of some strong emotion. "It was awful," the big man began, his voice shaking. "I found him in that horrible place, blood flowing from his mouth, dying! I picked him up and—"

"Enough, brother!" Raistlin's soft voice flicked like a whip. Caramon flinched. Tanis saw the young mage's golden eyes narrow, the thin hands clench. Caramon fell silent and gulped down his ale, glancing nervously at his brother. There was clearly a new strain, a tension between the twins.

Raistlin drew a deep breath and continued. "When I awoke," the mage said, "my skin had turned this color—a mark of my suffering. My body and my health are irretrievably shattered. And my eyes! I see through hourglass pupils and therefore I see time, as it affects all things. Even as I look at you now, Tanis," the mage whispered, "I see you dying, slowly, by inches. And so I see every living thing."

Raistlin's thin, clawlike hand gripped Tanis's arm. The half-elf shivered at the cold touch and started to pull away, but the golden eyes and the cold hand held him fast.

The mage leaned forward, his eyes glowing feverishly. "But I have power now!" he whispered. "Par-Salian told me the day would come when my strength would shape the world! I have power and"—he gestured—"the Staff of Magius."

Tanis looked to see a staff leaning against the vallenwood trunk within easy reach of Raistlin's hand. It was a plain wooden staff. A ball of bright crystal, clutched in a disembodied golden claw carved to resemble the talon of a dragon, gleamed at the top.

"Was it worth it?" Tanis asked quietly.

Raistlin stared at him, then his lips parted in a caricature of a grin. He withdrew his hand from Tanis's arm and folded his arms in the sleeves of his robe. "Of course!" the mage hissed. "Power is what I have long sought—and still seek." He leaned back and his thin figure melted into the dark shadow until all Tanis could see were the golden eyes, glittering in the firelight.

"Ale," said Flint, clearing his throat and licking his lips as if he would wash a bad taste out of his mouth. "Where is that kender? I suppose he stole the barmaid—"

"Here we are," cried Tas's cheerful voice. A tall, young, red-haired girl loomed behind him, carrying a tray of mugs.

Caramon grinned. "Now, Tanis," he boomed, "guess who this is. You, too, Flint. If you win, I'll buy this round."

Glad to take his mind off Raistlin's dark tale, Tanis stared at the laughing girl. Red hair curled around her face, her green eyes danced with fun, freckles were lightly smattered across her nose and cheeks. Tanis seemed to remember the eyes, but beyond that he was blank.

"I give up," he said. "But then, to elves humans seem to change so rapidly that we lose track. I am one hundred and two, yet seem no more than thirty to you. And to me those hundred years seem as thirty. This young woman must have been a child when we left."

"I was fourteen." The girl laughed and set the tray down on the table. "And Caramon used to say I was so ugly my father would have to pay someone to marry me."

"Tika!" Flint slammed his fist on the table. "You're buying, you great oaf!" He pointed at Caramon.

"No fair!" The giant laughed. "She gave you a clue."

"Well, the years have proved him wrong," Tanis said, smiling. "I've traveled many roads and you're one of the prettiest girls I've seen on Krynn."

Tika blushed with pleasure. Then her face darkened. "By the way, Tanis"—she reached in her pocket and drew forth a cylindrical object—"this arrived for you today. Under strange circumstances."

Tanis frowned and reached for the object. It was a small scrollcase made of black, highly polished wood. He slowly removed a thin piece of parchment and unrolled it. His heart thudded painfully at the sight of the bold, black handwriting.

"It's from Kitiara," he said finally, knowing his voice sounded strained and unnatural. "She's not coming."

There was a moment's silence. "That's done it," Flint said. "The circle is broken, the oath denied. Bad luck." He shook his head. "Bad luck."

3

Knight of Solamnia.
The old man's party.

Raistlin leaned forward. He and Caramon exchanged glances as thoughts passed wordlessly between them. It was a rare moment, for only great personal difficulty or danger ever made the twins' close kinship apparent. Kitiara was their older half-sister.

"Kitiara would not break her oath unless another, stronger oath bound her." Raistlin spoke their thoughts aloud.

"What does she say?" Caramon asked.

Tanis hesitated, then licked his dry lips. "Her duties with her new lord keep her busy. She sends her regrets and best wishes to all of us and her love—" Tanis felt his throat constrict. He coughed. "Her love to her brothers and to—" He paused, then rolled up the parchment. "That's all."

"Love to who?" Tasslehoff asked brightly. "Ouch!" He glared at Flint who had trod upon his foot. The kender saw

Tanis flush. "Oh," he said, feeling stupid.

"Do you know who she means?" Tanis asked the brothers. "What new lord does she talk about?"

"Who knows with Kitiara?" Raistlin shrugged his thin shoulders. "The last time we saw her was here, in the Inn, five years ago. She was going north with Sturm. We have not heard from her since. As for the new lord, I'd say we now know why she broke her oath to us: she has sworn allegiance to another. She is, after all, a mercenary."

"Yes," Tanis admitted. He slipped the scroll back into its case and looked up at Tika. "You say this arrived under strange circumstances? Tell me."

"A man brought it in, late this morning. At least I think it was a man." Tika shivered. "He was wrapped head to foot in clothing of every description. I couldn't even see his face. His voice was hissinglike and he spoke with a strange accent. 'Deliver this to one Tanis Half-Elven,' he said. I told him you weren't here and hadn't been here for several years. 'He will be,' the man said. Then he left." Tika shrugged. "That's all I can tell you. The old man over there saw him." She gestured to an old man sitting in a chair before the fire. "You might ask him if he noticed anything else."

Tanis turned to look at an old man who was telling stories to a dreamy-eyed child staring into the flames. Flint touched his arm.

"Here comes one who can tell you more," the dwarf said.

"Sturm!" Tanis said warmly, turning toward the door.

Everyone except Raistlin turned. The mage relapsed into the shadows once more.

At the door stood a straight-backed figure dressed in full plate armor and chain mail, the symbol of the Order of the Rose on the breastplate. A great many people in the Inn turned to stare, scowling. The man was a Solamnic knight, and the Knights of Solamnia had fallen into ill-repute up north. Rumors of their corruption had spread even this far south. The few who recognized Sturm as a long-time former resident of Solace shrugged and turned back to their drinking. Those who did not, continued to stare. In these days of peace, it was unusual enough to see a knight in full armor enter the Inn. But it was still more unusual to see a knight in full armor that dated back practically to the Cataclysm!

Sturm received the stares as accolades due his rank. He carefully smoothed his great, thick moustaches, which, being the ages-old symbol of the Knights, were as obsolete as his armor. He bore the trappings of the Solamnic Knights with unquestioned pride, and he had the sword-arm and the skill to defend that pride. Although people in the Inn stared, no one, after one look at the knight's calm, cold eyes, dared snicker or make a derogatory comment.

The knight held the door open for a tall man and a woman heavily cloaked in furs. The woman must have spoken a word of thanks to Sturm, for he bowed to her in a courtly, old-fashioned manner long dead in the modern world.

"Look at that." Caramon shook his head in admiration. "The gallant knight helps the lady fair. I wonder where he dragged up those two?"

"They're barbarians from the Plains," said Tas, standing on a chair, waving his arms to his friend. "That's the dress of the Que-shu tribe."

Apparently the two Plainsmen declined any offer Sturm made, for the knight bowed again and left them. He walked across the crowded Inn with a proud and noble air, such as he might have worn walking forward to be knighted by the king.

Tanis rose to his feet. Sturm came to him first and threw his arms around his friend. Tanis gripped him tightly, feeling the knight's strong, sinewy arms clasp him in affection. Then the two stood back to look at each other for a brief moment.

Sturm hasn't changed, Tanis thought, except that there are more lines around the sad eyes, more gray in the brown hair. The cloak is a little more frayed. There are a few more dents in the ancient armor. But the knight's flowing moustaches—his pride and joy—were as long and sweeping as ever, his shield was polished just as brightly, his brown eyes were just as warm when he saw his friends.

"And you have a beard," Sturm said with amusement.

Then the knight turned to greet Caramon and Flint. Tasslehoff dashed off after more ale, Tika having been called away to serve others in the growing crowd.

"Greetings, Knight," whispered Raistlin from his corner.

Sturm's face grew solemn as he turned to greet the other twin. "Raistlin," he said.

The mage drew back his hood, letting the light fall on his face. Sturm was too well-bred to let his astonishment show beyond a slight exclamation. But his eyes widened. Tanis realized the young mage was getting a cynical pleasure out of seeing his friends' discomfiture.

"Can I get you something, Raistlin?" Tanis asked.

"No, thank you," the mage answered, moving into the shadows once again.

"He eats practically nothing," Caramon said in a worried tone. "I think he lives on air."

"Some plants live on air," Tasslehoff stated, returning with Sturm's ale. "I've seen them. They hover up off the ground. Their roots suck food and water out of the atmosphere."

"Really?" Caramon's eyes were wide.

"I don't know who's the greater idiot," said Flint in disgust. "Well, we're all here. What news?"

"All?" Sturm looked at Tanis questioningly.

"Kitiara?"

"Not coming," Tanis replied steadily. "We were hoping perhaps you could tell us something."

"Not I." The knight frowned. "We traveled north together and parted soon after crossing the Sea Narrows into Old Solamnia. She was going to look up relatives of her father, she said. That was the last I saw of her."

"Well, I suppose that's that." Tanis sighed. "What of your relatives, Sturm? Did you find your father?"

Sturm began to talk, but Tanis only half-listened to Sturm's tale of his travels in his ancestral land of Solamnia. Tanis's thoughts were on Kitiara. Of all his friends, she had been the one he most longed to see. After five years of trying to get her dark eyes and crooked smile out of his mind, he discovered that his longing for her grew daily. Wild, impetuous, hot-tempered—the swordswoman was everything Tanis was not. She was also human, and love between human and elf always ended in tragedy. Yet Tanis could no more get Kitiara out of his heart than he could get his human half out of his blood. Wrenching his mind free of memories, he began listening to Sturm.

"I heard rumors. Some say my father is dead. Some say he's alive." His face darkened. "But no one knows where he is."

"Your inheritance?" Caramon asked.

Sturm smiled, a melancholy smile that softened the lines in his proud face. "I wear it," he replied simply. "My armor and my weapon."

Tanis looked down to see that the knight wore a splendid, if old-fashioned, two-handed sword.

Caramon stood up to peer over the table. "That's a beauty," he said. "They don't make them like that these days. My sword broke in a fight with an ogre. Theros Ironfeld put a new blade on it today, but it cost me dearly. So you're a knight now?"

Sturm's smile vanished. Ignoring the question, he caressed the hilt of his sword lovingly. "According to the legend, this sword will break only if I do," he said. "It was all that was left of my father's—"

Suddenly Tas, who hadn't been listening, interrupted. "Who are those people?" the kender asked in a shrill whisper.

Tanis looked up as the two barbarians walked past their table, heading for empty chairs that sat in the shadows of a corner near the firepit. The man was the tallest man Tanis had ever seen. Caramon—at six feet—would come only to this man's shoulder. But Caramon's chest was probably twice as big around, his arms three times as big. Although the man was bundled with the furs barbarian tribesmen live in, it was obvious that he was thin for his great height. His face, though dark-skinned, had the pale cast of one who has been ill or suffered greatly.

His companion—the woman Sturm had bowed to—was so muffled in a fur-trimmed cape and hood that it was difficult to tell much about her. Neither she nor her tall escort glanced at Sturm as they passed. The woman carried a plain staff trimmed with feathers in barbaric fashion. The man carried a well-worn knapsack. They sat down in the chairs, huddled in their cloaks, and talked together in low voices.

"I found them wandering around on the road outside of town," Sturm said. "The woman appeared near exhaustion, the man just as bad. I brought them here, told them they could get food and rest for the night. They are proud people and would have refused my help, I think, but they were lost and tired and"—Sturm lowered his voice—"there are things on the road these days that it is better not to face in the dark."

"We met some of them, asking about a staff," Tanis said grimly. He described their encounter with Fewmaster Toede.

Although Sturm smiled at the description of the battle, he shook his head. "A Seeker guard questioned me about a staff outside," he said. "Blue crystal, wasn't it?"

Caramon nodded and put his hand on his brother's thin arm. "One of the slimy guards stopped us," the warrior said. "They were going to impound Raist's staff, if you'll believe that—'for further investigation,' they said. I rattled my sword at them and they thought better of the notion."

Raistlin moved his arm from his brother's touch, a scornful smile on his lips.

"What would have happened if they had taken your staff?" Tanis asked Raistlin.

The mage looked at him from the shadows of his hood, his golden eyes gleaming. "They would have died horribly," the mage whispered, "and *not* by my brother's sword!"

The half-elf felt chilled. The mage's softly spoken words were more frightening than his brother's bravado. "I wonder what is so important about a blue crystal staff that goblins would kill to get it?" Tanis mused.

"There are rumors of worse to come," Sturm said quietly. His friends moved closer to hear him. "Armies are gathering in the north. Armies of strange creatures, not human. There is talk of war."

"But what? Who?" Tanis asked. "I've heard the same."

"And so have I," Caramon added. "In fact, I heard—"

As the conversation continued, Tasslehoff yawned and turned away. Easily bored, the kender looked around the Inn for some new amusement. His eyes went to the old man, still spinning tales for the child by the fire. The old man had a larger audience now—the two barbarians were listening, Tas noted. Then his jaw dropped.

The woman had thrown her hood back and the firelight shone on her face and hair. The kender stared in admiration. The woman's face was like the face of a marble statue—classic, pure, cold.

But it was her hair that captured the kender's attention. Tas had never before seen such hair, especially on the Plainsmen, who were usually dark-haired and dark-skinned. No jeweler spinning molten strands of silver and gold could have created the effect of this woman's silver-gold hair shining in the firelight.

One other person listened to the old man. This was a man dressed in the rich brown and golden robes of a Seeker. He sat at a small round table, drinking mulled wine. Several mugs stood empty before him and, even as the kender watched, he called sourly for another.

"That's Hederick," Tika whispered as she passed the companions' table. "The High Theocrat."

The man called out again, glaring at Tika. She bustled quickly over to help him. He snarled at her, mentioning poor service. She seemed to start to answer sharply, then bit her lip and kept silent.

The old man came to an end of his tale. The boy sighed. "Are all your stories of the ancient gods true, Old One?" he asked curiously.

Tasslehoff saw Hederick frown. The kender hoped he wouldn't bother the old man. Tas touched Tanis's arm to catch his attention, nodding his head toward the Seeker with a look that meant there might be trouble.

The friends turned. All were immediately overwhelmed by the beauty of the Plainswoman. They stared in silence.

The old man's voice carried clearly over the drone of the other conversation in the common room. "Indeed, my stories are true, child." The old man looked directly at the woman and her tall escort. "Ask these two. They carry such stories in their hearts."

"Do you?" The boy turned to the woman eagerly. "Can you tell me a story?"

The woman shrank back into the shadows, her face filled with alarm as she noticed Tanis and his friends staring at her. The man drew near her protectively, his hand reaching for his weapon. He glowered at the group, especially the heavily armed warrior, Caramon.

"Nervous bastard," Caramon commented, his hand straying to his own sword.

"I can understand why," Sturm said. "Guarding such a treasure. He *is* her bodyguard, by the way. I gathered from their conversation that she's some kind of royal person in their tribe. Though I imagine from the looks they exchanged that their relationship goes a bit deeper than that."

The woman raised her hand in a gesture of protest. "I'm sorry." The friends had to strain to hear her low voice. "I am not a teller of tales. I have not the art." She spoke the Common tongue, her accent thick.

The child's eager face filled with disappointment. The old man patted him on the back, then looked directly into the woman's eyes. "You may not be a teller of tales," he said pleasantly, "but you are a singer of songs, aren't you, Chieftain's Daughter? Sing the child your song, Goldmoon. You know the one."

From out of nowhere, apparently, a lute appeared in the old man's hands. He gave it to the woman who stared at him in fear and astonishment.

"How . . . do you know me, sir?" she asked.

"That is not important." The old man smiled gently. "Sing for us, Chieftain's Daughter."

The woman took the lute with hands that trembled visibly. Her companion seemed to make a whispered protest, but she did not hear him. Her eyes were held fast by the glittering black eyes of the old man. Slowly, as if in a trance, she began to strum the lute. As the melancholy chords drifted through the common room, conversations ceased. Soon, everyone was watching her, but she did not notice. Goldmoon sang for the old man alone.

The grasslands are endless,
And summer sings on,
And Goldmoon the princess
Loves a poor man's son.
Her father the chieftain
Makes long roads between them:
The grasslands are endless, and summer sings on.

The grasslands are waving,
The sky's rim is gray,
The chieftain sends Riverwind
East and away,

To search for strong magic
At the lip of the morning,
The grasslands are waving, the sky's rim is gray.

O Riverwind, where have you gone?
O Riverwind, autumn comes on.
I sit by the river
And look to the sunrise,
But the sun rises over the mountains alone.

The grasslands are fading,
The summer wind dies,
He comes back, the darkness
Of stones in his eyes.

He carries a blue staff
As bright as a glacier:
The grasslands are fading, the summer wind dies.

The grasslands are fragile,
As yellow as flame,
The chieftain makes mockery
Of Riverwind's claim.

He orders the people
To stone the young warrior:
The grasslands are fragile, as yellow as flame.

The grassland has faded,
And autumn is here.
The girl joins her lover,
The stones whistle near,

The staff flares in blue light
And both of them vanish:
The grasslands are faded, and autumn is here.

There was heavy silence in the room as her hand struck the final chord. Taking a deep breath, she handed the lute back to the old man and withdrew into the shadows once more.

"Thank you, my dear," the old man said, smiling.

"Now can I have a story?" the little boy asked wistfully.

"Of course," the old man answered and settled back in his chair. "Once upon a time, the great god, Paladine—"

"Paladine?" the child interrupted. "I've never heard of a god named Paladine."

A snorting sound came from the High Theocrat sitting at the nearby table. Tanis looked at Hederick, whose face was flushed and scowling. The old man appeared not to notice.

"Paladine is one of the ancient gods, child. No one has worshiped him for a long time."

"Why did he leave?" the little boy asked.

"He did not leave us," the old man answered, and his smile grew sad. "Men left him after the dark days of the Cataclysm. They blamed the destruction of the world on the gods, instead of on themselves, as they should have done. Have you ever heard the 'Canticle of the Dragon'?"

"Oh, yes," the boy said eagerly. "I love stories about dragons, though papa says dragons never existed. I believe in them, though. I hope to see one someday!"

The old man's face seemed to age and grow sorrowful. He stroked the young boy's hair. "Be careful what you wish, my child," he said softly. Then he fell silent.

"The story—" the boy prompted.

"Oh, yes. Well, once upon a time Paladine heard the prayer of a very great knight, Huma—"

"Huma from the Canticle?"

"Yes, that's the one. Huma became lost in the forest. He wandered and wandered until he despaired because he thought he would never see his homeland again. He prayed to Paladine for help, and there suddenly appeared before him a white stag."

"Did Huma shoot it?" the boy asked.

"He started to, but his heart failed him. He could not shoot an animal so magnificent. The stag bounded away. Then it stopped and looked back at him, as if waiting. Huma began to follow it. Day and night, he followed the stag until it led him to his homeland. He offered thanks to the god, Paladine."

"Blashphemy!" snarled a voice loudly. A chair crashed back.

Tanis put down his mug of ale, looking up. Everyone at the table stopped drinking to watch the drunken Theocrat.

"Blasphemy!" Hederick, weaving unsteadily on his feet, pointed at the old man. "Heretic! Corrupting our youth! I'll bring you before the counshel, old man." The Seeker fell back a step, then staggered forward again. He looked around the room with a pompous air. "Call the guardsh!" He made a grandiose gesture. "Have them arresht thish man and thish woman for singing lewd songsh. Obviously a witch! I'll confishcate thish staff!"

The Seeker lurched across the floor to the barbarian woman, who was staring at him in disgust. He reached clumsily for her staff.

"No," the woman called Goldmoon spoke coolly. "That is mine. You cannot take it."

"Witch!" the Seeker sneered. "I am the High Theocrat! I take what I want."

He started to make another grab for the staff. The woman's tall companion rose to his feet. "The Chieftain's Daughter says you will not take it," the man said harshly. He shoved the Seeker backward.

The tall man's push was not rough, but it knocked the drunken Theocrat completely off balance. His arms flailing wildly, he tried to catch himself. He lurched forward, too far, tripped over his official robes, and fell headfirst into the roaring fire.

There was a whoosh and a flare of light, then a sickening smell of burning flesh. The Theocrat's scream tore through the stunned silence as the crazed man leaped to his feet and started whirling around in a frenzy. He had become a living torch!

Tanis and the others sat, unable to move, paralyzed with the shock of the incident. Only Tasslehoff had wits enough to run forward, anxious to try and help the man. But the Theocrat was screaming and waving his arms, fanning the flames that were consuming his clothes and his body. There seemed no way that the little kender could help him.

"Here!" The old man grabbed the barbarian's feather-decorated staff and handed it to the kender. "Knock him down. Then we can smother the fire."

Tasslehoff took the staff. He swung it, using all his strength, and hit the Theocrat squarely in the chest. The man fell to the ground. There was a gasp from the crowd. Tasslehoff himself stood, open-mouthed, the staff clutched in his hand, staring down at the amazing sight at his feet.

The flames had died instantly. The man's robes were whole, undamaged. His skin was pink and healthy. He sat up, a look of fear and awe on his face. He stared down at his hands and his robes. There was not a mark on his skin. There was not the smallest cinder smoking on his robes.

"It healed him!" the old man proclaimed loudly. "The staff! Look at the staff!"

Tasslehoff's eyes went to the staff in his hands. It was made of blue crystal and was glowing with a bright blue light!

The old man began shouting. "Call the guards! Arrest the kender! Arrest the barbarians! Arrest their friends! I saw them come in with this knight." He pointed at Sturm.

"What?" Tanis leaped up. "Are you crazy, old man?"

"Call the guards!" The word spread. "Did you see—? The blue crystal staff? We've found it. Now they'll leave us alone. Call the guards!"

The Theocrat staggered to his feet, his face pale, blotched with red. The barbarian woman and her companion stood up, fear and alarm in their faces.

"Foul witch!" Hederick's voice shook with rage. "You have cured me with evil! Even as I burn to purify my flesh, you will burn to purify your soul!" With that, the Seeker reached out, and before anyone could stop him, he plunged his hand back into the flames! He gagged with the pain but did not cry out. Then, clutching his charred and blackened hand, he turned and staggered off through the murmuring crowd, a wild look of satisfaction on his pain-twisted face.

"You've got to get out of here!" Tika came running over to Tanis, her breath coming in gasps. "The whole town's been hunting for that staff! Those hooded men told the Theocrat they'd destroy Solace if they caught someone harboring the staff. The townspeople will turn you over to the guards!"

"But it's not our staff!" Tanis protested. He glared at the old man and saw him settle back into his chair, a pleased smile on his face. The old man grinned at Tanis and winked.

"Do you think they'll believe you!" Tika wrung her hands. "Look!"

Tanis looked around. People were glaring at them balefully. Some took a firm grip on their mugs. Others eased their hands onto the hilts of their swords. Shouts from down below drew his eyes back to his friends.

"The guards are coming!" exclaimed Tika.

Tanis rose. "We'll have to go out through the kitchen."

"Yes!" She nodded. "They won't look back there yet. But hurry. It won't take them long to surround the place."

Years of being apart had not affected the companions' ability to react as a team to threat of danger. Caramon had pulled on his shining helm, drawn his sword, shouldered his pack, and was helping his brother to his feet. Raistlin, his staff in his hand, was moving around the table. Flint had hold of his battle-axe and was frowning darkly at the onlookers, who seemed hesitant about rushing to attack such well-armed men. Only Sturm sat, calmly drinking his ale.

"Sturm!" Tanis said urgently. "Come on! We've got to get out of here!"

"Run?" The knight appeared astonished. "From this rabble?"

"Yes." Tanis paused; the knight's code of honor forbade running from danger. He had to convince him. "That man is a religious fanatic, Sturm. He'll probably burn us at the stake! And"—a sudden thought rescued him—"there is a lady to protect."

"The lady, of course." Sturm stood up at once and walked over to the woman. "Madam, your servant." He bowed; the courtly knight would not be hurried. "It seems we are all in this together. Your staff has placed us in considerable danger—you most of all. We are familiar with the area around here: we grew up here. You, I know, are strangers. We would be honored to accompany you and your gallant friend and guard your lives."

"Come on!" Tika urged, tugging on Tanis's arm. Caramon and Raistlin were already at the kitchen door.

"Get the kender," Tanis told her.

Tasslehoff stood, rooted to the floor, staring at the staff. It was rapidly fading back to its nondescript brown color. Tika grabbed Tas by his topknot and pulled him toward the kitchen. The kender shrieked, dropping the staff.

Goldmoon swiftly picked it up, clutching it close to her. Although frightened, her eyes were clear and steady as she looked at Sturm and Tanis; she was apparently thinking rapidly. Her companion said a harsh word in their language. She shook her head. He frowned and made a slashing motion with his hand. She snapped a quick reply and he fell silent, his face dark.

"We will go with you," Goldmoon said to Sturm in the Common tongue. "Thank you for the offer."

"This way!" Tanis herded them out through the swinging kitchen doors, following Tika and Tas. He glanced behind him and saw some of the crowd move forward, but in no great hurry.

The cook stared at them as they ran through the kitchen. Caramon and Raistlin were already at the exit, which was nothing more than a hole cut in the floor. A rope hung from a sturdy limb above the hole and dropped forty feet to the ground.

"Ah!" exclaimed Tas, laughing. "Here the ale comes up and the garbage goes down." He swung out onto the rope and shinnied down easily.

"I'm sorry about this," Tika apologized to Goldmoon, "but it is the only way out of here."

"I can climb down a rope." Then the woman smiled and added, "Though I admit it has been many years."

She handed her staff to her companion and grasped the stout rope. She began to descend, moving skillfully hand over hand. When she reached the bottom, her companion tossed the staff down, swung on the rope, and dropped through the hole.

"How are you going to get down, Raist?" Caramon asked, his face lined with concern. "I can carry you on my back—"

Raistlin's eyes flashed with an anger that startled Tanis. "I can get down myself!" the mage hissed. Before anyone could stop him, he stepped to the edge of the hole and leaped out into the air. Everyone gasped and peered down, expecting to see Raistlin splattered all over the ground. Instead, they saw the young mage gently floating down, his robes fluttering around him. The crystal on his staff glowed brightly.

"He shivers my skin!" Flint growled to Tanis.

"Hurry!" Tanis shoved the dwarf forward. Flint grabbed hold of the rope. Caramon followed, the big man's weight causing the limb the rope was tied around to creak.

"I will go last," Sturm said, his sword drawn.

"Very well." Tanis knew it was useless to argue. He slung the longbow and quiver of arrows over his shoulder, grabbed the rope, and started down. Suddenly his hands slipped. He slid down the rope, unable to stop it tearing the skin off his palms. He landed on the ground and looked, wincing, at his hands. His palms were raw and bleeding. But there was no time to think about them. Glancing up, he watched as Sturm descended.

Tika's face appeared in the opening. "Go to my house!" she mouthed, pointing through the trees. Then she was gone.

"I know the way," Tasslehoff said, his eyes glowing with excitement. "Follow me."

They hurried off after the kender, hearing the sounds of the guards climbing the stairway into the Inn. Tanis, unused to walking on the ground in Solace, was soon lost. Above him he could see the bridge-walks, the street lamps gleaming among the tree leaves. He was completely disoriented, but Tas kept pushing forward confidently, weaving in and out among the huge trunks of the vallenwood trees. The sounds of the commotion at the Inn faded.

"We'll hide at Tika's for the night," Tanis whispered to Sturm as they plunged through the underbrush. "Just in case someone recognized us and decides to search our homes. Everyone will have forgotten about this by morning. We'll take the Plainsmen to my house and let them rest a few days. Then we can send the barbarians on to Haven where the Council of High Seekers can talk with them. I think I might even go along—I'm curious about this staff."

Sturm nodded. Then he looked at Tanis and smiled his rare, melancholy smile. "Welcome home," the knight said.

"Same to you." The half-elf grinned.

They both came to a sudden halt, bumping into Caramon in the dark.

"We're here, I think," Caramon said.

In the light of the street lamps that hung in the tree limbs, they could see Tasslehoff climbing tree branches like a gully dwarf. The rest followed more slowly, Caramon assisting his brother. Tanis, gritting his teeth from the pain in his hands, climbed up slowly through the rapidly thinning autumn foliage. Tas pulled himself up over the porch railing with the skill of a burglar. The kender slipped over to the door and peered up and down the bridge-walk. Seeing no one on it, he motioned to the others. Then he studied the lock and smiled to himself in satisfaction. The kender slid something out of one of his pouches. Within seconds, the door of Tika's house swung open.

"Come in," he said, playing host.

They crowded inside the little house, the tall barbarian being forced to duck his head to avoid hitting the ceiling. Tas pulled the curtains shut. Sturm found a chair for the lady, and the tall barbarian went to stand behind her. Raistlin stirred up the fire.

"Keep watch," Tanis said. Caramon nodded. The warrior had already posted himself at a window, staring out into the darkness. The light from a street lamp gleamed through the curtains into the room, casting dark shadows on the walls. For long moments no one spoke, each staring at the others.

Tanis sat down. His eyes turned to the woman. "The blue crystal staff," he said quietly. "It healed that man. How?"

"I do not know." She faltered. "I—I haven't had it very long."

Tanis looked down at his hands. They were bleeding from where the rope had peeled off his skin. He held them out to her. Slowly, her face pale, the woman touched him with the staff. It began to glow blue. Tanis felt a slight shock tingle through his body. Even as he watched, the blood on his palms vanished, the skin became smooth and unscarred, the pain eased and soon left him completely.

"True healing!" he said in awe.

4

The open door.
Flight into darkness.

aistlin sat down on the hearth, rubbing his thin hands in the warmth of the small fire. His golden eyes seemed brighter than the flames as he stared intently at the blue crystal staff resting across the woman's lap.

"What do you think?" asked Tanis.

"If she's a charlatan, she's a good one," Raistlin commented thoughtfully.

"Worm! You dare to call the Chieftain's Daughter charlatan!" The tall barbarian stepped toward Raistlin, his dark brows contracted in a vicious scowl. Caramon made a low, rumbling sound in his throat and moved from the window to stand behind his brother.

"Riverwind . . ." The woman laid her hand on the man's arm as he drew near her chair. "Please. He meant no harm. It is right that they do not trust us. They do not know us."

43

"And we do not know them," the man growled.

"If I might examine it?" Raistlin said.

Goldmoon nodded and held out the staff. The mage stretched out his long, bony arm, his thin hands grasping for it eagerly. As Raistlin touched the staff, however, there was a bright flash of blue light and a crackling sound. The mage jerked his hand back, crying out in pain and shock. Caramon jumped forward, but his brother stopped him.

"No, Caramon," Raistlin whispered hoarsely, wringing his injured hand. "The lady had nothing to do with that."

The woman, indeed, was staring at the staff in amazement.

"What is it then?" Tanis asked in exasperation. "A staff that heals and injures at the same time?"

"It merely knows its own." Raistlin licked his lips, his eyes glittering. "Watch. Caramon, take the staff."

"Not me!" The warrior drew back as if from a snake.

"Take the staff!" Raistlin demanded.

Reluctantly, Caramon stretched out a trembling hand. His arm twitched as his fingers came closer and closer. Closing his eyes and gritting his teeth in anticipation of pain, he touched the staff. Nothing happened.

Caramon opened his eyes wide, startled. He gripped the staff, lifted it in his huge hand, and grinned.

"See there." Raistlin gestured like an illusionist showing off a trick to the crowd. "Only those of simple goodness, pure in heart"—his sarcasm was biting—"may touch the staff. It is truly a sacred staff of healing, blessed by some god. It is not magic. No magic objects that I have ever heard about have healing powers."

"Hush!" ordered Tasslehoff, who had taken Caramon's place by the window. "The Theocrat's guards!" he warned softly.

No one spoke. Now they could all hear goblin footsteps flapping on the bridge-walks that ran among the branches of the vallenwood trees.

"They're conducting a house-to-house search!" Tanis whispered incredulously, listening to fists banging on a neighboring door.

"The Seekers demand right of entry!" croaked a voice. There was a pause, then the same voice said, "No one home, do we kick the door in?"

"Naw," said another voice. "We'd better just report to the Theocrat, let him kick the door down. Now if it was unlocked, that'd be different, we're allowed to enter then."

Tanis looked at the door opposite him. He felt the hair rise on the back of his neck. He could have sworn they had shut and bolted the door . . . now it stood slightly open!

"The door!" he whispered. "Caramon—"

But the warrior had already moved over to stand behind the door, his back to the wall, his giant hands flexing.

The footsteps flapped to a stop outside. "The Seekers demand right of entry." The goblins began to bang on the door, then stopped in surprise as it swung open.

"This place is empty," said one. "Let's move on."

"You got no imagination, Grum," said the other. "Here's our chance to pick up a few pieces of silver."

A goblin head appeared around the open door. Its eyes focused on Raistlin, sitting calmly, his staff on his shoulder. The goblin grunted in alarm, then began to laugh.

"Oh, ho! Look what we've found! A staff!" The goblin's eyes gleamed. It took a step toward Raistlin, its partner crowding close behind. "Hand me that staff!"

"Certainly," the mage whispered. He held his own staff forth. "*Shirak*," he said. The crystal ball flared into light. The goblins shrieked and shut their eyes, fumbling for their swords. At that moment, Caramon jumped from behind the door, grabbed the goblins around their necks, and swept their heads together with a sickening thud. The goblin bodies crumpled into a stinking heap.

"Dead?" asked Tanis as Caramon bent over them, examining them by the light of Raistlin's staff.

"I'm afraid so." The big man sighed. "I hit them too hard."

"Well, that's torn it," Tanis said grimly. "We've murdered two more of the Theocrat's guards. He'll have the town up in arms. Now we can't just lie low for a few days—we've got to get out of here! And you two"—he turned to the barbarians—"had better come with us."

"Wherever we're going," muttered Flint irritably.

"Where were you headed?" Tanis asked Riverwind.

"We were traveling to Haven," the barbarian answered reluctantly.

"There are wise men there," Goldmoon said. "We hoped they could tell us about this staff. You see, the song I sang—it was true: the staff saved our lives—"

"You'll have to tell us later," Tanis interrupted. "When these guards don't report back, every goblin in Solace will be swarming up the trees. Raistlin, put out that light."

The mage spoke another word, *"Dumak."* The crystal glimmered, then the light died.

"What'll we do with the bodies?" Caramon asked, nudging a dead goblin with his booted foot. "And what about Tika? Won't she get into trouble?"

"Leave the bodies." Tanis's mind was working quickly. "And hack up the door. Sturm, knock over a few tables. We'll make it look as if we broke in here and got into a fight with these fellows. That way, Tika shouldn't be in too much trouble. She's a smart girl—she'll manage."

"We'll need food," Tasslehoff stated. He ran into the kitchen and began rummaging through the shelves, stuffing loaves of bread and anything else that looked edible into his pouches. He tossed Flint a full skin of wine. Sturm overturned a few chairs. Caramon arranged the bodies to make it look as if they had died in a ferocious battle. The Plainsmen stood in front of the dying fire, looking at Tanis uncertainly.

"Well?" said Sturm. "Now what? Where are we going?"

Tanis hesitated, running over the options in his mind. The Plainsmen had come from the east and—if their story was true and their tribe *had* been trying to kill them—they wouldn't want to go back that way. The group could travel south, into the elven kingdom, but Tanis felt a strange reluctance to go back to his homelands. He knew, too, that the elves would not be pleased to see these strangers enter their hidden city.

"We will travel north," he said finally. "We will escort these two until we come to the crossroads, then we can decide what to do from there. They can go on southwest to Haven, if they wish. I plan to travel farther north and see if the rumors about armies gathering are true."

"And perhaps run into Kitiara," Raistlin whispered slyly.

Tanis flushed. "Is that plan all right?" he asked, looking around.

"Though not the eldest among us, Tanis, you are the wisest," Sturm said. "We follow you—as always."

Caramon nodded. Raistlin was already heading for the door. Flint shouldered the wine skin, grumbling.

Tanis felt a gentle hand touch his arm. He turned and looked down into the clear blue eyes of the beautiful barbarian.

"We are grateful," Goldmoon said slowly, as if unused to expressing appreciation. "You risk your lives for us, and we are strangers."

Tanis smiled and clasped her hand. "I am Tanis. The brothers are Caramon and Raistlin. The knight is Sturm Brightblade. Flint Fireforge carries the wine and Tasslehoff Burrfoot is our clever locksmith. You are Goldmoon and he is Riverwind. There—we are strangers no longer."

Goldmoon smiled wearily. She patted Tanis's arm, then started out the door, leaning on the staff that once again seemed plain and nondescript. Tanis watched her, then glanced up to see Riverwind staring at him, the barbarian's dark face an impenetrable mask.

"Well," Tanis amended silently, "*some* of us are no longer strangers."

Soon everyone had gone, Tas leading the way. Tanis stood alone for a moment in the wrecked living room, staring at the bodies of the goblins. This was supposed to have been a peaceful homecoming after bitter years of solitary travel. He thought of his comfortable house. He thought of all the things he had planned to do—things he had planned to do together with Kitiara. He thought of long winter nights, with storytelling around the fire at the Inn, then returning home, laughing together beneath the fur blankets, sleeping through the snow-covered mornings.

Tanis kicked at the smoldering coals, scattering them. Kitiara had not come back. Goblins had invaded his quiet town. He was fleeing into the night to escape a bunch of religious fanatics, with every likelihood he could never return.

Elves do not notice the passage of time. They live for hundreds of years. For them, the seasons pass like brief rain showers. But Tanis was half human. He sensed change coming, felt the disquieting restlessness men feel before a thunderstorm.

He sighed and shook his head. Then he went out the shattered door, leaving it swinging crazily on one hinge.

5

Farewell to Flint. Arrows fly. Message in the stars.

anis swung over the porch and dropped down through the tree limbs to the ground below. The others waited, huddled in the darkness, keeping out of the light cast by street lamps swinging in the branches above them. A chill wind had sprung up, blowing out of the north. Tanis glanced behind him and saw other lights, lights of the search parties. He pulled his hood over his head and hurried forward.

"Wind's switched," he said. "There'll be rain by morning." He looked around at the small group, seeing them in the eerie, wildly dancing light of the wind-tossed lamps. Goldmoon's face was scarred with weariness. Riverwind's was a stoic mask of strength, but his shoulders sagged. Raistlin, shivering, leaned against a tree, wheezing for breath.

Tanis hunched his shoulders against the wind. "We've got to find shelter," he said. "Some place to rest."

"Tanis—" Tas tugged on the half-elf's cloak. "We could go by boat. Crystalmir Lake's only a short way. There're caves on the other side, and it will cut walking time tomorrow."

"That's a good idea, Tas, but we don't have a boat."

"No problem." The kender grinned. His small face and sharply pointed ears made him look particularly impish in the eerie light. Tas is enjoying all of this immensely, Tanis realized. He felt like shaking the kender, lecturing him sternly on how much danger they were in. But the half-elf knew it was useless: kender are totally immune to fear.

"The boat's a good idea," Tanis repeated, after a moment's thought. "You guide. And don't tell Flint," he added. "I'll take care of that."

"Right!" Tas giggled, then slipped back to the others. "Follow me," he called out softly, and he started off once more. Flint, grumbling into his beard, stumped after the kender. Goldmoon followed the dwarf. Riverwind cast a quick, penetrating glance around at everyone in the group, then fell into step behind her.

"I don't think he trusts us," Caramon observed.

"Would you?" Tanis asked, glancing at the big man. Caramon's dragon helm glinted in the flickering lights; his ring-mail armor was visible whenever the wind blew his cape back. A longsword clanked against his thick thighs, a short bow and a quiver of arrows were slung over his shoulder, a dagger protruded from his belt. His shield was battered and dented from many fights. The giant was ready for anything.

Tanis looked over at Sturm, who proudly wore the coat of arms of a knighthood that had fallen into disgrace three hundred years before. Although Sturm was only four years older than Caramon, the knight's strict, disciplined life, hardships brought on by poverty, and his melancholy search for his beloved father had aged the knight beyond his years. Only twenty-nine, he looked forty.

Tanis thought, I don't think I'd trust us either.

"What's the plan?" Sturm asked.

"We're going by boat," Tanis answered.

"Oh, ho!" Caramon chuckled. "Told Flint yet?"

"No. Leave that to me."

"Where are we getting the boat?" Sturm asked suspiciously.

"You'll be happier not knowing," the half-elf said.

The knight frowned. His eyes followed the kender, who was far ahead of them, flitting from one shadow to another. "I don't like this, Tanis. First we're murderers, now we're about to become thieves."

"I don't consider myself a murderer." Caramon snorted. "Goblins don't count."

Tanis saw the knight glare at Caramon. "I don't like any of this, Sturm," he said hastily, hoping to avoid an argument. "But it's a matter of necessity. Look at the Plainsmen—pride's the only thing keeping them on their feet. Look at Raistlin . . ." Their eyes went to the mage, who was shuffling through the dry leaves, keeping always in the shadows. He leaned heavily upon his staff. Occasionally, a dry cough racked his frail body.

Caramon's face darkened. "Tanis is right," he said softly. "Raist can't take much more of this. I must go to him." Leaving the knight and the half-elf, he hurried forward to catch up with the robed, bent figure of his twin.

"Let me help you, Raist," they heard Caramon whisper.

Raistlin shook his hooded head and flinched away from his brother's touch. Caramon shrugged and dropped his arm. But the big warrior stayed close to his frail brother, ready to help him if necessary.

"Why does he put up with that?" Tanis asked softly.

"Family. Ties of blood." Sturm sounded wistful. He seemed about to say more, then his eyes went to Tanis's elven face with its growth of human hair and he fell silent. Tanis saw the look, knew what the knight was thinking. Family, ties of blood—they were things the orphaned half-elf wouldn't know about.

"Come on," Tanis said abruptly. "We're dropping behind."

They soon left the vallenwood trees of Solace and entered the pine forest surrounding Crystalmir Lake. Tanis could faintly hear muffled shouts far behind them. "They've found the bodies," he guessed. Sturm nodded gloomily. Suddenly Tasslehoff seemed to materialize out of the darkness right beneath the half-elf's nose.

"The trail runs a little over a mile to the lake," Tas said. "I'll meet you where it comes out." He gestured vaguely, then disappeared before Tanis could say a word. The half-elf looked back at Solace. There seemed to be more lights, and they were moving in this direction. The roads were probably already blocked.

"Where's the kender?" Flint grumbled as they plunged through the forest.

"Tas is meeting us at the lake," Tanis replied.

"Lake?" Flint's eyes grew wide in alarm. "What lake?"

"There's only one lake around here, Flint," Tanis said, trying hard not to smile at Sturm. "Come on. We'd better keep going." His elvensight showed him the broad red outline of Caramon and the slighter red shape of his brother disappearing into the thick woods ahead.

"I thought we were just going to lie low in the woods for a while." Flint shoved his way past Sturm to complain to Tanis.

"We're going by boat." Tanis moved forward.

"Nope!" Flint growled. "I'm not getting in any boat!"

"That accident happened ten years ago!" Tanis said, exasperated. "Look, I'll make Caramon sit still."

"Absolutely not!" the dwarf said flatly. "No boats. I took a vow."

"Tanis," Sturm's voice whispered behind him. "Lights."

"Blast!" The half-elf stopped and turned. He had to wait a moment before catching sight of lights glittering through the trees. The search had spread beyond Solace. He hurried to catch up with Caramon, Raistlin, and the Plainsmen.

"Lights!" he called out in a piercing whisper. Caramon looked back and swore. Riverwind raised his hand in acknowledgment. "I'm afraid we're going to have to move faster, Caramon—" Tanis began.

"We'll make it," the big man said, unperturbed. He was supporting his brother now, his arm around Raistlin's thin body, practically carrying him. Raistlin coughed softly, but he was moving. Sturm caught up with Tanis. As they forced their way through the brush, they could hear Flint, puffing along behind, muttering angrily to himself.

"He won't come, Tanis," Sturm said. "Flint's been in mortal fear of boats ever since Caramon almost accidentally drowned him that time. You weren't there. You didn't see him after we hauled him out."

"He'll come," Tanis said, breathing hard. "He can't let us youngsters go off into danger without him."

Sturm shook his head, unconvinced.

Tanis looked back again. He saw no lights, but he knew they were too deep in the forest now to see them. Fewmaster Toede may not have impressed anybody with his brains, but it wouldn't take much intelligence to figure out that the group might take to the water. Tanis stopped abruptly to keep from bumping into someone. "What is it?" he whispered.

"We're here," Caramon answered. Tanis breathed a sigh of relief as he stared out across the dark expanse of Crystalmir Lake. The wind whipped the water into frothy whitecaps.

"Where's Tas?" He kept his voice low.

"There, I think." Caramon pointed at a dark object floating close to shore. Tanis could barely make out the warm red outline of the kender sitting in a large boat.

The stars gleamed with icy brightness in the blue-black sky. The red moon, Lunitari, was rising like a bloody fingernail from the water. Its partner in the night sky, Solinari, had already risen, marking the lake with molten silver.

"What wonderful targets we're going to make!" Sturm said irritably.

Tanis could see Tasslehoff turning this way and that, searching for them. The half-elf reached down, fumbling for a rock in the darkness. Finding one, he lobbed it into the water. It splashed just a few yards ahead of the boat. Tas, reacting to Tanis's signal, propelled the boat to shore.

"You're going to put all of us in one boat!" Flint said in horror. "You're mad, half-elf!"

"It's a big boat," Tanis said.

"No! I won't go. If it were one of the legendary white-winged boats of Tarsis, I still wouldn't go! I'd rather take my chances with the Theocrat!"

Tanis ignored the fuming dwarf and motioned to Sturm. "Get everyone loaded up. We'll be along in a moment."

"Don't take too long," Sturm warned. "Listen."

"I can hear," Tanis said grimly. "Go on."

"What are those sounds?" Goldmoon asked the knight as he came up to her.

"Goblin search parties," Sturm answered. "Those whistles

keep them in contact when they're separated. They're moving into the woods now."

Goldmoon nodded in understanding. She spoke a few words to Riverwind in their own language, apparently continuing a conversation Sturm had interrupted. The big Plainsman frowned and gestured back toward the forest with his hand.

He's trying to convince her to split with us, Sturm realized. Maybe he's got enough woodslore to hide from goblin search parties for days, but I doubt it.

"*Riverwind, gue-lando!*" Goldmoon said sharply. Sturm saw Riverwind scowl in anger. Without a word, he turned and stalked toward the boat. Goldmoon sighed and looked after him, deep sorrow in her face.

"Can I do anything to help, lady?" Sturm asked gently.

"No," she replied. Then she said sadly, as if to herself, "He rules my heart, but I am his ruler. Once, when we were young, we thought we could forget that. But I have been 'Chieftain's Daughter' too long."

"Why doesn't he trust us?" Sturm asked.

"He has all the prejudices of our people," Goldmoon replied. "The Plainsmen do not trust those who are not human." She glanced back. "Tanis cannot hide his elven blood beneath a beard. Then there are the dwarf, the kender."

"And what of you, lady?" Sturm asked. "Why do you trust us? Don't you have these same prejudices?"

Goldmoon turned to face him. He could see her eyes, dark and shimmering as the lake behind her. "When I was a girl," she said in her deep, low voice, "I was a princess of my people. I was a priestess. They worshiped me as a goddess. I believed in it. I adored it. Then something happened—" She fell silent, her eyes filled with memories.

"What was that?" Sturm prompted softly.

"I fell in love with a shepherd," Goldmoon answered, looking at Riverwind. She sighed and walked toward the boat.

Sturm watched Riverwind wade into the water to drag the boat closer to shore as Raistlin and Caramon reached the water's edge. Raistlin clutched his robes around him, shivering.

"I can't get my feet wet," he whispered hoarsely. Caramon did not reply. He simply put his huge arms around his brother, lifted him as easily as he would have lifted a child, and set Raistlin in the boat. The mage huddled in the aft part of the boat, not saying a word of thanks.

"I'll hold her steady," Caramon told Riverwind. "You get in." Riverwind hesitated a moment, then climbed quickly over the side. Caramon helped Goldmoon into the boat. Riverwind caught hold of her and steadied her as the boat rocked gently. The Plainsmen moved to sit in the stern, behind Tasslehoff.

Caramon turned to Sturm as the knight drew near. "What's happening back there?"

"Flint says he'll burn before he'll get in a boat—at least then he'll die warm instead of wet and cold."

"I'll go up and haul him down here," Caramon said.

"You'd only make things worse. You were the one that nearly drowned him, remember? Let Tanis handle it—he's the diplomat."

Caramon nodded. Both men stood, waiting in silence. Sturm saw Goldmoon look at Riverwind in mute appeal, but the Plainsman did not heed her glance. Tasslehoff, fidgeting on his seat, started to call out a shrill question, but a stern look from the knight silenced him. Raistlin huddled in his robes, trying to suppress an uncontrollable cough.

"I'm going up there," Sturm said finally. "Those whistles are getting closer. We don't dare take any more time." But at that moment, he saw Tanis shake hands with the dwarf, and begin to run toward the boat alone. Flint stayed where he was, near the edge of the woods. Sturm shook his head. "I told Tanis the dwarf wouldn't come."

"Stubborn as a dwarf, so the old saying goes," Caramon grunted. "And that one's had one hundred and forty-eight years to grow stubborner." The big man shook his head sadly. "Well, we'll miss him, that's for certain. He's saved my life more than once. Let me go get him. One punch on the jaw and he won't know whether he's in a boat or his own bed."

Tanis ran up, panting, and heard the last comment. "No, Caramon," he said. "Flint would never forgive us. Don't worry about him. He's going back to the hills. Get in the boat. There are more lights coming this way. We left a trail through the forest a blind gully dwarf could follow."

"No sense all of us getting wet," Caramon said, holding the side of the boat. "You and Sturm get in. I'll shove off."

Sturm was already over the side. Tanis patted Caramon on the back, then climbed in. The warrior pushed the boat out into the lake. He was up to his knees in water when they heard a call from the shore.

"Hold it!" It was Flint, running down from the trees, a vague moving shape of blackness against the moonlit shoreline. "Hang on! I'm coming!"

"Stop!" Tanis cried. "Caramon! Wait for Flint!"

"Look!" Sturm half-rose, pointing. Lights had appeared in the trees, smoking torches held by goblin guards.

"Goblins, Flint!" Tanis yelled. "Behind you! Run!" The dwarf, never questioning, put his head down and pumped for the shore, one hand on his helm to keep it from flying off.

"I'll cover him," Tanis said, unslinging his bow. With his elven sight, he was the only one who could see the goblins behind the torches. Fitting an arrow to his bow, Tanis stood as Caramon held the big boat steady. Tanis fired at the outline of the lead goblin. The arrow struck it in the chest and it pitched forward on its face. The other goblins slowed slightly, reaching for their own bows. Tanis fitted another arrow to his bow as Flint reached the shoreline.

"Wait! I'm coming!" the dwarf gasped and he plunged into the water and sank like a rock.

"Grab him!" Sturm yelled. "Tas, row back. There he is! See? The bubbles—" Caramon was splashing frantically in the water, hunting for the dwarf. Tas tried to row back, but the weight in the boat was too much for the kender. Tanis fired again, missed his mark, and swore beneath his breath. He reached for another arrow. The goblins were swarming down the hillside.

"I've got him!" Caramon shouted, pulling the dripping, spluttering dwarf out by the collar of his leather tunic. "Quit struggling," he told Flint, whose arms were flailing out in all directions. But the dwarf was in a complete state of panic. A goblin arrow thunked into Caramon's chain mail and stuck there like a scrawny feather.

"That does it!" The warrior grunted in exasperation and, with a great heave of his muscular arms, he pitched the dwarf into the boat as it moved out away from him. Flint caught hold of a seat and held on, his lower half sticking out over the

edge. Sturm grabbed him by the belt and dragged him aboard
as the boat rocked alarmingly. Tanis nearly lost his balance
and was forced to drop his bow and catch hold of the side to
keep from being thrown into the water. A goblin arrow stuck
into the gunwale, just barely missing Tanis's hand.

"Row back to Caramon, Tas!" Tanis yelled.

"I can't!" shouted the struggling kender. One swipe of an
out-of-control oar nearly knocked Sturm overboard.

The knight yanked the kender from his seat. He grabbed
the oars and smoothly brought the boat around to where
Caramon could get hold of the side.

Tanis helped the warrior climb in, then yelled to Sturm,
"Pull!" The knight pulled on the oars with all his strength,
leaning over backward as he thrust the oars deep into the
water. The boat shot away from shore, accompanied by the
howls of angry goblins. More arrows whizzed around the boat
as Caramon, dripping wet, plopped down next to Tanis.

"Goblin target practice tonight," Caramon muttered,
pulling the arrow from his mail shirt. "We show up beautifully against the water."

Tanis was fumbling for his dropped bow when he noticed
Raistlin sitting up. "Take cover!" Tanis warned, and Caramon
started to reach for his brother, but the mage, scowling at both
of them, slipped his hand into a pouch on his belt. His delicate fingers drew out a handful of something as an arrow
struck the seat next to him. Raistlin did not react. Tanis
started to pull the mage down, then realized he was lost in
the concentration necessary to a magic-user casting a spell.
Disturbing him now might have drastic consequences,
causing the mage to forget the spell or worse—to miscast
the spell.

Tanis gritted his teeth and watched. Raistlin lifted his thin,
frail hand and allowed the spell component he had taken from
his pouch to fall slowly from between his fingers onto the
deck of the boat. Sand, Tanis realized.

"*Ast tasarak sinuralan krynawi,*"Raistlin murmured, and
then moved his right hand slowly in an arc parallel to the
shore. Tanis looked back toward land. One by one, the goblins
dropped their bows and toppled over, as though Raistlin were
touching each in turn. The arrows ceased. Goblins farther

away howled in rage and ran forward. But by that time, Sturm's powerful strokes had carried the boat out of range.

"Good work, little brother!" Caramon said heartily. Raistlin blinked and seemed to return to the world, then the mage sank forward. Caramon caught him and held him for a moment. Then Raistlin sat up and sucked in a deep breath, which caused him to cough.

"I'll be all right," he whispered, withdrawing from Caramon.

"What did you do to them?" asked Tanis as he searched for enemy arrows to drop them overboard; goblins occasionally poisoned the arrowtips.

"I put them to sleep," Raistlin hissed through teeth that clicked together with the cold. "And now *I* must rest." He sank back against the side of the boat.

Tanis looked at the mage. Raistlin had, indeed, gained in power and skill. I wish I could trust him, the half-elf thought.

The boat moved across the star-filled lake. The only sounds to be heard were the soft, rhythmic splashing of the oars in the water and Raistlin's dry, wracking cough. Tasslehoff uncorked the wineskin, which Flint had somehow retained on his wild dash, and tried to get the chilled, shivering dwarf to swallow a mouthful. But Flint, crouched at the bottom of the boat, could only shudder and stare out across the water.

Goldmoon sank deeper into her fur cape. She wore the soft doeskin breeches of her people with a fringed overskirt and belted tunic. Her boots were made of soft leather. Water had sloshed over the edge of the boat when Caramon had thrown Flint aboard. The water made the doeskin cling to her, and soon she was chilled and shivering.

"Take my cape," Riverwind said in their language, starting to remove his bearskin cloak.

"No." She shook her head. "You have been suffering from the fever. I never get sick, you know that. But"—she looked up at him and smiled—"you may put your arm around me, warrior. The heat from our bodies will warm us both."

"Is that a royal command, Chieftain's Daughter?" Riverwind whispered teasingly, drawing her close to him.

"It is," she said, leaning against his strong body with a sigh of contentment. She looked up into the starry heavens, then stiffened and caught her breath in alarm.

"What is it?" Riverwind asked, staring up.

The others in the boat, although they had not understood the exchange, heard Goldmoon's gasp and saw her eyes transfixed by something in the night sky.

Caramon poked his brother and said, "Raist, what is it? I don't see anything."

Raistlin sat up, cast back his hood, then coughed. When the spasm passed, he searched the night sky. Then he stiffened, and his eyes widened. Reaching out with his thin, bony hand, Raistlin clutched Tanis's arm, holding onto it tightly as the half-elf involuntarily tried to pull away from the mage's skeletal grip. "Tanis . . ." Raistlin wheezed, his breath nearly gone. "The constellations . . ."

"What?" Tanis was truly startled by the pallor of the mage's metallic gold skin and the feverish luster of his strange eyes. "What about the constellations?"

"Gone!" rasped Raistlin and lapsed into a fit of coughing. Caramon put his arm around him, holding him close, almost as if the big man were trying to hold his brother's frail body together. Raistlin recovered, wiped his mouth with his hand. Tanis saw that his fingers were dark with blood. Raistlin took a deep breath, then spoke.

"The constellation known as the Queen of Darkness and the one called Valiant Warrior. Both gone. She has come to Krynn, Tanis, and he has come to fight her. All the evil rumors we have heard are true. War, death, destruction . . ." His voice died in another fit of coughing.

Caramon held him. "C'mon, Raist," he said soothingly. "Don't get so worked up. It's only a bunch of stars."

"Only a bunch of stars," Tanis repeated flatly. Sturm began to row again, pulling swiftly for the opposite bank.

6

Night in a cave.
Dissension. Tanis decides.

A chill wind began to blow across the lake. Storm clouds rolled across the sky from the north, obliterating the gaping black holes left by the fallen stars. The companions hunched down in the boat, pulling their cloaks tighter around them as the rain spattered down. Caramon joined Sturm at the oars. The big warrior tried to talk to the knight, but Sturm ignored him. He rowed in grim silence, occasionally muttering to himself in Solamnic.

"Sturm! There—between the great rocks to the left!" Tanis called out, pointing.

Sturm and Caramon pulled hard. The rain made sighting the landmark rocks difficult and, for a moment, it seemed that they had lost their way in the darkness. Then the rocks suddenly loomed ahead. Sturm and Caramon brought the boat around. Tanis sprang out over the side and pulled it to shore.

Torrents of rain lashed down. The companions climbed from the boat, wet and chilled. They had to lift the dwarf out—Flint was stiff as a dead goblin from fear. Riverwind and Caramon hid the boat in the thick underbrush. Tanis led the rest up a rocky trail to a small opening in the cliff face.

Goldmoon looked at the opening dubiously. It seemed to be no more than a large crack in the surface of the cliff. Inside, however, the cave was large enough for all of them to stretch out comfortably.

"Nice home." Tasslehoff glanced around. "Not much in the way of furniture."

Tanis grinned at the kender. "It will do for the night. I don't think even the dwarf will complain about this. If he does, we'll send him back to sleep in the boat!"

Tas flashed his own smile back at the half-elf. It was good to see the old Tanis back. He had thought his friend unusually moody and indecisive, not the strong leader he had remembered from earlier days. Yet, now that they were on the road, the glint was back in the half-elf's eyes. He had come out of his brooding shell and was taking charge, slipping back into his accustomed role. He needed this adventure to get his mind off his problems—whatever those might be. The kender, who had never been able to understand Tanis's inner turmoil, was glad this adventure had come along.

Caramon carried his brother from the boat and laid him down as gently as he could on the soft warm sand that covered the floor of the cave while Riverwind started a fire. The wet wood crackled and spit, but soon caught fire. The smoke curled up toward the ceiling and drifted out through a crack. The Plainsman covered the cave's entrance with brush and fallen tree branches, hiding the light of the fire and effectively keeping out the rain.

He fits in well, Tanis thought as he watched the barbarian work. He could almost be one of us. Sighing, the half-elf turned his attention to Raistlin. Kneeling down beside him, he looked at the young mage with concern. Raistlin's pale face reflected in the flickering firelight reminded the half-elf of the time he and Flint and Caramon had barely rescued Raistlin from a vicious mob, intent on burning the mage at the stake. Raistlin had attempted to expose a charlatan cleric who was bilking the villagers out of their money. Instead of turning on the cleric, the villagers had turned on Raistlin. As Tanis had told Flint—people wanted to believe in something.

Caramon busied himself around his brother, placing his own heavy cloak over his shoulders. Raistlin's body was wracked by coughing spasms, and blood trickled from his mouth. His eyes gleamed feverishly. Goldmoon knelt beside him, a cup of wine in her hand.

"Can you drink this?" she asked him gently.

Raistlin shook his head, tried to speak, coughed and pushed her hand away. Goldmoon looked up at Tanis. "Perhaps—my staff?" she asked.

"No." Raistlin choked. He motioned for Tanis to come near him. Even sitting next to him, Tanis could barely hear the mage's words; his broken sentences were interrupted by great gasps for air and fits of coughing. "The staff will not heal me, Tanis," he whispered. "Do not waste it on me. If it is a blessed artifact . . . its sacred power is limited. My body was my sacrifice . . . for my magic. This damage is permanent. Nothing can help. . . ." His voice died, his eyes closed.

The fire suddenly flared as wind whirled around the cavern. Tanis looked up to see Sturm pulling the brush aside and entering the cave, half-carrying Flint, who stumbled along on unsteady feet. Sturm dumped him down beside the fire. Both were soaking wet. Sturm was clearly out of patience with the dwarf and, as Tanis noted, with the entire group. Tanis watched him with concern, recognizing the signs of a dark depression that sometimes overwhelmed the knight. Sturm liked the orderly, the well-disciplined. The disappearance of the stars, the disturbance of the natural order of things, had shaken him badly.

Tasslehoff wrapped a blanket around the dwarf who sat huddled on the cave floor, his teeth chattering in his head so that his helm rattled. "B-b-b-boat . . ." was all he could say. Tas poured him a cup of wine which the dwarf drank greedily.

Sturm looked at Flint in disgust. "I'll take the first watch," he said and moved toward the mouth of the cave.

Riverwind rose to his feet. "I will watch with you," he said harshly.

Sturm froze, then turned slowly to face the tall Plainsman. Tanis could see the knight's face, etched in sharp relief by the firelight, dark lines carved around the stern mouth. Although shorter in stature than Riverwind, the knight's air of nobility and the rigidity of his stance made the two appear almost equal.

"I am a knight of Solamnia," Sturm said. "My word is my honor and my honor is my life. I gave my word, back in the Inn, that I would protect you and your lady. If you choose to dispute my word, you dispute my honor and therefore you insult me. I cannot allow that insult to remain between us."

"Sturm!" Tanis was on his feet.

Never taking his eyes from the Plainsman, the knight raised his hand. "Don't interfere, Tanis," Sturm said. "Well, what will it be, swords, knives? How do you barbarians fight?"

Riverwind's stoic expression did not change. He regarded the knight with intense, dark eyes. Then he spoke, choosing his words carefully. "I did not mean to question your honor. I do not know men and their cities, and I tell you plainly—I am afraid. It is my fear that makes me speak thus. I have been afraid ever since the blue crystal staff was given to me. Most of all, I am afraid for Goldmoon." The Plainsman looked over at the woman, his eyes reflecting the glowing fire. "Without her, I die. How could I trust—" His voice failed. The stoic mask cracked and crumbled from pain and weariness. His knees buckled and he pitched forward. Sturm caught him.

"You couldn't," the knight said. "I understand. You are tired, and you have been sick." He helped Tanis lay the Plainsman at the back of the cave. "Rest now. I will stand watch." The knight shoved aside the brush, and without saying another word, stepped outside into the rain.

Goldmoon had listened to the altercation in silence. Now she moved their meager possessions to the back of the cave and knelt down by Riverwind's side. He put his arm around her and held her close, burying his face in her silver-gold hair. The two settled in the shadows of the cave. Wrapped in Riverwind's fur cape, they were soon asleep, Goldmoon's head resting on her warrior's chest.

Tanis breathed a sigh of relief and turned back to Raistlin. The mage had fallen into a fitful sleep. Sometimes he murmured strange words in the language of magic, his hand reaching out to touch his staff. Tanis glanced around at the others. Tasslehoff was sitting near the fire, sorting through his "acquired" objects. He sat cross-legged, the treasures on the cave floor in front of him. Tanis could make out glittering rings, a few unusual coins, a feather from the goatsucker bird, pieces of twine, a bead necklace, a soap doll, and a whistle. One of the rings looked familiar. It was a ring of elven make, given Tanis a long time ago by someone he kept on the borders of his mind. It was a finely carved, delicate ring of golden, clinging ivy leaves.

Tanis crept over to the kender, walking softly to keep from waking the others. "Tas . . . " He tapped the kender on the shoulder and pointed. "My ring . . ."

"Is it?" asked Tasslehoff with wide-eyed innocence. "Is this yours? I'm glad I found it. You must have dropped it at the Inn."

Tanis took the ring with a wry smile, then settled down next to the kender. "Have you got a map of this area, Tas?"

The kender's eyes shone. "A map? Yes, Tanis. Of course." He swept up all his valuables, dumped them back into a pouch, and pulled a hand-carved, wooden scroll case from another pouch. He drew forth a sheaf of maps. Tanis had seen the kender's collection before, but it never failed to astonish him. There must have been a hundred, drawn on everything from fine parchment to soft kid leather to a huge palmetto leaf.

"I thought you knew every tree personally around these parts, Tanis." Tasslehoff sorted through his maps, his eyes occasionally lingering on a favorite.

The half-elf shook his head. "I've lived here many years," he said. "But, let's face it, I don't know any of the dark and secret paths."

"You won't find many to Haven." Tas pulled a map from his pile and smoothed it out on the cave floor. "The Haven Road through Solace Vale is quickest, that's for certain."

Tanis studied the map by the light of the dying campfire. "You're right," he said. "The road is not only quickest—it seems to be the only passable route for several miles ahead. Both south and north of us lie the Kharolis Mountains—no passes there." Frowning, Tanis rolled up the map and handed it back. "Which is exactly what the Theocrat will figure."

Tasslehoff yawned. "Well," he said, putting the map back carefully into the case, "it's a problem that will be solved by wiser heads than mine. I'm along for the fun." Tucking the case back into a pouch, the kender lay down on the cave floor, drew his legs up beneath his chin, and was soon sleeping the peaceful sleep of small children and animals.

Tanis looked at him with envy. Although aching with weariness, he couldn't relax enough for sleep. Most of the others had dropped off, all but the warrior watching over his brother. Tanis walked over to Caramon.

"Turn in," he whispered. "I'll watch Raistlin."

"No," the big warrior said. Reaching out, he gently pulled a cloak up closer around his brother's shoulders. "He might need me."

"But you've got to get some sleep."

"I will." Caramon grinned. "Go get some sleep yourself, nursemaid. Your children are fine. Look—even the dwarf is out cold."

"I don't have to look," Tanis said. "The Theocrat can probably hear him snoring in Solace. Well, my friend, this reunion was not much like we planned five years ago."

"What is?" Caramon asked softly, glancing down at his brother.

Tanis patted the man's arm, then lay down and rolled up in his own cloak and, at last, fell asleep.

The night passed—slowly for those on watch, swiftly for those asleep. Caramon relieved Sturm. Tanis relieved Caramon. The storm continued unabated all night, the wind whipping the lake into a white-capped sea. Lightning branched through the darkness like flaming trees. Thunder rumbled continually. The storm finally blew itself out by morning, and the half-elf watched day dawn, gray and chill. The rain had ended, but storm clouds still hung low. No sun appeared in the sky. Tanis felt a growing sense of urgency. He could see no end to the storm clouds massing to the north. Autumn storms were rare, especially ones with this ferocity. The wind was bitter, too, and it seemed odd that the storm came out of the north, when they generally swept east, across the Plains. Sensitive to the ways of nature, the strange weather upset Tanis nearly as much as Raistlin's fallen stars. He felt a need to get going, even though it was early morning yet. He went inside to wake the others.

The cave was chill and gloomy in the gray dawn, despite the crackling fire. Goldmoon and Tasslehoff were fixing breakfast. Riverwind stood in the back of the cave, shaking out Goldmoon's fur cloak. Tanis glanced at him. The Plainsman had been about to say something to Goldmoon as Tanis entered, but fell silent, contenting himself with staring at her meaningfully as he continued his work. Goldmoon kept her eyes lowered, her face pale and troubled. The barbarian regrets having let himself go last night, Tanis realized.

"There is not much food, I'm afraid," Goldmoon said, tossing cereal into a pot of boiling water.

"Tika's larder wasn't well stocked," Tasslehoff added in apology. "We've got a loaf of bread, some dried beef, half a moldy cheese, and the oatmeal. Tika must eat her meals out."

"Riverwind and I didn't bring any provisions," Goldmoon said. "We really didn't expect to make this trip."

Tanis was about to ask her more about her song and the staff, but the others started waking up as they smelled food. Caramon yawned, stretched, and stood up. Walking over to peer into the cook-pot, he groaned. "Oatmeal? Is that all?"

"There'll be less for dinner." Tasslehoff grinned. "Tighten your belt. You're gaining weight anyhow."

The big man sighed dismally.

The sparse breakfast was cheerless in the cold dawn. Sturm, refusing all offers of food, went outside to keep watch. Tanis could see the knight, sitting on a rock, staring gloomily at the dark clouds that trailed wispy fingers along the still water of the lake. Caramon ate his share of the food quickly, gulped down his brother's portion, and then appropriated Sturm's when the knight walked out. Then the big man sat, watching wistfully while the rest finished.

"You gonna eat that?" he asked, pointing to Flint's share of bread. The dwarf scowled. Tasslehoff, seeing the warrior's eyes roam over to his plate, crammed his bread into his mouth, nearly choking himself in the process. At least it kept him quiet, Tanis thought, glad for the respite from the kender's shrill voice. Tas had been teasing Flint unmercifully all morning, calling him "Seamaster" and "Shipmate," asking him the price of fish, and how much he would charge to ferry them back across the lake. Flint finally threw a rock at him, and Tanis sent Tas down to the lake to scrub out the pans.

The half-elf walked to the back of the cave.

"How are you this morning, Raistlin?" he asked. "We're going to have to be moving out soon."

"I am much better," the mage replied in his soft, whispering voice. He was drinking some herbal concoction of his own making. Tanis could see small, feathery green leaves floating in steaming water. It gave off a bitter, acrid odor and Raistlin grimaced as he swallowed it.

Tasslehoff came bounding back into the cave, pots and tin plates clattering loudly. Tanis gritted his teeth at the noise, started to reprimand the kender, then changed his mind. It wouldn't do any good.

Flint, seeing the tension on Tanis's face, grabbed the pots from the kender and began packing them away. "Be serious," the dwarf hissed at Tasslehoff. "Or I'll take you by the topknot and tie you to a tree as a warning to all kender—"

Tas reached out and plucked something from the dwarf's beard. "Look!" the kender held it up gleefully. "Seaweed!" Flint, roaring, made a grab for the kender, but Tas skipped out of his way agilely.

There was a rustling sound as Sturm shoved aside the brush covering the doorway. His face was dark and brooding.

"Stop this!" Sturm said, glowering at Flint and Tas, his moustaches quivering. His dour gaze turned on Tanis. "I could hear these two clear down by the lake. They'll have every goblin in Krynn on us. We've got to get out of here. Well, which way are we headed?"

An uneasy silence fell. Everyone stopped what he was doing and looked at Tanis, with the exception of Raistlin. The mage was wiping his cup out with a white cloth, cleaning it fastidiously. He continued working, eyes downcast, as though totally uninterested.

Tanis sighed and scratched his beard. "The Theocrat in Solace is corrupt. We know that now. He is using the goblin scum to take control. If he had the staff, he would use it for his own profit. We've searched for a sign of the true gods for years. It seems we may have found one. I am not about to hand it over to that Solace fraud. Tika said she believed the Highseekers in Haven were still interested in the truth. They may be able to tell us about the staff, where it came from, what its powers are. Tas, give me the map."

The kender, spilling the contents of several pouches onto the floor, finally produced the parchment requested.

"We are here, on the west bank of Crystalmir," Tanis continued. "North and south of us are branches of the Kharolis Mountains which form the boundaries of Solace Vale. There are no known passes through either range except through Gateway Pass south of Solace—"

"Almost certainly held by the goblins," muttered Sturm.

"There are passes to the northeast—"

"That's across the lake!" Flint said in horror.

"Yes"—Tanis kept a straight face—"across the lake. But those lead to the Plains, and I don't believe you want to go that direction." He glanced at Goldmoon and Riverwind. "The west road goes through the Sentinel Peaks and Shadow Canyon to Haven. That seems to me the obvious direction to take."

Sturm frowned. "And if the Highseekers there are as bad as the one in Solace?"

"Then we continue south to Qualinesti."

"Qualinesti?" Riverwind scowled. "The Elven Lands? No! Humans are forbidden to enter. Besides, the way is hidden—"

A rasping, hissing sound cut into the discussion. Everyone turned to face Raistlin as he spoke. "There is a way." His voice was soft and mocking; his golden eyes glittered in the cold light of dawn. "The paths of Darken Wood. They lead right to Qualinesti."

"Darken Wood?" Caramon repeated in alarm. "No, Tanis!" The warrior shook his head. "I'll fight the living any day of the week—but not the dead!"

"The dead?" Tasslehoff asked eagerly. "Tell me, Caramon—"

"Shut up, Tas!" Sturm snapped. "Darken Wood is madness. None who enter have ever returned. You would have us take this prize there, mage?"

"Hold!" Tanis spoke sharply. Everyone fell silent. Even Sturm quieted. The knight looked at Tanis's calm, thoughtful face, the almond-shaped eyes that held the wisdom of his many years of wandering. The knight had often tried to resolve within himself why he accepted Tanis's leadership. He was nothing more than a bastard half-elf, after all. He did not come of noble blood. He wore no armor, carried no shield with a proud emblem. Yet Sturm followed him, and loved him and respected him as he respected no other living man.

Life was a dark shroud to the Solamnic knight. He could not pretend to ever know or understand it except through the code of the knights he lived by. *"Est Sularus oth Mithas"*—"My honor is life." The code defined honor and was more complete and detailed and strict than any known on Krynn. The code had held true for seven hundred years, but Sturm's secret fear was that, someday, in the final battle, the code would have no answers. He knew that if that day came, Tanis would be at his side, holding the crumbling world together. For while Sturm followed the code, Tanis lived it.

Tanis's voice brought the knight's thoughts back to the present. "I remind all of you that this staff is not our 'prize.' The staff rightfully belongs to Goldmoon—if it belongs to anyone. We have no more right to it than the Theocrat in Solace." Tanis turned to Goldmoon. "What is your will, lady?"

Goldmoon stared from Tanis to Sturm, then she looked at Riverwind. "You know my mind," he said coldly. "But—you are Chieftain's Daughter." He rose to his feet. Ignoring her pleading gaze, he stalked outside.

"What did he mean?" Tanis asked.

"He wants us to leave you, take the staff to Haven," Goldmoon answered, her voice low. "He says you are adding to our danger. We would be safer on our own."

"Adding to your danger!" Flint exploded. "Why we wouldn't be here, I wouldn't have nearly drowned—again!—if it hadn't been for—for—" The dwarf began to sputter in his rage.

Tanis held up his hand. "Enough." He scratched his beard. "You will be safer with us. Will you accept our help?"

"I will," Goldmoon answered gravely, "for a short distance at least."

"Good," Tanis said. "Tas, you know your way through Solace Vale. You are our guide. And remember, we're not on a picnic!"

"Yes, Tanis," the kender said, subdued. He gathered his many pouches, hung them around his waist and over his shoulders. Passing Goldmoon, he knelt swiftly and patted her hand, then he was out the cave entrance. The rest hastily gathered their gear together and followed.

"It's going to rain again," Flint grumbled, glancing up at the lowering clouds. "I should have stayed in Solace." Muttering, he walked off, adjusting his battle-axe on his back. Tanis, waiting for Goldmoon and Riverwind, smiled and shook his head. At least some things never changed, dwarves among them.

Riverwind took their packs from Goldmoon and slung them over his shoulder. "I have made certain the boat is well-hidden and secure," he told Tanis. The stoic mask was in place again this morning. "In case we need it."

"A good idea," Tanis said. "Thank—"

"If you will go ahead." Riverwind motioned. "I will come behind and cover our tracks."

Tanis started to speak, to thank the Plainsman. But Riverwind had already turned his back and was beginning his work. Walking up the path, the half-elf shook his head. Behind him, he could hear Goldmoon speaking softly in her own language. Riverwind replied—one, harsh word. Tanis heard Goldmoon sigh, then all other words were lost in the sound of crackling brush as Riverwind obliterated all traces of their passing.

7

The story of the staff. Strange clerics. Eerie feelings.

The thick woods of Solace Vale were a green mass of vibrant life. Beneath the dense roof of the vallen-woods flourished thistlebrush and greenwall. The ground was crisscrossed with the bothersome tangleshoot vines. These had to be trod on with great care or they would suddenly snake around an ankle, trapping the helpless victim until he was devoured by one of the many predatory animals lurking in the Vale, thus providing tangleshoot with what it needed to live—blood.

It took over an hour of hacking and chopping through the brush to get to the Haven Road. All of them were scratched, torn, and tired, and the long stretch of smooth-packed dirt that carried travelers to Haven or beyond was a welcome sight. It wasn't until they stopped just in sight of the road and rested that they realized there were no sounds. A hush had fallen over the land, as if every creature were holding its breath, waiting. Now that they had reached the road, no one was particularly eager to step out of the shelter of the brush.

"Do you think it's safe?" Caramon asked, peering through a hedge.

"Safe or not, it's the way we have to go," Tanis snapped, "unless you can fly or unless you want to go back into the forest. It took us an hour to travel a few hundred yards. We ought to reach the crossroads next week at that pace."

The big man flushed, chagrined. "I didn't mean—"

"I'm sorry." Tanis sighed. He too looked down the road. The vallenwoods formed a dark corridor in the gray light. "I don't like it any better than you do."

"Do we separate or stay together?" Sturm interrupted what he considered idle chatter with cold practicality.

"We stay together," Tanis replied. Then, after a moment, he added, "Still, someone ought to scout—"

"I will, Tanis," Tas volunteered, popping up out of the brush beneath Tanis's elbow. "No one would ever suspect a kender traveling alone."

Tanis frowned. Tas was right—no one would suspect him. Kender were all afflicted with wanderlust, traveling throughout Krynn in search of adventure. But Tas had the disconcerting habit of forgetting his mission and wandering off if something more interesting caught his attention.

"Very well," Tanis said finally. "But, remember, Tasslehoff Burrfoot, keep your eyes open and your wits about you. No roaming off the road and above all"—Tanis fixed the kender's eye with his own sternly—"keep your hands out of other people's belongings."

"Unless they're bakers," Caramon added.

Tas giggled, pushed his way through the final few feet of brush, and started off down the road, his hoopak staff digging holes in the mud, his pouches jouncing up and down as he walked. They heard his voice lift in a kender trailsong.

Your one true love's a sailing ship
That anchors at our pier.
We lift her sails, we man her decks,
We scrub the portholes clear;

And yes, our lighthouse shines for her,
And yes, our shores are warm;
We steer her into harbor,
Any port in a storm.

The sailors stand upon the docks,
The sailors stand in line,
As thirsty as a dwarf for gold
Or centaurs for cheap wine.

For all the sailors love her,
And flock to where she's moored,
Each man hoping that he might
Go down, all hands on board.

Tanis, grinning, allowed a few minutes to pass after hearing the last verse of Tas's song before starting out. Finally they stepped out on the road with as much fear as a troupe of unskilled actors facing a hostile audience. It felt as if every eye on Krynn was on them.

The deep shade under the flame-colored leaves made it impossible to see anything in the woods even a few feet from the road. Sturm walked ahead of the group, alone, in bitter silence. Tanis knew that though the knight held his head proudly, he was slogging through his own darkness. Caramon and Raistlin followed. Tanis kept his eyes on the mage, concerned about his ability to keep up.

Raistlin had experienced some difficulty in getting through the brush, but he was moving along well now. He leaned on his staff with one hand, holding open a book with the other. Tanis at first wondered what the mage was studying, then realized it was his spellbook. It is the curse of the magi that they must constantly study and recommit their spells to memory every day. The words of magic flame in the mind, then flicker and die when the spell is cast. Each spell burns up some of the magician's physical and mental energy until he is totally exhausted and must rest before he can use his magic again.

Flint stumped along on the other side of Caramon. The two began to argue softly about the ten-year-old boating accident.

"Trying to catch a fish with your bare hands—" Flint grumbled his disgust.

Tanis came last, walking next to the Plainsmen. He turned his attention to Goldmoon. Seeing her clearly in the flecked gray light beneath the trees, he noticed lines around her eyes that made her appear older than her twenty-nine years.

"Our lives have not been easy," Goldmoon confided to him as they walked. "Riverwind and I have loved each other many years, but it is the law of my people that a warrior who wants to marry his chieftain's daughter must perform some great feat to prove himself worthy. It was worse with us. Riverwind's family was cast out of our tribe years ago for refusing to worship our ancestors. His grandfather believed in ancient gods who had existed before the Cataclysm, though he could find little evidence of them left on Krynn.

"My father was determined I should not marry so far beneath my station. He sent Riverwind on an impossible quest, to find some object with holy properties that would prove the existence of these ancient gods. Of course, my father didn't believe such an object existed. He hoped Riverwind would meet his death, or that I would come to love another." She looked up at the tall warrior walking beside her and smiled. But his face was hard, his eyes staring far away. Her smile faded. Sighing, she continued her story, speaking softly, more to herself than Tanis.

"Riverwind was gone long years. And my life was empty. I sometimes thought my heart would die. Then, just a week ago, he returned. He was half-dead, out of his mind with a raging fever. He stumbled into camp and fell at my feet, his skin burning to the touch. In his hand, he clutched this staff. We had to pry his fingers loose. Even unconscious, he would not release it.

"He raved in his fever about a dark place, a broken city where death had black wings. Then, when he was nearly wild with fear and terror and the servants had to tie his arms to the bed, he remembered a woman, a woman dressed in blue light. She came to him in the dark place, he said, and healed him and gave him the staff. When he remembered her, he grew calmer and his fever broke.

"Two days ago—" She paused, had it really been only two days? It seemed a lifetime! Sighing, she continued. "He presented the staff to my father, telling him it had been given to him by a goddess, though he did not know her name. My father looked at this staff"—Goldmoon held it up—"and commanded it to do something, anything. Nothing happened. He threw it back to Riverwind, proclaiming him a fraud, and ordered the people to stone him to death as punishment for his blasphemy!"

Goldmoon's face grew pale as she spoke, Riverwind's face dark and shadowed.

"The tribe bound Riverwind and dragged him to the Grieving Wall," she said, barely speaking above a whisper. "They started hurling rocks. He looked at me with so much love and he shouted that not even death would separate us. I couldn't bear the thought of living my life alone, without him. I ran to him. The rocks struck us—" Goldmoon put her hand to her forehead, wincing in remembered pain, and Tanis's attention was drawn to a fresh, jagged scar on her tanned skin. "There was a blinding flash of light. When Riverwind and I could see again, we were standing on the road outside of Solace. The staff glowed blue, then dimmed and faded until it is as you see it now. It was then we determined to go to Haven and ask the wise men at the temple about the staff."

"Riverwind," Tanis asked, troubled, "what do you remember of this broken city? Where was it?"

Riverwind didn't answer. He glanced at Tanis out of the corner of his dark eyes, and it was obvious his thoughts had been far away. Then he stared off into the shadowy trees.

"Tanis Half-Elven," he finally said. "That is your name?"

"Among humans, that is what I am called," Tanis answered. "My elvish name is long and difficult for humans to pronounce."

Riverwind frowned. "Why is it," he asked, "that you are called half-elf and not half-man?"

The question struck Tanis like a blow across the face. He could almost envision himself sprawling in the dirt and had to force himself to stop and swallow an angry retort. He knew Riverwind was asking this question for a reason. It had not been meant as an insult. This was a test, Tanis realized. He chose his words carefully.

"According to humans, half an elf is but part of a whole being. Half a man is a cripple."

Riverwind considered this, finally nodded once, abruptly, and answered Tanis's question.

"I wandered many long years," he replied. "Often I had no idea where I was. I followed the sun and the moons and the stars. My last journey is like a dark dream." He was silent for a moment. When he spoke, it was as if he were talking from some great distance. "It was a city once beautiful, with white buildings supported by tall columns of marble. But it is now as if some great hand had picked up the city and cast it down a mountainside. The city is now very old and very evil."

"Death on black wings," Tanis said softly.

"It rose like a god from the darkness, its creatures worshiped it, shrieking and howling." The Plainsman's face paled beneath his sun-baked skin. He was sweating in the chill morning air. "I can speak of it no more!" Goldmoon laid her hand on his arm, and the tension in his face eased.

"And out of the horror came a woman who gave you the staff?" Tanis pursued.

"She healed me," Riverwind said simply. "I was dying."

Tanis stared intently at the staff Goldmoon held in her hand. It was just a plain, ordinary staff that he never noticed until his attention was called to it. A strange device was carved on the top, and feathers—such as the barbarians admire—were tied around it. Yet he had seen it glow blue! He had felt its healing powers. Was this a gift from ancient gods—come to aid them in their time of need? Or was it evil? What did he know of these barbarians anyway? Tanis thought about Raistlin's claim that the staff could only be touched by those pure of heart. He shook his head. It sounded good. He wanted to believe it. . . .

Tanis, lost in thought, felt Goldmoon touch his arm. He looked up to see Sturm and Caramon signaling. The half-elf suddenly realized he and the Plainsmen had fallen far behind the others. He broke into a run.

"What is it?"

Sturm pointed. "The scout returns," he said dryly.

Tasslehoff was running down the road toward them. He waved his arm three times.

"Into the brush!" Tanis ordered. The group hurriedly left the road and plunged into the bushes and scrub trees growing along the south edge, all except Sturm.

"Come on!" Tanis put his hand on the knight's arm. Sturm pulled away from the half-elf.

"I will not hide in a ditch!" the knight stated coldly.

"Sturm—" Tanis began, fighting to control his rising anger. He choked back bitter words that would do no good and might cause irreparable harm. Instead, he turned from the knight, his lips compressed, and waited in grim silence for the kender.

Tas came dashing up, pouches and packs bouncing wildly as he ran. "Clerics!" he gasped. "A party of clerics. Eight."

Sturm sniffed. "I thought it was a battalion of goblin guards at the least. I believe we can handle a party of clerics."

"I don't know," Tasslehoff said, dubiously. "I've seen clerics from every part of Krynn and I've never seen any like these." He glanced down the road apprehensively, then gazed up at Tanis, unusual seriousness in his brown eyes. "Do you remember what Tika said about the strange men in Solace—hanging around with Hederick? How they were hooded and dressed in heavy robes? Well, that describes these clerics exactly! And, Tanis, they gave me an eerie feeling." The kender shuddered. "They'll be in sight in a few moments."

Tanis glanced at Sturm. The knight raised his eyebrows. Both of them knew that kenders did not feel the emotion of fear, yet were extremely sensitive to other creatures' natures. Tanis couldn't remember when the sight of any being on Krynn had ever given Tas an "eerie feeling"—and he had been with the kender in some tight spots.

"Here they come," Tanis said suddenly. He and Sturm and Tas moved back into the shadows of the trees to the left, watching as the clerics slowly rounded a bend in the road. They were too far away for the half-elf to be able to tell much about them, except that they were moving very slowly, dragging a large handcart behind them.

"Maybe you should talk to them, Sturm," Tanis said softly. "We need information about the road ahead. But be careful, my friend."

"I'll be careful." Sturm said, smiling. "I have no intention of throwing my life away needlessly."

The knight gripped Tanis's arm a moment in silent apology, then dropped his hand to loosen his sword in its antique scabbard. He walked across to the other side of the road and leaned up against a broken-down wooden fence, head bowed, as though resting. Tanis stood a moment, irresolute, then turned and made his way through the brush, Tasslehoff at his heels.

"What is it?" Caramon grunted as Tanis and Tas appeared. The big warrior shifted his girth, causing his arsenal of weapons to clank loudly. The rest of the companions were huddled together, concealed behind thick clumps of brush, yet able to get a clear view of the road.

"Hush." Tanis knelt down between Caramon and Riverwind, who crouched in the brush a few feet to Tanis's left. "Clerics," he whispered. "A group of them coming down the road. Sturm's going to question them."

"Clerics!" Caramon snorted derisively and settled back comfortably on his heels. But Raistlin stirred restlessly.

"Clerics," he whispered thoughtfully. "I do not like this."

"What do you mean?" asked Tanis.

Raistlin peered at the half-elf from the dark shadows of his hood. All Tanis could see were the mage's golden hourglass eyes, narrow slits of cunning and intelligence.

"Strange clerics," Raistlin spoke with elaborate patience, as one speaks to a child. "The staff has healing, clerical powers—such powers as have not been seen on Krynn since the Cataclysm! Caramon and I saw some of these cloaked and hooded men in Solace. Don't you find it odd, my friend, that these clerics and this staff turned up at the same time, in the same place, when neither has been seen before? Perhaps this staff is truly theirs—by right."

Tanis glanced at Goldmoon. Her face was shadowed with worry. Surely she must be wondering the same thing. He looked back at the road again. The cloaked figures were moving at a crawling pace, pulling the cart. Sturm sat on the fence, stroking his moustaches.

The companions waited in silence. Gray clouds massed overhead, the sky grew darker and soon water began to drip through the branches of the trees.

"There, it's raining," Flint grumbled. "It isn't enough that I have to squat in a bush like a toad, now I get soaked to the skin—"

Tanis glared at the dwarf. Flint mumbled and fell silent. Soon the companions could hear nothing but the rain splatting against the already wet leaves, drumming on shield and helm. It was a cold, steady rain, the kind that seeps through the thickest cloak. It ran off Caramon's dragon helm and trickled down his neck. Raistlin began to shiver and cough, covering his mouth with his hand to muffle the sound as everyone stared at him in alarm.

Tanis looked out to the road. Like Tas, he had never seen anything to compare to these clerics in his hundred years of life on Krynn. They were tall, about six feet in height. Long robes shrouded their bodies, hooded cloaks covered the robes. Even their feet and hands were wrapped in cloth, like bandages covering leprous wounds. As they neared Sturm, they glanced around warily. One of them stared straight into the brush where the companions were hiding. They could see only dark glittering eyes through a swath of cloth.

"Hail, Knight of Solamnia," the lead cleric said in the Common tongue. His voice was hollow, lisping, an inhuman voice. Tanis shivered.

"Greetings, brethren," Sturm answered, also in Common. "I have traveled many miles this day and you are the first travelers I have passed. I have heard strange rumors, and I seek information about the road ahead. Where do you come from?"

"We come from the east originally," the cleric answered. "But today we travel from Haven. It is a chill, bitter day for journeying, knight, which is perhaps why you find the road empty. We ourselves would not undertake such a journey save we are driven by necessity. We did not pass you on the road, so you must be traveling from Solace, Sir Knight."

Sturm nodded. Several of the clerics standing at the rear of the cart turned their hooded faces toward each other, muttering. The lead cleric spoke to them in a strange, guttural language. Tanis looked at his companions. Tasslehoff shook his head, as did the rest of them; none of them had heard it before. The cleric switched back to Common. "I am curious to hear these rumors you speak of, knight."

"There is talk of armies in the north," Sturm replied. "I am traveling that way, to my homeland of Solamnia. I would not want to run into a war to which I had not been invited."

"We have not heard these rumors," the cleric answered. "So far as we know, the road to the north is clear."

"Ah, that's what comes of listening to drunken companions." Sturm shrugged. "But what is this necessity you speak of that drives the brethren out into such foul weather?"

"We seek a staff," the cleric answered readily. "A blue crystal staff. We heard that it had been sighted in Solace. Do you know aught of it?"

"Yes," Sturm answered. "I heard of such a staff in Solace. I heard of the armies to the north from the same companions. Am I to believe these stories or not?"

This appeared to confound the cleric for a moment. He glanced around, as if uncertain how to react.

"Tell me," said Sturm, lounging back against the fence, "why do you seek a blue crystal staff? Surely one of plain, sturdy wood would suit you reverend gentlemen better."

"It is a sacred staff of healing," the cleric replied gravely. "One of our brothers is sorely ill; he will die without the blessed touch of this holy relic."

"Healing?" Sturm raised his eyebrows. "A sacred staff of healing would be of great value. How did you come to misplace such a rare and wonderful object?"

"We did not misplace it!" the cleric snarled. Tanis saw the man's wrapped hands clench in anger. "It was stolen from our holy order. We tracked the foul thief to a barbarian village in the Plains, then lost his trail. There are rumors of strange doings in Solace, however, and it is there we go." He gestured to the back of the cart. "This dismal journey is but little sacrifice for us compared to the pain and agony our brother endures."

"I'm afraid I cannot help—" Sturm began.

"I can help you!" called a clear voice from beside Tanis. He reached out, but he was too late. Goldmoon had risen from the brush and was walking determinedly to the road, pushing aside tree branches and brambles. Riverwind jumped to his feet and crashed through the shrubbery after her.

"Goldmoon!" Tanis risked a piercing whisper.

"I must know!" was all she said.

The clerics, hearing Goldmoon's voice, glanced at each other knowingly, nodding their hooded heads. Tanis sensed trouble, but before he could say anything, Caramon jumped to his feet.

"The Plainsmen are not leaving me behind in a ditch while they have all the fun!" Caramon stated, plunging through the thicket after Riverwind.

"Has everyone gone mad?" Tanis growled. He grabbed Tasslehoff by his shirt collar, dragging the kender back as he was about to leap joyfully after Caramon. "Flint, watch the kender. Raistlin—"

"No need to worry about me, Tanis," the mage whispered. "I have no intention of going out there."

"Right. Well, stay here." Tanis rose to his feet and slowly started forward, an "eerie feeling" creeping over him.

8

Search for truth. Unexpected answers.

can help you." Goldmoon's clear voice rang out like a pure, silver bell. The Chieftain's Daughter saw Sturm's shocked face; she understood Tanis's warning.

But this was not the act of a foolish, hysterical woman. Goldmoon was far from that. She had ruled her tribe in all but name for ten years, ever since sickness had struck her father like a lightning bolt, leaving him unable to speak clearly or to move his right arm and leg. She had led her people in times of war with neighboring tribes and in times of peace. She had confounded attempts to wrest her power from her. She knew that what she was doing now was dangerous. These strange clerics filled her with loathing. But they obviously knew something about this staff, and she had to know the answer.

"I am the bearer of the blue crystal staff," Goldmoon said, approaching the leader of the clerics, her head held proudly.

81

"But we did not steal it; the staff was given to us."

Riverwind stepped to one side of her, Sturm to the other. Caramon came charging through the brush and stood behind her, his hand on his sword hilt, an eager grin on his face.

"So you say," the cleric said in a soft, sneering voice. He stared at the plain brown staff in her hand with avid, black, gleaming eyes, then reached out his wrapped hand to take it. Goldmoon swiftly clasped the staff to her body.

"The staff was carried out of a place of great evil," she said. "I will do what I can to help your dying brother, but I will not relinquish this staff to you or to anyone else until I am firmly convinced of your rightful claim to it."

The cleric hesitated, glanced back at his fellows. Tanis saw them make nervous, tentative gestures toward the wide cloth belts they wore tied around their flowing robes. Unusually wide belts, Tanis noticed, with strange bulges beneath them—not, he was sure, made by prayer books. He swore in frustration, wishing Sturm and Caramon were paying attention. But Sturm seemed completely relaxed and Caramon was nudging him as though sharing a private joke. Tanis raised his bow cautiously and put an arrow to the string.

The cleric finally bowed his head in submission, folding his hands in his sleeves. "We will be grateful for whatever aid you can give our poor brother," he said, his voice muffled. "And then I hope you and your companions will return with us to Haven. I promise you that you will be convinced that the staff has come into your possession wrongly."

"We'll go where we've a mind to, brother," Caramon growled.

Fool! Tanis thought. The half-elf considered shouting a warning, then decided to remain hidden in case his growing fears were realized.

Goldmoon and the leader of the cloaked men passed the cart, Riverwind next to her. Caramon and Sturm remained near the front of it, watching with interest. As Goldmoon and the cleric reached the back, the cleric put out a wrapped hand and drew Goldmoon toward the cart. She pulled away from his touch and stepped forward by herself. The cleric bowed humbly, then lifted up a cloth covering the back of the cart. Holding the staff in front of her, Goldmoon peered in.

Tanis saw a flurry of movement. Goldmoon screamed. There was a flash of blue light and a cry. Goldmoon sprang backward as Riverwind jumped in front of her. The cleric lifted a horn to his lips and blew long, wailing notes.

"Caramon! Sturm!" Tanis called, raising his bow. "It's a tra—" A great weight dropped on the half-elf from above, knocking him to the ground. Strong hands groped for his throat, shoving his face deep into the wet leaves and mud. The man's fingers found their hold and began squeezing. Tanis fought to breathe, but his nose and mouth were filled with mud. Seeing starbursts, he tore frantically at the hands that were trying to crush his windpipe. The man's grip was incredibly strong. Tanis felt himself losing consciousness. He tensed his muscles for one final, desperate struggle, then he heard a hoarse cry and a bone-crushing thump. The hands relaxed their grip and the heavy weight was dragged off him.

Tanis staggered to his knees, his breath coming in painful gasps. Wiping mud from his face, he looked up to see Flint with a log in his hand. But the dwarf's eyes were not on him. They were on the body at his feet.

Tanis followed the astonished dwarf's gaze, and the half-elf recoiled in horror. It wasn't a man! Leathery wings sprang from its back. It had the scaly flesh of a reptile; its large hands and feet were clawed, but it walked upright in the manner of men. The creature wore sophisticated armor that allowed it the use of its wings. It was the creature's face, however, that made him shudder, it was not the face of any living being he had ever seen before, either on Krynn or in his darkest nightmares. The creature had the face of a man, but it was as if some malevolent being had twisted it into that of a reptile!

"By all the gods," Raistlin breathed, creeping up to Tanis. "What is that?"

Before Tanis could answer, he saw out of the corner of his eye a brilliant flash of blue light and he heard Goldmoon calling.

For one instant, as Goldmoon had looked into the cart, she had wondered what terrible disease could turn a man's flesh into scales. She had moved forward to touch the pitiful cleric with her staff, but at that moment the creature sprang out at her, grasping for the staff with a clawed hand. Goldmoon stumbled backward, but the creature was swift and its clawed hand closed around the staff. There was a blinding flash of blue light. The creature shrieked in pain and fell back, wringing its blackened hand. Riverwind, sword drawn, had leaped in front of his Chieftain's Daughter.

But now she heard him gasp and she saw his sword arm drop weakly. He staggered backward, making no effort to defend himself. Rough wrapped hands grabbed her from behind. A horrible scaled hand was clapped over her mouth. Struggling to free herself, she caught a glimpse of Riverwind. He was staring wide-eyed in terror at the thing in the cart, his face deathly white, his breathing swift and shallow—a man who wakes from a nightmare to discover it is reality.

Goldmoon, strong child of a warrior race, kicked backward at the cleric holding her, her foot aiming for his knee. Her skillful kick caught her opponent off guard and crushed his kneecap. The instant the cleric eased his grip on her, Goldmoon whirled around and struck him with her staff. She was amazed to see the cleric slump to the ground, seemingly felled by a blow even the mighty Caramon might have envied. She looked at her staff in astonishment, the staff that now glowed a bright blue. But there was no time to wonder—other creatures surrounded her. She swung her glistening staff in a wide arc, holding them at bay. But for how long?

"Riverwind!"

Goldmoon's cry woke the Plainsman from his terror. Turning, he saw her backing into the forest, keeping the cloaked clerics away with the staff. He grabbed one of the clerics from behind and threw him heavily to the ground. Another jumped at him while a third sprang toward Goldmoon.

There was a blinding blue flash.

A moment ahead of Tanis's cry, Sturm had realized the clerics had set a trap and drew his sword. He had seen, through the slats of the old wooden cart, a clawed hand grabbing for the staff. Lunging forward, he had gone to back up Riverwind. But the knight was totally unprepared for the Plainsman's reaction at sight of the creature in the cart. Sturm saw Riverwind stagger backward, helpless, as the creature grabbed a battleaxe in its uninjured hand and sprang directly at the barbarian. Riverwind made no move to defend himself. He just stared, his weapon dangling in his hand.

Sturm plunged his sword into the creature's back. The thing screamed and whirled around to attack, wrenching the sword from the knight's hand. Slavering and gurgling in its dying rage, the creature wrapped its arms around the startled knight and bore him into the muddy road. Sturm knew the thing that grasped him was dying and fought to beat down the terror and revulsion he felt at the touch of its slimy skin. The screaming stopped, and he felt the creature go rigid. The knight shoved the body over and quickly started to pull his sword from the creature's back. The weapon didn't budge! He stared at it in disbelief, then yanked on the sword with all his might, even putting his booted foot against the body to gain leverage. The weapon was stuck fast. Furious, he beat at the creature with his hands, then drew back in fear and loathing. The thing had turned to stone!

"Caramon!" Sturm yelled as another of the strange clerics leaped toward him, swinging an axe. Sturm ducked, felt a slashing pain, and then was blinded when blood flowed into his eyes. He stumbled, unable to see, and a crushing weight bore him to the ground.

Caramon, standing near the front of the cart, started to go to Goldmoon's aid when he heard Sturm's cry. Then two of the creatures bore down on him. Swinging his shortsword to force them to keep their distance, Caramon drew his dagger with his left hand. One cleric jumped for him and Caramon slashed out, his blade biting deep into flesh. He smelled a foul, rotting stench and saw a sickly green stain appear on the cleric's robes, but the wound appeared just to enrage the creature. It kept coming, saliva dripping from jaws that were the jaws of a reptile—not a man. For a moment, panic engulfed Caramon. He had fought trolls and goblins, but these horrible clerics completely unnerved him. He felt lost and alone, then he heard a reassuring whisper next to him.

"I am here, my brother." Raistlin's calm voice filled his mind.

"About time," Caramon gasped, threatening the creature with his sword. "What sort of foul clerics are these?"

"Don't stab them!" Raistlin warned swiftly. "They'll turn to stone. They're not clerics. They are some sort of reptile man. That is the reason for the robes and hoods."

Though different as light and shadow, the twins fought well as a team. They exchanged few words during battle, their thoughts merging faster than tongues could translate. Caramon dropped his sword and dagger and flexed his huge arm muscles. The creatures, seeing Caramon drop his weapons, charged forward. Their rags had fallen loose and fluttered about them grotesquely. Caramon grimaced at the sight of the scaled bodies and clawed hands.

"Ready," he said to his brother.

"*Ast tasark simiralan krynawi*," said Raistlin softly, and he threw a handful of sand into the air. The creatures stopped their wild rush, shook their heads groggily as magical sleep stole over them . . . but then blinked their eyes. Within moments, they had regained their senses and started forward again!

"Magic resistant!" Raistlin murmured in awe. But that brief interlude of near sleep was long enough for Caramon. Encircling their scrawny, reptilian necks with his huge hands, the warrior swept their heads together. The bodies tumbled to the ground—lifeless statues. Caramon looked up to see two more clerics crawling over the stony bodies of their brethren, curved swords gleaming in their wrapped hands.

"Stand behind me," ordered Raistlin in a hoarse whisper. Caramon reached down and grabbed dagger and sword. He dodged behind his brother, fearful for his twin's safety, yet knowing Raistlin could not cast his spell if he stood in the way.

Raistlin stared intently at the creatures, who—recognizing a magic-user—slowed and glanced at each other, hesitant to approach. One dropped to the ground and crawled under the cart. The other sprang forward, sword in hand, hoping to impale the mage before his spell was cast, or at least break the concentration that was so necessary to the spellcaster. Caramon bellowed. Raistlin seemed not to hear or see any of them. Slowly he raised his hands. Placing his thumbs together, he spread his thin fingers in a fanlike pattern and spoke, "*Kair tangus miopiar.*" Magic coursed through his frail body, and the creature was engulfed in flame.

Tanis, recovering from his initial shock, heard Sturm's yell and crashed through the brush out onto the road. He swung the flat of his sword blade like a club and struck the creature that had Sturm pinned to the ground. The cleric fell over with a shriek and Tanis was able to drag the wounded knight into the brush.

"My sword," Sturm mumbled, dazed. Blood poured down his face; he tried unsuccessfully to wipe it away.

"We'll get it," Tanis promised, wondering how. Looking down the road, he could see more creatures swarming out of the woods and heading toward them. Tanis's mouth was dry. We've got to get out of here, he thought, fighting down panic. He forced himself to pause and draw a deep breath. Then he turned to Flint and Tasslehoff who had run up behind him.

"Stay here and guard Sturm," he instructed. "I'm going to get everyone together. We'll head back into the woods."

Not waiting for an answer, Tanis dashed out into the road, but then the flames from Raistlin's spell flared out and he was forced to fling himself to the ground.

The cart began to smoke as the straw pallet the creature had been lying on inside caught fire.

"Stay here and guard Sturm. Humpf!" Flint muttered, getting a firm grip on his battle-axe. For the moment, the creatures coming down the road did not seem to notice the dwarf or the kender or the wounded knight lying in the shadows of the trees. Their attention was on the two small knots of battling warriors. But Flint knew it was only a matter of time. He planted his feet more firmly. "Do something for Sturm," he said to Tas irritably. "Make yourself useful for once."

"I'm trying," Tasslehoff replied in a hurt tone. "But I can't get the bleeding stopped." He wiped the knight's eyes with a moderately clean handkerchief. "There, can you see now?" he asked anxiously.

Sturm groaned and tried to sit up, but pain flashed through his head and he sank back. "My sword," he said.

Tasslehoff looked over to see Sturm's two-handed weapon sticking out of the back of the stone cleric. "That's fantastic!" the wide-eyed kender said. "Look, Flint! Sturm's sword—"

"I know, you fog-brained idiot kender!" Flint roared as he saw a creature running toward them, its blade drawn.

"I'll just go get it," Tas said cheerfully to Sturm as he knelt beside him. "I won't be a moment."

"No—" Flint yelled, realizing the attacking cleric was out of Tas's line of vision. The creature's wicked, curved sword lashed out in a flashing arc, aimed for the dwarf's neck. Flint swung his axe, but at that moment, Tasslehoff—his eyes on Sturm's sword—rose to his feet. The kender's hoopak staff struck the dwarf in the back of the knees, causing Flint's legs to buckle beneath him. The creature's sword whistled harmlessly overhead as the dwarf gave a startled yell and fell over backward on top of Sturm.

Tasslehoff, hearing the dwarf shout, looked back, astonished at an odd sight: a cleric was attacking Flint and, for some reason, the dwarf was lying on his back, legs flailing, when he should have been up fighting.

"What *are* you doing, Flint?" Tas shouted. He nonchalantly struck the creature in the midsection with his hoopak, struck it again on the head as it toppled forward, and watched it fall to the ground, unconscious.

"There!" he said irritably to Flint. "Do I have to fight your battles for you?" The kender turned and headed back toward Sturm's sword.

"Fight! For me!" The dwarf, sputtering with rage, struggled wildly to stand up. His helm had slipped over his eyes, blinding him. Flint shoved it back just as another cleric bowled into him, knocking the dwarf off his feet again.

Tanis found Goldmoon and Riverwind standing back to back, Goldmoon fending off the creatures with her staff. Three of them lay dead at her feet, their stony remains blackened from the staff's blue flame. Riverwind's sword was caught fast in the guts of another statue. The Plainsman had unslung his only remaining weapon—his short bow—and had an arrow nocked and ready. The creatures were, for the moment, hanging back, discussing their strategy in low, indecipherable tones. Knowing they must rush the Plainsmen in a moment, Tanis leaped toward them and smote one of the creatures from behind, using the flat of his sword, then made a backhand swing at another.

"Come on!" he shouted to the Plainsmen. "This way!"

Some of the creatures turned at this new attack; others hesitated. Riverwind fired an arrow and felled one, then he grabbed Goldmoon's hand and together they ran toward Tanis, jumping over the stone bodies of their victims.

Tanis let them get past him, fending off the creatures with the flat of his sword. "Here, take this dagger!" he shouted to

Riverwind as the barbarian ran by. Riverwind grabbed it, reversed it, and struck one of the creatures in the jaw. Jabbing upward with the hilt, he broke its neck. There was another flash of blue flame as Goldmoon used her staff to knock another creature out of the way. Then they were into the woods.

The wooden cart was burning fiercely now. Peering through the smoke, Tanis caught glimpses of the road. A shiver ran through him as he saw dark winged forms floating to the ground about a half mile away on either side of them. The road was cut off in both directions. They were trapped unless they escaped into the woods immediately.

He reached the place where he had left Sturm. Goldmoon and Riverwind were there, so was Flint. Where was everyone else? He stared around in the thick smoke, blinking back tears.

"Help Sturm," he told Goldmoon. Then he turned to Flint, who was trying unsuccessfully to yank his axe out of the chest of a stone creature. "Where are Caramon and Raistlin? And where's Tas? I told him to stay here—"

"Blasted kender nearly got me killed!" Flint exploded. "I hope they carry him off! I hope they use him for dog meat! I hope—"

"In the name of the gods!" Tanis swore in exasperation. He made his way through the smoke toward where he had last seen Caramon and Raistlin and stumbled across the kender, dragging Sturm's sword back along the road. The weapon was nearly as big as Tasslehoff and he couldn't lift it, so he was dragging it through the mud.

"How did you get that?" Tanis asked in amazement, coughing in the thick smoke that boiled around them.

Tas grinned, tears streaming down his face from the smoke in his eyes. "The creature turned to dust," he said happily. "Oh, Tanis, it was wonderful. I walked up and pulled on the sword and it wouldn't come out, so I pulled again and—"

"Not now! Get back to the others!" Tanis grabbed the kender and shoved him forward. "Have you seen Caramon and Raistlin?"

But just then he heard the warrior's voice boom out of the smoke. "Here we are," Caramon panted. He had his arm around his brother, who was coughing uncontrollably. "Have we destroyed them all?" the big man asked cheerfully.

"No, we haven't," Tanis replied grimly. "In fact, we've got to get away through the woods to the south." He put his arm around Raistlin and together they hurried back to where the others were huddled by the road, choking in the smoke, yet thankful for its enveloping cover.

Sturm was on his feet, his face pale, but the pain in his head was gone and the wound had quit bleeding.

"The staff healed him?" Tanis asked Goldmoon.

She coughed. "Not completely. Enough so that he can walk."

"It has . . . limits," Raistlin said, wheezing.

"Yes—" Tanis interrupted. "Well, we're heading south, into the woods."

Caramon shook his head. "That's Darken Wood—" he began.

"I know—you'd rather fight the living," Tanis interrupted. "How do you feel about that now?"

The warrior did not answer.

"More of those creatures are coming from both directions. We can't fight off another assault. But we won't enter Darken Wood if we don't have to. There's a game trail not far from here we can use to reach Prayer's Eye Peak. There we can see the road to the north, as well as all other directions."

"We could go north as far as the cave. The boat's hidden there." Riverwind suggested.

"No!" yelled Flint in a strangled voice. Without another word, the dwarf turned and plunged into the forest, running south as fast as his short legs could carry him.

9

Flight! The white stag.

he companions stumbled through the thick woods as fast as they could and soon reached the game trail. Caramon took the lead, sword in hand, eyeing every shadow. His brother followed, one hand on Caramon's shoulder, his lips set in grim determination. The rest came after, their weapons drawn.

But they saw no more of the creatures.

"Why aren't they chasing us?" Flint asked after they had traveled about an hour.

Tanis scratched his beard—he had been wondering about the same thing. "They don't need to," he said finally. "We are trapped. They've undoubtedly blocked all the exits from this forest. With the exception of Darken Wood . . ."

"Darken Wood!" Goldmoon repeated softly. "Is it truly necessary to go that way?"

91

"It may not be," Tanis said. "We'll get a look around from Prayer's Eye Peak."

Suddenly they heard Caramon, walking ahead of them, shout. Running forward, Tanis found Raistlin had collapsed.

"I'll be all right," the mage whispered. "But I must rest."

"We can all use rest," Tanis said.

No one answered. All sank down wearily, catching their breath in quick, sharp gasps. Sturm closed his eyes and leaned against a moss-covered rock. His face was a ghastly shade of grayish white. Blood had matted his long moustaches and caked his hair. The wound was a jagged slash, turning slowly purple. Tanis knew that the knight would die before he said a word of complaint.

"Don't worry," Sturm said harshly. "Just give me a moment's peace." Tanis gripped the knight's hand briefly, then went to sit beside Riverwind.

Neither spoke for long minutes, then Tanis asked, "You've fought those creatures before, haven't you?"

"In the broken city." Riverwind shuddered. "It all came back to me when I looked inside the cart and saw that thing leering at me! At least—" He paused, shook his head. Then he gave Tanis a half-smile. "At least I know now that I'm not going insane. Those horrible creatures really do exist—I had wondered sometimes."

"I can imagine," Tanis murmured. "So these creatures are spreading all over Krynn, unless your broken city was near here."

"No. I came into Que-shu out of the east. It was far from Solace, beyond the Plains of my homeland."

"What do you suppose those creatures meant, saying they had tracked you to our village?" Goldmoon asked slowly, laying her cheek on his leather tunic sleeve, slipping her hand around his arm.

"Don't worry," Riverwind said, taking her hand in his. "The warriors there would deal with them."

"Riverwind, do you remember what you were going to say?" she prompted.

"Yes, you are right," Riverwind replied, stroking her silver-gold hair. He looked at Tanis and smiled. For an instant, the expressionless mask was gone and Tanis saw warmth deep within the man's brown eyes. "I give my thanks to you, Half-Elven, and to all of you." His glance flickered over everyone. "You have saved our lives more than once and I have been ungrateful. But"—he paused—"it's all so strange!"

"It's going to get stranger." Raistlin's voice was ominous.

The companions were drawing nearer Prayer's Eye Peak. They had been able to see it from the road, rising above the forests. Its split peak looked like two hands pressed together in prayer—thus the name. The rain had stopped. The woods were deathly quiet. The companions began to think that the forest animals and birds had vanished from the land, leaving an eerie, empty silence behind. All of them felt uneasy—except perhaps Tasslehoff, and kept peering over their shoulders or drawing their swords at shadows.

Sturm insisted on walking rear guard, but he began lagging behind as the pain in his head increased. He was becoming dizzy and nauseated. Soon he lost all conception of where he was and what he was doing. He knew only that he must keep walking, placing one foot in front of the other, moving forward like one of Tas's automatons.

How did Tas's story go? Sturm tried to remember it through a haze of pain. These automatons served a wizard who had summoned a demon to carry the kender away. It was nonsense, like all the kender's stories. Sturm put one foot in front of the other. Nonsense. Like the old man's stories—the old man in the Inn. Stories of the White Stag and ancient gods—Paladine. Stories of Huma. Sturm clasped his hands on his throbbing temples as if he could hold his splitting head together. Huma . . .

As a boy, Sturm had fed on stories of Huma. His mother, daughter of a Knight of Solamnia, married to a Knight—had known no other stories to tell her son. Sturm's thoughts turned to his mother, his pain making him think of her tender ministrations when he was sick or hurt. Sturm's father had sent his wife and their son into exile because the boy—his only heir—was a target for those who would see the Knights of Solamnia banished forever from the face of Krynn. Sturm and his mother took refuge in Solace. Sturm made friends readily, particularly with one other boy, Caramon, who shared his interest in all things military. But Sturm's proud mother considered the people beneath her. And so, when the fever consumed her, she had died alone except for her teenage son. She had commended the boy to his father—if his father still lived, which Sturm was beginning to doubt.

After his mother's death, the young man became a seasoned warrior under the guidance of Tanis and Flint, who adopted Sturm as they had unofficially adopted Caramon and Raistlin. Together with Tasslehoff, the travel-loving kender, and, on occasion, the twins' wild and beautiful half-sister, Kitiara, Sturm and his friends escorted Flint on his journeys through the lands of Abanasinia, plying his trade as metalsmith.

Five years ago, however, the companions decided to separate to investigate reports of evil growing in the land. They vowed to meet again at the Inn of the Last Home.

Sturm had traveled north to Solamnia, determined to find his father and his heritage. He found nothing, and only narrowly escaped with his life—and his father's sword and armor. The journey to his homeland was a harrowing experience. Sturm had known the Knights were reviled, but he had been shocked to realize just how deep the bitterness against them ran. Huma, Lightbringer, Knight of Solamnia, had driven back the darkness years ago, during the Age of Dreams, and thus began the Age of Might. Then came the Cataclysm, when the gods abandoned man, according to the popular belief. The people had turned to the Knights for help, as they had turned to Huma in the past. But Huma was long dead. The Knights could only watch helplessly as terror rained down from heaven and Krynn was smote asunder. The people had cried to the Knights, but they could do nothing, and the people had never forgiven them. Standing in front of his family's ruined castle, Sturm vowed that he would restore the honor of the Knights of Solamnia—if it meant that he must sacrifice his life in the attempt.

But how could he do that fighting a bunch of clerics, he wondered bitterly, the trail dimming before his eyes. He stumbled, caught himself quickly. Huma had fought dragons. Give me dragons, Sturm dreamed. He lifted his eyes. The leaves blurred into a golden mist and he knew he was going to faint. Then he blinked. Everything came sharply into focus.

Before him rose Prayer's Eye Peak. He and his companions had arrived at the foot of the old, glacial mountain. He could see trails twisting and winding up the wooded slope, trails used by Solace residents to reach picnic spots on the eastern side of the Peak. Next to one of the well-worn paths stood a white stag. Sturm stared. The stag was the most magnificent animal the knight had ever seen. It was huge, standing several hands taller than any other stag the knight had hunted. It held its head proudly, its splendid rack gleaming like a crown. Its eyes were deep brown against its pure white fur, and it gazed at the knight intently, as if it knew him. Then, with a slight shake of its head, the stag bounded away to the southwest.

"Stop!" the knight called out hoarsely.

The others whirled around in alarm, drawing weapons. Tanis came running back to him. "What is it, Sturm?"

The knight involuntarily put his hand to his aching head.

"I'm sorry, Sturm," Tanis said. "I didn't realize you were as sick as this. We can rest. We're at the foot of Prayer's Eye Peak. I'm going to climb the mountain and see—"

"No! Look!" The knight gripped Tanis's shoulder and turned him around. He pointed. "See it? The white stag!"

"The white stag?" Tanis stared in the direction the knight indicated. "Where? I don't—"

"There," Sturm said softly. He took a few steps forward, toward the animal who had stopped and seemed to be waiting for him. The stag nodded its great head. It darted away again, just a few steps, then turned to face the knight once more. "He wants us to follow him," Sturm gasped. "Like Huma!"

The others had gathered around the knight now, regarding him with expressions that ranged from deeply concerned to obviously skeptical.

"I see no stag of any color," Riverwind said, his dark eyes scanning the forest.

"Head wound." Caramon nodded like a charlatan cleric. "C'mon, Sturm, lie down and rest while—"

"You great blithering idiot!" the knight snarled at Caramon. "With your brains in your stomach, it is just as well you do not see the stag. You would probably shoot it and cook it! I tell you this—we must follow it!"

"The madness of the head wound," Riverwind whispered to Tanis. "I have seen it often."

"I'm not sure," Tanis said. He was silent for a few moments. When he spoke, it was with obvious reluctance. "Though I have not seen the white stag myself, I have been with one who has and I have followed it, like in the old man's story." His hand absently fingered the ring of twisted ivy leaves that he wore on his left hand, his thoughts with the golden-haired elfmaiden who wept when he left Qualinesti.

"You're suggesting we follow an animal we can't even see?" Caramon said, his jaw going slack.

"It would not be the strangest thing we have done," Raistlin commented sarcastically in his whispering voice. "Though, remember, it was the old man who told the tale of the White Stag and the old man who got us into this—"

"It was our own choice got us into this," Tanis snapped. "We could have turned the staff over to the High Theocrat and talked our way out of the predicament; we've talked our way out of worse. I say we follow Sturm. He has been chosen, apparently, just as Riverwind was chosen to receive the staff—"

"But it's not even leading us in the right direction!" Caramon argued. "You know as well as I do there are no trails through the western part of the woods. No one ever goes there."

"All the better," Goldmoon said suddenly. "Tanis said those creatures must have the paths blocked. Maybe this is a way out. I say we follow the knight." She turned and started off with Sturm, not even glancing back at the others—obviously accustomed to being obeyed. Riverwind shrugged and shook his head, scowling darkly, but he walked after Goldmoon and the others followed.

The knight left the well-trodden paths of Prayer's Eye Peak behind, moving in a southwesterly direction up the slope. At first it appeared Caramon was right—there were no trails. Sturm was crashing through the brush like a madman. Then, suddenly, a smooth wide trail opened up ahead of them. Tanis stared at it in amazement.

"What or who cleared this trail?" he asked Riverwind, who was also examining it with a puzzled expression.

"I don't know," the Plainsman said. "It's old. That felled tree has lain there long enough to sink over halfway into the dirt and it's covered with moss and vines. But there are no tracks—other than Sturm's. There's no sign of anyone or any animal passing through here. Yet why isn't it overgrown?"

Tanis couldn't answer and he couldn't take time to think about it. Sturm forged ahead rapidly; all the party could do was try to keep him in sight.

"Goblins, boats, lizard men, invisible stags—what next?" complained Flint to the kender.

"I wish I could see the stag," Tas said wistfully.

"Get hit on the head." The dwarf snorted. "Although with you, we probably couldn't tell the difference."

The companions followed Sturm, who was climbing with a wild kind of elation, his pain and wound forgotten. Tanis had difficulty catching up with the knight. When he did, he was alarmed at the feverish gleam in Sturm's eye. But the knight was obviously being guided by something. The trail led them up the slope of Prayer's Eye Peak. Tanis saw that it was taking them to the gap between the "hands" of stone, a gap that as far as he knew no one had ever entered before.

"Wait a moment," he gasped, running to catch up with Sturm. It was nearly midday, he guessed, though the sun was still hidden by jagged gray clouds. "Let's rest. I'm going to take a look at the land from over there." He pointed to a rock ledge that jutted out from the side of the peak.

"Rest . . ." repeated Sturm vaguely, stopping and catching his breath. He stared ahead for a moment, then turned to Tanis. "Yes. We'll rest." His eyes gleamed brightly.

"Are you all right?"

"Fine," Sturm said absently and paced around the grass, gently stroking and smoothing his moustaches. Tanis looked at him a moment, irresolute, then went back to the others who were just coming over the crest of a small rise.

"We're going to rest here," the half-elf said. Raistlin breathed a sigh of relief and sank down in the wet leaves.

"I'm going to have a look north, see what's moving back on the road to Haven," Tanis added.

"I'll come with you," Riverwind offered.

Tanis nodded and the two left the path, heading for the rock ledge. Tanis glanced at the tall warrior as they walked together. He was beginning to feel comfortable with the stern, serious

Plainsman. A deeply private person himself, Riverwind respected the privacy of others and would never think of probing the boundaries Tanis set around his soul. This was as relaxing to the half-elf as a night's unbroken sleep. He knew that his friends—simply because they were his friends and had known him for years—were speculating on his relationship with Kitiara. Why had he chosen to break it off so abruptly five years ago? And why, then, his obvious disappointment when she failed to join them? Riverwind, of course, knew nothing about Kitiara, but Tanis had the feeling that if he did, it would be all the same to the Plainsman: it was Tanis's business, not his.

When they were within sight of the Haven Road, they crawled the last few feet, inching their way along the wet rock until they came to the rim of the ledge. Tanis, looking below and to the east, could see the old picnic paths disappearing around the side of the mountain. Riverwind pointed, and Tanis realized there were creatures moving along the picnic trails! That explained the uncanny hush in the forest. Tanis pressed his lips together grimly. The creatures must be waiting to ambush them. Sturm and his white stag had probably saved their lives. But it wouldn't take the creatures long to find this new trail. Tanis glanced below him and blinked— there was no trail! There was nothing but thick, impenetrable forest. The trail had closed behind them! I must be imagining things, he thought, and he turned his eyes back to Haven Road and the many creatures moving along it. It hadn't taken them long to get organized, he thought. He gazed farther to the north and saw the still, peaceful waters of Crystalmir Lake. Then his glance traveled to the horizon.

He frowned. There was something wrong. He couldn't place it immediately, so he said nothing to Riverwind but stared at the skyline. Storm clouds massed in the north more thickly than ever, long gray fingers raking the land. And reaching up to meet them—that was it! Gripping Riverwind's arm, Tanis stabbed his finger northward. Riverwind looked, squinting, seeing nothing at first. Then he saw it, black smoke drifting into the sky. His thick, heavy brows contracted.

"Campfires," Tanis said.

"Many hundred campfires," Riverwind amended softly. "The fires of war. That is an army encampment."

"So the rumors are confirmed," Sturm said when they returned. "There *is* an army to the north."

"But what army? Whose? And why? What are they going to attack?" Caramon laughed incredulously. "No one would send an army after this staff." The warrior paused. "Would they?"

"The staff is but a part of this," Raistlin hissed. "Remember the fallen stars!"

"Children's stories!" Flint sniffed. He upended the empty wineskin, shook it, and sighed.

"My stories are not for children," Raistlin said viciously, twisting up from the leaves like a snake. "And you would do well to heed my words, dwarf!"

"There it is! There's the stag!" Sturm said suddenly, his eyes staring straight at a large boulder—or so it seemed to his companions. "It is time to go."

The knight began walking. The others hastily gathered their gear together and hurried after him. As they climbed ever farther up the trail—which seemed to materialize before them as they went—the wind switched and began blowing from the south. It was a warm breeze, carrying with it the fragrance of late-blooming autumn wildflowers. It drove back the storm clouds and just as they came to the cleft between the two halves of the Peak, the sun broke free.

It was well past midday when they stopped to rest for one more brief period before attempting the climb through the narrow gap between the walls of Prayer's Eye Peak through which Sturm said they must go. The stag had led the way, he insisted.

"It'll be suppertime soon," Caramon said. He heaved a gusty sigh, staring at his feet. "I could eat my boots!"

"They're beginning to look good to me, too," Flint said grumpily. "I wish that stag was flesh and blood. It might be useful for something besides getting us lost!"

"Shut up!" Sturm turned on the dwarf in a sudden rage, his fists clenched. Tanis rose quickly, put his hand on the knight's shoulder, holding him back.

Sturm stood glaring at the dwarf, moustaches quivering, then he jerked away from Tanis. "Let's go," he muttered.

As the companions entered the narrow defile, they could see clear blue sky on the other side. The south wind whistled across the steep white walls of the Peak soaring above them. They walked carefully, small stones causing their feet to slip more than once. Fortunately, the way was so narrow that they could easily regain their balance by catching themselves against the steep walls.

After about thirty minutes of walking, they came out on the other side of Prayer's Eye Peak. They halted, staring down into a valley. Lush, grassy meadowland flowed in green waves below them to lap on the shores of a light-green aspen forest far to the south. The storm clouds were behind them, and the sun shone brightly in a clear, azure sky.

For the first time, they found their cloaks too heavy, except for Raistlin who remained huddled in his red, hooded cape. Flint had spent the morning complaining about the rain and now started in on the sunshine, it was too bright, glaring into his eyes. It was too hot, beating down on his helm.

"I say we throw the dwarf off the mountain," growled Caramon to Tanis.

Tanis grinned. "He'd rattle all the way down and give away our position."

"Who's down there to hear him?" Caramon said, gesturing toward the valley with his broad hand. "I bet we're the first living beings to set eyes on this valley."

"First *living* beings," Raistlin breathed. "You are right there, my brother. For you look on Darken Wood."

No one spoke. Riverwind shifted uncomfortably; Goldmoon crept over to stand beside him, staring down into the green trees, her eyes wide. Flint cleared his throat and fell silent, stroking his long beard. Sturm regarded the forest calmly. So did Tasslehoff. "It doesn't look bad at all," the kender said cheerfully. Sitting cross-legged on the ground, a sheaf of parchment spread out on his knees, he was drawing a map with a bit of charcoal, attempting to trace their way up Prayer's Eye Peak.

"Looks are as deceptive as light-fingered kender," Raistlin whispered harshly.

Tasslehoff frowned, started to retort, then caught Tanis's eye and went back to his drawing. Tanis walked over to Sturm. The knight stood out on a ledge, the south wind blowing back his long hair and whipping his frayed cape about him.

"Sturm, where is the stag? Do you see it now?"

"Yes," Sturm answered. He pointed downward. "It walked across the meadow; I can see its trail in the tall grass. It has gone into the aspens there."

"Gone into Darken Wood," Tanis murmured.

"Who says that is Darken Wood?" Sturm turned to face Tanis.

"Raistlin."

"Bah!"

"He is magi," Tanis said.

"He is crazed," Sturm replied. Then he shrugged. "But stay here rooted on the side of the Peak if you like, Tanis. I will follow the stag—as did Huma—even if it leads me into Darken Wood." Wrapping his cloak around him, Sturm climbed down the ledge and began to walk along a winding trail that led down the mountainside.

Tanis returned to the others. "The stag's leading him on a straight path right into the forest," he said. "How certain are you that this forest is Darken Wood, Raistlin?"

"How certain is one of anything, Half-Elven?" the mage replied. "I am not certain of drawing my next breath. But go ahead. Walk into the wood that no living man has ever walked out of. Death is life's one great certainty, Tanis."

The half-elf felt a sudden urge to throw Raistlin off the side of the mountain. He stared after Sturm, who was nearly halfway down into the valley.

"I'm going with Sturm," he said suddenly. "But I'll be responsible for no one else in this decision. The rest of you may follow as you choose."

"I'm coming!" Tasslehoff rolled his map up and slipped it into his scroll case. He scrambled to his feet, sliding in the loose rock.

"Ghosts!" Flint scowled at Raistlin, snapped his fingers derisively, then stumped over to stand beside the half-elf. Goldmoon followed unhesitatingly, though her face was pale. Riverwind joined the group more slowly, his face thoughtful. Tanis was relieved—the barbarians had many frightening legends of Darken Wood, he knew. And finally, Raistlin moved forward so rapidly he took his brother completely by surprise.

Tanis regarded the mage with a slight smile. "Why do you come?" he couldn't help asking.

"Because you will need me, Half-Elven," the mage hissed. "Besides, where would you have us go? You have allowed us to be led this far, there can be no turning back. It is the Ogre's Choice you offer us, Tanis—'Die fast or die slow.' " He set off down the side of the Peak. "Coming, brother?"

The others glanced uneasily at Tanis as the brothers passed. The half-elf felt like a fool. Raistlin was right, of course. He'd let this go far beyond his control, then made it seem as if it were their decision, not his, allowing him to go forward with a clear conscience. Angrily he picked up a rock and hurled it far down the mountainside. Why was it his responsibility in the first place? Why had he gotten involved, when all he had wanted was to find Kitiara and tell her his mind was made up—he loved her and wanted her. He could accept her human frailties as he had learned to accept his own.

But Kit hadn't come back to him. She had a "new lord." Maybe that's why he'd—

"Ho, Tanis!" The kender's voice floated up to him.

"I'm coming," he muttered.

The sun was just beginning to dip into the west when the companions reached the edge of the forest. Tanis figured they had at least three or four hours of daylight left. If the stag continued to lead them on smooth, clear trails, they might be able to get through this forest before darkness fell.

Sturm waited for them beneath the aspens, resting comfortably in the leafy, green shade. The companions left the meadow slowly, none of them in any hurry to enter the woods.

"The stag entered here," Sturm said, rising to his feet and pointing into the tall grass.

Tanis saw no tracks. He took a drink of water from his nearly empty waterskin and stared into the forest. As Tasslehoff had said, the wood did not seem sinister. In fact, it looked cool and inviting after the harsh brilliance of the autumn sunshine.

"Maybe there'll be some game in here," Caramon said, rocking back on his heels. "Not stags, of course," he added hastily. "Rabbits, maybe."

"Shoot nothing. Eat nothing. Drink nothing in Darken Wood," Raistlin whispered.

Tanis looked at the mage, whose hourglass eyes were dilated. The metallic skin shone a ghastly color in the strong sunlight. Raistlin leaned upon his staff, shivering as if from a chill.

"Children's stories," Flint muttered, but the dwarf's voice lacked conviction. Although Tanis knew Raistlin's flair for the dramatic, he had never seen the mage affected like this before.

"What do you sense, Raistlin?" he asked quietly.

"There is a great and powerful magic laid on this wood," whispered Raistlin.

"Evil?" asked Tanis.

"Only to those who bring evil in with them," the mage stated.

"Then you are the only one who need fear this forest," Sturm told the mage coldly.

Caramon's face flushed an ugly red; his hand fumbled for his sword. Sturm's hand went to his blade. Tanis gripped Sturm's arm as Raistlin touched his brother. The mage stared at the knight, his golden eyes glimmering.

"We shall see," Raistlin said, the words nothing more than hissing sounds flicking between his teeth. "We shall see." Then, leaning heavily upon his staff, Raistlin turned to his brother. "Coming?"

Caramon glared angrily at Sturm, then entered the wood, walking beside his twin. The others moved after them, leaving only Tanis and Flint standing in the long, waving grass.

"I'm getting too old for this, Tanis," the dwarf said suddenly.

"Nonsense," the half-elf replied, smiling. "You fought like a—"

"No, I don't mean the bones or the muscles"—the dwarf looked at his gnarled hands—"though they're old enough. I mean the spirit. Years ago, before the others were born, you and I would have walked into a magicked wood without giving it a second thought. Now . . ."

"Cheer up," Tanis said. He tried to sound light, though he was deeply disturbed by the dwarf's unusual somberness. He studied Flint closely for the first time since meeting outside

Solace. The dwarf looked old, but then Flint had always looked old. His face, what could be seen through the mass of gray beard and moustaches and overhanging white eyebrows, was brown and wrinkled and cracked like old leather. The dwarf grumbled and complained, but then Flint had always grumbled and complained. The change was in the eyes. The fiery luster was gone.

"Don't let Raistlin get to you," Tanis said. "We'll sit around the fire tonight and laugh at his ghost stories."

"I suppose so." Flint sighed. He was silent a moment, then said, "Someday I'll slow you up, Tanis. I don't ever want you to think, why do I put up with this grumbling old dwarf?"

"Because I need you, grumbling old dwarf," Tanis said, putting his hand on the dwarf's heavy-set shoulder. He motioned into the wood, after the others. "I need you, Flint. They're all so . . . so young. You're like a solid rock that I can set my back against as I wield my sword."

Flint's face flushed in pleasure. He tugged at his beard, then cleared his throat gruffly. "Yes, well, you were always sentimental. Come along. We're wasting time. I want to get through this confounded forest as fast as possible." Then he muttered, "Just glad it's daylight."

10

DARKEN WOOD.
The dead walk. Raistlin's magic.

The only thing Tanis felt on entering the forest was relief at being out of the glare of the autumn sun. The half-elf recalled all the legends he had heard about Darken Wood— stories of ghosts told around the fire at night—and he kept in mind Raistlin's foreboding. But all Tanis felt was that the forest was so much more alive than any other he had ever entered.

There was no deathly hush as they had experienced earlier. Small animals chattered in the brush. Birds fluttered in the high branches above them. Insects with gaily colored wings flitted past. Leaves rustled and stirred, flowers swayed though no breeze touched them—as if the plants reveled in being alive.

All of the companions entered the forest with their hands on their weapons, wary and watchful and distrustful. After a time of trying to avoid making leaves crunch, Tas said it seemed "kind of silly," and they relaxed—all except Raistlin.

They walked for about two hours, traveling at a smooth but rapid easy pace along a smooth and clear trail. Shadows lengthened as the sun made its downward slide. Tanis felt at peace in this forest. He had no fear that the awful, winged creatures could follow them here. Evil seemed out of place, unless, as Raistlin said, one brought one's own evil into the wood. Tanis looked at the mage. Raistlin walked alone, his head bowed. The shadows of the forest trees seemed to gather thickly around the young mage. Tanis shivered and realized that the air was turning cool as the sun dropped below the treetops. It was time to begin thinking about making camp for the night.

Tanis pulled out Tasslehoff's map to study it once more before the light faded. The map was of elven design and written across the forest in flowing script were the words "Darken Wood." But the woods themselves were only vaguely outlined, and Tanis couldn't be certain if the words pertained to this forest or one farther south. Raistlin must be wrong, Tanis decided—this can't be Darken Wood. Or, if so, its evil was simply a product of the mage's imagination. They walked on.

Soon it was twilight, that time of evening when the dying light makes everything most vivid and distinct. The companions began to lag. Raistlin limped, and his breath came in wheezing gasps. Sturm's face turned ashen. The half-elf was just about to call a halt for the night when—as if anticipating his wishes—the trail led them right to a large, green glade. Clear water bubbled up from underground and trickled down smooth rocks to form a shallow brook. The glade was blanketed with thick, inviting grass; tall trees stood guard duty on the edges. As they saw the glade, the sun's light reddened, then faded, and the misty shades of night crept around the trees.

"Do not leave the path," Raistlin intoned as his companions started to enter the glade.

Tanis sighed. "Raistlin," he said patiently—"we'll be all right. The path is in plain sight, not ten feet away. Come on. You've got to rest. We all do. Look"—Tanis held out the map— "I don't think this is Darken Wood. According to this—"

Raistlin ignored the map with disdain. The rest of the companions ignored the mage and, moving off the path, began setting up camp. Sturm sank down against a tree, his eyes closed in pain, while Caramon stared at the smaller, fleeting shadows with a hungry eye. At a signal from Caramon, Tasslehoff slipped off into the forest after firewood.

Watching them, the mage's face twisted in a sardonic smile. "You are all fools. This is Darken Wood, as you will see before the night is ended." He shrugged. "But, as you say, I need rest. However, *I* will not leave the path." Raistlin sat down on the trail, his staff beside him.

Caramon flushed in embarrassment as he saw the others exchanging amused glances. "Aw, Raist," the big man said, "join us. Tas has gone for wood and maybe I can shoot a rabbit."

"*Shoot* nothing!" Raistlin actually spoke above a whisper, making everyone start. "*Harm* nothing in Darken Wood! Neither plant nor tree, bird nor animal!"

"I agree with Raistlin," Tanis said. "We have to spend the night here and I don't want to kill any animal in this forest if we don't have to."

"Elves never want to kill period," Flint grumbled. "The magician scares us to death and you starve us. Well, if anything does attack us tonight, I hope it's edible!"

"You and me both, dwarf." Caramon heaved a sigh, went over to the creek, and began trying to assuage his hunger by drowning it.

Tasslehoff returned with firewood. "I didn't cut it," he assured Raistlin. "I just picked it up."

But even Riverwind couldn't make the wood catch fire. "The wood's wet," he stated finally and tossed his tinderbox back into his pack.

"We need light," Flint said uneasily as night's shadows closed in thickly. Sounds in the woods that had been innocent in the daytime now seemed sinister and threatening.

"Surely you do not fear children's stories," Raistlin hissed.

"No!" snapped the dwarf. "I just want to make certain the kender doesn't rifle my pack in the dark."

"Very well," said Raistlin with unusual mildness. He spoke his word of command: "*Shirak*." A pale, white light shone from the crystal on the tip of the mage's staff. It was a ghostly light and did little to brighten the darkness. In fact, it seemed to emphasize the menace in the night.

"There, you have light," the mage whispered softly. He thrust the bottom of the staff into the wet ground.

It was then Tanis realized his elven vision was gone. He should have been able to see the warm, red outlines of his companions, but they were nothing more than darker shadows against the starry darkness of the glade. The half-elf didn't say anything to the others, but the peaceful feeling he had been enjoying was pierced by a sliver of fear.

"I'll take the first watch," Sturm offered heavily. "I shouldn't sleep with this head wound, anyway. I once knew a man who did, he never woke up."

"We'll watch in twos," Tanis said. "I'll take first watch with you."

The others opened packs and began making up beds on the grass, except for Raistlin. He remained sitting on the trail, the light of his staff shining on his bowed, hooded head. Sturm settled down beneath a tree. Tanis walked over to the brook and drank thirstily. Suddenly he heard a strangled cry behind him. He drew his sword and stood, all in one motion. The others had their weapons drawn. Only Raistlin sat, unmoving.

"Put your swords away," he said. "They will do you no good. Only a weapon of powerful magic could harm these."

An army of warriors surrounded them. That alone would have been enough to chill anyone's blood. But the companions could have dealt with that. What they couldn't handle was the horror that overwhelmed and numbed their senses. Each one recalled Caramon's flippant comment: "I'll fight the living any day of the week, but not the dead."

These warriors were dead.

Nothing more than fleeting, fragile white light outlined their bodies. It was as if the human warmth that had been theirs while they lived lingered on horribly after death. The flesh had rotted away, leaving behind the body's image as remembered by the soul. The soul apparently remembered other things, too. Each warrior was dressed in ancient, remembered armor. Each warrior carried remembered weapons that could inflict well-remembered death. But the undead needed no weapons. They could kill from fear alone, or by the touch of their grave-cold hands.

How can we fight these things? Tanis thought wildly, he who had never felt such fear in the face of flesh and blood enemies. Panic engulfed him, and he considered yelling for the others to turn and run for it.

Angrily, the half-elf forced himself to calm down, to get a grip on reality. Reality! He almost laughed at the irony. Running was useless; they would get lost, separated. They had to stay and deal with this—somehow. He began to walk toward the ghostly warriors. The dead said nothing, made no threatening moves. They simply stood, blocking the path. It was impossible to count them since some glimmered into being while others faded, only to return when their comrades dimmed. Not that it makes any difference, Tanis admitted to himself, feeling sweat chill his body. One of these undead warriors could kill all of us simply by lifting its hand.

As the half-elf drew nearer to the warriors, he saw a gleam of light—Raistlin's staff. The mage, leaning on his staff, stood in front of the huddle of companions. Tanis came to stand beside him. The pale crystal light reflected on the mage's face, making it seem nearly as ghostly as the faces of the dead before him.

"Welcome to Darken Wood, Tanis," the mage said.

"Raistlin—" Tanis choked. He had to try more than once to get his dry throat to form a sound. "What are these—"

"Spectral minions," the mage whispered without taking his eyes from them. "We are fortunate."

"Fortunate?" Tanis repeated incredulously. "Why?"

"These are the spirits of men who gave their pledge to perform some task. They failed in that pledge, and it is their doom to keep performing the same task over and over until they win their release and find true rest in death."

"How in the name of the Abyss does that make us fortunate?" Tanis whispered harshly, releasing his fear in anger. "Perhaps they pledged to rid the forest of all who entered!"

"That is possible"—Raistlin flickered a glance at the half-elf—"though I do not think it likely. We will find out."

Before Tanis could react, the mage stepped away from the group and faced the spectres.

"Raist!" Caramon said in a strangled voice, starting to shove forward.

"Keep him back, Tanis," Raistlin commanded harshly. "Our lives depend on this."

Gripping the warrior's arm, Tanis asked Raistlin, "What are you going to do?"

"I am going to cast a spell that will enable us to communicate with them. I will perceive their thoughts. They will speak through me."

The mage threw his head back, his hood slipping off. He stretched out his arms and began to speak. "*Ast bilak parbilakar. Suh tangus moipar?*" he murmured, then repeated that phrase three times. As Raistlin spoke, the crowd of warriors parted and a figure more awesome and terrifying than the rest appeared. The spectre was taller than the rest and wore a shimmering crown. His pallid armor was richly decorated with dark jewels. His face showed the most terrible grief and anguish. He advanced upon Raistlin.

Caramon choked and averted his eyes. Tanis dared not speak or cry out, fearful of disturbing the mage and breaking the spell. The spectre raised a fleshless hand, reached out slowly to touch the young mage. Tanis trembled—the spectre's touch meant certain death. But Raistlin, entranced, did not move. Tanis wondered if he even saw the chill hand coming toward his heart. Then Raistlin spoke.

"You who have been long dead, use my living voice to tell us of your bitter sorrow. Then give us leave to pass through this forest, for our purpose is not evil, as you will see if you read our hearts."

The spectre's hand halted abruptly. The pale eyes searched Raistlin's face. Then, shimmering in the darkness, the spectre bowed before the mage. Tanis sucked in his breath; he had sensed Raistlin's power, but this . . !

Raistlin returned the bow, then moved to stand beside the spectre. His face was nearly as pale as that of the ghostly figure next to him. The living dead and the dead living, Tanis thought, shuddering.

When Raistlin spoke, his voice was no longer the wheezing whispering of the fragile mage. It was deep and dark and commanding and rang through the forest. It was cold and hollow and might have come from below the ground. "Who are you who trespass in Darken Wood?"

Tanis tried to answer, but his throat had dried up completely. Caramon, next to him, couldn't even lift his head. Then Tanis felt movement at his side. The kender! Cursing himself, he reached out to grab for Tasslehoff, but it was too late. The small figure, topknot dancing, ran out into the light of Raistlin's staff and stood before the spectre.

Tasslehoff bowed respectfully. "I am Tasslehoff Burrfoot," he said. "My friends"—he waved his small hand at the group—"call me Tas. Who are you?"

"It matters little," the sepulchral voice intoned. "Know only that we are warriors from a time long forgotten."

"Is it true that you broke a pledge and that's how you come to be here?" Tas asked with interest.

"It is. We pledged to guard this land. Then came the smoldering mountain from the heavens. The land was ripped apart. Evil things crept out from the bowels of the earth and we dropped our swords and fled in terror until bitter death overtook us. We have been called to fulfill our oath, as evil once more stalks the land. And here will we remain until evil is driven back and balance is restored again."

Suddenly Raistlin gave a shriek and flung back his head, his eyes rolling upward until the watching companions could see only the whites. His voice became a thousand voices crying out at once. This startled even the kender, who stepped back a pace and looked around uneasily for Tanis.

The spectre raised his hand in a commanding gesture, and the tumult ceased as though swallowed by the darkness. "My men demand to know the reason you enter Darken Wood. If it is for evil, you will find that you have brought evil upon yourselves, for you will not live to see the moons rise."

"No, not evil. Certainly not," Tasslehoff said hurriedly. "It's kind of a long story, you see, but we're obviously not going anywhere in a big hurry and you're obviously not either, so I'll tell it to you.

"To begin with, we were in the Inn of the Last Home in Solace. You probably don't know it. I'm not sure how long it's been there, but it wasn't around during the Cataclysm and it sounds like you were. Well, there we were, listening to the old man talking of Huma and he—the old man, not Huma—told Goldmoon to sing her song and she said what song and then she sang and a Seeker decided to be a music critic and Riverwind, that's the tall man over there—shoved the Seeker into the fire. It was an accident—he didn't mean to. But the Seeker went up like a torch! You should have seen it! Anyway, the old man handed me the staff and said hit him and I did and the staff turned to blue crystal and the flames died and—"

"Blue crystal!" The spectre's voice echoed hollowly from Raistlin's throat as he began to walk toward them. Tanis and Sturm both jumped forward, grabbing Tas and dragging him out of the way. But the spectre seemed intent only on examining the group. His flickering eyes focused on Goldmoon. Raising a pale hand, he motioned her forward.

"No!" Riverwind tried to prevent her from leaving his side, but she pushed away gently and walked over to stand before the spectre, the staff in her hand. The ghostly army encircled them.

Suddenly the spectre drew his sword from its pallid sheath. He held it high overhead and white light tinged with blue flame flickered from the blade.

"Look at the staff!" Goldmoon gasped.

The staff glowed pale blue, as if answering the sword.

The ghostly king turned to Raistlin and reached his pale hand toward the entranced mage. Caramon gave a hoarse bellow and broke free of Tanis's grip. Drawing his sword, he lunged at the undead warrior. The blade pierced the flickering body, but it was Caramon who screamed in pain and dropped, writhing, to the ground. Tanis and Sturm knelt beside him. Raistlin stared ahead, his expression unchanged, unmoving.

"Caramon, where—" Tanis held him, trying frantically to see where the big man was injured.

"My hand!" Caramon rocked back and forth, sobbing, his left hand—his sword hand—thrust tightly under his right arm.

"What's the matter?" Tanis asked. Then, seeing the warrior's sword on the ground, he knew: Caramon's sword was rimed with frost.

Tanis looked up in horror and saw the spectre's hand close tightly around Raistlin's wrist. A shudder wracked the mage's frail body; his face twisted in pain, but he did not fall. The mage's eyes closed, the lines of cynicism and bitterness smoothed away and the peace of death descended on him. Tanis watched in awe, only partially aware of Caramon's hoarse cries. He saw Raistlin's face transform again, this time imbued with ecstasy. The mage's aura of power intensified until it glowed around him with an almost palpable brilliance.

"We are summoned," Raistlin said. The voice was his own and yet like none Tanis had ever heard him use. "We must go."

The mage turned his back on them and walked into the woods, the ghostly king's fleshless hand still grasping his wrist. The circle of undead parted to let him pass.

"Stop them," Caramon moaned. He staggered to his feet.

"We can't!" Tanis fought to restrain him, and finally the big man collapsed in the half-elf's arms, weeping like a child. "We'll follow him. He'll be all right. He's magi, Caramon—we can't understand. We'll follow—"

The eyes of the undead flickered with an unholy light as they watched the companions pass them and enter the forest. The spectral army closed ranks behind them.

The companions stepped into a raging battle. Steel rang; wounded men shrieked for help. So real was the clash of armies in the darkness that Sturm drew his sword reflexively. The tumult deafened him; he ducked and dodged unseen blows that he knew were aimed at him. He swung his sword in desperation at black air, knowing that he was doomed and there was no escape. He began to run, and he suddenly stumbled out of the forest into a barren, wasted glade. Raistlin stood before him, alone.

The mage's eyes were closed. He sighed gently, then collapsed to the ground. Sturm ran to him, then Caramon appeared, nearly knocking Sturm over to reach his brother and gather him tenderly in his arms. One by one, the others ran as if driven into the glade. Raistlin was still murmuring strange, unfamiliar words. The spectres vanished.

"Raist!" Caramon sobbed brokenly.

The mage's eyelids flickered and opened. "The spell . . . drained me. . . ." he whispered. "I must rest. . . ."

"And rest ye shall!" boomed a voice—a living voice!

Tanis breathed a sigh of relief even as he put his hand on his sword. Quickly he and the others jumped protectively in

113

front of Raistlin, turning to face outward, staring into the darkness. Then the silver moon appeared, suddenly, as if a hand had produced it from beneath a black silk scarf. Now they could see the head and shoulders of a man standing amid the trees. His bare shoulders were as large and heavy as Caramon's. A mane of long hair curled around his neck; his eyes were bright and glittered coldly. The companions heard a rustling in the brush and saw the flash of a spear tip being raised, pointing at Tanis.

"Put thy puny weapons down," the man warned. "Ye be surrounded and have not a chance."

"A trick," Sturm growled, but even as he spoke there was a tremendous crashing and cracking of tree limbs. More men appeared, surrounding them, all armed with spears that glinted in the moonlight.

The first man strode forward then, and the companions stared in amazement, their hands on their weapons going slack.

The man wasn't a man at all, but a centaur! Human from the waist up, he had the body of a horse from the waist down. He cantered forward with easy grace, powerful muscles rippling across his barrel chest. Other centaurs moved into the path at his commanding gesture. Tanis sheathed his sword. Flint sneezed.

"Thee must come with us," the centaur ordered.

"My brother is ill," Caramon growled. "He can't go anywhere."

"Place him upon my back," the centaur said coolly. "In fact, if any of you be tired, thee may ride to where we go."

"Where are you taking us?" Tanis asked.

"Thee is in no position to ask questions." The centaur reached out and prodded Caramon's back with his spear. "We travel far and fast. I suggest thee ride. But fear not." He bowed before Goldmoon, extending his foreleg and touching his hand to his shaggy hair. "Harm will not come to thee this night."

"Can I ride, Tanis, please?" begged Tasslehoff.

"Don't trust them!" Flint sneezed violently.

"I *don't* trust them," Tanis muttered, "but we don't seem to have a whole lot of choice in the matter—Raistlin can't walk. Go on, Tas. The rest of you, too."

Caramon, scowling at the centaurs suspiciously, lifted his brother in his arms and set him upon the back of one of the half-man, half-animals. Raistlin slumped forward weakly.

"Climb up," the centaur said to Caramon. "I can bear the weight of thee both. Thy brother will need thy support, for we ride swiftly tonight."

Flushing with embarrassment, the big warrior clambered onto the centaur's broad back, his huge legs dangling almost to the ground. He put an arm around Raistlin as the centaur galloped down the path. Tasslehoff, giggling with excitement, jumped onto a centaur and promptly slid off the other side into the mud. Sturm, sighing, picked up the kender and set him on the centaur's back. Then, before Flint could protest, the knight lifted the dwarf up behind Tas. Flint tried to speak but could only sneeze as the centaur moved away. Tanis rode with the first centaur, who seemed to be the leader.

"Where are you taking us?" Tanis asked again.

"To the Forestmaster," the centaur answered.

"The Forestmaster?" Tanis repeated. "Who is he, one like yourselves?"

"She is the Forestmaster," the centaur replied and began to canter down the trail.

Tanis started to ask another question, but the centaur's quickened pace jolted him, and he nearly bit through his tongue as he came down hard on the centaur's back. Feeling himself start to slide backward as the centaur trotted faster and faster, Tanis threw his arms around the centaur's broad torso.

"Nay, thee doesn't need to squeeze me in two!" The centaur glanced back, his eyes glittering in the moonlight. "It be my job to see thee stays on. Relax. Put thy hands on me rump to balance thyself. There, now. Grip with thy legs."

The centaurs left the trail and plunged into the forest. The moonlight was immediately swallowed up by the dense trees. Tanis felt branches whip past, swiping at his clothing. The centaur never swerved or slowed in his gallop, however, and Tanis could only assume he knew the trail well, a trail the half-elf couldn't see.

Soon the pace began to slacken and the centaur finally came to a stop. Tanis could see nothing in the smothering darkness. He knew his companions were near only because he could hear Raistlin's shallow breathing, Caramon's jingling armor, and Flint's unabated sneezing. Even the light from Raistlin's staff had died.

"A powerful magic is laid on this forest," the mage whispered weakly when Tanis asked him about it. "This magic dispels all others."

Tanis's uneasiness grew. "Why are we stopping?"

"Because thee art here. Dismount," the centaur ordered gruffly.

"Where is here?" Tanis slid off the centaur's broad back onto the ground. He stared around him but could see nothing. Apparently the trees kept even the smallest glimmer of moonlight or starlight from penetrating through to the trail.

"Thee stands in the center of Darken Wood," the centaur replied. "And now I bid thee farewell—or fare evil, depending on how the Forestmaster judges thee."

"Wait a minute!" Caramon called out angrily. "You can't just leave us here in the middle of this forest, blind as newborn kittens—"

"Stop them!" Tanis ordered, reaching for his sword. But his weapon was gone. An explosive oath from Sturm indicated the knight had discovered the same thing.

The centaur chuckled. Tanis heard hooves beat into soft earth and tree branches rustled. The centaurs were gone.

"Good riddance!" Flint sneezed.

"Are we all here?" Tanis asked, reaching out his hand and feeling Sturm's strong, reassuring grasp.

"I'm here," piped Tasslehoff. "Oh, Tanis, wasn't it wonderful? I—"

"Hush, Tas!" Tanis snapped. "The Plainsmen?"

"We're here," said Riverwind grimly. "Weaponless."

"No one has a weapon?" Tanis asked. "Not that it would do us much good in this cursed blackness," he amended bitterly.

"I have my staff," Goldmoon's low voice said softly.

"And a formidable weapon that is, daughter of Que-shu," came a deep voice. "A weapon for good, intended to combat illness and injury and disease." The unseen voice grew sad. "In these times it will also be used as a weapon against the evil creatures who seek to find and banish it from the world."

II

The Forestmaster.
A peaceful interlude.

W ho are you?" Tanis called. "Show yourself!"

"We will not harm you," bluffed Caramon.

"Of course you won't." Now the deep voice was amused. "You have no weapons. I will return them when the time is propitious. No one brings weapons into Darken Wood, not even a knight of Solamnia. Do not fear, noble knight. I recognize your blade as ancient and most valuable! I will keep it safe. Forgive this apparent lack of trust, but even the great Huma laid the Dragonlance at my feet."

"Huma!" Sturm gasped. "Who are you?"

"I am the Forestmaster." Even as the deep voice spoke, the darkness parted. A gasp of awe, gentle as a spring wind, swept the company as they stared before them. Silver moonlight shone brightly on a high rock ledge. Standing on the ledge was a unicorn. She regarded them coolly, her intelligent eyes gleaming with infinite wisdom.

The unicorn's beauty pierced the heart. Goldmoon felt swift tears spring to her eyes and she was forced to close them against the animal's magnificent radiance. Her fur was the silver of moonlight, her horn was shining pearl, her mane like seafoam. The head might have been sculpted from glistening marble, but no human or even dwarven hand could capture the elegance and grace that lived in the fine lines of the powerful neck and muscular chest. The legs were strong but delicate, the hooves small and cloven like those of a goat. In later days, when Goldmoon walked dark paths and her heart was bleak with despair and hopelessness, she had only to shut her eyes and remember the unicorn to find comfort.

The unicorn tossed her head and then lowered it in grave welcome. The companions, feeling awkward and clumsy and confused, bowed in return. The unicorn suddenly whirled and left the rock ledge, cantering down the rocks toward them.

Tanis, feeling a spell lifted from him, looked around. The bright silver moonlight lit a sylvan glade. Tall trees surrounded them like giant, beneficent guardians. The half-elf was aware of a deep abiding sense of peace here. But there was also a waiting sadness.

"Rest yourselves," the Forestmaster said as she came among them. "You are tired and hungry. Food will be brought and fresh water for cleansing. You may put aside your watchfulness and fears for this evening. Safety exists here, if it exists anywhere in this land tonight."

Caramon, his eyes lighting up at the mention of food, eased his brother to the ground. Raistlin sank into the grass against the trunk of a tree. His face was deathly pale in the silver moonlight, but his breathing was easy. He did not seem ill so much as just terribly exhausted. Caramon sat next to him, looking around for food. Then he heaved a sigh.

"Probably more berries anyway," the warrior said unhappily to Tanis. "I crave meat—roasted deer haunch, a nice sizzling bit of rabbit—"

"Hush," Sturm remonstrated softly, glancing at the Forestmaster. "She'd probably consider roasting you first!"

Centaurs came out of the forest bearing a clean, white cloth, which they spread on the grass. Others placed clear crystal globe lights on the cloth, illuminating the forest.

Tasslehoff stared at the lights curiously. "They're bug lights!"

The crystal globes held thousands of tiny bugs, each one having two brightly glowing spots on its back. They crawled around inside the globes, apparently content to explore their surroundings.

Next, the centaurs brought bowls of cool water and clean white cloths to bathe their faces and hands. The water refreshed their bodies and minds as it washed away the stains of battle. Other centaurs placed chairs, which Caramon stared at dubiously. They were crafted of one piece of wood that curved around the body. They appeared comfortable, except that each chair had only one leg!

"Please be seated," said the Forestmaster graciously.

"I can't sit in that!" the warrior protested. "I'll tip over." He stood at the edge of the tablecloth. "Besides, the tablecloth is spread on the grass. I'll sit on the grass with it."

"Close to the food," muttered Flint into his beard.

The others glanced uneasily at the chairs, the strange crystal bug lamps, and the centaurs. The Chieftain's Daughter, however, knew what was expected of guests. Although the outside world might have considered her people barbarians, Goldmoon's tribe had strict rules of politeness that must be religiously observed. Goldmoon knew that to keep your host waiting was an insult to both the host and his bounty. She sat down with regal grace. The one-legged chair rocked slightly, adjusting to her height, crafting itself for her alone.

"Sit at my right hand, warrior," she said formally, conscious of the many eyes upon them. Riverwind's face showed no emotion, though he was a ludicrous sight trying to bend his tall body to sit in the seemingly fragile chair. But, once seated, he leaned back comfortably, almost smiling in disbelieving approval.

"Thank you all for waiting until I was seated," Goldmoon said hastily, to cover the others' hesitation. "You may all sit now."

"Oh, that's all right," began Caramon, folding his arms across his chest. "I wasn't waiting. I'm not going to sit in these weird chair—" Sturm's elbow dug sharply into the warrior's ribs.

"Gracious lady," Sturm bowed and sat down with knightly dignity.

"Well, if he can do it, so can I," muttered Caramon, his decision hastened by the fact that the centaurs were bringing in food. He helped his brother to a seat and then sat down gingerly, making certain the chair bore his weight.

Four centaurs positioned themselves at each of the four corners of the huge white cloth spread out upon the ground. They lifted the cloth to the height of a table, then released it. The cloth remained floating in place, its delicately embroidered surface as hard and sturdy as one of the solid tables in the Inn of the Last Home.

"How splendid! How do they do that?" Tasslehoff cried, peering underneath the cloth. "There's nothing under there!" he reported, his eyes wide.

The centaurs laughed uproariously and even the Forestmaster smiled. Next the centaurs laid down plates made of beautifully cut and polished wood. Each guest was given a knife and fork fashioned from the horns of a deer. Platters of hot roasted meat filled the air with a tantalizing smoky aroma. Fragrant loaves of bread and huge wooden bowls of fruit glistened in the soft lamplight.

Caramon, feeling secure in his chair, rubbed his hands together. Then he grinned broadly and picked up his fork. "Ahhhh!" He sighed in appreciation as one of the centaurs set before him a platter of roasted deer meat. Caramon plunged his fork in, sniffing in rapture at the steam and juice that gushed forth from the meat. Suddenly he realized everyone was staring at him. He stopped and looked around.

"Wha—?" he asked, blinking. Then his eyes rested on the Forestmaster and he flushed and hurriedly removed his fork. "I . . . I beg your pardon. This deer must have been someone you knew—I mean—one of your subjects."

The Forestmaster smiled gently. "Be at ease, warrior," she said. "The deer fulfills his purpose in life by providing sustenance for the hunter—be it wolf or man. We do not mourn the loss of those who die fulfilling their destinies."

It seemed to Tanis that the Forestmaster's dark eyes went

to Sturm as she spoke, and there was a deep sadness in them that filled the half-elf's heart with cold fear. But when he turned back to the Forestmaster, he saw the magnificent animal smiling once more. "My imagination," he thought.

"How do we know, Master," Tanis asked hesitantly, "whether the life of any creature has fulfilled its destiny? I have known the very old to die in bitterness and despair. I have seen young children die before their time but leave behind such a legacy of love and joy that grief for their passing was tempered by the knowledge that their brief lives had given much to others."

"You have answered your own question, Tanis Half-Elven, far better than I could," the Forestmaster said gravely. "Say that our lives are measured not by gain but by giving."

The half-elf started to reply, but the Forestmaster interrupted. "Put your cares aside for now. Enjoy the peace of my forest while you may. Its time is passing."

Tanis glanced sharply at the Forestmaster, but the great animal had turned her attention away from him and was staring far off into the woods, her eyes clouded with sorrow. The half-elf wondered what she meant, and he sat, lost in dark thoughts, until he felt a gentle hand touch his.

"You should eat," Goldmoon said. "Your cares won't vanish with the meal—and, if they do, so much the better."

Tanis smiled at her and began to eat with a sharp appetite. He took the Forestmaster's advice and relegated his worries to the back of his mind for a while. Goldmoon was right: they weren't likely to go away.

The rest of the companions did the same, accepting the strangeness of their surroundings with the aplomb of seasoned travelers. Though there was nothing to drink but water—much to Flint's disappointment—the cool, clear liquid washed the terrors and doubts from their hearts as it had cleansed the blood and dirt from their hands. They laughed, talked, and ate, enjoying each other's companionship. The Forestmaster spoke to them no more but watched each in turn.

Sturm's pale face had regained some color. He ate with grace and dignity. Sitting next to Tasslehoff, he answered the kender's inexhaustible store of questions about his homeland. He also, without calling undue attention to the fact, removed from Tasslehoff's pouch a knife and fork that had unaccountably made their way there. The knight sat as far from Caramon as possible and did his best to ignore him.

The big warrior was obviously enjoying his meal. He ate three times more than anyone else, three times as fast, and three times as loudly. When not eating, he described to Flint a fight with a troll, using the bone he was chewing on as a sword to illustrate his thrusts and parries. Flint ate heartily and told Caramon he was the biggest liar in Krynn.

Raistlin, sitting beside his brother, ate very little, taking nibbles of only the tenderest meat, a few grapes, and a bit of bread he soaked in water first. He said nothing but listened intently to everyone, absorbing all that was said into his soul, storing it for future reference and use.

Goldmoon ate her meal delicately, with practiced ease. The Que-shu princess was accustomed to eating in public view and could make conversation easily. She chatted with Tanis, encouraging him to describe the elven lands and other places he had visited. Riverwind, next to her, was acutely uncomfortable and self-conscious. Although not a boisterous eater like Caramon, the Plainsman was obviously more accustomed to eating at the campfires of his fellow tribesmen than in royal halls. He handled cutlery with awkward clumsiness, and he knew that he appeared crude beside Goldmoon. He said nothing, seeming willing to fade into the background.

Finally everyone began shoving plates away and settling back in the strange wooden chairs, ending their dinner with pieces of sweet shortcake. Tas began to sing his kender trailsong, to the delight of the centaurs. Then suddenly Raistlin spoke. His soft, whispering voice slithered through the laughter and loud talk.

"Forestmaster"—the mage hissed the name—"today we fought loathsome creatures that we have never seen before on Krynn. Can you tell us of these?"

The relaxed and festive mood was smothered as effectively as if covered by a shroud. Everyone exchanged grim looks.

"These creatures walk like men," Caramon added, "but look like reptiles. They have clawed hands and feet and wings and"—his voice dropped—"they turn to stone when they die."

The Forestmaster regarded them with sadness as she rose to her feet. She seemed to expect the question.

"I know of these creatures," she answered. "Some of them entered the Darken Wood with a party of goblins from Haven a week ago. They wore hoods and cloaks, no doubt to disguise their horrible appearance. The centaurs followed them in secret, to make certain they harmed no one before the spectral minions dealt with them. The centaurs reported that the creatures call themselves 'draconians' and speak of belonging to the 'Order of Draco.' "

Raistlin's brow furrowed. "Draco," he whispered, puzzled. "But who are they? What race or species?"

"I do not know. I can tell you only this: they are not of the animal world, and they belong to none of the races of Krynn."

This took a moment for everyone to assimilate. Caramon blinked. "I don't—" he began.

"She means, my brother, that they are not of this world," Raistlin explained impatiently.

"Then where'd they come from?" Caramon asked, startled.

"That's the question, isn't it?" Raistlin said coldly. "Where did they come from—and why?"

"I cannot answer that." The Forestmaster shook her head. "But I can tell you that before the spectral minions put an end to these draconians, they spoke of 'armies to the north.' "

"I saw them." Tanis rose to his feet. "Campfires—" His voice caught in his throat as he realized what the Forestmaster had been about to say. "Armies! Of these draconians? There must be thousands!" Now everyone was standing and talking at once.

"Impossible!" the knight said, scowling.

"Who's behind this? The Seekers? By the gods," Caramon bellowed, "I've got a notion to go to Haven and bash—"

"Go to Solamnia, not to Haven," Sturm advised loudly.

"We should travel to Qualinost," Tanis argued. "The elves—"

"The elves have their own problems," the Forestmaster interrupted, her cool voice a calming influence. "As do the Highseekers of Haven. No place is safe. But I will tell you where you must go to find answers to your questions."

"What do you mean you will tell us where to go?" Raistlin stepped forward slowly, his red robes rippling around him as he walked. "What do you know of us?" The mage paused, his eyes narrowing with a sudden thought.

"Yes, I was expecting you," the Forestmaster replied in answer to Raistlin's thoughts. "A great and shining being appeared to me in the wilderness this day. He told me that the one bearing the blue crystal staff would come this night to Darken Wood. The spectral minions would let the staff-bearer and her companions pass—though they have allowed no human or elf or dwarf or kender to enter Darken Wood since the Cataclysm. I was to give the bearer of the staff this message: 'You must fly straight away across the Eastwall Mountains. In two days the staffbearer must be within Xak Tsaroth. There, if you prove worthy, you shall receive the greatest gift given to the world.' "

"Eastwall Mountains!" The dwarf's mouth dropped open. "We'll need to fly all right, to reach Xak Tsaroth in two days time. Shining being! Hah!" He snapped his fingers.

The rest glanced uneasily at each other. Finally Tanis said hesitantly, "I'm afraid the dwarf is right, Forestmaster. The journey to Xak Tsaroth would be long and perilous. We would have to go back through lands we know are inhabited by goblins and these draconians."

"And then we would have to pass through the Plains," Riverwind spoke for the first time since meeting the Forestmaster. "Our lives are forfeit." He gestured toward Goldmoon. "The Que-shu are fierce fighters and they know the land. They are waiting. We would never get through safely." He looked at Tanis. "And my people have no love for elves."

"And why go to Xak Tsaroth anyway?" Caramon rumbled. "Greatest gift—what could that be? A powerful sword? A chest of steel coins? That would come in handy, but there's a battle brewing up north apparently. I'd hate to miss it."

The Forestmaster nodded gravely. "I understand your dilemma," she said. "I offer what help is in my power. I will see to it that you reach Xak Tsaroth in two days. The question is, will you go?"

Tanis turned to the others. Sturm's face was drawn. He met Tanis's look and sighed. "The stag led us here," he said slowly, "perhaps to receive this advice. But my heart lies north, in my homeland. If armies of these draconians are preparing to attack, my place is with those Knights who will surely band together to fight this evil. Still, I do not want to desert you, Tanis, or you, lady." He nodded to Goldmoon, then slumped down, his aching head in his hands.

Caramon shrugged. "I'll go anywhere, fight anything, Tanis. You know that. What say you, brother?"

But Raistlin, staring into the darkness, did not answer.

Goldmoon and Riverwind were speaking together in low voices. They nodded to each other, then Goldmoon said to Tanis, "We will go to Xak Tsaroth. We appreciate everything you've done for us—"

"But we ask for no man's help any longer," Riverwind stated proudly. "This is the completion of our quest. As we began alone, so we will finish it alone."

"And you will die alone!" Raistlin said softly.

Tanis shivered. "Raistlin," he said, "a word with you."

The mage turned obediently and walked with the half-elf into a small thicket of gnarled and stunted trees. Darkness closed around them.

"Just like the old days," Caramon said, his eyes following his brother uneasily.

"And look at all the trouble we got into then," Flint reminded him, plopping down onto the grass.

"I wonder what they talk about?" Tasslehoff said. Long ago, the kender had tried to eavesdrop on these private conversations between the mage and the half-elf, but Tanis had always caught him and shooed him away. "And why can't they discuss it with us?"

"Because we'd probably rip Raistlin's heart out," Sturm answered, in a low, pain-filled voice. "I don't care what you say, Caramon, there's a dark side to your brother, and Tanis has seen it. For which I'm grateful. He can deal with it. I couldn't."

Uncharacteristically, Caramon said nothing. Sturm stared at the warrior, startled. In the old days, the fighter would have leaped to his brother's defense. Now he sat silent, preoccupied, his face troubled. So there is a dark side to Raistlin, and now Caramon, too, knows what it is. Sturm shuddered, wondering what had happened in these past five years that cast such a dark shadow across the cheerful warrior.

Raistlin walked close to Tanis. The mage's arms were crossed in the sleeves of his robes, his head bowed in thought. Tanis could feel the heat of Raistlin's body radiate through the red robes, as though he were being consumed by an inner fire. As usual, Tanis felt uncomfortable in the young mage's presence. Yet, right now, he knew of no one else he could turn to for advice. "What do you know of Xak Tsaroth?" Tanis asked.

"There was a temple there—a temple to the ancient gods," Raistlin whispered. His eyes glittered in the eerie light of the red moon. "It was destroyed in the Cataclysm and its people fled, certain that the gods had abandoned them. It passed from memory. I did not know it still existed."

"What did you see, Raistlin?" Tanis asked softly, after a long pause. "You looked far away—what did you see?"

"I am magi, Tanis, not a seer."

"Don't give me that," Tanis snapped. "It's been a long time, but not that long. I know you don't have the gift of foresight. You were thinking, not scrying. And you came up with answers. I want those answers. You've got more brains than all of us put together, even if—" He stopped.

"Even if I am twisted and warped." Raistlin's voice rose with harsh arrogance. "Yes, I am smarter than you—all of you. And someday I will prove it! Someday you—with all your strength and charm and good looks—you, all of you, will call me master!" His hands clenched to fists inside his robes, his eyes flared red in the crimson moonlight. Tanis, who was accustomed to this tirade, waited patiently. The mage relaxed, his hands unclenched. "But for now, I give you my advice. What did I see? These armies, Tanis, armies of draconians, will overrun Solace and Haven and all the lands of your fathers. That is the reason we must reach Xak Tsaroth. What we find there will prove this army's undoing."

"But why are there armies?" Tanis asked. "What would anyone want with control of Solace and Haven and the Plains to the east? Is it the Seekers?"

"Seekers! Hah!" Raistlin snorted. "Open your eyes, Half-Elf. Someone or something powerful created these creatures—these draconians. Not the idiot Seekers. And no one goes to all that trouble to take over two farm cities or even to look for a blue crystal staff. This is a war of conquest, Tanis. Someone seeks to conquer Ansalon! Within two days time, life on Krynn as we have known it will come to an end. This is the portent of the fallen stars. The Queen of Darkness has returned. We face a foe who seeks—at the very least—to enslave us, or perhaps destroy us completely."

"Your advice?" Tanis asked reluctantly. He felt change coming and, like all elves, he feared and detested change.

Raistlin smiled his crooked, bitter smile, reveling in his moment of superiority. "That we go to Xak Tsaroth immediately. That we leave tonight, if possible, by whatever means this Forestmaster has planned. If we do not acquire this gift within two days—the armies of draconians will."

"What do you think the gift might be?" Tanis wondered aloud. "A sword or coins, like Caramon said?"

"My brother's a fool," Raistlin stated coldly. "You don't believe that and neither do I."

"Then what?" Tanis pursued.

Raistlin's eyes narrowed. "I have given you my advice. Act upon it as you will. I have my own reasons for going. Let us leave it at that, Half-Elf. But it will be dangerous. Xak Tsaroth was abandoned three hundred years ago. I do not think it will have remained abandoned long."

"That is true," Tanis mused. He stood silently for long moments. The mage coughed once, softly. "Do you believe we were chosen, Raistlin?" Tanis asked.

The mage did not hesitate. "Yes. So I was given to know in the Towers of Sorcery. So Par-Salian told me."

"But why?" Tanis questioned impatiently. "We are not the stuff of heroes—well, maybe Sturm—"

"Ah," said Raistlin. "But *who* chose us? And for what purpose? Consider that, Tanis Half-Elven!"

The mage bowed to Tanis, mockingly, and turned to walk back through the brush to the rest of the group.

12

Winged sleep. Smoke in the east.
Dark memories.

ak Tsaroth," Tanis said. "That is my decision."

"Is that what the mage advises?" Sturm asked sullenly.

"It is," Tanis answered, "and I believe his advice is sound. If we do not reach Xak Tsaroth within two days, others will and this 'greatest gift' may be lost forever."

"The greatest gift!" Tasslehoff said, his eyes shining. "Just think, Flint! Jewels beyond price! Or maybe—"

"A keg of ale and Otik's fried potatoes," the dwarf muttered. "And a nice warm fire. But no—Xak Tsaroth!"

"I guess we're all in agreement, then," Tanis said. "If you feel you are needed in the north, Sturm, of course you—"

"I will go with you to Xak Tsaroth." Sturm sighed. "There is nothing in the north for me. I have been deluding myself. The knights of my order are scattered, holed up in crumbling fortresses, fighting off the debt collectors."

The knight's face twisted in agony and he lowered his head. Tanis suddenly felt tired. His neck hurt, his shoulders and back ached, his leg muscles twitched. He started to say something more, then felt a gentle hand touch his shoulder. He looked up to see Goldmoon's face, cool and calm in the moonlight.

"You are weary, my friend," she said. "We all are. But we are glad you are coming, Riverwind and I." Her hand was strong. She looked up, her clear gaze encompassing the entire group. "We are glad all of you are coming with us."

Tanis, glancing at Riverwind, wasn't certain the tall Plainsman agreed with her.

"Just another adventure," Caramon said, flushing with embarrassment. "Eh, Raist?" He nudged his brother. Raistlin, ignoring his twin, looked at the Forestmaster.

"We must leave immediately," the mage said coldly. "You mentioned something about helping us cross the mountains."

"Indeed," the Forestmaster replied, nodding gravely. "I, too, am glad you have made this decision. I hope you find my aid welcome."

The Forestmaster raised her head, looking up into the sky. The companions followed her gaze. The night sky, seen through the canopy of tall trees, glittered brilliantly with stars. Soon the companions became aware of something flying up there, winking out the stars in passing.

"I'll be a gully dwarf," Flint said solemnly. "Flying horses. What next?"

"Oh!" Tasslehoff drew in a deep breath. The kender was transfixed with wonder as he watched the beautiful animals circle above them, descending lower and lower with each turn, their fur radiating blue-white in the moonlight. Tas clasped his hands together. Never in his wildest kender imaginings had he dreamed of flying. This was worth fighting all the draconians on Krynn.

The pegasi dipped to the ground, their feathery wings creating a wind that tossed the tree branches and laid the grass flat. A large pegasus with wings that touched the ground when he walked bowed reverently to the Forestmaster. His bearing was proud and noble. Each of the other beautiful creatures bowed in turn.

"You have summoned us?" the leader asked the Forestmaster.

"These guests of mine have urgent business to the east. I bid you bear them with the swiftness of the winds across the Eastwall Mountains."

The pegasus regarded the companions with astonishment. He walked with stately mien over to stare first at one, then another. When Tas raised his hand to pet the steed's nose, both of the animal's ears swiveled forward and he reared his great head back. But when he got to Flint, he snorted in disgust and turned to the Forestmaster. "A kender? Humans? And a *dwarf!*"

"Don't do *me* any favors, horse!" Flint sneezed.

The Forestmaster merely nodded and smiled. The pegasus bowed in reluctant assent. "Very well, Master," he replied. With powerful grace, he walked over to Goldmoon and started to bend his foreleg, dipping low before her to assist her in mounting.

"No, do not kneel, noble animal," she said. "I have ridden horses since before I could walk. I need no such assistance." Handing Riverwind her staff, Goldmoon threw her arm around the pegasus's neck and pulled herself astride his broad back. Her silver-gold hair blew feathery white in the moonlight, her face was pure and cold as marble. Now she truly looked like the princess of a barbarian tribe.

She took her staff from Riverwind. Raising it in the air, she lifted her voice in song. Riverwind, his eyes shining with admiration, leaped up behind her on the back of the winged horse. Putting his arms around her, he added his deep baritone voice to hers.

Tanis had no idea what they were singing, but it seemed a song of victory and triumph. It stirred his blood and he would have willingly joined in. One of the pegasi cantered up to him. He pulled himself up and settled himself on his broad back, sitting in front of the powerful wings.

Now all the companions, caught up in the elation of the moment, mounted, Goldmoon's song adding wings to their souls as the pegasi spread their huge wings and caught the wind currents. They soared higher and higher, circling above the forest. The silver moon and the red bathed the valley below and the clouds above in an eerie, beautiful, purplish glow that receded into a deeper purple night. As the forest fell away from them, the last thing the companions saw was the Forestmaster, glimmering like a star fallen from the heavens, shining lost and alone in a darkening land.

One by one, the companions felt drowsiness overcome them.

Tasslehoff fought this magically induced sleep longest. Enchanted by the rush of wind against his face, spellbound by the sight of the tall trees that normally loomed over him reduced to child's toys, Tas struggled to remain awake long after everyone else. Flint's head rested against his back, the dwarf snoring loudly. Goldmoon was cradled in Riverwind's arms. His head drooped over her shoulder. Even in his sleep, he held her protectively. Caramon slumped over his horse's neck, breathing stentoriously. His brother rested against his twin's broad back. Sturm slept peacefully, the lines of pain gone from his face. Even Tanis's bearded face was clear of care and worry and responsibility.

Tas yawned. "No," he mumbled, blinking rapidly and pinching himself.

"Rest now, little kender," his pegasus said in amusement. "Mortals were not meant to fly. This sleep is for your protection. We do not want you to panic and fall off."

"I won't," Tas protested, yawning again. His head sank forward. The pegasus's neck was warm and comfortable, the fur was fragrant and soft. "I won't panic," Tas whispered sleepily. "Never panic . . ." He slept.

The half-elf woke with a start to find that he was lying in a grassy meadow. The leader of the pegasi stood above him, staring off to the east. Tanis sat up.

"Where are we?" he began. "This isn't a city." He looked around. "Why—we haven't even crossed the mountains yet!"

"I am sorry." The pegasus turned to him. "We could not take you as far as the Eastwall Mountains. There is great trouble brewing in the east. A darkness fills the air, such a darkness as I have not felt in Krynn for countless—" He stopped, lowered his head and pawed the ground restlessly. "I dare not travel farther."

"Where are we? " the confused half-elf repeated. "And where are the other pegasi?"

"I sent them home. I remained to guard your sleep. Now that you are awake, I must return home as well." The pegasus gazed sternly at Tanis. "I know not what awakened this great evil on Krynn. I trust it was not you and your companions."

He spread his great wings.

"Wait!" Tanis scrambled to his feet. "What—"

The pegasus leaped into the air, circled twice, then was gone, flying rapidly back to the west.

"What evil?" Tanis asked glumly. He sighed and looked around. His companions were sleeping soundly, lying on the ground around him in various poses of slumber. He studied the horizon, trying to get his bearings. It was nearly dawn, he realized. The sun's light was just beginning to illuminate the east. He was standing on a flat prairie. There was not a tree in sight, nothing but rolling fields of tall grass as far as he could see.

Wondering what the pegasus had meant about trouble to the east, Tanis sat down to watch the sun rise and wait for his friends to wake. He wasn't particularly worried about where he was, for he guessed Riverwind knew this land down to the last blade of grass. So he stretched out on the ground, facing the east, feeling more relaxed after that strange sleep than he had in many nights.

Suddenly he sat upright, his relaxed feeling gone, a tightness clutching at his throat like an unseen hand. For there, snaking up to meet the bright new morning sun, were three thick, twisting columns of greasy, black smoke. Tanis stumbled to his feet. He ran over and shook Riverwind gently, trying to wake the Plainsman without disturbing Goldmoon.

"Hush," Tanis whispered, putting a warning finger on his lips and nodding toward the sleeping woman as Riverwind blinked at the half-elf. Seeing Tanis's dark expression, the barbarian was instantly awake. He stood up quietly and moved off with Tanis, glancing around him.

"What's this?" he whispered. "We're in the Plains of Abanasinia. Still about a half day's journey from the Eastwall Mountains. My village lies to the east—"

He stopped as Tanis pointed silently eastward. Then he gave a shallow, ragged cry as he saw the smoke curling into the sky. Goldmoon jerked awake. She sat up, gazed at

Riverwind sleepily, then with growing alarm. Turning, she followed his horrified stare.

"No," she moaned. "No!" she cried again. Quickly rising, she began to gather their possessions. The others woke at her cry.

"What is it?" Caramon jumped up.

"Their village," Tanis said softly, gesturing with his hand. "It's burning. Apparently the armies are moving quicker than we thought."

"No," said Raistlin. "Remember—the draconian clerics mentioned they had traced the staff to a village in the Plains."

"My people," Goldmoon murmured, energy draining from her. She slumped in Riverwind's arms, staring at the smoke. "My father . . ."

"We'd better get going." Caramon glanced around uneasily. "We show up like a jewel in a gypsy dancer's navel."

"Yes," Tanis said. "We've definitely got to get out of here. But where do we go?" he asked Riverwind.

"Que-shu," Goldmoon's tone allowed no contradiction. "It's on our way. The Eastwall Mountains are just beyond my village." She started through the tall grass.

Tanis glanced at Riverwind.

"Marulina!" the Plainsman called out to her. Running forward, he caught hold of Goldmoon's arm. *"Nikh pat-takh merilar!"* he said sternly.

She stared up at him, her eyes blue and cold as the morning sky. "No," she said resolutely, "I am going to our village. It is our fault if something has happened. I don't care if there are thousands of those monsters waiting. I will die with our people, as I should have done." Her voice failed her. Tanis, watching, felt his heart ache with pity.

Riverwind put his arm around her and together they began walking toward the rising sun.

Caramon cleared his throat. "I hope I do meet a thousand of those things," he muttered, hoisting his and his brother's packs. "Hey," he said in astonishment. "They're full." He peered in his pack. "Provisions. Several days' worth. And my sword's back in my scabbard!"

"At least that's one thing we won't have to worry about," Tanis said grimly. "You all right, Sturm?"

"Yes," the knight answered. "I feel much better after that sleep."

"Right, then. Let's go. Flint, where's Tas?" Turning, Tanis nearly fell over the kender who had been standing right behind him.

"Poor Goldmoon," Tas said softly. Tanis patted him on the shoulder. "Maybe it won't be as bad as we fear," the half-elf said, following the Plainsmen through the rippling grass. "Maybe the warriors fought them off and those are victory fires."

Tasslehoff sighed and looked up at Tanis, his brown eyes wide. "You're a rotten liar, Tanis," the kender said. He had the feeling it was going to be a very long day.

Twilight. The pale sun set. Shafts of yellow and tan streaked the western sky, then faded into dreary night. The companions sat huddled around a fire that offered no warmth, for there existed no flame on Krynn that would drive the chill from their souls. They did not speak to each other, but each sat staring into the fire, trying to make some sense of what they had seen, trying to make sense of the senseless.

Tanis had lived through much that was horrible in his life. But the ravaged town of Que-shu would always stand out in his mind as a symbol of the horrors of war.

Even so, remembering Que-shu, he could only grasp fleeting images, his mind refusing to encompass the total awful vision. Oddly enough, he remembered the melted stones of Que-shu. He remembered them vividly. Only in his dreams did he recall the twisted and blackened bodies that lay among the smoking stones.

The great stone walls, the huge stone temples and edifices, the spacious stone buildings with their rock courtyards and statuary, the large stone arena—all had melted, like butter on a hot summer day. The rock still smoldered, though it was obvious that the village must have been attacked well over a sunrise ago. It was as if a white-hot, searing flame had engulfed the entire village. But what fire was there on Krynn that could melt rock?

He remembered a creaking sound, remembered hearing it and being puzzled by it, and wondering what it was until locating the source of the only sound in the deathly still town became an obsession. He ran through the ruined village until he located the source. He remembered that he shouted to the others until they came. They stood staring into the melted arena.

Huge stone blocks had poured down from the side of the bowl-shaped depression, forming molten ripples of rock around the bottom of the dish. In the center—on grass that was blackened and charred—stood a crude gibbet. Two stout posts had been driven into the burned ground by unspeakable force, their bases splintered by the impact. Ten feet above the ground, a crosspiece pole was lashed to the two posts. The wood was charred and blistered. Scavenger birds perched on the top. Three chains, made of what appeared to be iron before it had melted and run together, swung back and forth. This was the cause of the creaking sound. Suspended from each chain, apparently by the feet, was a corpse. The corpses were not human; they were hobgoblin. On top of the gruesome structure was a shield stuck to the crosspiece with a broken swordblade. Roughly clawed on the battered shield were words written in a crude form of Common.

"This is what happens to those who take prisoners against my commands. Kill or be killed." It was signed, *Verminaard.*

Verminaard. The name meant nothing to Tanis.

Other images. He remembered Goldmoon standing in the center of her father's ruined house trying to put back together the pieces of a broken vase. He remembered a dog— the only living thing they found in the entire village—curled around the body of a dead child. Caramon stopped to pet the small dog. The animal cringed, then licked the big man's hand. It then licked the child's cold face, looking up at the warrior hopefully, expecting this human to make everything all right, to make his little playmate run and laugh again. He remembered Caramon stroking the dog's soft fur with his huge hands.

He remembered Riverwind picking up a rock, holding it, aimlessly, as he stared around his burned and blasted village.

He remembered Sturm, standing transfixed before the gibbet, staring at the sign, and he remembered the knight's lips moving as though in prayer or perhaps a silent vow.

He remembered the sorrow-lined face of the dwarf, who had seen so much tragedy in his long lifetime, as he stood in the center of the ruined village, patting Tasslehoff gently on the back after finding the kender sobbing in a corner.

He remembered Goldmoon's frantic search for survivors. She crawled through the blackened rubble, screaming out names, listening for faint answers to her calls until she was hoarse and Riverwind finally convinced her it was hopeless. If there were any survivors, they had long since fled.

He remembered standing alone, in the center of the town, looking at piles of dust with arrow heads in them, and recognizing them as bodies of draconians.

He remembered a cold hand touching his arm and the mage's whispering voice. "Tanis, we must leave. There is nothing more we can do and we must reach Xak Tsaroth. Then we will have our revenge."

And so they left Que-shu. They traveled far into the night, none of them wanting to stop, each wanting to push his body to the point of exhaustion so that, when they finally slept, there would be no evil dreams.

But the dreams came anyway.

13

Chill dawn. Vine bridges.
Dark water.

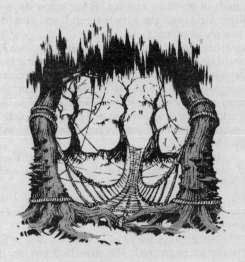

 anis felt clawed hands clutching at his throat. He struggled and fought, then woke to find Riverwind bending over him in the darkness, shaking him roughly.

"What . . . ?" Tanis sat up.

"You were dreaming," the Plainsman said grimly. "I had to wake you. Your shouts would draw an army down on us."

"Yes, thanks," Tanis muttered. "I'm sorry." He sat up, trying to shake off the nightmare. "What time is it?"

"Still several hours till dawn," Riverwind said wearily. He returned to where he had been sitting, his back against the trunk of a twisted tree. Goldmoon lay sleeping on the ground beside him. She began to murmur and shake her head, making small, soft, moaning cries like a wounded animal. Riverwind stroked her silver-gold hair, and she quieted.

"You should have wakened me earlier," Tanis said. He stood up, rubbing his shoulders and neck. "It's my watch."

"Do you think I could sleep?" asked Riverwind bitterly.

"You've got to," Tanis answered. "You'll slow us up if you don't."

"The men in my tribe can travel for many days without sleep," Riverwind said. His eyes were dull and glazed, and he seemed to stare at nothing.

Tanis started to argue, then sighed and kept quiet. He knew that he could never truly understand the agony the Plainsman was suffering. To have friends and family—an entire life—utterly destroyed, must be so devastating that the mind shrank from even imagining it. Tanis left him and walked over to where Flint was sitting carving at a piece of wood.

"You might as well get some sleep," Tanis told the dwarf. "I'll watch for a while."

Flint nodded. "I heard you yelling over there." He sheathed his dagger and thrust the piece of wood into a pouch. "Defending Que-shu?"

Tanis frowned at the memory. Shivering in the chill night, he wrapped his cloak around him, drew up his hood. "Any idea where we are?" he asked Flint.

"The Plainsman says we're on a road known as Sageway East," the dwarf answered. He stretched out on the cold ground, dragging a blanket up around his shoulders. "Some old highway. It's been around since before the Cataclysm."

"I don't suppose we'd be fortunate enough to have this road take us into Xak Tsaroth?"

"Riverwind doesn't seem to think so," the dwarf mumbled sleepily. "Says he's only followed it a short distance. But at least it gets us through the mountains." He gave a great yawn and turned over, pillowing his head on his cloak.

Tanis breathed deeply. The night seemed peaceful enough. They hadn't run into any draconians or goblins in their wild flight from Que-shu. As Raistlin said, apparently the draconians had attacked Que-shu in search of the staff, not as part of any preparations for battle. They had struck and then withdrawn. The Forestmaster's time limit still held good, Tanis supposed—Xak Tsaroth within two days. And one day had already passed.

Shivering, the half-elf walked back over to Riverwind. "Do you have any idea how far we have to go and in what direction?" Tanis crouched down next to the Plainsman.

"Yes," Riverwind nodded, rubbing his burning eyes. "We must go to the northeast, toward Newsea. That is where the city is rumored to be. I have never been there—" He frowned, then shook his head. "I've never been there," he repeated.

"Can we reach it by tomorrow?" Tanis asked.

"Newsea is said to be two days' journey from Que-shu." The barbarian sighed. "If Xak Tsaroth exists, we should be able to reach it in a day, though I have heard that the land from here to Newsea is swampy and difficult to travel."

He shut his eyes, his hand absently stroking Goldmoon's hair. Tanis fell silent, hoping the Plainsman would sleep. The half-elf moved quietly to sit beneath the tree, staring into the night. He made a mental note to ask Tasslehoff in the morning if he had a map.

The kender did have a map, but it wasn't much help, dating, as it did, before the Cataclysm. Newsea wasn't on the map since it had appeared after the land had been torn apart and the waters of Turbidus Ocean had rushed in to fill it. Still, the map showed Xak Tsaroth only a short distance from the highway marked Sageway East. They should reach it some time that afternoon, if the territory they had to cross wasn't impassable.

The companions ate a cheerless breakfast, most forcing the food down without appetite. Raistlin brewed his foul-smelling herbal drink over the small fire, his strange eyes lingering on Goldmoon's staff.

"How precious it has become," he commented softly— "now that it has been purchased by the blood of innocents."

"Is it worth it? Is it worth the lives of my people?" Goldmoon asked, staring at the nondescript brown staff dully. She seemed to have aged during the night. Gray circles smudged the skin beneath her eyes.

None of the companions answered, each looking away in awkward silence. Riverwind stood up abruptly and stalked off into the woods by himself. Goldmoon lifted her eyes and stared after him, then her head sank into her hand and she began to weep silently. "He blames himself." She shook her head. "And I am not helping him. It wasn't his fault."

"It's not anyone's fault," Tanis said slowly, walking over to her. He put his hand on her shoulder, rubbing out the tenseness he felt in the bunched muscles of her neck. "We can't understand. We've just got to keep going and hope we find the answer in Xak Tsaroth."

She nodded and wiped her eyes, drew a deep breath, and blew her nose on a handkerchief Tasslehoff handed her.

"You're right," she said, swallowing. "My father would be ashamed of me. I must remember—I am Chieftain's Daughter."

"No," came Riverwind's deep voice from where he stood behind her in the shadows of the trees. "You are Chieftain."

Goldmoon gasped. She twisted to her feet to stare, wide-eyed, at Riverwind. "Perhaps I am," she faltered—"but it is meaningless. Our people are dead—"

"I saw tracks," Riverwind answered. "Some managed to flee. They have probably gone into the mountains. They will return, and you will be their ruler."

"Our people . . . still alive!" Goldmoon's face became radiant.

"Not many. Maybe none now. It would depend on whether or not the draconians followed them into the mountains." Riverwind shrugged. "Still, you are now their ruler"—bitterness crept into his voice—"and I will be husband of Chieftain."

Goldmoon cringed, as though he had struck her. She blinked, then shook her head. "No, Riverwind," she said softly. "I . . . we've talked—"

"Have we?" he interrupted. "I was thinking about it last night. I've been gone so many years. My thoughts were of you, as a woman. I did not realize—" He swallowed and then drew a deep breath. "I left Goldmoon. I returned to find Chieftain's Daughter."

"What choice did I have?" Goldmoon cried angrily. "My father wasn't well. I had to rule or Loreman would have taken over the tribe. Do you know what's it like—being Chieftain's Daughter? Wondering at every meal if this morsel is the one with the poison? Struggling every day to find the money in the treasury to pay the soldiers so that Loreman would have no excuse to take over! And all the time I must act as Chieftain's Daughter, while my father sits and drools and mumbles." Her voice choked with tears.

Riverwind listened, his face stern and unmoving. He stared at a point above her head. "We should get started," he said coldly. "It's nearly dawn."

The companions had traveled only a few miles on the old, broken road when it dumped them, literally, into a swamp. They had noticed that the ground was getting spongier and the tall, sturdy trees of the mountain canyon forests dwindled. Strange, twisted trees rose up before them. A miasma blotted out the sun, and the air became foul to breathe. Raistlin began to cough and he covered his mouth with a handkerchief. They stayed on the broken stones of the old road, avoiding the dank, swampy ground next to it.

Flint was walking in front with Tasslehoff when suddenly the dwarf gave a great shout and disappeared into the muck. They could see only his head.

"Help! The dwarf!" Tas shouted, and the others ran up.

"It's dragging me under!" Flint flailed about the black, oozing mud in panic.

"Hold still," Riverwind cautioned. "You have fallen in deathmirk. Don't go in after him!" he warned Sturm who had leaped forward. "You'll both die. Get a branch."

Caramon grabbed a young sapling, took a deep breath, grunted, and pulled. They could hear its roots snapping and creaking as the huge warrior dragged it out of the ground. Riverwind stretched out flat, extending the branch to the dwarf. Flint, nearly up to his nose in the slimy muck, thrashed about and finally grabbed hold of it. The warrior hauled the tree out of the deathmirk, the dwarf clinging to it.

"Tanis!" The kender clutched at the half-elf and pointed. A snake, as big around as Caramon's arm, slithered into the ooze right where the dwarf had been floundering.

"We can't walk through this!" Tanis gestured at the swamp. "Maybe we should turn back."

"No time," Raistlin whispered, his hourglass eyes glittering.

"And there is no other way," Riverwind said. His voice sounded strange. "And we can get through—I know a path."

"What?" Tanis turned to him. "I thought you said—"

"I've been here," the Plainsman said in a strangled voice. "I can't remember when, but I've been here. I know the way through the swamp. And it leads to—" He licked his lips.

"Leads to a broken city of evil?" Tanis asked grimly when the Plainsman did not finish his sentence.

"Xak Tsaroth!" Raistlin hissed.

"Of course," Tanis said softly. "It makes sense. Where would we go to find answers about the staff—except to the place where the staff was given you?"

"And we must go now!" said Raistlin insistently. "We must be there by midnight tonight!"

The Plainsman took the lead. He found firm ground around the black water and, making them all walk single file, led them away from the road and deeper into the swamp. Trees that he called ironclaw rose out of the water, their roots standing exposed, twisting into the mud. Vines drooped from their branches and trailed across the faint path. The mist closed in, and soon no one could see beyond a few feet. They were forced to move slowly, testing every step. A false move and they would have plunged into the stinking morass that lay foul and stagnant all around them.

Suddenly the trail came to an end in dark swamp water.

"Now what?" Caramon asked gloomily.

"This," Riverwind said, pointing. A crude bridge, made out of vines twisted into ropes, was attached to a tree. It spanned the water like a spider web.

"Who built it?" Tanis asked.

"I don't know," Riverwind said. "But you will find them all along the path, wherever it becomes impassable."

"I told you Xak Tsaroth would not remain abandoned," Raistlin whispered.

"Yes, well—I suppose we shouldn't throw stones at a gift of the gods," replied Tanis. "At least we don't have to swim!"

The journey across the vine bridge was not pleasant. The vines were coated with slimy moss, which made walking precarious. The structure swayed alarmingly when touched, and its motion became erratic when anyone crossed. They made it safely to the other side but had walked only a short distance before they were forced to use another bridge. And always below them and around them was the dark water, where strange eyes watched them hungrily. Then they reached a point where the firm ground ended and there were no vine bridges. Ahead was nothing but slimy water.

"It isn't very deep," Riverwind muttered. "Follow me. Step only where I step."

Riverwind took a step, then another step, feeling his way, the rest keeping right behind him, staring into the water. They stared in disgust and alarm as unknown and unseen things slithered past their legs. When they reached firm ground again, their legs were coated with slime; all of them gagged from the smell. But this last journey seemed, perhaps, to have been the worst. The jungle growth was not as thick, and they could even see the sun shining faintly through a green haze.

The farther north they traveled, the firmer the terrain became. By midday, Tanis called a halt when he found a dry patch of ground beneath an ancient oak tree. The companions sank down to eat lunch and speak hopefully of leaving the swamp behind them. All except Goldmoon and Riverwind. They spoke not at all.

Flint's clothes were sopping wet. He shook with the cold and began complaining about pains in his joints. Tanis grew worried. He knew the dwarf was subject to rheumatism and remembered what Flint had said about fearing to slow them up. Tanis tapped the kender and gestured him over to one side.

"I know you've got something in one of your pouches that would take the chill off the dwarf's bones, if you know what I mean," Tanis said softly.

"Oh, sure, Tanis," Tas said, brightening. He fumbled around, first in one pouch, then another, and finally came up with a gleaming silver flask. "Brandy. Otik's finest."

"I don't suppose you paid for it?" Tanis asked, grinning.

"I will," the kender replied, hurt. "Next time I'm there."

"Sure." Tanis patted him on the shoulder. "Share some with Flint. Not too much," he cautioned. "Just warm him up."

"All right. And we'll take the lead—we mighty warriors." Tas laughed and skipped over to the dwarf as Tanis returned to the others. They were silently packing up the remains of lunch and preparing to move out. All of us could use some of Otik's finest, he thought. Goldmoon and Riverwind had not spoken to each other all morning. Their mood spread a pall on everyone. Tanis could think of nothing to do that would end the torture these two were experiencing. He could only hope that time would salve the wounds.

The companions continued along the trail for about an hour after lunch, moving more quickly since the thickest part of the jungle had been left behind. Just as they thought they had left the swamp, however, the firm ground came abruptly to an end. Weary, sick with the smell, and discouraged, the companions found themselves wading through the muck once again.

Only Flint and Tasslehoff were unaffected by the return to the swamp. These two had ranged far ahead of the others. Tasslehoff soon "forgot" Tanis's warning about drinking only a little of the brandy. The liquid warmed the blood and took the edge off the gloomy atmosphere, so the kender and dwarf passed the flask back and forth many times until it was empty and they were traipsing along, making jokes about what they would do if they encountered a draconian.

"I'd turn it to stone, all right," the dwarf said, swinging an imaginary battle-axe. "Wham!—right in the lizard's gizzard."

"I'll bet Raistlin could turn one to stone with a look!" Tas imitated the mage's grim face and dour stare. They both laughed loudly, then hushed, giggling, peering back unsteadily to see if Tanis had heard them.

"I'll bet Caramon'd stick a fork in one and eat it!" Flint said.

Tas choked with laughter and wiped tears from his eyes. The dwarf roared. Suddenly the two came to the end of the spongy ground. Tasslehoff grabbed hold of the dwarf as Flint nearly plunged head-first into a pool of swamp water so wide that a vine bridge would not span it. A huge ironclaw tree lay across the water, its thick trunk making a bridge wide enough for two people to walk across side-by-side.

"Now *this* is a bridge!" Flint said, stepping back a pace and trying to bring the log into focus. "No more spider crawling on those stupid green webs. Let's go."

"Shouldn't we wait for the others?" Tasslehoff asked mildly. "Tanis wouldn't want to us to get separated."

"Tanis? Humpf!" The dwarf sniffed. "We'll show him."

"All right," Tasslehoff agreed cheerfully. He leaped up onto the fallen tree. "Careful," he said, slipping slightly, then easily catching his balance. "It's slick." He took a few quick steps, arms outstretched, his feet pointed out like a rope walker he'd seen once at a summer fair.

The dwarf clambered up after the kender, Flint's thick boots clumping clumsily on the log. A voice in the unbrandied part of Flint's mind told him he could never have done this cold sober. It also told him he was a fool for crossing the bridge without waiting for the others, but he ignored it. He was feeling positively young again.

Tasslehoff, enchanted with pretending he was Mirgo the Magnificent, looked up and discovered that he did, indeed, have an audience—one of those draconian things leaped onto the log in front of him. The sight sobered Tas up rapidly. The kender was not given to fear, but he was certainly amazed. He had presence of mind enough to do two things. First he yelled out loudly—"Tanis, ambush!" Then he lifted his hoopak staff and swung it in a wide arc.

The move took the draconian by surprise. The creature sucked in its breath and jumped back off the log to the bank below. Tas, momentarily off balance, regained his feet quickly and wondered what to do next. He glanced around and saw another draconian on the bank. They were, he was puzzled to notice, not armed. Before he could consider this oddity, he heard a roar behind him. He had forgotten the dwarf.

"What is it?" Flint shouted.

"Draco-thing-a-ma-jiggers," Tas said, gripping his hoopak and peering through the mists. "Two ahead! Here they come!"

"Well, confound it, get out of my way!" Flint snarled. Reaching behind, he fumbled for his axe.

"Where am I supposed to go?" Tas shouted wildly.

"Duck!" yelled the dwarf.

The kender ducked, throwing himself down on the log as one of the draconians came toward him, its clawed hands outstretched. Flint swung his axe in a mighty blow that would have decapitated the draconian if it had come anywhere near it. Unfortunately, the dwarf miscalculated and the blade whistled harmlessly in front of the draconian who was waving its hands in the air and chanting strange words.

The momentum of Flint's swing spun the dwarf around. His feet slipped on the slimy log, and, with a loud cry, the dwarf tumbled backward into the water.

Tasslehoff, having been around Raistlin for years, recognized that the draconian was casting a magic spell. Lying face down on the log, his hoopak staff clutched in his hand, the kender figured he had about one and a half seconds to consider what to do. The dwarf was gasping and spluttering in the water beneath him. Not inches away, the draconian was clearly reaching a stunning conclusion to his spellcasting. Deciding that anything was better than being magicked, Tas took a deep breath and dove off the log.

"Tanis! Ambush!"

"Damn!" swore Caramon as the kender's voice floated to them out of the mist somewhere ahead.

They all began running toward the sound, cursing the vines and the tree branches that blocked their way. Crashing out through the forest, they saw the fallen ironclaw bridge. Four draconians ran out of the shadows, blocking their path.

Suddenly the companions were plunged into darkness too thick to see their own hands, much less their comrades.

"Magic!" Tanis heard Raistlin hiss. "These are magic-users. Stand aside. You cannot fight them."

Then Tanis heard the mage cry out in agony.

"Raist!" Caramon shouted. "Where—ugh—" There was a groan and the sound of a heavy body thudding to the ground.

Tanis heard the draconians chanting. Even as he fumbled for his sword, he was suddenly covered, head to toe, in a thick, gooey substance that clogged up his nose and mouth. Struggling to free himself, he only enmeshed himself further. He heard Sturm swearing next to him, Goldmoon cried out, Riverwind's voice was choked off, then drowsiness overcame him. Tanis sank to his knees, still fighting to free himself from the weblike substance that glued his hands to his sides. Then he fell forward on his face and sank into an unnatural sleep.

14

PRISONERS OF THE DRACONIANS.

ying on the ground, panting for breath, Tasslehoff watched as the draconians prepared to carry off his unconscious friends. The kender was well-hidden beneath a bush near the swamp. The dwarf was stretched out next to him, knocked out cold. Tas glanced at him in remorse. He'd had no choice. In his panic, Flint had dragged the kender down in the cold water. If he hadn't clunked the dwarf over the head with his hoopak staff, neither of them would have surfaced alive. He'd hauled the comatose dwarf up out of the water and hidden him beneath a bush.

Then Tasslehoff watched helplessly as the draconians bound his friends magically in what looked like strong spider webs. Tas saw they were all apparently unconscious—or dead—because they didn't struggle or put up a fight.

The kender did get a certain amount of grim amusement out of watching the draconians try to pick up Goldmoon's staff. Evidently they recognized it, for they croaked over it in their guttural language and made gestures of glee. One—presumably the leader—reached out to grasp it. There was a flash of blue light. Giving a screeching cry, the draconian dropped the staff and hopped up and down on the bank, uttering words Tas assumed were impolite. The leader finally came up with an ingenious idea. Pulling a fur blanket from Goldmoon's pack, the draconian laid it down on the ground. The creature picked up a stick and used it to roll the staff onto the blanket. Then it gingerly wrapped the staff in the fur and lifted it up triumphantly. The draconians lifted the webbed bodies of the kender's friends and bore them away. Other draconians followed behind, carrying the companions' packs and their weapons.

As the draconians marched along a path very near the hidden kender, Flint suddenly groaned and stirred. Tas clamped his hand over the dwarf's mouth. The draconians didn't seem to hear and kept moving. Tas could see his friends clearly in the fading afternoon light as the draconians passed. They seemed to be sound asleep. Caramon was even snoring. The kender remembered Raistlin's sleep spell and figured that was what the draconians had used on his friends.

Flint groaned again. One of the draconians near the end of the line stopped and peered into the brush. Tas picked up his hoopak and held it over the dwarf's head—just in case. But it wasn't needed. The draconian shrugged and muttered to itself, then hurried to catch up with its squad. Sighing in relief, Tas took his hand off the dwarf's mouth. Flint blinked and opened his eyes.

"What happened?" The dwarf moaned, his hand on his head.

"You fell off the bridge and hit your head on a log," Tas said glibly.

"I did?" Flint looked suspicious. "I don't remember that. I remember one of those draconian things coming at me and I remember falling into the water—"

"Well, you did, so don't argue," Tas said hurriedly, getting to his feet. "Can you walk?"

"Of course I can walk," the dwarf snapped. He stood up, a little wobbly, but erect. "Where is everybody?"

"The draconians captured them and carried them off."

"All of them?" Flint's mouth fell open. "Just like that?"

"These draconians were magic-users," Tas said impatiently, anxious to get started. "They cast spells, I guess. They didn't hurt them, except for Raistlin. I think they did something terrible to him. I saw him as they passed. He looked awful. But he's the only one." The kender tugged on the dwarf's wet sleeve. "Let's go—we've got to follow them."

"Yeah, sure," Flint mumbled, looking around. Then he put his hand on his head again. "Where's my helm?"

"At the bottom of the swamp," Tas said in exasperation. "Do you want to go in after it?"

The dwarf gave the murky water a horrified glance, shivered, and turned away hurriedly. He put his hand to his head again and felt a large bump. "I sure don't remember hitting my head," he muttered. Then a sudden thought struck him. He felt around his back wildly. "My axe!" he cried.

"Hush!" Tas scolded. "At least you're alive. Now we've got to rescue the others."

"And how do you propose to do that without any weapons except that overgrown slingshot?" Flint grumbled, stumping along after the fast-moving kender.

"We'll think of something," Tas said confidently, though he felt as if his heart were getting tangled up in his feet, it had sunk so low.

The kender picked up the draconians' trail without any trouble. It was obviously an old and well-used trail; it looked as though hundreds of draconian feet had tramped along it. Tasslehoff, examining the tracks, suddenly realized that they might be walking into a large camp of the monsters. He shrugged. No use worrying about such minor details.

Unfortunately, Flint didn't share the same philosophy. "There's a whole damn army up there!" the dwarf gasped, grabbing the kender by the shoulder.

"Yes, well—" Tas paused to consider the situation. He brightened. "That's all the better. The more of *them* there are, the less chance they'll have of seeing *us*." He started off again. Flint frowned. There was something wrong with that logic, but right now he couldn't figure out what, and he was too wet and chilled to argue. Besides, he was thinking the same thing the kender was: the only other choice they had was to escape into the swamp themselves and leave their friends in the hands of the draconians. And that was no choice at all.

They walked another half hour. The sun sank into the mist, giving it a blood-red tinge, and night fell swiftly in the mirky swamp.

Soon they saw a blazing light ahead of them. They left the trail and sneaked into the brush. The kender moved silently as a mouse; the dwarf stepped on sticks that snapped beneath his feet, ran into trees, and blundered through the brush. Fortunately, the draconian camp was celebrating and probably wouldn't have heard an army of dwarves approaching. Flint and Tas knelt just beyond the firelight and watched. The dwarf suddenly grabbed the kender with such violence that he nearly pulled him over.

"Great Reorx!" Flint swore, pointing. "A dragon!"

Tas was too stunned to say anything. He and the dwarf watched in amazed horror as the draconians danced and prostrated themselves before a giant black dragon. The creature lurked inside the remaining half shell of a crumbled domed ruin. Its head was higher than the treetops, its wing span was enormous. One of the draconians, wearing robes, bent before the dragon, gesturing to the staff as it lay on the ground with the captured weapons.

"There's something strange about that dragon," Tas whispered after watching for a few moments.

"Like they're not supposed to exist?"

"That's just the point," Tas said. "Look at it. The creature isn't moving or reacting to anything. It's just sitting there. I always thought that dragons would be more lively, don't you know?"

"Go up and tickle its foot!" Flint snorted. "Then you'll see lively!"

"I think I'll do that," the kender said. Before the dwarf could say a word, Tasslehoff crept out of the brush, flitting from shadow to shadow as he drew near the camp. Flint could have torn his beard out in frustration, but it would have been disastrous to try and stop him now. The dwarf could do nothing but follow.

"Tanis!"

The half-elf heard someone calling him from across a huge chasm. He tried to answer, but his mouth was stuffed with something sticky. He shook his head. Then he felt an arm around his shoulders, helping him sit up. He opened his eyes. It was night. Judging by the flickering light, a huge fire blazed brightly somewhere. Sturm's face, looking concerned, was near his. Tanis sighed and reached out his hand to clasp the knight's shoulder. He tried to speak and was forced to pull off bits of the sticky substance that clung to his face and mouth like cobwebs.

"I'm all right," Tanis said when he could talk. "Where are we?" He glanced around. "Is everyone here? Anyone hurt?"

"We're in a draconian camp," Sturm said, helping the half-elf stand. "Tasslehoff and Flint are missing and Raistlin's hurt."

"Badly?" Tanis asked, alarmed by the serious expression on Sturm's face.

"Not good," the knight replied.

"Poisoned dart," Riverwind said. Tanis turned toward the Plainsman and got his first clear look at their prison. They were inside a cage made of bamboo. Draconian guards stood outside, their long, curved swords drawn and ready. Beyond the cage, hundreds of draconians milled around a campfire. And above the campfire . . .

"Yes," Sturm said, seeing Tanis's startled expression. "A dragon. More children's stories. Raistlin would gloat."

"Raistlin—" Tanis went over to the mage who was lying in a corner of the cage, covered in his cloak. The young mage was feverish and shaking with chills. Goldmoon knelt beside him, her hand on his forehead, stroking back the white hair. He was unconscious. His head tossed fitfully, and he murmured strange words, sometimes shouting out garbled commands. Caramon, his face nearly as pale as his brother's, sat beside him. Goldmoon met Tanis's questioning gaze and shook her head sadly, her eyes large and gleaming in the reflected firelight. Riverwind came over to stand beside Tanis.

"She found this in his neck," he said, carefully holding up a feathered dart between thumb and forefinger. He glanced at the mage without love but with a certain amount of pity. "Who can say what poison burns in his blood?"

"If we had the staff—" Goldmoon said.

"Right," Tanis said. "Where is it?"

"There," Sturm said, his mouth twisting wryly. He pointed. Tanis peered past hundreds of draconians and saw the staff lying on Goldmoon's fur blanket in front of the black dragon.

Reaching out, Tanis grasped a bar of the cage. "We could break out," he told Sturm. "Caramon could snap this like a twig."

"Tasslehoff could snap it like a twig if he were here," Sturm said. "Of course, then we've only got a few hundred of these creatures to take care of—not to mention the dragon."

"All right. Don't rub it in." Tanis sighed. "Any idea what happened to Flint and Tas?"

"Riverwind said he heard a splash just after Tas yelled out that we were being ambushed. If they were lucky, they dived off the log and escaped into the swamp. If not—" Sturm didn't finish.

Tanis closed his eyes to shut out the firelight. He felt tired— tired of fighting, tired of killing, tired of slogging through the muck. He thought longingly of lying down and sinking back into sleep. Instead, he opened his eyes, stalked over to the cage, and rattled the bars. A draconian guard turned around, sword raised.

"You speak Common?" Tanis asked in the very lowest, crudest form of the Common language used on Krynn.

"I speak Common. Apparently better than you do, elven scum," the draconian sneered. "What do you want?"

"One of our party is injured. We ask that you treat him. Give him an antidote to this poison dart."

"Poison?" The draconian peered into the cage. "Ah, yes, the magic-user." The creature gurgled deep in its throat, a sound obviously meant to be laughter. "Sick, is he? Yes, the poison acts swiftly. Can't have a magic-user around. Even behind bars they're deadly. But don't worry. He won't be lonely—the rest of you will be joining him soon enough. In fact, you should envy him. Your deaths will not be nearly so quick."

The draconian turned its back and said something to its partner, jerking its clawed thumb in the direction of the cage. Both of them croaked their gurgling laughter. Tanis, feeling disgust and rage welling up deep inside of him, looked back at Raistlin.

The mage was rapidly growing worse. Goldmoon put her hand on Raistlin's neck, feeling for the life beat, and then shook her head. Caramon made a moaning sound. Then his glance shifted to the two draconians, laughing and talking together outside.

"Stop—Caramon!" Tanis yelled, but it was too late.

With a roar like a wounded animal, the huge warrior leaped toward the draconians. Bamboo gave way before him, the shards splintering and cutting into his skin. Mad with the desire to kill, Caramon never noticed. Tanis jumped on his back as the warrior crashed past him, but Caramon shook him off as easily as a bear shakes off an annoying fly.

"Caramon, you fool—" Sturm grunted as he and Riverwind both threw themselves on the warrior. But Caramon's rage carried him on.

Whirling, one draconian raised its sword, but Caramon sent the weapon flying. The creature hit the ground, knocked senseless by a blow from the big man's fist. Within seconds, there were six draconians, bows and arrows in their hands, surrounding the warrior. Sturm and Riverwind wrestled Caramon to the ground. Sturm, sitting on him, shoved his face into the mud until he felt Caramon relax beneath him and heard him give a strangled sob.

At that instant, a high-pitched, shrill voice screeched through the camp. "Bring the warrior to me!" said the dragon.

Tanis felt the hair rise on his neck. The draconians lowered their weapons and turned to face the dragon, staring in astonishment and muttering among themselves. Riverwind and Sturm got to their feet. Caramon lay on the ground, choking with sobs. The draconian guards glanced at each other uneasily, while those standing near the dragon backed off hurriedly and formed an immense semicircle around it.

One of the creatures, whom Tanis supposed by the insignia on its armor to be some sort of captain, stalked up to a robed draconian who was staring, open-mouthed, at the black dragon.

"What's going on?" the captain demanded. The draconian spoke in the Common tongue. Tanis, listening closely, realized they were of different species—the robed draconians were apparently the magic-users and the priests. Presumably, the two could not communicate in their own languages. The military draconian was clearly upset.

"Where is that Bozak priest of yours? He must tell us what to do!"

"The higher of my order is not here." The robed draconian quickly regained his composure. "One of *them* flew here and took him to confer with Lord Verminaard about the staff."

"But the dragon never speaks when the priest is not here." The captain lowered his voice. "My boys don't like it. You'd better do something quickly!"

"What is this delay?" The dragon's voice shrieked like a wailing wind. "Bring me the warrior!"

"Do as the dragon says." The robed draconian motioned quickly with a clawed hand. Several draconians rushed over, shoved Tanis and Riverwind and Sturm back into the shattered cage, and lifted the bleeding Caramon up by the arms. They dragged him over to stand before the dragon, his back to the blazing fire. Near him lay the blue crystal staff, Raistlin's staff, their weapons, and their packs.

Caramon raised his head to confront the monster, his eyes blurred with tears and blood from the many cuts the bamboo had inflicted on his face. The dragon loomed above him, seen dimly through the smoke rising from the bonfire.

"We mete out justice swiftly and surely, human scum," the dragon hissed. As it spoke, it beat its huge wings, fanning them slowly. The draconians gasped and began to back up, some stumbling over themselves as they hurried to get out of the monster's way. Obviously they knew what was coming.

Caramon stared at the creature without fear. "My brother is dying," he shouted. "Do what you will to me. I ask only one thing. Give me my sword so that I can die fighting!"

The dragon laughed shrilly; the draconians joined it, gurgling and croaking horribly. As the dragon's wings beat the air, it began to rock back and forth, seemingly preparing to leap on the warrior and devour him.

"This will be fun. Let him have his weapon," the dragon commanded. Its flapping wings caused a wind to whip through the camp, scattering sparks from the fire.

Caramon shoved the draconian guards aside. Wiping his hand across his eyes, he walked over to the pile of weapons and pulled out his sword. Then he turned to face the dragon, resignation and grief etched into his face. He raised his sword.

"We can't let him die out there by himself!" Sturm said harshly, and he took a step forward, prepared to break out.

Suddenly a voice came from the shadows behind them.

"Hssst . . . Tanis!"

The half-elf whirled around. "Flint!" he exclaimed, then glanced apprehensively at the draconian guards, but they were absorbed in watching the spectacle of Caramon and the dragon. Tanis hurried to the back of the bamboo cage where the dwarf stood.

"Get out of here!" the half-elf ordered. "There's nothing you can do. Raistlin's dying, and the dragon—"

"Is Tasslehoff ," Flint said succinctly.

"What?" Tanis glared at the dwarf. "Make sense."

"The dragon is Tasslehoff," Flint repeated patiently.

For once Tanis was speechless. He stared at the dwarf.

"The dragon's made of wicker," the dwarf whispered hurriedly. "Tasslehoff sneaked behind it and looked inside. It's rigged! Anyone sitting inside the dragon can make the wings flap and speak through a hollow tube. I guess that's how the priests keep order around here. Anyway, Tasslehoff's the one flapping his wings and threatening to eat Caramon."

Tanis gasped. "But what do we do? There's still a hundred draconians around. Sooner or later they're going to realize what's going on."

"Get over to Caramon, you and Riverwind and Sturm. Grab your weapons and packs and the staff. I'll help Goldmoon carry Raistlin into the woods. Tasslehoff's got something in mind. Just be ready."

Tanis groaned.

"I don't like it any better than you do," the dwarf growled. "Trusting our lives to that rattle-brained kender. But, well, he *is* the dragon, after all."

"He certainly is," Tanis said, eyeing the dragon who was shrieking and wailing and flapping its wings and rocking back and forth. The draconians were staring at it in open-mouthed wonder. Tanis grabbed Sturm and Riverwind and huddled down near Goldmoon, who had not left Raistlin's side. The half-elf explained what was happening. Sturm looked at him as if he were as crazed as Raistlin. Riverwind shook his head.

"Well, have you got a better plan?" Tanis asked.

Both of them looked at the dragon, then back at Tanis, and shrugged.

"Goldmoon goes with the dwarf," Riverwind said.

She started to protest. He looked at her, his eyes expressionless, and she swallowed and fell silent.

"Yes," Tanis said. "Stay with Raistlin, lady, please. We'll bring the staff to you."

"Hurry then," she said through white lips. "He is very nearly gone."

"We'll hurry," Tanis said grimly. "I have a feeling that once things get started out there, we're going to be moving very fast!" He patted her hand. "Come on." He stood up and took a deep breath.

Riverwind's eyes were still on Goldmoon. He started to speak, then shook his head irritably and turned without a word to stand beside Tanis. Sturm joined them. The three crept up behind the draconian guards.

Caramon lifted his sword. It flashed in the firelight. The dragon went into a wild frenzy, and all of the draconians fell back, braying and beating their swords against their shields. Wind from the dragon's wings blew up ashes and sparks from the fire, setting some nearby bamboo huts on fire. The draconians did not notice, so eager were they for the kill. The dragon shrieked and howled, and Caramon felt his mouth go dry and his stomach muscles clench. It was the first time he had ever gone into battle without his brother; the thought made his heart throb painfully. He was about to leap forward and attack when Tanis, Sturm, and Riverwind appeared out of nowhere to stand by his side.

"We will not let our friend die alone!" the half-elf cried defiantly at the dragon. The draconians cheered wildly.

"Get out of here, Tanis!" Caramon scowled, his face flushed and streaked with tears. "This is my fight."

"Shut up and listen!" Tanis ordered. "Get your sword and mine, Sturm. Riverwind, grab your weapons and the packs and any draconian weapons you can pick up to replace those we lost. Caramon, pick up the two staffs."

Caramon stared at him. "What—"

"Tasslehoff's the dragon," Tanis said. "There isn't time to explain. Just do as I say! Get the staff and take it into the woods. Goldmoon's waiting." He laid his hand on the warrior's shoulder. Tanis shoved him. "Go! Raistlin's almost finished! You're his only chance."

This statement reached Caramon's mind. He ran to the pile of weapons and grabbed the blue crystal staff and Raistlin's Staff of Magius, while the draconians yelled. Sturm and Riverwind armed themselves, Sturm bringing Tanis his sword.

"And now, prepare to die, humans!" the dragon screamed. Its wings gave a great lurch and suddenly the creature was flying, hovering in midair. The draconians croaked and cried out in alarm, some breaking for the woods, others hurling themselves flat on the ground.

"Now!" yelled Tanis. "Run, Caramon!"

The big warrior broke for the woods, running swiftly toward where he could see Goldmoon and Flint waiting for him. A draconian appeared in front of him, but Caramon hurled it out of his way with a thrust of his great arm. He could hear a wild commotion behind him, Sturm chanting a Solamnic war cry, draconians yelling. Other draconians leaped at Caramon. He used the blue crystal staff as he had seen Goldmoon use it, swinging it in a wide arc with his huge right hand. It flashed blue flame and the draconians fell back.

Caramon reached the woods and found Raistlin lying at Goldmoon's feet, barely breathing. Goldmoon grabbed the staff from Caramon and laid it on the mage's inert body. Flint watched, shaking his head. "It won't work," muttered the dwarf. "It's used up."

"It has to work," Goldmoon said firmly. "Please," she murmured, "whoever is master of this staff, heal this man. Please." Unknowing, she repeated it over and over. Caramon watched for a moment, blinking his eyes. Then the woods around him were lit by a gigantic burst of flame.

"Name of the Abyss!" Flint breathed. "Look at that!"

Caramon turned just in time to see the great black wicker dragon crash headlong into the blazing bonfire. Flaming logs flew into the air, showering sparks over the camp. The draconians' bamboo huts, some already ablaze, began burning fiercely. The wicker dragon gave a final, horrifying shriek and then it, too, caught fire.

"Tasslehoff!" Flint swore. "That blasted kender—he's inside there!" Before Caramon could stop him, the dwarf ran out into the blazing draconian camp.

"Caramon . . ." Raistlin murmured. The big warrior knelt beside his brother. Raistlin was still pale, but his eyes were open and clear. He sat up, weakly, leaning against his brother, and stared out at the raging fire. "What's going on?"

"I'm not sure," Caramon said. "Tasslehoff turned into a dragon and after that things get real confused. You just rest." The warrior stared into the smoke, his sword drawn and ready in case any draconians came for them.

But the draconians now had little interest in the prisoners. The smaller breed, panic stricken, were fleeing into the forest as their great god-dragon went up in flames. A few of the robed draconians, bigger and apparently more intelligent than the other species, were trying desperately to bring order to the fearful chaos raging around them.

Sturm fought and slashed his way through the draconians without encountering any organized resistance. He had just reached the edge of the clearing, near the bamboo cage, when Flint passed him, running back toward the camp!

"Hey! Where—" Sturm yelled at the dwarf.

"Tas, in the dragon!" The dwarf didn't stop.

Sturm turned and saw the black wicker dragon burning with flames that shot high into the air. Thick smoke boiled up, blanketing the camp, the dank heavy swamp air preventing it from rising and drifting away. Sparks showered down as part of the blazing dragon exploded into the camp. Sturm ducked and batted out sparks that landed on his cape, then ran after the dwarf, catching up with the short-legged Flint easily.

"Flint," he panted, grasping the dwarf's arm. "It's no use. Nothing could live in that furnace! We've got to get back to the others—"

"Let go of me!" Flint roared so furiously that Sturm let go in amazement. The dwarf ran for the burning dragon again. Sturm heaved a sigh and ran after him, his eyes beginning to water in the smoke.

"Tasslehoff Burrfoot!" Flint called. "You idiotic kender! Where are you?"

There was no answer.

"Tasslehoff!" Flint screamed. "If you wreck this escape, I'll murder you. So help me—" Tears of frustration and grief and anger and smoke coursed down the dwarf's cheeks.

The heat was overwhelming. It seared Sturm's lungs, and the knight knew they couldn't breathe much more of this or they would perish themselves. He took hold of the dwarf firmly, intending to knock him out if necessary, when suddenly he saw movement near the edge of the blaze. He rubbed his eyes and looked closer.

The dragon lay on the ground, the head still connected to the blazing body by a long wicker neck. The head had not caught fire yet, but flames were starting to eat into the wicker neck. The head would soon be ablaze, too. Sturm saw the movement again.

"Flint! Look!" Sturm ran toward the head, the dwarf pounding along behind. Two small legs encased in bright blue pants were sticking out of the dragon's mouth, kicking feebly.

"Tas!" Sturm yelled. "Get out! The head's going to burn!"

"I can't! I'm stuck!" came a muffled voice.

Sturm stared at the head, frantically trying to figure out how to free the kender, while Flint just grabbed hold of Tas's legs and pulled.

"Ouch! Stop!" yelled Tas.

"No good," the dwarf puffed. "He's stuck fast."

The inferno crept up the dragon's neck.

Sturm drew his sword. "I may cut off his head," he muttered to Flint, "but it's his only chance." Estimating the size of the kender, guessing where his head would be, and hoping his hands weren't stretched out over his head, Sturm lifted his sword above the dragon's neck.

Flint closed his eyes.

The knight took a deep breath and brought his blade crashing down on the dragon, severing the head from the neck.

There was a cry from the kender inside but whether from pain or astonishment, Sturm couldn't tell.

"Pull!" he yelled at the dwarf.

Flint grabbed hold of the wicker head and pulled it away from the blazing neck. Suddenly a tall, dark shape loomed out of the smoke. Sturm whipped around, sword ready, then saw it was Riverwind.

"What are you—" The Plainsman stared at the dragon's head. Perhaps Flint and Sturm had gone mad.

"The kender's stuck in there!" Sturm yelled. "We can't take the head apart out here, surrounded by draconians! We've got to—"

His words were lost in a roar of flame, but Riverwind finally saw the blue legs sticking out of the dragon's mouth. He grabbed hold of one side of the dragon's head, thrusting his hands in one of the eyesockets. Sturm got hold of the other, and together they lifted the head—kender inside—and began running through the camp. Those few draconians they encountered took one look at the terrifying apparition and fled.

"C'mon, Raist," Caramon said solicitously, his arm around his brother's shoulder. "You've got to try and stand. We have to be ready to move out of here. How do you feel?"

"How do I ever feel?" whispered Raistlin bitterly. "Help me up. There! Now leave me in peace for a moment." He leaned against a tree, shivering but standing.

"Sure, Raist," Caramon said, hurt, backing off. Goldmoon glanced at Raistlin in disgust, remembering Caramon's grief when he thought his brother was dying. She turned away to watch for the others, staring through the gathering smoke.

Tanis appeared first, running so fast he crashed into Caramon. The big warrior caught him in his huge arms, breaking the half-elf's forward momentum and keeping him on his feet.

"Thanks!" Tanis gasped. He leaned over, hands on his knees, to catch his breath. "Where are the others?"

"Weren't they with you?" Caramon frowned.

"We got separated." Tanis drew in huge gulps of air, then coughed as the smoke flew down his lungs.

"*SuTorakh!*" interrupted Goldmoon in an awed voice. Tanis and Caramon both spun around in alarm, staring out into the smoke-filled camp to see a grotesque sight emerging from the swirling smoke. A dragon's head with a forked blue tongue was lunging at them. Tanis blinked in disbelief, then he heard a sound behind him that nearly made him leap into a tree in panic. He whirled around, heart in his throat, sword in his hand.

Raistlin was laughing.

Tanis had never heard the mage laugh before, even when Raistlin was a child, and he hoped he would never hear it again. It was weird, shrill, mocking laughter. Caramon stared at his brother in amazement, Goldmoon in horror. Finally the sound of Raistlin's laughter died until the mage was laughing silently, his golden eyes reflecting the glow of the draconian camp going up in flames.

Tanis shuddered and turned back around to see that in fact the dragon's head was carried by Sturm and Riverwind. Flint raced along in front, a draconian helm on his head. Tanis ran forward to meet them.

"What in the name of—"

"The kender's stuck in here!" Sturm said. He and Riverwind dropped the head to the ground, both of them breathing heavily. "We've got to get him out." Sturm eyed the laughing Raistlin warily. "What's the matter with him? Still poisoned?"

"No, he's better," Tanis said, examining the dragon's head.

"A pity," Sturm muttered as he knelt beside the half-elf.

"Tas, are you all right?" Tanis called out, lifting the huge mouth to see inside.

"I think Sturm chopped off my hair!" the kender wailed.

"Lucky it wasn't your head!" Flint snorted.

"What's holding him?" Riverwind leaned down to peer inside the dragon's mouth.

"I'm not sure," Tanis said, swearing softly. "I can't see in all this blasted smoke." He stood up, sighing in frustration. "And we've got to get out of here! The draconians will get organized soon. Caramon, come here. See if you can rip off the top."

The big warrior came over to stand in front of the wicker dragon's head. Bracing himself, he got hold of the two eye-sockets, closed his eyes, took a deep breath, then grunted and heaved. For a minute nothing happened. Tanis watched the muscles bulge on the big man's arms, saw his thigh muscles absorb the strain. Blood rushed to Caramon's face. Then there was the ripping and snapping sound of wood splintering. The top of the dragon's head gave way with a sharp crack. Caramon staggered backward as the top half of the head suddenly came off in his hands.

Tanis reached in, grabbed Tas's hand, and jerked him free. "Are you all right?" he asked. The kender seemed wobbly on his feet, but his grin was wide as ever.

"I'm fine," Tas said brightly. "Just a little singed." Then his face darkened. "Tanis," he said, his face crinkling with unusual worry. He felt at his long topknot. "My hair?"

"All there," Tanis said, smiling.

Tas breathed a sigh of relief. Then he began to talk. "Tanis, it was the most wonderful thing—flying like that. And the look on Caramon's face—"

"The story will have to wait," Tanis said firmly. "We've got to get out of here. Caramon? Can you and your brother make it all right?"

"Yeah, go on," Caramon said.

Raistlin stumbled forward, accepting the support of his brother's strong arm. The mage glanced behind at the sundered dragon's head and he wheezed, his shoulders shaking in silent, grim amusement.

15

Escape. The well.
Death on black wings.

S moke from the burning draconian camp hung over the black swamplands, shielding the companions from the eyes of the strange, evil creatures. The smoke floated wraithlike through the swamps, drifting across the silver moon and obscuring the stars. The companions dared not risk a light—even the light from Raistlin's staff—for they could hear horns blowing all around them as the draconian leaders tried to reestablish order.

Riverwind led them. Although Tanis had always prided himself on his own woodland skills, he completely lost all sense of direction in the black misty mire. An occasional fleeting glimpse of the stars, whenever the smoke lifted, showed him that they were bearing north.

They hadn't gone far when Riverwind missed a step and plunged knee-deep into muck. After Tanis and Caramon

163

dragged the Plainsman out of the water, Tasslehoff crept ahead, testing the ground with his hoopak staff. It sank every time.

"We have no choice but to wade," Riverwind said grimly.

Choosing a path where the water seemed shallower, the company left firm ground and splashed into the muck. At first it was only ankle deep, then they sank to their knees. Soon they sank deeper still; Tanis was forced to carry Tasslehoff, the giggling kender grasping him around the neck. Flint steadfastly refused all offers of help, even when the tip of his beard got wet. Then he vanished. Caramon, following him, fished the dwarf out of the water and slung him over his shoulder like a wet sack, the dwarf too tired and frightened to grumble. Raistlin staggered, coughing, through the water, his robes dragging him down. Weary and still sick from the poison, the mage finally collapsed. Sturm grabbed hold of him and half-dragged, half-carried the mage through the swamp.

After an hour of floundering in the icy water, they finally reached firm ground and sank down to rest, shivering with the cold.

The trees began to creak and groan, their branches bending as a sharp wind sprang up from the north. The wind blew the mists into wispy rags. Raistlin, lying on the ground, looked up. The mage caught his breath. He sat up, alarmed.

"Storm clouds." He choked, coughing, and fought to speak. "They come from the north. We have no time. No time! We must reach Xak Tsaroth. Hurry! Before the moon sets!"

Everyone looked up. A gathering darkness was moving out of the north, swallowing up the stars. Tanis could feel the same sense of urgency that was driving the mage. Wearily, he rose to his feet. Without a word, the rest of the group rose and stumbled forward, Riverwind taking the lead. But dark swamp water blocked their path once more.

"Not again!" Flint moaned.

"No, we do not have to wade again. Come look," Riverwind said. He led the way to the water's edge. There, amid many other ruins protruding from the dank ground, lay an obelisk that had either fallen or been pushed over to form a bridge across to the other bank of the swamp.

"I'll go first," Tas volunteered, hopping energetically onto the long stone. "Hey, there's writing on this thing. Runes of some sort."

"I must see!" Raistlin whispered, hurrying over. He spoke his word of command, "*Shirak*," and the crystal on the tip of his staff burst into light.

"Hurry!" Sturm growled. "You've just told everything within a twenty-mile radius we're here."

But Raistlin would not be rushed. He held the light over the spidery runes, studying them intently. Tanis and the others climbed onto the obelisk and joined the mage.

The kender bent down, tracing the runes with his small hand. "What does it say, Raistlin? Can you read it? The language seems very old."

"It is old," the mage whispered. "It dates from before the Cataclysm. The runes say, 'The Great City of Xak Tsaroth, whose beauty surrounds you, speaks to the good of its people and their generous deeds. The gods reward us in the grace of our home'."

"How awful!" Goldmoon shuddered, looking at the ruin and desolation around her.

"The gods rewarded them indeed," Raistlin said, his lips parting in a cynical smile. No one spoke. Then Raistlin whispered, "*Dulak*," and extinguished the light. Suddenly the night seemed much blacker. "We must keep going," the mage said. "Surely there is more than a fallen monument to mark what this place once stood for."

They crossed the obelisk into thick jungle. At first there seemed to be no trail, then Riverwind, searching diligently, found a trail cut through the vines and the trees. He bent down to study it. His face was grim when he rose.

"Draconians?" Tanis asked.

"Yes," he said heavily. "The tracks of many clawed feet. And they lead north, straight to the city."

Tanis asked in an undertone, "Is this the broken city, where you were given the staff?"

"And where death had black wings," Riverwind added. He closed his eyes, wiping his hand over his face. Then he drew a deep, ragged breath. "I don't know. I can't remember—but I am afraid without knowing why."

Tanis put his hand on Riverwind's arm. "The elves have a saying: 'Only the dead are without fear.' "

Riverwind startled him by suddenly clasping the half-elf's hand with his. "I have never known an elf," the Plainsman said. "My people distrust them, saying that the elves have no care for Krynn or for humans. I think my people may have been mistaken. I am glad I met you, Tanis of Qualinost. I count you as a friend."

Tanis knew enough of Plains lore to realize that, with this statement, Riverwind had declared himself willing to sacrifice everything for the half-elf—even his life. A vow of friendship was a solemn vow among the Plainsmen. "You are my friend, too, Riverwind," Tanis said simply. "You and Goldmoon both are my friends."

Riverwind turned his eyes to Goldmoon who stood near them, leaning on her staff, her eyes closed, her face drawn with pain and exhaustion. Riverwind's face softened with compassion as he looked at her. Then it hardened, pride drawing the stern mask over it again.

"Xak Tsaroth is not far off," he said coolly. "And these tracks are old." He led the way into the jungle. After only a short walk, the northern trail suddenly changed to cobblestones.

"A street!" exclaimed Tasslehoff.

"The outskirts of Xak Tsaroth!" Raistlin breathed.

"About time!" Flint stared all around in disgust. "What a mess! If the greatest gift ever given to man is here, it must be well hidden!"

Tanis agreed. He had never seen a more dismal place. As they walked, the broad street took them into an open-paved courtyard. To the east stood four tall, free-standing columns that supported nothing; the building lay in ruins around them. A huge unbroken circular stone wall rose about four feet above the ground. Caramon, going over to inspect it, announced that it was a well.

"Deep at that," he said. He leaned over and peered down into it. "Smells bad, too."

North of the well stood what appeared to be the only building to have escaped the destruction of the Cataclysm. It was finely constructed of pure white stone, supported by tall, slender columns. Large golden double doors gleamed in the moonlight.

"That was a temple to the ancient gods," Raistlin said,

more to himself than anyone else. But Goldmoon, standing near him, heard his soft whisper.

"A temple?" she repeated, staring at the building. "How beautiful." She walked toward it, strangely fascinated.

Tanis and the rest searched the grounds and found no other buildings intact. Fluted columns lay on the ground, their broken pieces aligned to show their former beauty. Statues lay broken and, in some cases, grotesquely defaced. Everything was old, so old it made even the dwarf feel young.

Flint sat down on a column. "Well, we're here." He blinked at Raistlin and yawned. "What now, mage?"

Raistlin's thin lips parted, but before he could reply, Tasslehoff yelled, "Draconian!"

Everyone spun around, weapons in their hands. A draconian, ready to move, was glaring at them from the edge of the well.

"Stop it!" Tanis shouted. "It will alert others!"

But before anyone could reach it, the draconian spread its wings and flew *into* the well. Raistlin, his golden eyes flaring in the moonlight, ran to the well and peered over the edge. Raising his hand as if to cast a spell, he hesitated, then dropped his hand limply to his side. "I can't," he said. "I can't think. I can't concentrate. I must sleep!"

"We're all tired," Tanis said wearily. "If something's down there, it warned it. There's nothing we can do now. We've got to rest."

"It *has* gone to warn something," Raistlin whispered. He huddled in his cloak and stared around, his eyes wide. "Can't you feel it? Any of you? Half-Elf? Evil about to waken and come forth."

Silence fell.

Then Tasslehoff climbed up on the stone wall and peered down. "Look! The draconian is floating down, just like a leaf. His wings don't flap—"

"Be quiet!" Tanis snapped.

Tasslehoff glanced at the half-elf in surprise—Tanis's voice sounded strained and unnatural. The half-elf was staring at the well, his hands clenching nervously. Everything was still. Too still. The storm clouds massed to the north, but there was no wind. Not a branch creaked, not a leaf stirred. The silver moon and the red cast twin shadows that made things seen from the corner of the eye unreal and distorted.

Then, slowly, Raistlin backed away from the well, raising his hands before him as if to ward off some dreadful danger.

"I feel it, too." Tanis swallowed. "What is it?"

"Yes, what is it?" Tasslehoff, leaning over, stared eagerly into the well. It looked as deep and dark as the mage's hour-glass eyes.

"Get him away from there!" Raistlin cried.

Tanis, infected by the mage's fear and his own growing sense that something was terribly wrong, started to run for Tas. Even as he began to move, though, he felt the ground shake beneath his feet. The kender gave a startled cry as the ancient stone wall of the well cracked and gave way beneath him. Tas felt himself sliding into the terrible blackness below him. He scrabbled frantically with his hands and feet, trying to clutch the crumbling rocks. Tanis lunged desperately, but he was too far away.

Riverwind had started moving when he heard Raistlin's cry, and the tall man's long, swift strides carried him quickly to the well. Catching hold of Tas by his collar, the Plainsman plucked him from the wall just as the stones and mortar tumbled down into the blackness below.

The ground trembled again. Tanis tried to force his numb mind to figure out what was happening. Then a blast of cold air burst from the well. The wind swept dirt and leaves from the courtyard into the air, stinging his face and eyes.

"Run!" Tanis tried to yell, but he choked on the foul stench erupting from the well.

The columns left standing after the Cataclysm began to shake. The companions stared fearfully at the well. Then Riverwind tore his gaze away. "Goldmoon . . ." he said, looking around. He dropped Tas to the ground. "Goldmoon!" He stopped as a high-pitched shriek rose from the depths of the well. The sound was so loud and shrill that it pierced the head. Riverwind searched frantically for Goldmoon, calling her name.

Tanis was stunned by the noise. Unable to move, he saw Sturm, hand on his sword, slowly back away from the well. He saw Raistlin—the mage's ghastly face glistening metallic yellow, his golden eyes red in the red moon's light—scream something Tanis couldn't hear. He saw Tasslehoff staring at the well in wide-eyed wonder. Sturm ran across the courtyard, scooped up the kender under one arm, and ran on to the trees. Caramon ran to his exhausted brother, caught him up, and headed for cover. Tanis knew some monstrous evil was coming up out of the well, but he could not move. The words "run, fool, run" screamed in his brain.

Riverwind, too, stayed near the well, fighting the fear that was growing within him: he couldn't find Goldmoon! Distracted by rescuing the kender from tumbling into the well, he had not seen Goldmoon approach the unbroken temple. He looked around wildly, struggling to keep his balance as the ground shook beneath his feet. The high-pitched shrieking noise, the throbbing and trembling of the ground, brought back hideous, nightmarish memories. "Death on black wings." He began to sweat and shake, then forced his mind to concentrate on Goldmoon. She needed him; he knew—and he alone knew— that her show of strength only masked her fear, doubt, uncertainty. She would be terribly afraid, and he had to find her.

As the stones of the well began to slide, Riverwind moved away and caught sight of Tanis. The half-elf was shouting and pointing past Riverwind toward the temple. Riverwind knew Tanis was saying something, but he couldn't hear above the shrieking sound. Then he knew! Goldmoon! Riverwind turned to go to her, but he lost his balance and fell to his knees. He saw Tanis start to run toward him.

Then the horror burst from the well, the horror of his fevered nightmares. Riverwind closed his eyes and saw no more.

It was a dragon.

Tanis, in those first few moments when the blood seemed to drain from his body, leaving him limp and lifeless, looked at the dragon as it burst forth from the well and thought, "How beautiful . . . how beautiful. . . ."

Sleek and black, the dragon rose, her glistening wings folded close to her sides, her scales gleaming. Her eyes glowed red-black, the color of molten rock. Her mouth opened in a snarl, teeth flashing white and wicked. Her long,

red tongue curled as she breathed the night air. Clear of the
well's confines, the dragon spread her wings, blotting out
stars, obliterating moonlight. Each wing was tipped with a
pure, white claw that shone blood-red in the light of Lunitari.

Fear such as Tanis had never imagined shriveled his stomach. His heart throbbed painfully; he couldn't catch his breath.
He could only stare in horror and awe and marvel at the creature's deadly beauty. The dragon circled higher and higher
into the night sky. Then, just as Tanis felt the paralyzing fear
start to recede, just as he began to fumble for his bow and
arrows, the dragon spoke.

One word she said—a word in the language of magic—and
a thick, terrible darkness fell from the sky, blinding them all.
Tanis instantly lost all grasp on where he was. He only knew
there was a dragon above him about to attack. He was power-
less to defend himself. All he could do was crouch down,
crawl among the rubble, and try desperately to hide.

Deprived of his sense of sight, the half-elf concentrated on
his sense of hearing. The shrieking noise had stopped as the
darkness fell. Tanis could hear the slow, gentle flap of the
dragon's leathery wings and knew it was circling above them,
rising gradually. Then he couldn't hear even the flapping anymore; the wings had quit beating. He visualized a great, black
bird of prey, hovering alone, waiting.

Then there was a very gentle rustling sound, the sound of
leaves shivering as the wind rises before a storm. The sound
grew louder and louder until it was the rushing of wind when
the storm hits, and then it was the shrieking of the hurricane.
Tanis pressed his body close against the crumbled well and
covered his head with his arms.

The dragon was attacking.

She could not see through the darkness she had cast, but
Khisanth knew that the intruders were still in the courtyard
below. Her minions, the draconians, had warned her that a
group walked the land, carrying the blue crystal staff. Lord
Verminaard wanted that staff, wanted it kept safe with her,
never to be seen in human lands. But she had lost it, and Lord
Verminaard had not been pleased. She had to get it back.
Therefore, Khisanth had waited an instant before casting her

darkness spell, studying the intruders carefully, searching for the staff. Unaware that already it had passed beyond her sight, she was pleased. She had only to destroy.

The attacking dragon dropped from the sky, her leathery wings curving back like the blade of a black dagger. She dove straight for the well, where she had seen the intruders running for their lives. Knowing that they would be paralyzed by dragonfear, Khisanth was certain she could kill them all with one pass. She opened her fanged mouth.

Tanis heard the dragon coming nearer. The great rushing sound grew louder and louder, then stopped for an instant. He could hear huge tendons creaking, lifting and spreading giant wings. Then he heard a great gasping sound as of air being drawn into a gaping throat, then a strange sound that reminded him of steam escaping from a boiling kettle. Something liquid splashed near him. He could hear rocks splitting and cracking and bubbling. Drops of the liquid splashed on his hand, and he gasped as a searing pain penetrated his being.

Then Tanis heard a scream. It was a deep-voiced scream, a man's scream—Riverwind. So terrible, so agonized was the scream that Tanis dug his fingernails into his palms to keep from adding his own voice to that horrible wail and revealing himself to the dragon. The screaming seemed to go on and on and then it died into a moan. Tanis felt the rush of a large body swoosh past him in the darkness. The stones he pressed his body against shook. Then the tremor of the dragon's passage sank lower and lower into the depths of the well. Finally the ground was still.

There was silence.

Tanis drew a painful breath and opened his eyes. The darkness was gone. The stars shone; the moons glowed in the sky. For a moment the half-elf could do nothing but breathe and breathe again, trying to calm his shaking body. Then he was on his feet, running toward a dark form lying in the stone courtyard.

Tanis was the first to reach the Plainsman's body. He took one look, then choked and turned away.

What remained of Riverwind no longer resembled anything human. The man's flesh had been seared from his body.

The white of bone was clearly visible where skin and muscle had melted from his arms. His eyes ran like jelly down the fleshless, cadaverous cheeks. His mouth gaped open in a silent scream. His ribcage lay exposed, hunks of flesh and charred cloth clinging to the bones. But—most horrible—the flesh on his torso had been burned away, leaving the organs exposed, pulsing red in the garish red moonlight.

Tanis sank down, vomiting. The half-elf had seen men die on his sword. He had seen them hacked to pieces by trolls. But this . . . this was horribly different, and Tanis knew the memory of this would haunt him forever. A strong arm gripped him by the shoulders, offering silent comfort and sympathy and understanding. The nausea passed. Tanis sat back and breathed. He wiped his mouth and nose, then tried to force himself to swallow, gagging painfully.

"You all right?" Caramon asked with concern.

Tanis nodded, unable to speak. Then he turned at the sound of Sturm's voice.

"May the true gods have mercy! Tanis, he's still alive! I saw his hand move!" Sturm choked. He could say no more.

Tanis rose to his feet and walked shakily toward the body. One of the charred and blackened hands had risen from the stones, plucking horribly at the air.

"End it!" Tanis said hoarsely, his throat raw from bile. "End it! Sturm—"

The knight had already drawn his sword. Kissing the hilt, he raised the blade to the sky and stood before Riverwind's body. He closed his eyes and mentally withdrew into an old world where death in battle had been glorious and fine. Slowly and solemnly, he began to recite the ancient Solamnic Death Chant. As he spoke the words that laid hold of the warrior's soul and transported it to realms of peace beyond, he reversed the blade of the sword and held it poised above Riverwind's chest.

"Return this man to Huma's breast
Beyond the wild, impartial skies;
Grant to him a warrior's rest
And set the last spark of his eyes
Free from the smothering clouds of wars,

Upon the torches of the stars.
Let the last surge of his breath
Take refuge in the cradling air
Above the dreams of ravens, where
Only the hawk remembers death.
Then let his shade to Huma rise,
Beyond the wild, impartial skies."

The knight's voice sank.

Tanis felt the peace of the gods wash over him like cool, cleansing water, easing his grief and submerging the horror. Caramon, beside him, wept silently. As they watched, moonlight flashed on the sword blade.

Then a clear voice spoke. "Stop. Bring him to me."

Both Tanis and Caramon sprang up to stand in front of the man's tortured body, knowing that Goldmoon must be spared this hideous sight. Sturm, lost in tradition, came back to reality with a start and reversed his killing stroke. Goldmoon stood, a tall, slender shadow silhouetted against the golden, moonlit doors of the temple. Tanis started to speak, but he felt suddenly the cold hand of the mage grip his arm. Shivering, he jerked away from Raistlin's touch.

"Do as she says," the mage hissed. "Carry him to her."

Tanis's face contorted with fury at the sight of Raistlin's expressionless face, uncaring eyes.

"Take him to her," Raistlin said coldly. "It is not for us to choose death for this man. That is for the gods."

16

A bitter choice.
The greatest gift.

anis stared at Raistlin. Not the quiver of an eyelid betrayed his feelings—if the mage had any feelings. Their eyes met and, as always, Tanis felt that the mage saw more than was visible to him. Suddenly Tanis hated Raistlin, hated him with a passion that shocked the half-elf, hated him for not feeling this pain, hated him and envied him at the same time.

"We must do something!" Sturm said harshly. "He's not dead and the dragon may return!"

"Very well," Tanis said, his voice catching in his throat. "Wrap him in a blanket. . . . But give me a moment alone with Goldmoon."

The half-elf walked slowly across the courtyard. His footsteps echoed in the stillness of the night as he climbed marble steps to a wide porch where Goldmoon stood in front of the shining golden doors. Glancing behind him, Tanis could see his friends wrapping blankets from their packs around tree limbs to make a battlefield stretcher. The man's body was nothing more than a dark, shapeless mass in the moonlight.

"Bring him to me, Tanis," Goldmoon repeated as the half-elf came up to her. He took hold of her hand.

"Goldmoon," Tanis said, "Riverwind is horribly injured. He is dying. There is nothing you can do—not even the staff—"

"Hush, Tanis," Goldmoon said gently.

The half-elf fell silent, seeing her clearly for the first time. In astonishment, he realized that the Plainswoman was tranquil, calm, uplifted. Her face in the moonlight was the face of the sailor who has fought the stormy seas in his fragile boat and drifted at last into peaceful waters.

"Come inside the temple, my friend," Goldmoon said, her beautiful eyes looking intently into Tanis's. "Come inside and bring Riverwind to me."

Goldmoon had not heard the approach of the dragon, had not seen its attack on Riverwind. When they entered the broken courtyard of Xak Tsaroth, Goldmoon had felt a strange and powerful force drawing her into the temple. She walked across the rubble and up the stairs, oblivious to everything but the golden doors shimmering in the silver-red moonlight. She approached them and stood before them for a moment. Then she became aware of the commotion behind her and heard Riverwind calling her name. "Goldmoon . . ." She paused, unwilling to leave Riverwind and her friends, knowing a terrible evil was rising from the well.

"Come inside, child," a gentle voice called to her.

Goldmoon lifted her head and stared at the doors. Tears came to her eyes. The voice was her mother's. Tearsong, priestess of Que-shu, had died long ago, when Goldmoon was very young.

"Tearsong?" Goldmoon choked. "Mother—"

"The years have been many and sad for you, my daughter"—her mother's voice was not heard so much as felt in her heart—"and I fear your burden will not soon ease. Indeed, if you continue on you will leave this darkness only to enter a deeper darkness. Truth will light your way, my daughter, though you may find its light shines dimly in the vast and terrible night ahead. Still, without the truth, all will perish and be lost. Come here inside the temple with me, daughter. You will find what you seek."

"But my friends, Riverwind." Goldmoon looked back at the well and saw Riverwind stumble on the shaking cobblestones. "They cannot fight this evil. They will die without me. The staff could help! I cannot leave!" She started to turn back as the darkness fell.

"I can't see them! . . . Riverwind! . . . Mother, help me," she cried in agony.

But there was no answer. This isn't fair! Goldmoon screamed silently, clenching her fists. We never wanted this! We only wanted to love each other, and now—now we may lose that! We have sacrificed so much and none of it has made any difference. I am thirty years old, mother! Thirty and childless. They have taken my youth, they have taken my people. And I have nothing to show in return. Nothing—except this! She shook the staff. And now I am being asked once again to give still more.

Her anger calmed. Riverwind—had he been angry all those long years he searched for answers? All he had found was this staff, and it brought only more questions. No, he hadn't been angry, she thought. His faith is strong. I am the weak one. Riverwind was willing to die for his faith. It seems I must be willing to live—even if it means living without him.

Goldmoon leaned her head against the golden doors, their metal surface cool to her skin. Reluctantly, she made her bitter decision. I will go forward, mother—though if Riverwind dies, my heart dies, too. I ask only one thing: If he dies, let him know, somehow, that I will continue his search.

Leaning upon her staff, the Chieftain of the Que-shu pushed open the golden doors and entered the temple. The doors shut behind her at the precise moment the black dragon burst from the well.

Goldmoon stepped inside soft, enfolding darkness. She could see nothing at first, but a memory of being held very close in her mother's warm embrace played through her mind. A pale light began to shine around her. Goldmoon saw she was under a vast dome that rose high above an intricately inlaid tile floor. Beneath the dome, in the center of the room, stood a marble statue of singular grace and beauty. The light in the room emanated from this statue. Goldmoon, entranced, moved toward it. The statue was of a woman in flowing robes. Her marble face bore an expression of radiant hope, tempered with sadness. A strange amulet hung around her neck.

"This is Mishakal, goddess of healing, whom I serve," said her mother's voice. "Listen to her words, my daughter."

Goldmoon stood directly in front of the statue, marveling at its beauty. But it seemed unfinished, incomplete. Part of the statue was missing, Goldmoon realized. The marble woman's hands were curved, as if they had been holding a long slender pole, but the hands were empty. Without conscious thought, with only the need to complete such beauty, Goldmoon slid her staff into the marble hands.

It began to gleam with a soft blue light. Goldmoon, startled, backed away. The staff's light grew into a blinding radiance. Goldmoon shielded her eyes and fell to her knees. A great and loving power filled her heart. She bitterly regretted her anger.

"Do not be ashamed of your questioning, beloved disciple. It was your questioning that led you to us, and it is your anger that will sustain you through the many trials ahead. You come seeking the truth and you shall receive it.

"The gods have not turned away from man—it is man who turned away from the true gods. Krynn is about to face its greatest trial. Men will need the truth more than ever. You, my disciple, must return the truth and power of the true gods to man. It is time to restore the balance of the universe. Evil now has tipped the scales. For as the gods of good have returned to man, so have the gods of evil—constantly striving for men's souls. The Queen of Darkness has returned, seeking that which will allow her to walk freely in this land once more. Dragons, once banished to the nether regions, walk the land."

Dragons, thought Goldmoon dreamily. She found it difficult to concentrate and grasp the words that flooded her mind. It would not be until later that she would fully comprehend the message. Then she would remember the words forever.

"To gain the power to defeat them, you will need the truth of the gods, this is the greatest gift of which you were told. Below this temple,

*in the ruins haunted by the glories of ages past, rest the Disks of
Mishakal; circular disks made of gleaming platinum. Find the Disks
and you can call upon my power, for I am Mishakal, goddess of healing.*

"*Your way will not be easy. The gods of evil know and fear the
great power of the truth. The ancient and powerful black dragon,
Khisanth, known to men as Onyx, guards the Disks. Her lair is in
the ruined city of Xak Tsaroth below us. Danger lies ahead of you if
you choose to try and recover the Disks. Therefore I bless this staff.
Present it boldly, never wavering, and you shall prevail.*"

The voice faded. It was then Goldmoon heard Riverwind's
death cry.

Tanis entered the temple and felt as if he had walked backward into memory. The sun was shining through the trees in
Qualinost. He and Laurana and her brother, Gilthanas, were
lying on the riverbank, laughing and sharing dreams after
some childish game. Happy childhood days had been few for
Tanis—the half-elf learned early that he was different from the
others. But that day had been a day of golden sunshine and
warm friendship. The remembered peace washed over him,
easing his grief and horror.

He turned to Goldmoon, standing silently beside him.
"What is this place?"

"That is a story whose telling must wait," Goldmoon answered. With a light hand on Tanis's arm, she drew him across
the shimmering tile floor until they both stood before the shining marble statue of Mishakal. The blue crystal staff cast a brilliant glow throughout the chamber.

But even as Tanis's lips parted in wonder, a shadow darkened the room. He and Goldmoon turned toward the door.
Caramon and Sturm entered, bearing the body of Riverwind
between them on the makeshift litter. Flint and Tasslehoff—
the dwarf looking old and weary, the kender unusually subdued—stood on either side of the litter, an odd sort of honor
guard. The somber procession moved slowly inside. Behind
them came Raistlin, his hood pulled over his head, his hands
folded in his robes—the spectre of death itself.

They moved across the marble floor, intent on the burden
they bore, and came to a halt before Tanis and Goldmoon.
Tanis, looking down at the body at Goldmoon's feet, shut his

eyes. Blood had soaked through the thick blanket, spreading in great dark splotches across the fabric.

"Remove the blanket," Goldmoon commanded. Caramon looked at Tanis pleadingly.

"Goldmoon—" Tanis began gently.

Suddenly, before anyone could stop him, Raistlin bent down and tore the blood-stained blanket from the body.

Goldmoon gave a strangled gasp at the sight of Riverwind's tortured body, turning so pale that Tanis reached out a steadying hand, fearing she might faint. But Goldmoon was the daughter of a strong, proud people. She swallowed, drew a deep, shuddering breath. Then she turned and walked up to the marble statue. She lifted the blue crystal staff carefully from the goddess's hands, then she returned to kneel beside Riverwind's body.

"*Kan-tokah,*" she said softly. "My beloved." Reaching out a shaking hand, she touched the dying Plainsman's forehead. The sightless face moved toward her as if he heard. One of the blackened hands twitched feebly, as if he would touch her. Then he gave a great shudder and lay perfectly still. Tears streamed unheeded down Goldmoon's cheeks as she lay the staff across Riverwind's body. Soft blue light filled the chamber. Everyone the light touched felt rested and refreshed. The pain and exhaustion from the day's toil left their bodies. The horror of the dragon's attack lifted from their minds, as the sun burns through fog. Then the light of the staff dimmed and faded. Night settled over the temple, lit once more only by the light emanating from the marble statue.

Tanis blinked, trying once more to re-accustom his eyes to the dark. Then he heard a deep voice.

"*Kan-tokah neh sirakan.*"

He heard Goldmoon cry out in joy. Tanis looked down at what should have been Riverwind's corpse. Instead, he saw the Plainsman sit up, holding out his arms for Goldmoon. She clung to him, laughing and crying at the same time.

"And so," Goldmoon told them, coming to the end of her story, "we must find a way down into the ruined city that lies somewhere below the temple, and we must remove the Disks from the dragon's lair."

They were eating a frugal dinner, sitting on the floor in the main chamber of the temple. A quick inspection of the building revealed that it was empty, although Caramon told of finding draconian tracks on the staircase, as well as the tracks of some other creature the warrior couldn't identify.

It was not a large building. Two worship rooms were located on opposite sides of the hallway that led to the main chamber where the statue stood. Two circular rooms branched off the main chamber to the north and south. They were decorated with frescoes that were now covered with fungus and faded beyond recognition. Two sets of golden double doors led to the east. Caramon reported finding a staircase there that led down into the wrecked city below. The faint sound of surf could be heard, reminding them that they were perched on top of a great cliff, overlooking Newsea.

The companions sat, each preoccupied with his own thoughts, trying to assimilate the news Goldmoon had given them. Tasslehoff, however, continued to poke around the rooms, peering into dark corners. Finding little of interest, the kender grew bored and returned to the group, holding an old helmet in his hand. It was too big for him; kenderfolk never wore helmets anyway, considering them bothersome and restrictive. He tossed it to the dwarf.

"What's this?" Flint asked suspiciously, holding it up to the light cast by Raistlin's staff. It was a helm of ancient design, well crafted by a skilled metalsmith. Undoubtedly a dwarf, Flint decided, rubbing his hands over it lovingly. A long tail of animal hair decorated the top. Flint tossed the draconian helm he had been wearing to the floor. Then he put the new-found helm on his head. It fit perfectly. Smiling, he took it off, once more admiring the workmanship. Tanis watched him with amusement.

"That's horsehair," he said, pointing to the tassel.

"No, it's not!" the dwarf protested, frowning. He sniffed at it, wrinkling his nose. Failing to sneeze, he glanced at Tanis in triumph. "It's hair from the mane of a griffon."

Caramon guffawed. "Griffon!" He snorted. "There's about as many griffons on Krynn as there are—"

"Dragons," interjected Raistlin smoothly.

The conversation died abruptly.

Sturm cleared his throat. "We'd better get some sleep," he said. "I'll take first watch."

"No one need keep watch this night," Goldmoon said softly. She sat close to Riverwind. The tall Plainsman had not spoken much since his brush with death. He had stared for a long time at the statue of Mishakal, recognizing the woman in blue light who had given him the staff, but he refused to answer any questions or discuss it.

"We are safe here," Goldmoon affirmed, glancing at the statue.

Caramon raised his eyebrows. Sturm frowned and stroked his moustaches. Both men were too polite to question Goldmoon's faith, but Tanis knew that neither warrior would feel safe if watches weren't set. Yet there weren't many hours left until dawn and they all needed rest. Raistlin was already asleep, wrapped in his robes in a dark corner of the chamber.

"I think Goldmoon is right," Tasslehoff said. "Let's trust these old gods, since it seems we have found them."

"The elves never lost them; neither did the dwarves," Flint protested, scowling. "I don't understand any of this! Reorx is one of the ancient gods, presumably. We have worshiped him since before the Cataclysm."

"Worship?" Tanis asked. "Or cry to him in despair because your people were shut out of the Kingdom under the Mountain. No, don't get mad—" Tanis, seeing the dwarf's face flush an ugly red, held up his hand. "The elves are no better. We cried to the gods when our homeland was laid waste. We know of the gods and we honor their memories—as one would honor the dead. The elven clerics vanished long ago, as did the dwarven clerics. I remember Mishakal the Healer. I remember hearing the stories of her when I was young. I remember hearing stories of dragons, too. Children's tales, Raistlin would say. It seems our childhood has come back to haunt us—or save us, I don't know which. I have seen two miracles tonight, one of evil and one of good. I must believe in both, if I am to trust the evidence of my senses. Yet . . ." The half-elf sighed. "I say we take turns on watch tonight. I am sorry, lady. I wish my faith were as strong as yours."

Sturm took first watch. The rest wrapped themselves in their blankets and lay on the tile floor. The knight walked through the moonlit temple, checking the quiet rooms, more from force of habit than because he felt any threat. He could hear the wind blow chill and fierce outside, sweeping out from the north. But inside it was strangely warm and comfortable—too comfortable.

Sitting at the base of the statue, Sturm felt a sweet peacefulness creep over him. Startled, he sat bolt upright and realized, chagrined, that he had nearly fallen asleep on watch. That was inexcusable! Berating himself severely, the knight determined that he would walk his watch—the full two hours—as punishment. He started to rise, then stopped. He heard singing, a woman's voice. Sturm stared around wildly, his hand on his sword. Then his hand slipped from the hilt. He recognized the voice and the song. It was his mother's voice. Once more Sturm was with her. They were fleeing Solamnia, traveling alone except for one trusted retainer—and he would be dead before they reached Solace. The song was one of those wordless lullabies that were older than dragons. Sturm's mother held her child close, and tried to keep her fear from him by singing this gentle, soothing song. Sturm's eyes closed. Sleep blessed him, blessed all of the companions.

The light from Raistlin's staff glowed brightly, keeping away the darkness.

17

The Paths of the Dead.
Raistlin's new friends.

he sound of metal crashing against the tile floor jolted Tanis out of a deep sleep. He sat up, alarmed, his hand fumbling for his sword.

"Sorry," Caramon said, grinning shamefacedly. "I dropped my breastplate."

Tanis drew a deep breath that turned into a yawn, stretched, and lay back down on his blanket. The sight of Caramon putting on his armor—with Tasslehoff's help—reminded the half-elf of what they faced today. He saw Sturm buckling his armor on as well, while Riverwind polished the sword he had picked up. Tanis firmly put the thought of what might happen to them today out of his mind.

That was not an easy task, especially for the elven part of Tanis—elves revere life and, although they believe that death is simply a movement into a higher plane of existence, death of any creature is seen to diminish life on this plane. Tanis forced the human side of him to take possession of his soul today. He would have to kill, and perhaps he would have to accept the death of one or more of these people he loved. He remembered how he had felt yesterday, when he thought he might lose Riverwind. The half-elf frowned and sat up suddenly, feeling as if he had awakened from a bad dream.

"Is everyone up? " he asked, scratching his beard.

Flint stumped over and handed him a hunk of bread and some dried strips of venison. "Up and breakfasted," the dwarf grumbled. "You could have slept through the Cataclysm, Half-Elf."

Tanis took a bite of venison without appetite. Then, wrinkling his nose, he sniffed. "What's that funny smell?"

"Some concoction of the mage's." The dwarf grimaced, plopping down next to Tanis. Flint pulled out a block of wood and began carving, hacking away furiously, making chips fly. "He pounded up some sort of powder in a cup and added water. Stirred it up and drank it, but not before it made that gullymudge smell. I'm happier not knowing what it was."

Tanis agreed. He chewed on the venison. Raistlin was now reading his spellbook, murmuring the words over and over until he had committed them to memory. Tanis wondered what kind of spell Raistlin had that might be useful against a dragon. From what little he remembered about dragonlore—learned ages ago from the elven bard, Quivalen Soth—only the spells of the very greatest mages had a chance of affecting dragons, who could work their own magic—as they had witnessed.

Tanis looked at the frail young man absorbed in his spellbook and shook his head. Raistlin might be powerful for his age, and he was certainly devious and clever. But dragons were ancient. They had been in Krynn before the first elves—the oldest of the races—walked the land. Of course, if the plan the companions discussed last night worked out, they wouldn't even encounter the dragon. They hoped simply to find the lair and escape with the Disks. It was a good plan, Tanis thought, and probably worth about as much as smoke on the wind. Despair began to creep over him like a dank fog.

"Well, I'm all set," Caramon announced cheerfully. The big warrior felt immeasurably better in his armor. The dragon seemed a very small annoyance this morning. He tunelessly whistled an old marching song as he stuffed his mud-stained clothing into his pack. Sturm, his armor carefully adjusted, sat apart from the companions, his eyes closed, performing whatever secret ritual knights performed, preparing himself mentally for combat. Tanis stood up, stiff and cold, moving around to get the circulation going and ease the soreness from his muscles. Elves did nothing before battle, except ask forgiveness for taking life.

"We, too, are ready," Goldmoon said. She was dressed in a heavy gray tunic made of soft leather trimmed with fur. She had braided her long silver-gold hair in a twist around her head—a precaution against an enemy using her hair to gain a handhold.

"Let's get this over with." Tanis sighed as he picked up the longbow and quiver of arrows Riverwind had taken from the draconian camp and slung them over his shoulder. In addition, Tanis was armed with a dagger and his longsword. Sturm had his two-handed sword. Caramon carried his shield, a longsword, and two daggers Riverwind had scrounged. Flint had replaced his lost battle-axe with one from the draconian camp. Tasslehoff had his hoopak and a small dagger he had discovered. He was very proud of it and was deeply wounded when Caramon told him it would be of use if they ran into any ferocious rabbits. Riverwind bore his longsword strapped to his back and still carried Tanis's dagger. Goldmoon bore no weapon other than the staff. We're well armed, Tanis thought gloomily. For all the good it will do us.

The companions left the chamber of Mishakal, Goldmoon coming last. She gently touched the statue of the goddess with her hand as she passed, whispering a silent prayer.

Tas led the way, skipping merrily, his topknot bouncing behind him. He was going to see a real live dragon! The kender couldn't imagine anything more exciting.

Following Caramon's directions, they headed east, passing through two more sets of golden double doors, and came to a large circular room. A tall, slime-coated pedestal stood in the center—so tall not even Riverwind could see what, if anything, was on it. Tas stood beneath it, staring up at it wistfully.

"I tried to climb it last night," he said—"but it was too slippery. I wonder what's up there?"

"Well, whatever it is will have to stay forever beyond the reach of kenders," Tanis snapped irritably. He walked over to investigate the staircase that spiraled down into the darkness. The stairs were broken and covered with rotting plants and fungus.

"The Paths of the Dead," Raistlin said suddenly.

"What?" Tanis started.

"The Paths of the Dead," the mage repeated. "That's what this staircase is called."

"How in the name of Reorx do you know that?" Flint growled.

"I have read something of this city," Raistlin replied in his whispering voice.

"This is the first we've heard of it," Sturm said coldly. "What else do you know that you haven't told us?"

"A great many things, knight," Raistlin returned, scowling. "While you and my brother played with wooden swords, I spent my time in study."

"Yes, study of that which is dark and mysterious," the knight sneered. "What really happened in the Towers of High Sorcery, Raistlin? You didn't gain these wonderful powers of yours without giving something in return. What did you sacrifice in that Tower? Your health—or your soul!"

"I was with my brother in the Tower," Caramon said, the warrior's normally cheerful face now haggard. "I saw him battle powerful mages and wizards with only a few simple spells. He defeated them, though they shattered his body. I carried him, dying, from the terrible place. And I—" The big man hesitated.

Raistlin stepped forward quickly and placed his cold, thin hand on his twin's arm.

"Be careful what you say," he hissed.

Caramon drew a ragged breath and swallowed. "I know what he sacrificed," the warrior said in a husky voice. Then he lifted his head proudly. "We are forbidden to speak of it. But you have known me many years, Sturm Brightblade, and I give you my word of honor, you may trust my brother as you trust me. If ever a time comes when that is not so, may my death—and his—be not far behind."

Raistlin's eyes narrowed at this vow. He regarded his brother with a thoughtful, somber expression. Then Tanis saw the mage's lip curl, the serious mien wiped out by his customary cynicism. It was a startling change. For a moment, the twins' resemblance to each other had been remarkable. Now they were as different as opposite sides of a coin.

Sturm stepped forward and clasped Caramon's hand, gripping it tightly, wordlessly. Then he turned to face Raistlin, unable to regard him without obvious disgust. "I apologize, Raistlin," the knight said stiffly. "You should be thankful you have such a loyal brother."

"Oh, I am," Raistlin whispered.

Tanis glanced at the mage sharply, wondering if he had only imagined sarcasm in the mage's hissing voice. The half-elf licked his dry lips, a sudden, bitter taste in his mouth. "Can you guide us through this place?" he asked abruptly.

"I could have," Raistlin answered, "if we had come here prior to the Cataclysm. The books I studied dated back hundreds of years. During the Cataclysm, when the fiery mountain struck Krynn, the city of Xak Tsaroth was cast down the side of a cliff. I recognize this staircase because it is still intact. As for beyond—" He shrugged.

"Where do the stairs lead?"

"To a place known as the Hall of the Ancestors. Priests and kings of Xak Tsaroth were buried in crypts there."

"Let's get moving," Caramon said gruffly. "All we're doing here is scaring ourselves."

"Yes." Raistlin nodded. "We must go and go quickly. We have until nightfall. By tomorrow, this city will be overrun by the armies moving from the north."

"Bah!" Sturm frowned. "You may know lots of things as you claim, mage, but you can't know that! Caramon is right, though—we have stayed here too long. I will take the lead."

He started down the stairs, moving carefully to keep from slipping on the slimy surface. Tanis saw Raistlin's eyes—narrow, golden slits of enmity—follow Sturm down.

"Raistlin, go with him and light the way," Tanis ordered, ignoring the angry glance Sturm flashed up at him. "Caramon, walk with Goldmoon. Riverwind and I will take rear guard."

"And where does that leave us?" Flint grumbled to the kender as they followed behind Goldmoon and Caramon. "In the middle, as usual. Just more useless baggage—"

"There might be anything up there," Tas said, looking back to the pedestal. He obviously hadn't heard a word of what had been said. "A crystal ball of farseeing, a magic ring like I once had. Did I ever tell you about my magic ring?" Flint groaned. Tanis heard the kender's voice prattling on as the two disappeared down the stairs.

The half-elf turned to Riverwind. "You were here—you must have been. We have seen the goddess who gave you the staff. Did you come down here?"

"I don't know," Riverwind said wearily. "I remember nothing about it. Nothing—except the dragon."

Tanis fell silent. The dragon. It all came down to the dragon. The creature loomed large in everyone's thoughts. And how feeble the small group seemed against a monster who had sprung full grown from Krynn's darkest legends. Why us? Tanis thought bitterly. Was there ever a more unlikely group of heroes—bickering, grumbling, arguing—half of us not trusting the other half. "We were chosen." That thought brought little comfort. Tanis remembered Raistlin's words: "Who chose us—and why!" The half-elf was beginning to wonder.

They moved silently down the steep stairway that curled ever deeper into the hillside. At first it was intensely dark as they spiraled down. Then the way began to get lighter, until Raistlin was able to extinguish the light on his staff. Soon Sturm raised his hand, halting the others behind him. Beyond stretched a short corridor, no more than a few feet long. This led to a large arched doorway that revealed a vast open area. A pale gray light filtered into the corridor, as did the odor of dankness and decay.

The companions stood for long moments, listening carefully. The sound of rushing water seemed to come from below and beyond the door, nearly drowning out all other sounds. Still, Tanis thought he had heard something else—a sharp crack—and he had felt more than heard a thumping and throbbing on the floor. But it didn't last long, and the sharp crack wasn't repeated. Then, more puzzling still, came a metallic scraping sound punctuated by an occasional shrill screech. Tanis glanced at Tasslehoff questioningly.

The kender shrugged. "I haven't a clue," he said, cocking his head and listening closely. "I've never heard anything like it, Tanis, except once—" He paused, then shook his head. "Do you want me to go look?" he asked eagerly.

"Go."

Tasslehoff crept down the short corridor, flitting from shadow to shadow. A mouse running across thick carpet makes more noise than a kender when he wants to escape notice. He reached the door and peered out. Ahead of him stretched what must once have been a vast ceremonial hall. Hall of the Ancestors, that's what Raistlin called it. Now it was a Hall of Ruins. Part of the floor to the east had fallen into a hole from which a foul-smelling white mist boiled up. Tas noticed other huge holes gaping in the floor, while chunks of large stone tile stuck up like grave markers. Carefully testing the floor beneath his feet, the kender stepped out into the hall. Through the mist he could faintly distinguish a dark doorway on the south wall . . . and another on the north. The strange screeching sound came from the south. Tas turned and began walking in that direction.

He suddenly heard the thumping and throbbing sound again to the north, behind him, and felt the floor start to tremble. The kender hurriedly dashed back into the stairwell. His friends had heard the sound and were flattened against the wall, weapons in hand. The thumping sound grew into a loud whoosh. Then ten or fifteen squat, shadowy figures rushed past the arched doorway. The floor shook. They heard hard breathing and an occasional muttered word. Then the figures vanished in the mist, heading south. There was another sharp cracking sound, then silence.

"What in the name of the Abyss was that?" Caramon exclaimed. "Those weren't draconians, unless they've come up with a short, fat breed. And where'd they come from?"

"They came from the north end of the hall," Tas said. "There's a doorway there and one to the south. The weird screeching sounds come from the south, where those things were headed."

"What's east?" Tanis asked.

"Judging by the sound of falling water I could hear, about a thousand-foot drop," the kender replied. "The floor's caved in. I wouldn't recommend walking over there."

Flint sniffed. "I smell something . . . something familiar. I can't place it."

189

"I smell death," Goldmoon said, shivering, holding her staff close.

"Naw, this is something worse," Flint muttered. Then his eyes opened wide and his face grew red with rage and anger. "I've got it!" he roared. "Gully dwarf!" He unslung his axe. "That's what those miserable little things were. Well, they won't be gully dwarves for long. They'll be stinking corpses!"

He dashed forward. Tanis, Sturm, and Caramon leaped after him just as he reached the end of the corridor and dragged him back.

"Keep quiet!" Tanis ordered the sputtering dwarf. "Now, how sure are you that they are gully dwarves?"

The dwarf angrily shook himself from Caramon's grasp. "Sure!" he started to roar, then dropped it to a loud whisper. "Didn't they hold me prisoner for three years?"

"Did they?" Tanis asked, startled.

"That's why I never told you where I was these last five years," the dwarf said, flushing with embarrassment. His face darkened. "But I swore I'd get revenge. I'll kill every living gully dwarf I come across."

"Wait a minute," Sturm interrupted. "Gully dwarves aren't evil, not like goblins at any rate. What could they be doing living here with draconians?"

"Slaves," Raistlin answered coolly. "Undoubtedly the gully dwarves have lived here many years, probably ever since the city was abandoned. When the draconians were sent, perhaps, to guard the Disks, they found the gully dwarves and used them as slave labor."

"They might be able to help us then," Tanis murmured.

"Gully dwarves!" Flint exploded. "You'd trust those filthy little—"

"No," Tanis said. "We cannot trust them, of course. But nearly every slave is willing to betray his master, and gully dwarves—like most dwarves—feel little loyalty to anyone except their own chieftains. As long as we don't ask them to do anything that might endanger their own dirty skins, we might be able to buy their aid."

"Well, I'll be an ogre's hind end!" Flint said in disgust. He hurled his axe to the ground, tore his pack off, and slumped down against the wall, arms folded. "Go on. Go ask your new friends to help you. I'll not be with you! They'll help you, all right. Help you right up the dragon's snout!"

Tanis and Sturm exchanged concerned glances, remembering the boat incident. Flint could be incredibly stubborn, and Tanis thought it quite likely that this time the dwarf would prove immovable.

"I dunno." Caramon sighed and shook his head. "It's too bad the dwarf's staying behind. If we do get the gully dwarves to help us, who'll keep the scum in line?"

Amazed that Caramon could be so subtle, Tanis smiled and picked up on the warrior's lead. "Sturm, I guess."

"Sturm!" The dwarf bounded to his feet. "A knight who won't stab an enemy in the back? You need someone who knows these foul creatures—"

"You're right, Flint," Tanis said gravely. "I guess you'll have to come with us."

"You bet," Flint grumbled. He grabbed his things and stumped off down the corridor. He turned around. "You coming?"

Hiding their smiles, the companions followed the dwarf out into the Hall of the Ancestors. They kept close to the wall, avoiding the treacherous floor. They headed south, following the gully dwarves, and entered a dimly lit passage that ran south only a few hundred feet, then turned sharply east. Once again they heard the cracking noise. The metallic screeching had stopped. Suddenly, they heard behind them the sound of pounding feet.

"Gully dwarves!" growled Flint.

"Back!" Tanis ordered. "Be ready to jump them. We can't let them raise an alarm!"

Everyone flattened himself against the wall, sword drawn and ready. Flint held his battle-axe, a look of eager anticipation on his face. Staring back into the vast hall, they saw another group of short fat figures running toward them.

Suddenly, the leader of the gully dwarves looked up and saw them. Caramon leaped out in front of the small running figures, his huge arm raised commandingly. "Halt!" he said. The gully dwarves glanced up at him, swarmed around him, and disappeared around the corner to the east. Caramon turned around to stare after them in astonishment.

"Halt . . . " he said half-heartedly.

A gully dwarf popped back around the corner, glared at Caramon, and put a grubby finger to his lips. "Shhhhh!" Then the squat figure vanished. They heard the cracking sound and the screeching noise started up again.

"What do you suppose is going on?" Tanis asked softly.

"Do they all look like that?" Goldmoon said, her eyes wide. "They're so filthy and ragged, and there are sores all over their bodies."

"And they have the brains of a doorknob," Flint grunted.

The group cautiously rounded the corner, hands on their weapons. A long, narrow corridor extended east, lit by torches that flickered and smoked in the stifling air. The light reflected off walls wet with condensed moisture. Arched doorways revealing only blackness opened up off the hallway.

"The crypts," Raistlin whispered.

Tanis shivered. Water dripped on him from the ceiling. The metallic screeching was louder and nearer. Goldmoon touched the half-elf's arm and pointed. Tanis saw, down at the far end of the corridor, a doorway. Beyond the opening was another passageway forming a T-intersection. The corridor was filled with gully dwarves.

"I wonder why the little guys are lined up," Caramon said.

"This is our chance to find out," Tanis said. He was starting forward when he felt the mage's hand on his arm.

"Leave this to me," Raistlin whispered.

"We had better come with you," Sturm stated, "to cover you, of course."

"Of course," Raistlin sniffed. "Very well, but do not disturb me."

Tanis nodded. "Flint, you and Riverwind guard this end of the corridor." Flint opened his mouth to protest, then scowled and fell back to stand opposite the Plainsmen.

"Stay well behind me," Raistlin ordered, then moved down the corridor, his red robes rustling around his ankles, the Staff of Magius thumping softly on the floor at each step. Tanis and Sturm followed, moving along the side of the dripping walls. Cold air flowed from the crypts. Peering inside one, Tanis could see the dark outline of a sarcophagus reflected in the sputtering torchlight. The coffin was elaborately carved, decorated with gold that shone no longer. An oppressive air hung over the crypts. Some of the tombs appeared to have been broken into and plundered. Tanis caught a glimpse of a skull grinning out of the darkness. He wondered if these ancient dead were planning their revenge for having their rest disturbed. Tanis forced himself to return to reality. It was bleak enough.

Raistlin stopped when he neared the end of the corridor. The gully dwarves watched him curiously, ignoring the others behind him. The mage did not speak. He reached into a pouch on his belt and drew out several golden coins. The gully dwarves' eyes brightened. One or two at the front of the line edged toward Raistlin to get a better view. The mage held up a coin so they all could see it. Then he threw it high into the air and . . . it vanished!

The gully dwarves gasped. Raistlin opened his hand with a flourish to reveal the coin. There was scattered applause. The gully dwarves crept closer, mouths gaping in wonder.

Gully dwarves—or Aghar—as their race was known, were truly a miserable lot. The lowest caste in dwarven society, they were to be found all over Krynn, living in filth and squalor in places that had been abandoned by most other living creatures, including animals. Like all dwarves, they were clannish, and several clans often lived together, following the rule of their chieftains or one particularly powerful clan leader. Three clans lived in Xak Tsaroth—the Sluds, the Bulps, and the Glups. Members of all three clans now surrounded Raistlin. There were both males and females, though it was not easy to tell the sexes apart. The females lacked whiskers on their chins but had them on their cheeks. They wore a tattered overskirt wrapped around their waists extending to their bony knees. Otherwise, they were every bit as ugly as their male counterparts. Despite their wretched appearance, gully dwarves generally led a cheerful existence.

Raistlin, with marvelous dexterity, made the coin dance over his knuckles, flipping it in and out of his fingers. Then he made it disappear, only to reappear inside the ear of some startled gully dwarf who stared at the mage in amazement. This last trick produced a momentary interruption in the performance as the Aghar's friends grabbed him and peered intently into his ear, one of them even sticking his finger inside to see if more coins might be forthcoming. This interesting activity ceased, though, when Raistlin reached into another pouch and removed a small scroll of parchment. Spreading it open with his long, thin fingers, the mage began to read from it, chanting softly, *"Suh tangus moipar, ast akular kalipad."* The gully dwarves watched in total fascination.

When the mage finished reading, the spidery-looking words on the scroll began to burn. They flared, then disappeared, leaving traces of green smoke.

"What was that all about?" Sturm asked suspiciously.

"They are now spellbound," Raistlin replied. "I have cast over them a spell of friendship."

The gully dwarves were enthralled and, Tanis noticed, the expressions on their faces had changed from interest to open, unabashed affection for the mage. They reached out and patted him with their dirty hands, jabbering away in their shapeless language. Sturm glanced at Tanis in alarm. Tanis knew what the knight was thinking: Raistlin could have cast that spell on any of them at any time.

Hearing the sound of running feet, Tanis looked quickly back to where Riverwind stood guard. The Plainsman pointed to the gully dwarves, then held up his hands, fingers spread. Ten more were heading their way. Soon, the new Aghar trotted into view, passing Riverwind without so much as a glance. They pulled up short on seeing the commotion around the mage.

"What happening?" said one, staring at Raistlin. The spellbound gully dwarves were gathered around the mage, tugging on his robe and dragging him down the hall.

"Friend. This our friend," they all chattered wildly in a crude form of Common.

"Yes," Raistlin said in a soft and gentle voice, so smooth and winning that Tanis was momentarily taken aback. "You are all my friends," the mage continued. "Now, tell me, my friends, where does this corridor lead?" Raistlin pointed to the east. There was an immediate babble of answers.

"Corridor lead that way," said one, pointing east.

"No, it lead that way!" said another, pointing west.

A scuffle broke out, the gully dwarves pushing and shoving. Soon fists were flying and then one gully dwarf had another on the ground, kicking him, yelling, "That way! That way!" at the top of his lungs.

Sturm turned to Tanis. "This is ridiculous! They'll bring every draconian in the place down on us. I don't know what that crazy magician has done, but you've got to stop him."

Before Tanis could intervene, however, one female gully dwarf took matters into her own hands. Dashing into the melee, she grabbed the two combatants, knocked their heads together smartly, and dumped them on the floor. The others, who had been cheering them on, immediately hushed, and the newcomer turned to Raistlin. She had a thick, bulbous nose and her hair stood up wildly on her head. She wore a patched and ragged dress, thick shoes, and stockings that collapsed around her ankles. But she seemed to be a leader among the gully dwarves, for they all eyed her with respect. This may have been because she carried a huge, heavy bag slung over one shoulder. The bag dragged along the ground as she walked, occasionally tripping her. But the bag was apparently of great importance to her. When one of the other gully dwarves attempted to touch it, she whirled around and smacked him across the face.

"Corridor lead to big bosses," she said, nodding her head toward the east.

"Thank you, my dear," Raistlin said, reaching out to touch her cheek. He spoke a few words, *"Tan-tago, musalah."*

The female gully dwarf watched, fascinated, as he spoke. Then she sighed and gazed up at him in adoration.

"Tell me, little one," Raistlin said. "How many bosses?"

The gully dwarf frowned, concentrating. She raised a grubby hand. "One," she said, holding up one finger. "And one, and one, and one." Looking up at Raistlin triumphantly, she held up four fingers and said, "Two."

"I'm beginning to agree with Flint," Sturm growled.

"Shhhh," Tanis said. Just then the screeching noise stopped. The gully dwarves looked down the corridor uneasily as into the silence came the harsh cracking sound again.

"What is that noise?" Raistlin asked his spellbound adorer.

"Whip," the female gully dwarf said emotionlessly. Reaching out her filthy hand, she took hold of Raistlin's robe and started to pull him toward the east end of the corridor. "Bosses get mad. We go."

"What is it you do for the bosses?" Raistlin asked, holding back.

"We go. You see." The gully dwarf tugged on him. "We down. They up. Down. Up. Down. Up. Come. You go. We give ride down."

Raistlin, being carried along on a tide of Aghar, looked back at Tanis, motioning with his hand. Tanis signaled to Riverwind and Flint, and everyone started moving down the hall behind the gully dwarves. Those Raistlin had charmed remained clustered around him, trying to stay as close as possible, while the rest ran off down the corridor when the whip cracked again. The companions followed Raistlin and the gully dwarves down to the corner, where the screeching noise started up once again, much louder now.

The female gully dwarf brightened as she heard it. She and the rest of the gully dwarves halted. Some of them slouched against the slime-covered walls, others plopped on the floor like sacks. The female stayed near Raistlin, holding the hem of his sleeve in her small hand. "What is it? " he asked. "Why have we stopped?"

"We wait. Not our turn yet," she informed him.

"What will we do when it is our turn?" he asked patiently.

"Go down," she said, staring up at him adoringly.

Raistlin looked at Tanis, shook his head. The mage decided to try a new approach.

"What is your name, little one?" he asked.

"Bupu."

Caramon snorted and quickly clapped his hand over his mouth.

"Now, Bupu," Raistlin said in dulcet tones, "do you know where the dragon's lair is?"

"Dragon?" Bupu repeated, astounded. "You want dragon?"

"No," Raistlin said hastily, "we don't want the dragon—just the dragon's lair, where the dragon lives."

"Oh, me not know that." Bupu shook her head. Then, seeing disappointment on Raistlin's face, she clutched his hand. "But me take you to the great Highbulp. He know everything."

Raistlin raised his eyebrows. "And how do we get to the Highbulp?"

"Down!" she said, grinning happily. The screeching sound stopped. There was a crack of a whip. "It our turn to go down now. You come. You come now. Go see Highbulp."

"Just a moment." Raistlin extricated himself from the gully

dwarf's grasp. "I must talk to my friends." He walked over to Tanis and Sturm. "This Highbulp is probably head of the clan, maybe head of several clans."

"If he's as intelligent as this lot, he won't know where his own wash bowl is, let alone the dragon," Sturm growled.

"He'll know, most likely," Flint spoke up grudgingly. "They're not smart, but gully dwarves remember everything they see or hear if you can just get them to put it into words of more than one syllable."

"We better go see the great Highbulp then," Tanis said ruefully. "Now, if we could just figure out what this up and down business is and that squeaking noise—"

"I know!" said a voice.

Tanis looked around. He had completely forgotten about Tasslehoff. The kender came running back in from around the corner, his topknot dancing, eyes shining with merriment. "It's a lift, Tanis," he said. "Like in dwarven mines. I was in a mine, once. It was the most wonderful thing. They had a lift that took rock up and down. And this is just like it. Well, almost like it. You see—" He was suddenly overcome with giggles and couldn't go on. The rest glaring at him, the kender made a violent effort to control himself

"They're using a giant lard-rendering pot! The gully dwarves that have been standing in line here run out when one of the draco-thing-ama-jiggers cracks this big whip. They all jump into the pot that's attached to a huge chain wrapped around a spoked wheel with teeth that fit into the links of the chain—that's what's squeaking! The wheel turns and down they go, and pretty soon up comes another pot—"

"Big bosses. Pot full of big bosses," Bupu said.

"Filled with draconians!" Tanis repeated in alarm.

"Not come here," Bupu said. "Go that way—" She waved a hand vaguely.

Tanis remained uneasy. "So these are the bosses. How many draconians are there by the pot?"

"Two," said Bupu, holding Raistlin's sleeve securely. "Not more than two."

"Actually, there are four," Tas said with an apologetic glance for contradicting the gully dwarf. "They're the little ones, not the big ones that cast spells."

197

"Four." Caramon flexed his huge arms. "We can handle four."

"Yes, but we've got to time it so that fifteen more aren't arriving," Tanis pointed out.

The whip cracked again.

"Come!" Bupu tugged urgently on Raistlin's sleeve. "We go. Bosses get mad."

"I'd say this is as good a time as any," Sturm said, shrugging. "Let the gully dwarves run as usual. We'll follow and overwhelm the bosses in the confusion. If one pot is up here waiting to be loaded with gully dwarves, the other has to be on the ground level."

"I suppose," Tanis said. He turned to the gully dwarves. "When you get to the lift—er, pot—don't jump in. Just dodge aside and keep out of the way. All right?"

The gully dwarves stared at Tanis with deep suspicion. The half-elf sighed and looked at Raistlin. Smiling slightly, the mage repeated Tanis's instructions. Immediately the gully dwarves began to smile and nod enthusiastically.

The whip cracked again and the companions heard a harsh voice. "Quit loafing, you scum, or we'll chop your nasty feet off and give you an excuse for being slow!"

"We'll see whose feet get chopped off," Caramon said.

"This be some fun!" said one of the gully dwarves solemnly. The Aghar dashed down the corridor.

18

Fight at the lift.
Bupu's cure for a cough.

ot mist rose from two large holes in the floor, swirling around whatever was nearby. Between the two holes was a large wheel, around which ran a gigantic chain. A tremendous black iron pot hung suspended from the chain over one of the holes. The other end of the chain disappeared through the other hole. Four armor-clad draconians, two of them swinging leather whips and armed with curved swords, stood around the pot. They were visible only briefly, then mist hid them from view. Tanis could hear the whip crack and a guttural voice bellowing.

"You louse-ridden dwarf vermin! What're you doing, holding back there. Get into this pot before I flay the filthy flesh from your nasty bones! I—ulp!"

The draconian stopped in midsentence, its eyes bulging out of its reptilian head as Caramon emerged from the mist, roaring his battle cry. The draconian let out a yell that changed into a choking gurgle as Caramon grabbed the creature around its scrawny neck, lifted it off its clawed feet, and hurled it back against the wall. Gully dwarves scattered as the body hit the wall with a bone-crushing thump.

Even as Caramon attacked, Sturm—swinging his great two-handed sword—yelled out the knight's salute to an enemy and lopped the head off a draconian who never saw what was coming. The severed head rolled on the floor with a crunching sound as it changed to stone.

Unlike goblins, who attack anything that moves without strategy or thought, draconians are intelligent and quick-thinking. The two remaining by the pot had no intention of taking on five skilled and well-armed warriors. One of them immediately jumped into the pot, yelling instructions to its companion in their guttural language. The other draconian dashed over to the wheel and freed the mechanism. The pot began to drop through the hole.

"Stop it!" Tanis yelled. "It's going for reinforcements!"

"Wrong!" shouted Tasslehoff, peering over the edge. "The reinforcements are already on the way up in the other pot. There must be twenty of them!"

Caramon ran to stop the draconian operating the lift, but he was too late. The creature left the mechanism turning and dashed toward the pot. With a great bound, it leaped in after its companion. Caramon, on the principle of don't let the enemy get away, jumped right into the pot after it! The gully dwarves cheered and hooted, some dashing over to the edge to get a better view.

"That big idiot!" Sturm swore. Shoving gully dwarves aside to look down, he saw swinging fists and flashing armor as Caramon and the draconians flailed away at each other. Caramon's added weight caused the pot to fall faster.

"They'll cut the lummox to jerky down there," Sturm muttered. "I'm going after him," he yelled to Tanis. Launching himself into the air, he grabbed hold of the chain and slid right down it into the pot.

"Now we've lost both of them!" Tanis groaned. "Flint, come with me. Riverwind, stay up here with Raistlin and Goldmoon. See if you can reverse that damned wheel! No, Tas, not you!"

Too late. The kender, screaming enthusiastically, leaped onto the chain and began shinnying down. Tanis and Flint jumped into the hole, too. Tanis wrapped his arms and legs around the chain, hanging on just above the kender, but the dwarf missed his hold, landing in the pot helmet first. Caramon promptly stepped on him.

The draconians in the pot pinned the warrior against the side. He punched one, sending it slamming to the other side, and drew his dagger on the other as it fumbled for its sword. Caramon stabbed before the draconian could get the sword free, but the warrior's dagger glanced off the creature's armor and was jarred out of Caramon's grasp. The draconian went for his face, trying to gouge his eyes out with its clawed hands. Grabbing the draconian's wrists in a crushing grip, Caramon succeeded in wrenching its hands away from his face. The two powerful beings—human and draconian—struggled against the side of the pot.

The other draconian recovered from Caramon's blow and seized its sword. But its dive for the warrior came to an abrupt halt when Sturm, sliding down the chain, kicked it hard in the face with his heavy boot. The draconian reeled backwards, the sword flying from its grasp. Sturm leaped and tried to club the creature with the flat of his sword, but the draconian thrust the blade aside with its hands.

"Get off me!" Flint roared from the bottom of the pot. Blinded by his helm, he was being slowly crushed by Caramon's big feet. In a spurt of ferocious anger, the dwarf straightened his helm, then heaved himself up, causing Caramon to lose his footing and tumble forward into the draconian. The creature sidestepped while Caramon staggered into the huge chain. The draconian swung its sword wildly. Caramon ducked and the sword clanged uselessly against the chain, notching the blade. Flint hurled himself at the draconian, hitting it squarely in the stomach with his head. The two fell against the side.

The pot gained momentum, swirling the foul mists around them.

Keeping his eyes on the action below, Tanis lowered himself down the chain. "Stay put!" he snarled at Tasslehoff. Letting go his grip, Tanis dropped down and landed in the midst of the melee. Tas, disappointed but reluctant to disobey Tanis, clung to the chain with one hand while he reached into his pouch and pulled out a rock, ready to drop it—on the head of an enemy, he hoped.

The pot began to sway as the combatants fell against the sides in their struggles, all the while dropping lower and lower, causing the other pot—filled with screaming and cursing draconians—to rise higher and higher.

Riverwind, standing at the hole with the gully dwarves, could see very little through the mist. He could, however, hear thumps and curses and groans from the pot holding his friends. Then out of the mist rose the other pot. Draconians stood, swords in their hands, staring, open-mouthed, up at him, their long red tongues panting in anticipation. In moments, he and Goldmoon, Raistlin, and fifteen gully dwarves would be facing about twenty angry draconians!

He spun around, stumbled over a gully dwarf, regained his balance, and ran to the mechanism. Somehow he had to stop that pot from rising. The huge wheel was turning slowly, the chain screeching through the spokes. Riverwind stared at it with the idea of grabbing the chain in his bare hands. A flurry of red shoved him aside. Raistlin watched the wheel for an instant, timing its rotation, then he jammed the Staff of Magius in between the wheel and the floor. The staff shivered for an instant and Riverwind held his breath, fearing the staff would snap. But it held! The mechanism shuddered to a stop.

"Riverwind!" Goldmoon yelled from where she had remained by the hole. The Plainsman ran over to the edge, Raistlin following. The gully dwarves, lined up around the hole, were having a wonderful time, thoroughly enjoying one of the most interesting events to occur in their lives. Only Bupu moved away from the edge—she trotted after Raistlin, grasping his robe whenever possible.

"*Khark-umat!*" breathed Riverwind as he looked down into the swirling mist.

Caramon tossed overboard the draconian he had been fighting. It fell with a shriek into the mist. The big warrior had claw marks on his face and a sword slash on his right arm. Sturm, Tanis, and Flint still battled the second draconian who seemed willing to kill regardless of the consequences. When it finally became clear that hitting was not enough, Tanis stabbed it with his dagger. The creature sank down, immediately turning to rock, holding Tanis's weapon fast in its stony corpse.

Then the pot lurched to a halt, jolting everyone.

"Look out! Neighbors!" yelled Tasslehoff, dropping off the chain. Tanis looked over to see the other pot, filled with draconians, swinging only about twenty feet away. Armed to the teeth, the draconians were preparing a boarding maneuver. Two clambered up onto the edge of the pot, ready to leap across the misty gap. Caramon leaned over the edge of the pot and made a wild and vicious swing with his sword in an attempt to slash one of the boarders. He missed and the momentum of his swing set the pot rotating on its chain.

Caramon lost his balance and fell forward, his great weight tipping the pot dangerously. He found himself staring directly down at the ground far below him. Sturm grabbed hold of Caramon's collar and yanked him back, causing the pot to rock erratically. Tanis slipped, landing on his hands and knees at the bottom of the pot where he discovered that the stone draconian had decayed into dust, allowing him to retrieve his dagger.

"Here they come!" Flint yelled, hauling Tanis to his feet.

One draconian launched itself toward them and caught hold of the edge of the pot with its clawed hands. The pot tilted precariously once again.

"Get over there!" Tanis shoved Caramon to the opposite side, hoping the warrior's weight would keep the pot stable. Sturm hacked at the draconian's hands, trying to force it to let go. Then another draconian flew over, gauging its distance better than the first. It landed in the pot next to Sturm.

"Don't move!" Tanis screamed at Caramon as the warrior instinctively charged into combat. The pot tilted. The big man quickly returned to his position. The pot righted itself. The draconian hanging onto the edge, its fingers oozing green, let go, spread its wings, and floated down into the mist.

Tanis spun around to fight the draconian that had landed in the pot and fell over Flint, knocking the dwarf off his feet again. The half-elf staggered against the side. As the pot rocked, he stared down. The mists parted and he saw the

ruined city of Xak Tsaroth far below him. When he drew back,
feeling sick and disoriented, he saw Tasslehoff fighting the
draconian. The little kender crawled up the creature's back
and bashed it on the head with a rock. At the bottom of the
pot, Flint picked up Caramon's dropped dagger and stabbed
the same creature in the leg. The draconian screamed as the
blade bit deep. Knowing more draconians were about to fly
over, Tanis looked up in despair. But the despair turned to
hope when he saw Riverwind and Goldmoon staring down
through the mist.

"Bring us back up!" Tanis yelled frantically, then something hit him on the head. The pain was excruciating. He felt
himself falling and falling and falling. . . .

Raistlin did not hear Tanis's yell—the mage had already
gone into action.

"Come here, my friends," Raistlin said swiftly. The spellbound gully dwarves gathered eagerly around him. "Those
bosses down there want to hurt me," he said softly.

The gully dwarves growled. Several frowned darkly. A few
shook their fists at the potful of draconians.

"But you can help," Raistlin said. "You can stop them."

The gully dwarves stared at the mage dubiously. Friendship—after all—went only so far.

"All you must do," Raistlin said patiently, "is run over and
jump on that chain." He pointed at the chain attached to the
draconians' pot.

The gully dwarves' faces brightened. That didn't sound
bad. In fact, it was something they did almost daily when they
missed catching hold of the pot.

Raistlin waved his arm. "Go!" he ordered.

The gully dwarves—all except Bupu—glanced at each
other, then dashed to the edge of the hole and, yelling wildly,
flung themselves onto the chain above the draconians, clinging to it with marvelous dexterity.

The mage ran over to the wheel, Bupu trotting along after
him. Grabbing the Staff of Magius, he tugged it free. The wheel
shivered and began to move once again, turning more and
more rapidly as the weight of the gully dwarves caused the
draconian pot to plummet back down into the mists.

Several of the draconians who had been perched on the

edge about to jump into the other pot were caught off guard by the sudden jolt. They lost their balance and fell. Though their wings stopped their fall, they shrieked in rage as they drifted to the ground below, their cries contrasting oddly with the gleeful shouts of the gully dwarves.

Riverwind leaned out over the edge of the hole and caught hold of the companions' pot as it reached the wheel.

"Are you all right?" Goldmoon asked anxiously, leaning over to help Caramon out. "Tanis is hurt," Caramon said, supporting the half-elf.

"It's just a bump," Tanis protested groggily. He felt a large lump rising on the back of his skull. "I thought I was falling out of that thing." He shuddered at the memory.

"We can't get down that way!" Sturm said, climbing out of the pot. "And we can't stay around up here. It won't take them long to get this lift back in operation and then they'll be after us. We'll have to go back."

"No! Don't go!" Bupu clutched at Raistlin. "I know way to Highbulp!" She tugged at his sleeve, pointing north. "Good way! Secret way! No bosses," she said softly, stroking his hand. "I not let bosses get you. You pretty."

"We don't seem to have much choice. We've got to get down there," Tanis said, wincing when Goldmoon's staff touched him. Then the healing power flowed through his body. He relaxed as the pain eased and sighed. "As you said, they've lived here for years."

Flint growled and shook his head as Bupu started down the corridor, heading north.

"Stop! Listen!" Tasslehoff called softly. They heard the sound of clawed feet coming toward them.

"Draconians!" said Sturm. "We've got to get out of here! Head back west."

"I knew it," Flint grumbled, scowling. "That gully dwarf's led us right into those lizards!"

"Wait!" Goldmoon gripped Tanis's arm. "Look at her!"

The half-elf turned to see Bupu remove something limp and shapeless from the bag she carried over her shoulder. Stepping up to the wall, she waved the thing in front of the stone slab and muttered a few words. The wall shivered, and within seconds, a doorway appeared, leading into darkness.

The companions exchanged uneasy glances.

"No choice," Tanis muttered. The rattle and clank of armored draconians could be heard clearly, marching down the corridor toward them. "Raistlin, light," he ordered.

The mage spoke and the crystal on his staff flared. He and Bupu and Tanis quickly passed through the secret door. The rest followed, and the other door slid shut behind them. The mage's staff revealed a small, square room decorated with wall carvings so covered with green slime that they were impossible to distinguish. They stood in silence as they heard draconians pass in the corridor.

"They must have heard the fight," Sturm whispered. "It won't take them long to get the lift in motion, then we'll have the whole draconian force after us!"

"I know way down." Bupu waved her hand deprecatingly. "No worry."

"How did you open the door, little one?" Raistlin asked curiously, kneeling beside Bupu.

"Magic," she said shyly and she held out her hand. Lying in the gully dwarf's grubby palm was a dead rat, its teeth fixed in a permanent grimace. Raistlin raised his eyebrows, then Tasslehoff touched his arm.

"It's not magic, Raistlin," the kender whispered. "It's a simple, hidden floor lock. I saw it when she pointed at the wall and I was about to say something when she went through this magic rigmarole. She steps on it when she gets close to the door and waves that thing." The kender giggled. "She probably tripped it once, accidentally, while carrying the rat."

Bupu gave the kender a scathing glance. "Magic!" she stated, pouting and stroking the rat lovingly. She popped it back into her bag and said—"Come, you go." She led them north, passing through broken, slime-coated rooms. Finally she came to a halt in a room filled with rock dust and debris. Part of the ceiling had collapsed and the floor was littered with broken tiles. The gully dwarf jabbered and pointed at something in the northeast corner of the room.

"Go down!" she said.

Tanis and Raistlin walked over to inspect. They found a four-foot-wide pipe, one end sticking up out of the crumbling floor. Apparently it had fallen through the ceiling, caving in the northeast section of the room. Raistlin thrust his staff down inside the pipe and peered inside.

"Come, you go!" Bupu said, pointing and tugging at Raistlin's sleeve urgently. "Bosses can't follow."

"That's probably true," Tanis said. "Not with their wings."

"But there's not room enough to swing a sword," Sturm said, frowning. "I don't like it—"

Suddenly everyone stopped talking. They heard the wheel creak and the chain start to screech. The companions looked at each other.

"Me first!" Tasslehoff grinned. Poking his head into the pipe, he crawled forward on his hands and knees.

"Are you sure I'll fit?" Caramon asked, staring at the opening anxiously.

"Don't worry," Tas's voice floated out. "It's so slick with slime you'll slip through like a greased pig."

This cheerful statement did not seem to impress Caramon. He continued to regard the pipe gloomily as Raistlin, led by Bupu, clutched his robes around him and slid inside, his staff lighting the way. Flint climbed in next. Goldmoon followed, grimacing in disgust as her hands slipped in the thick, green slime. Riverwind slid in after her.

"This is insane—I hope you know that!" Sturm muttered in disgust.

Tanis didn't answer. He clapped Caramon on the back. "Your turn," he said, listening to the sound of the chain moving faster and faster.

Caramon groaned. Getting down on his hands and knees, the big warrior crawled forward into the pipe opening. His sword hilt caught on the edge. Backing out, he fumbled to readjust the sword, then he tried again. This time his rump stuck up too far making his back scrape along the top. Tanis planted his foot firmly on the big warrior's rear end and shoved.

"Flatten down!" the half-elf ordered.

Caramon collapsed like a wet sack with another groan. He squirmed in, head first, shoving his shield in front of him, his armor dragging along the metal pipe with a shrill, scraping sound that set Tanis's teeth on edge.

The half-elf reached out and grasped the top of the pipe. Thrusting his legs in first, he began to slide in the foul-smelling

slime. He twisted his head around to look back at Sturm, who
came last.

"Sanity ended when we followed Tika into the kitchen of
the Inn of the Last Home," he said.

"True enough," the knight agreed with a sigh.

Tasslehoff, enthralled by the new experience of crawling
down the pipe, suddenly saw dark figures at the bottom end.
Scrabbling for a handhold, he slid to a stop.

"Raistlin!" the kender whispered. "Something's coming up
the pipe!"

"What is it?" the mage started to ask, but the foul, moist air
caught in his throat and he began to cough. Trying to catch his
breath, he shone the staff's light down the pipe to see who
approached.

Bupu took one look and sniffed. "Gulp-pulphers!" she
muttered. Waving her hand, she shouted. "Go back! Go back!"

"We go up—ride lift! Big bosses get mad!" yelled one.

"We go down. See Highbulp!" Bupu said importantly.

At this, the other gully dwarves began backing down, muttering and swearing.

But Raistlin couldn't move for a moment. He clutched his
chest, hacking, the sound echoing alarmingly in the stillness
of the narrow pipe. Bupu gazed at him anxiously, then thrust
her small hand into her bag, fished around for several moments, and came up with an object that she held up to the
light, She squinted at it, then sighed and shook her head.
"This not what I want," she mumbled.

Tasslehoff, catching sight of a brilliant, colorful flash, crept
closer. "What is that?" he asked, even though he knew the
answer. Raistlin, too, was staring at the object with wide glittering eyes.

Bupu shrugged. "Pretty rock," she said without interest,
searching through the bag once more.

"An emerald!" Raistlin wheezed.

Bupu glanced up. "You like?" she asked Raistlin.

"Very much!" the mage gasped.

"You keep." Bupu put the jewel in the mage's hand. Then,
with a cry of triumph, she brought out what she had been
searching for. Tas, leaning up close to see the new wonder,

drew back in disgust. It was a dead—very dead—lizard. There was a piece of chewed-on leather cord tied around the lizard's stiff tail. Bupu held it toward Raistlin.

"You wear around neck," she said. "Cure cough."

The mage, accustomed to handling much more unpleasant objects than this, smiled at Bupu and thanked her, but declined the cure, assuring her that his cough was much improved. She looked at him dubiously, but he did seem better—the spasm had passed. After a moment, she shrugged and put the lizard back into her bag. Raistlin, examining the emerald with expert eyes, stared coldly at Tasslehoff. The kender, sighing, turned his back and continued down the pipe. Raistlin slipped the stone into one of the secret inner pockets sewn into his robes.

When a branch pipe joined theirs, Tas looked questioningly at the gully dwarf. Bupu hesitantly pointed south, into the new pipe. Tas entered slowly. "This is stee—" he gasped as he began to slide rapidly down. He tried to slow his descent, but the slime was too thick. Caramon's explosive oath, echoing down the pipe from behind him, told the kender that his companions were having the same problem. Suddenly Tas saw light ahead of him. The tunnel was coming to an end, but where? Tas had a vivid vision of bursting out five hundred feet above nothing. But there wasn't anything he could do to stop himself. The light grew brighter, and Tasslehoff shot out the end of the pipe with a small shriek.

Raistlin slid out of the pipe, nearly falling on Bupu. The mage, looking around, thought for an instant that he had tumbled into a fire. Great, billowing clouds of white rolled around the room. Raistlin began to cough and gasp for breath.

"Wha—?" Flint flew out of the end of the pipe, falling on his hands and knees. He peered through the cloud. "Poison?" He gasped crawling over to the mage. Raistlin shook his head, but he couldn't answer. Bupu clutched the mage, dragging him toward the door. Goldmoon slid out on her stomach, knocking the breath from her body. Riverwind tumbled out, twisting his body to avoid hitting Goldmoon. There was a clanging bang as Caramon's shield shot from the pipe. Caramon's spiked armor and broad girth had slowed him enough so that he was able to crawl out of the pipe. But he was bruised and battered and covered with green filth. By the time Tanis arrived, everyone was gagging in the powdery atmosphere.

"What in the name of the Abyss?" Tanis said, astonished, then promptly choked as he inhaled a lungful of the white stuff. "Get out of here," he croaked. "Where's that gully dwarf?"

Bupu appeared in the doorway. She had taken Raistlin out of the room and was now motioning to the others. They emerged thankfully into the unclouded air and slumped down to rest among the ruins of a street. Tanis hoped they weren't waiting for an army of draconians. Suddenly he looked up. "Where's Tas?" he asked in alarm, staggering to his feet.

"Here I am," said a choked and miserable voice.

Tanis whirled around.

Tasslehoff—at least Tanis presumed it was Tasslehoff—stood before him. The kender was covered from topknot to toes in a thick, white, pasty substance. All Tanis could see of him were two brown eyes blinking out of a white mask.

"What happened?" the half-elf asked. He had never seen anyone quite so miserable as the bedraggled kender.

Tasslehoff didn't answer. He just pointed back inside.

Tanis, fearing something disastrous, ran over and peered cautiously through the crumbling doorway. The white cloud had dissipated so that he could see around the room now. Over in one corner—directly opposite the pipe opening—stood a number of large, bulging sacks. Two of them had been split open, spilling a mass of white onto the floor.

Then Tanis understood. He put his hand over his face to hide his smile. "Flour," he murmured.

19

The broken city.
Highbulp Phudge I, the Great.

The night of the Cataclysm had been a night of horror for the city of Xak Tsaroth. When the fiery mountain struck Krynn, the land split apart. The ancient and beautiful city of Xak Tsaroth slid down the face of a cliff into a vast cavern formed by the huge rents in the ground. Thus, underground, it was lost to the sight of men, and most people believed the city had vanished entirely, swallowed up by Newsea. But it still existed, clinging to the rough sides of the cavern walls, spread out upon the floor of the cavern—there were ruined buildings on several different levels. The building the companions had fallen into, which Tanis assumed must have been a bakery, was on the middle level, caught by rocks and held up against the sheer cliff face. Water from underground streams flowed down the sides of the rock and ran into the street, swirling among the ruins.

Tanis's gaze followed the course of the water. It ran down the middle of the cracked cobblestone street, running past other small shops and houses where people had once lived and gone about their business. When the city fell, the tall buildings that once lined the street toppled against one another, forming a crude archway of broken marble slabs above the cobblestones. Doors and broken shop windows yawned into the street. All was still and quiet, except for the noise of the dripping water. The air was heavy with the odor of decay. It weighed upon the spirit. And though the air was warmer down beneath the ground level than up above, the gloomy atmosphere chilled the blood. No one spoke. They washed the slime from their bodies (and the flour from Tas) as best they could, then refilled their water skins. Sturm and Caramon searched the area but saw no draconians. After a few moments of rest, the companions rose and moved on.

Bupu led them south, down the street, beneath the archway of ruined buildings. The street opened into a plaza—here the water in the streets became a river, flowing west.

"Follow river." Bupu pointed.

Tanis frowned, hearing above the noise of the river another sound, the crashing and roaring of a great waterfall. But Bupu insisted, so the heroes edged their way around the plaza river, occasionally plunging ankle deep in the water. Reaching the end of the street, the companions discovered the waterfall. The street dropped off into air, and the river gushed out from between broken columns to fall nearly five hundred feet into the bottom of the cavern. There rested the remainder of the ruined city of Xak Tsaroth.

They could see by the dim light that filtered through cracks in the cavern roof far above that the heart of the ancient city lay scattered about on the floor of the cavern in many states of decay. Some of the buildings were almost completely intact. Others, however, were nothing but rubble. A chill fog, created by the many waterfalls plunging down into the cavern, hung over the city. Most of the streets had become rivers, which combined to flow into a deep abyss to the north. Peering through the mists, the companions could see the huge chain hanging only a few hundred feet away, slightly north of their present position. They realized that the lift raised and lowered people at least one thousand feet.

"Where does the Highbulp live?" Tanis asked, looking down into the dead city below him.

"Bupu says he lives over there"—Raistlin gestured—"in those buildings on the western side of the cavern."

"And who lives in the reconstructed buildings right below us?" Tanis asked.

"Bosses," Bupu replied, scowling.

"How many bosses?"

"One, and one, and one." Bupu counted until she had used up all her fingers. "Two," she said. "Not more than two."

"Which could be anything from two hundred to two thousand," Sturm muttered. "How do we get to see the Highwhoop."

"Highbulp!" Bupu glared at him. "Highbulp Phudge I. The great."

"How do we get to him, without the bosses catching us?"

In answer, Bupu pointed upward to the rising pot full of draconians. Tanis looked blank, glanced at Sturm who shrugged disgustedly. Bupu sighed in exasperation and turned to Raistlin, obviously considering the others incapable of understanding. "Bosses go up. We go down," she said.

Raistlin stared at the lift through the mist. Then he nodded in understanding. "The draconians probably believe that we are trapped up there with no way to get down into the city. If most of the draconians are up above, that would allow us to move safely below."

"All right," Sturm said. "But how in the name of Istar do we get down? Most of us can't fly!"

Bupu spread her hands. "Vines!" she said. Seeing everyone's look of confusion, the gully dwarf stumped over to the edge of the waterfall and pointed down. Thick, green vines hung over the edge of the rocky cliff like giant snakes. The leaves on the vines were torn, tattered, and, in some places, stripped off entirely, but the vines themselves appeared thick and tough, even if they were slippery.

Goldmoon, unusually pale, crept toward the edge, peered over, and backed away hurriedly. It was a five-hundred-foot drop straight down to a rubble-strewn cobblestone street. Riverwind put his arm around her, comfortingly.

"I've climbed worse," Caramon said complacently.

"Well, I don't like it," said Flint. "But anything's better than sliding down a sewer." Grabbing hold of the vine, he swung himself over the ledge and began to inch slowly down hand over hand. "It's not bad," he shouted up.

Tasslehoff slid down a vine after Flint, traveling rapidly and with such skill that he received a grunt of approbation from Bupu.

The gully dwarf turned to look at Raistlin, pointing at his long, flowing robes and frowning. The mage smiled at her reassuringly. Standing on the edge of the cliff, he said softly, *"Pveathrfall."* The crystal ball on top of his staff flared and Raistlin leaped off the edge of the cliff, disappearing into the mist below. Bupu shrieked. Tanis caught her, fearing the adoring gully dwarf might throw herself over.

"He'll be fine," the half-elf assured her, feeling a flash of pity when he saw the look of genuine anguish on her face. "He is magi," he said. "Magic. You know."

Bupu obviously did *not* know because she stared at Tanis suspiciously, threw her bag around her neck, grabbed hold of a vine, and began scrabbling down the slippery rock. The rest of the companions were preparing to follow when Goldmoon whispered brokenly, "I can't."

Riverwind took her hands. *"Kan-toka,"* he said softly, "it will be all right. You heard what the dwarf said. Just don't look down."

Goldmoon shook her head, her chin quivering. "There must be another way," she said stubbornly. "We will search for it!"

"What's the problem?" Tanis asked. "We should hurry—"

"She's afraid of heights," Riverwind said.

Goldmoon shoved him away. "How dare you tell him that!" she shouted, her face flushed with anger.

Riverwind stared at her coldly. "Why not?" he said, his voice grating. "He's not your subject. You can let him know you're human, that you have human frailties. You have only one subject to impress now, Chieftain, and that is me!"

If Riverwind had stabbed her, he could have inflicted no more terrible pain. The color drained from Goldmoon's lips. Her eyes grew wide and staring, like the eyes of a corpse. "Please secure the staff on my back," she said to Tanis.

"Goldmoon, he didn't mean—" he began.

"Do as I command!" she ordered curtly, her blue eyes blazing in anger.

Tanis, sighing, tied the staff to her back with a length of rope. Goldmoon did not even glance at Riverwind. When the staff was fastened tightly, she started toward the edge of the cliff. Sturm jumped in front of her.

"Allow me to go down the vine ahead of you," he said. "If you slip—"

"If I slip and fall, you'd fall with me. The only thing we'd accomplish would be to die together," she snapped. Leaning down, she took a firm grip on the vine and swung herself over the edge. Almost immediately, her sweating hands slipped. Tanis's breath caught in his throat. Sturm lunged forward, though he knew there wasn't anything he could do. Riverwind stood watching, not a sign of emotion on his face. Goldmoon clutched frantically at the vines and thick leaves. She caught hold and clung to them tightly, unable to breathe, unwilling to move. She pressed her face against the wet leaves, shuddering, her eyes closed to block out the sight of the terrifying drop to the ground below. Sturm went over the edge and climbed down to her.

"Leave me alone," Goldmoon said to him through clenched teeth. She drew a trembling breath, cast a proud, defiant glance at Riverwind, then began to lower herself down the vine.

Sturm stayed near her, keeping an eye on her, as he skillfully climbed down the cliff face. Tanis, standing next to Riverwind, wanted to say something to the Plainsman but feared to do more harm. Saying nothing, therefore, he went over the edge. Riverwind followed silently.

The half-elf found the climb easy, though he slipped the last few feet, landing in an inch of water. Raistlin, he noticed, was shivering with the cold, his cough worsening in the damp air. Several gully dwarves stood around the mage, staring at him with admiring eyes. Tanis wondered how long the charm spell would last.

Goldmoon leaned against the wall, shaking. She did not look at Riverwind as he reached the ground and moved away from her, his face still expressionless.

"Where are we?" Tanis shouted above the noise of the waterfall. The mist was so thick he couldn't see anything except broken columns, overgrown with vines and fungus.

"Great Plaza that way." Bupu urgently jabbed her grubby finger toward the west. "Come. You follow. Go see Highbulp!"

She started off. Tanis reached out his hand and caught hold of her, dragging her to a stop. She glared at him, deeply offended. The half-elf removed his hand. "Please. Just listen a moment! What about the dragon? Where's the dragon?"

Bupu's eyes widened. "You want dragon?" she asked.

"No!" yelled Tanis. "We don't want the dragon. But we need to know if the dragon comes into this part of the city—" He felt Sturm's hand on his shoulder and gave up. "Forget it. Never mind," he said wearily. "Go on."

Bupu regarded Raistlin with deep sympathy for having to put up with these insane people, then she took the mage's hand and trotted off down the street to the west, the other gully dwarves trailing along behind. Half-deafened by the thundering noise of the waterfall, the companions waded after, glancing about them uneasily, dark windows loomed above them, dark doorways threatened. At each moment, they expected scaly, armored draconians to appear. But the gully dwarves did not seem concerned. They sloshed along the street, keeping as close to Raistlin as possible, and jabbering in their uncouth language.

Eventually the sounds of the waterfall faded in the distance. The mist continued to swirl around them, however, and the silence of the dead city was oppressive. Dark water gushed and gurgled past their feet along the cobblestone riverbed. Suddenly the buildings came to an end and the street opened into a huge, circular plaza. Through the water they could see the remnants in the plaza of flagstone paving in an intricate sunburst design. In the center of the plaza, the river was joined by another stream rushing in from the north. They formed a small whirlpool as the waters met and swirled before joining and continuing west between another group of tumble-down buildings.

Here, light streamed into the plaza from a crack in the cavern roof hundreds of feet above, illuminating the ghostly mists, dancing off the surface of the water whenever the mists parted.

"Other side Great Plaza," Bupu pointed.

The companions came to a halt in the shadows of the ruined buildings. All of them had the same thought: The plaza

216

was over one hundred feet across without a scrap of shelter. Once they ventured out, there would be no hiding.

Bupu, trotting along without concern, suddenly realized no one was following her except other gully dwarves. She looked back, irritated at the delay. "You come, Highbulp this way."

"Look!" Goldmoon grasped Tanis's arm.

On the other side of the great flagstone plaza were great, tall marble columns that supported a stone roof. The columns were cracked and shattered, letting the roof sag. The mists parted and Tanis caught a glimpse of a courtyard behind the columns. Dark forms of tall, domed buildings were visible beyond the courtyard. Then the mists closed around them. Though now sunk into degradation and ruin, this structure must have once been the most magnificent in Xak Tsaroth.

"The Royal Palace," Raistlin confirmed, coughing.

"Shhhh!" Goldmoon shook Tanis's arm. "Can't you see? No, wait—"

The mists flowed in front of the pillars. For a moment the companions could not see anything. Then the fog swirled away. The companions shrank back into the dark doorway. The gully dwarves came to a skidding halt in the plaza and, whirling around, raced back to cower behind Raistlin.

Bupu peered at Tanis from under the mage's sleeve. "That dragon," she said. "You want?"

It was the dragon.

Sleek and shining black, her leathery wings folded at her side, Khisanth slithered out from under the roof, ducking her head to fit beneath the sagging stone facade. Her clawed front feet clicked on the marble stairs as she stopped and stared into the floating mist with her bright red eyes. Her back legs and heavy reptilian tail were not visible, the dragon's body extending thirty feet or more back into the courtyard. A cringing draconian walked beside her, the two apparently deep in conversation.

Khisanth was angry. The draconian had brought her disturbing news—it was impossible that any of the strangers could have survived her attack at the well! But now the captain of her guard reported strangers in the city! Strangers who attacked her forces with skill and daring, strangers bearing a brown staff whose description was known to every draconian serving in this part of the Ansalon continent.

"I cannot believe this report! None could have escaped me." Khisanth's voice was soft, almost purring, yet the draconian trembled as he heard it. "The staff was not with them. I would have sensed its presence. You say these intruders are still above, in the upper chambers? Are you certain?"

The draconian gulped and nodded. "There is no way down, royal one, except the lift."

"There are other ways, you lizard," Khisanth sneered. "These miserable gully dwarves crawl around the place like parasites. The intruders have the staff, and they are trying to get down into the city. That means only one thing—they are after the Disks! How could they have learned of them?" The dragon snaked her head around and up and down as if she could see those who threatened her plans through the blinding mists. But the mists swirled past, thicker than ever.

Khisanth snarled in irritation. "The staff! That miserable staff! Verminaard should have foreseen this with those clerical powers he touts so highly, then it could have been destroyed. But, no, he is busy with his war while I must rot here in this dank tomb of a city." Khisanth gnawed a talon as she pondered.

"You could destroy the Disks," the draconian suggested, greatly daring.

"Fool, don't you think we've tried?" Khisanth muttered. She lifted her head. "No, it is far too dangerous to stay here longer. If these intruders know of the secret, others must also. The Disks should be removed to a safe place. Inform Lord Verminaard that I am leaving Xak Tsaroth. I will join him in Pax Tharkas and I will bring the intruders with me for questioning."

"*Inform* Lord Verminaard?" the draconian asked, shocked.

"Very well," Khisanth responded sarcastically. "If you insist on the charade, *ask* my Lord's permission. I suppose you have sent most of the troops up to the top?"

"Yes, royal one." The draconian bowed.

Khisanth considered the matter. "Perhaps you are not such an idiot after all," she mused. "I can handle things below. Concentrate your search in the upper parts of the city. When you find these intruders, bring them straight to me. Do not hurt them any more than necessary to subdue them. And be careful of that staff!"

The draconian fell to its knees before the dragon, who sniffed in derision and crept back into the dark shadows out of which she had come.

The draconian ran down the stairs where it was joined by several more creatures who appeared out of the mist. After a brief, muffled exchange in their own language, the draconians started up the north street. They walked nonchalantly, laughing at some private joke, and soon vanished into the mist.

"They're not worried, are they?" Sturm said.

"No," Tanis agreed grimly. "They think they've got us."

"Let's face it, Tanis. They're right," Sturm said. "This plan we've been discussing has one major flaw. If we sneak in without the dragon knowing, and *if* we get the Disks—we still have to get out of this godforsaken city with draconians crawling all over the upper levels."

"I asked you before and I'll ask you now," Tanis said. "Have you got a better plan?"

"I've got a better plan," Caramon said gruffly. "No disrespect, Tanis, but we all know how elves feel about fighting." The big man gestured toward the palace. "That's obviously where the dragon lives. Let's lure it out as we planned, only this time we'll fight it, not creep around its lair like thieves. When the dragon's disposed of, then we can get the Disks."

"My dear brother," Raistlin whispered, "your strength lies in your sword-arm, not in your mind. Tanis is wise, as the knight said when we started on this little adventure. You would do well to pay attention to him. What do you know of dragons, my brother? You have seen the effects of its deadly breath." Raistlin was overcome by a fit of coughing. He dragged a soft cloth out from the sleeve of his robe. Tanis saw that the cloth was stained with blood.

After a moment, Raistlin continued. "You could defend yourself against that, perhaps, and against the sharp claws and fangs, and the slashing tail, which can knock down those pillars. But what will you use, dear brother, against her magic? Dragons are the most ancient of magic-users. She could charm you as I have charmed my little friend. She could put you to sleep with a word, then murder you while you dreamed."

"All right," Caramon muttered, chagrined. "I didn't know

219

any of that. Damn it, who does know anything about these creatures!"

"There is much lore on the dragons in Solamnia," Sturm said softly.

He wants to fight the dragon, too, Tanis realized. He is thinking of Huma, the perfect knight, called Dragonbane.

Bupu tugged on Raistlin's robe. "Come. You go. No more bosses. No more dragon." She and the other gully dwarves started splashing across the flagstone plaza.

"Well?" Tanis said, looking at the two warriors.

"It seems we have no choice," Sturm said stiffly. "We do not face the enemy, we hide behind gully dwarves! Sooner or later a time must come when we face these monsters!" He spun on his heel and walked off, his back straight, his moustaches bristling. The companions followed.

"Maybe we're worrying needlessly." Tanis scratched his beard, glancing back at the palace that was now obscured by the mist. "Perhaps this is the only dragon left in Krynn—one that survived the Age of Dreams."

Raistlin's lips twisted. "Remember the stars, Tanis," he murmured. "The Queen of Darkness has returned. Recall the words of the Canticle: 'swarm of her shrieking hosts.' Her hosts were dragons, according to the ancient ones. She has returned and her hosts have come with her."

"This way!" Bupu clutched at Raistlin, pointing down a street branching off to the north. "This home!"

"At least it's dry," Flint grumbled. Turning right, they left the river behind them. Mist closed in around the companions as they entered another nest of ruined buildings. This section of town must have been the poorer part of the city of Xak Tsaroth, even in its glory days—the buildings were in the last stages of decay and collapse. The gully dwarves began whooping and hollering as they ran down the street. Sturm looked at Tanis in alarm at the noise.

"Can't you get them to be quieter?" Tanis asked Bupu. "So the draconians, er, bosses won't find us."

"Pooh!" She shrugged. "No bosses. They not come here. Afraid of the great Highbulp."

Tanis had his doubts about that, but, glancing around, he couldn't see any signs of the draconians. From what he had observed, the lizardlike men seemed to lead a well-ordered, militaristic life. By contrast, the streets in this part of town were cluttered with trash and filth. The disreputable buildings erupted with gully dwarves. Males, females, and dirty, ragged children stared at them curiously as they walked down the street. Bupu and the other spellbound gully dwarves swarmed around Raistlin, practically carrying him.

The draconians were undeniably smart, Tanis thought. They allowed their slaves to live their private lives in peace— so long as they didn't stir up trouble. A good idea, considering that gully dwarves outnumbered draconians about ten to one. Though they were basically cowards, gully dwarves had a reputation as very nasty fighters when backed into a corner.

Bupu brought the group to a halt in front of one of the darkest, dingiest, filthiest alleys Tanis had ever seen. A foul mist flowed out from it. The buildings leaned over, holding each other up like drunks stumbling out of a tavern. As he watched, small dark creatures skittered out of the alley and gully dwarf children began chasing after them.

"Dinner," shrieked one, smacking his lips.

"Those are rats!" Goldmoon cried in horror.

"Do we have to go in there?" Sturm growled, staring at the tottering buildings.

"The smell alone is enough to knock a troll dead," Caramon added. "And I'd rather die under the dragon's claw than have a gully dwarf hovel fall on top of me."

Bupu gestured down the alley. "The Highbulp!" she said, pointing to the most dilapidated building on the block.

"Stay here and keep watch if you want," Tanis told Sturm. "I'll go talk with the Highbulp."

"No." The knight scowled, gesturing the half-elf into the alley. "We're in this together."

The alley ran several hundred feet to the east, then it twisted north and came suddenly to a dead end. Ahead of them was a decaying brick wall and no way out. Their return was blocked by gully dwarves who had run in after them.

"Ambush!" Sturm hissed and drew his sword. Caramon began to rumble deep in his throat. The gully dwarves, seeing the flash of cold steel, panicked. Falling all over themselves and each other, they whirled and fled back down the alley.

Bupu glared at Sturm and Caramon in disgust. She turned to Raistlin. "You make them stop!" she demanded, pointing to the warriors. "Or I not take to Highbulp."

"Put your sword away, knight," Raistlin hissed, "unless you think you've found a foe worthy of your attention."

Sturm glowered at Raistlin, and for a moment Tanis thought he might attack the mage, but then the knight thrust his sword away. "I wish I knew what your game was, magician," Sturm said coldly. "You were so eager to come to this city, even before we knew about the Disks. Why? What are you after?"

Raistlin did not reply. He stared at the knight malevolently with his strange golden eyes, then turned to Bupu. "They will not trouble you further, little one," he whispered.

Bupu looked around to make certain they were properly cowed, then she walked forward and knocked twice on the wall with her grubby fist. "Secret door," she said importantly.

Two knocks answered Bupu's knock.

"That signal," she said. "Three knocks. Now they let in."

"But she only knocked twice—" Tas began, giggling.

Bupu glared at him.

"Shhh!" Tanis nudged the kender.

Nothing happened. Bupu, frowning, knocked twice more. Two knocks answered. She waited. Caramon, his eyes on the alley opening, began moving restlessly from one foot to the other. Bupu knocked twice again. Two knocks answered.

Finally Bupu yelled at the wall. "I knock secret code knock. You let in!"

"Secret knock five knocks," answered a muffled voice.

"I knock five knocks!" Bupu stated angrily. "You let in!"

"You knock six knocks."

"I count eight knocks," argued another voice.

Bupu suddenly pushed on the wall with both hands. It opened easily. She peered inside. "I knock four knocks. You let in!" she said, raising a clenched fist.

"All right," the voice grumbled.

Bupu shut the door, knocked twice. Tanis, hoping to avoid any more incidents and delays, glared at the kender, who was writhing with suppressed laughter.

The door swung open—again. "You come in," the guard said sourly. "But that not four knocks," he whispered to Bupu loudly. She ignored him as she swept disdainfully past him, dragging her bag along the floor.

"We see Highbulp," she announced.

"You take this lot to Highbulp?" One of the guards gasped, staring at the giant Caramon and the tall Riverwind with wide eyes. His companion began backing up.

"See Highbulp," Bupu said proudly.

The gully dwarf guard, never taking his eyes off the formidable-looking group, backed into a stinking, filthy hallway, then broke into a run. He began shouting at the top of his lungs. "An army! An army has broken in!" They could hear his shouts echo down the hallway.

"Bah!" Bupu sniffed. "Glup-phunger spawn! Come. See Highbulp."

She started down the hallway, clutching her bag to her chest. The companions could still hear the shouts of the gully dwarf echoing down the corridor.

"An army! An army of giants! Save the Highbulp!"

The great Highbulp, Phudge I, was a gully dwarf among gully dwarves. He was almost intelligent, rumored to be fabulously wealthy, and a notorious coward. The Bulps had long been the elite clan of Xak Tsaroth—or "Th" as they called it— ever since Nulph Bulp fell down a shaft one night in a drunken stupor and discovered the city. Upon sobering up the next morning, he claimed it for his clan. The Bulps promptly moved in and, in later years, graciously allowed the clans Slud and Glup to occupy the city as well.

Life was good in the ruined city—by gully dwarf standards, anyway. The outside world left them alone (since the outside world hadn't the foggiest notion they were there and wouldn't have cared if it did). The Bulps had no trouble maintaining their dominance over the other clans, mostly because it was a Bulp (Glunggu) with a scientific turn of mind (certain jealous members of the Slud clan whispered that his mother had been a gnome) who developed the lift, putting to use the two enormous iron pots used by the city's former residents for rendering lard. The lift enabled the gully dwarves to extend their scavenging activities to the jungle above the sunken city, greatly improving their standard of living. Glunggu Bulp became a hero and was proclaimed Highbulp by unanimous decision. The chieftainship of the clans had remained in the Bulp family ever since.

The years passed and then, suddenly, the outside world took an interest in Xak Tsaroth. The arrival of the dragon and the draconians put a sad crimp on the gully dwarf lifestyle. The draconians had initially intended to wipe out the filthy little nuisances, but the gully dwarves—led by the great Phudge—had cringed and cowered and whimpered and wailed and prostrated themselves so abjectly that the draconians were merciful and simply enslaved them.

So it was that the gully dwarves—for the first time in several hundred years of living in Xak Tsaroth—were forced to work. The draconians repaired buildings, put things into military order, and generally made life miserable for the gully dwarves who had to cook and clean and repair things.

Needless to say, the great Phudge was not pleased with this state of affairs. He spent long hours thinking up ways to remove the dragon. He knew the location of the dragon's lair, of course, and had even discovered a secret route leading there. He had actually sneaked in once, when the dragon was away. Phudge had been awestruck by the vast amount of pretty rocks and shining coins gathered in the huge underground room. The great Highbulp had traveled some in his wild youth and he knew that folk in the outside world coveted these pretty rocks and would give vast amounts of colorful and gaudy cloth (Phudge had a weakness for fine clothes) in return. On the spot, the Highbulp drew up a map so he wouldn't forget how to get back to the treasure. He even had the presence of mind to swipe a few of the smaller rocks.

Phudge dreamed of this wealth for months afterward, but he never found another opportunity to return. This was due to two factors: one, the dragon never left again and, two, Phudge couldn't make heads nor tails of his map.

If only the dragon would leave permanently, he thought, or if some hero would come along and conveniently stick a sword into it! These were the Highbulp's fondest dreams, and this was the state of affairs when the great Phudge heard his guards proclaiming that an army was attacking.

Thus it came to pass that—when Bupu finally dragged the great Phudge out from under his bed and convinced him that he was not about to be set upon by an army of giants—Highbulp Phudge I began to believe that dreams could come true.

"And so you're here to kill the dragon," said the great Highbulp, Phudge I, to Tanis Half-Elven.

"No," Tanis said patiently, "we're not."

The companions stood in the Court of the Aghar before the throne of a gully dwarf Bupu had introduced as the great Highbulp. Bupu kept an eye on the companions as they entered the throne room, eagerly anticipating their looks of stunned awe. Bupu was not disappointed. The looks on the companions' faces as they entered might well be described as stunned.

The city of Xak Tsaroth had been stripped of its finery by the early Bulps who used it to decorate the throne room of their lord. Following the philosophy that if one yard of gold cloth is good, forty yards is better, and totally uninhibited by good taste, the gully dwarves turned the throne room of the great Highbulp into a masterpiece of confusion. Heavy, frayed gold cloth swirled and draped every available inch of wall space. Huge tapestries hung from the ceiling (some of them upside-down). The tapestries must have once been beautiful, delicate-colored threads blending to show scenes of city life, or portray stories and legends from the past. But the gully dwarves, wanting to liven them up, painted over the cloth in garish, clashing colors.

Thus Sturm was shocked to the core of his being when confronted by a bright red Huma battling a purple-spotted dragon beneath an emerald-green sky.

Graceful, nude statues, standing in all the wrong places, adorned the room as well. These, too, the gully dwarves had enhanced, considering pure white marble drab and depressing. They painted the statues with enough realism and attention to detail that Caramon—with an embarrassed glance at Goldmoon—flushed bright red and kept his eyes on the floor.

The companions, in fact, had problems maintaining their serious mien when ushered into this gallery of artistic horrors. One failed utterly: Tasslehoff was immediately overcome by the giggles so severely that Tanis was forced to send the kender back to the Waiting Place outside the Court to try and compose himself. The rest of the group bowed solemnly to the great Phudge—with the exception of Flint who stood bolt upright, his hands fingering his battle-axe, without the trace of a smile on his aged face.

The dwarf had laid his hand on Tanis's arm before they entered the court of the Highbulp. "Don't be taken in by this foolery, Tanis," Flint warned. "These creatures can be treacherous."

The Highbulp was somewhat flustered when the companions entered, especially at the sight of the tall fighters. But Raistlin made a few well-chosen remarks that considerably mollified and reassured (if disappointed) the Highbulp.

The mage, interrupted by fits of coughing, explained that they did not want to cause trouble, they simply planned to retrieve an object of religious value from the dragon's lair and leave, preferably without disturbing the dragon.

This, of course, didn't fit in with Phudge's plans. He therefore assumed he hadn't heard correctly. Cocooned in gaudy robes, he leaned back in the chipped gold-leaf throne and repeated calmly—"You here. Got swords. Kill dragon."

"No," said Tanis again. "As our friend, Raistlin, explained, the dragon is guarding an object that belongs to our gods. We want to remove the object and escape the city before the dragon is aware that it is gone."

The Highbulp frowned. "How me know you not take all treasure, leave Highbulp only one mad dragon? There be lot of treasure, pretty rocks."

Raistlin looked up sharply, his eyes gleaming. Sturm, fidgeting with his sword, glanced at the mage in disgust.

"We will bring you the pretty rocks," Tanis assured the Highbulp. "Help us and you will get all the treasure. We want only to find this relic of our gods."

It had become obvious to the Highbulp that he was dealing with thieves and liars, not the heroes he had expected. This group was apparently as frightened of the dragon as he was and that gave the Highbulp an idea. "What you want from Highbulp?" he asked, trying to subdue his glee and appear subtle.

Tanis sighed in relief. At last they seemed to be getting somewhere. "Bupu"—he indicated the female gully dwarf clinging to Raistlin's sleeve—"told us that you were the only one in the city who could lead us to the dragon's lair."

"Lead!" The great Phudge lost his composure for a moment and clutched his robes around him. "No lead! Great Highbulp not expendable. People need me!"

"No, no. I didn't mean lead," Tanis amended hastily. "If you had a map or could send someone to show us the way."

"Map!" Phudge mopped the sweat off his brow with the sleeve of his robe. "Should say so in first place. Map. Yes. I send for map. Meantime, you eat. Guests of the Highbulp. Guards take to mess hall."

"No, thank you," Tanis said politely, unable to look at the others. They had passed the gully dwarf mess hall on their way to see the Highbulp. The smell alone had been enough to ruin even Caramon's appetite.

"We have our own food," Tanis continued. "We would like some time to ourselves to rest and discuss our plans further."

"Certainly." The Highbulp scooted forward to the front of the throne. Two of his guards came over to help him down since his feet didn't touch the floor. "Go back to Waiting Place. Sit. Eat. Talk. I send map. Maybe you tell Phudge plans?"

Tanis glanced swiftly at the gully dwarf and saw the Highbulp's squinty eyes gleam with cunning. The half-elf felt cold, suddenly realizing this gully dwarf was no buffoon. Tanis began to wish he had talked more with Flint. "Our plans are hardly formed yet, your majesty," the half-elf said.

The great Highbulp knew better. Long ago he had drilled a hole through the wall of the room known as Waiting Place so that he could eavesdrop on his subjects as they waited for an audience with him, discovering what they intended to bother him about in advance. Thus he knew a great deal about the companions' plans already, so he let the matter drop. The use of the term "your majesty" may have had something to do with this; the Highbulp had never heard anything quite so suitable.

"Your majesty," Phudge repeated, sighing with pleasure. He poked one of his guards in the back. "You remember. From now on, say 'Your Majesty.'"

"Y-yes, y-your, uh, majesty," the gully dwarf stuttered. The great Phudge waved his filthy hand graciously and the companions bowed their way out. Highbulp, Phudge I, stood for a moment beside his throne, smiling in what he considered a charming manner until his guests were gone. Then his expression changed, transforming into a smile so shrewd and devious his guards crowded around him in eager anticipation.

"You," he said to one. "Go to quarters. Bring map. Give to fools in next room."

The guard saluted and ran off. The other guard remained close, waiting in open-mouthed expectation. Phudge glanced around, then drew the guard even nearer, considering exactly how to phrase his next command. He needed some heroes and if he had to create his own out of whatever scum came along, then he would do so. If they died, it was no great loss. If they succeeded in killing the dragon, so much the better. The gully dwarves would get what was—to them—more precious than all the pretty rocks in Krynn: a return to the sweet, halcyon days of freedom! And so, enough of this nonsense about sneaking around.

Phudge leaned over and whispered in the guard's ear. "You go to dragon. Give her best regards of his majesty, High-bulp, Phudge I, and tell her . . ."

20

The Highbulp's Map.
A spellbook of Fistandantilus.

I don't trust that little bastard any farther than I can stand the smell of him," Caramon growled.

"I agree," Tanis said quietly. "But what choice do we have? We've agreed to bring him the treasure. He has everything to lose and nothing to gain if he betrays us."

They sat on the floor in the Waiting Place, a filthy antechamber outside the throne room. The decorations in this room were just as vulgar as in the Court. The companions were nervous and tense, speaking little and forcing themselves to eat.

Raistlin refused food. Curled up on the floor apart from the others, he prepared and drank down the strange herbal mixture that eased his cough. Then he wrapped himself in his robes and stretched out, eyes closed, on the floor. Bupu sat curled up near him, munching on something from her bag.

Caramon, going over to check on his brother, was horrified to see a tail disappear into her mouth with a slurp.

Riverwind sat by himself. He did not take part in the hushed conversation as the friends went over their plans once again. The Plainsman stared moodily at the floor. When he felt a light touch on his arm, he didn't even lift his head. Goldmoon, her face pale, knelt beside him. She tried to speak, failed, then cleared her throat.

"We must talk," she said firmly in their language.

"Is that a command?" he asked bitterly.

She swallowed. "Yes," she answered, barely audible.

Riverwind rose to his feet and walked over to stand in front of a garish tapestry. He did not look at Goldmoon or even speak to her. His face was drawn into a stern mask, but underneath, Goldmoon could see the searing pain in his soul. She gently laid her hand on his arm.

"Forgive me," she said softly.

Riverwind regarded her in astonishment. She stood before him, her head bowed, an almost childlike shame on her face. He reached out to stroke the silver-gold hair of the one he loved more than life itself. He felt Goldmoon tremble at his touch and his heart ached with love. Moving his hand from her head to her neck, he very gently and tenderly drew the beloved head to his chest and then suddenly clasped her in his arms.

"I've never heard you say those words before," he said, smiling to himself, knowing she could not see him.

"I have never said them," she gulped, her cheek pressed against his leather shirt. "Oh, my beloved, I am sorrier than I can say that you came home to Chieftain's Daughter and not Goldmoon. But I've been so afraid."

"No," he whispered, "I am the one who should ask forgiveness." He raised his hand to wipe away her tears. "I didn't realize what you had gone through. All I could think of was myself and the dangers I had faced. I wish you had told me, heart's dearest."

"I wished you had asked," she replied, looking up at him earnestly. "I have been Chieftain's Daughter so long it is the only thing I know how to be. It is my strength. It gives me courage when I am frightened. I don't think I can let go."

"I don't want you to let go." He smiled at her, smoothing wayward strands of hair from her face. "I fell in love with Chieftain's Daughter the first time I saw you. Do you remember? At the games held in your honor."

"You refused to bow to receive my blessing," she said. "You acknowledged my father's leadership but denied that I was a goddess. You said man could not make gods of other men." Her eyes looked back so many, many years. "How tall and proud and handsome you were, talking of ancient gods that did not exist to me then."

"And how furious you were," he recalled, "and how beautiful! Your beauty was a blessing to me in itself. I needed no other. You wanted me thrown out of the games."

Goldmoon smiled sadly. "You thought I was angry because you had shamed me before the people, but that was not so."

"No? What was it then, Chieftain's Daughter?"

Her face flushed a dusky rose, but she lifted her clear blue eyes to him. "I was angry because I knew when I saw you standing there, refusing to kneel before me, that I had lost part of myself and that, until you claimed it, I would never be whole again."

For reply, the Plainsman pressed her to him, kissing her hair gently.

"Riverwind," she said, swallowing, "Chieftain's Daughter is still here. I don't think she can ever leave. But you must know that Goldmoon is underneath and, if this journey ever ends and we come to peace at last, then Goldmoon will be yours forever and we will banish Chieftain's Daughter to the winds."

A thump at the Highbulp's door caused everyone to start nervously as a gully dwarf guard stumbled into the room. "Map," he said, thrusting a crumpled piece of paper at Tanis.

"Thank you," said the half-elf gravely. "And extend our thanks to the Highbulp."

"His *Majesty*, the Highbulp," the guard corrected with an anxious glance toward a tapestry-covered wall. Bobbing clumsily, he backed into the Highbulp's quarters.

Tanis spread the map flat. Everyone gathered around it, even Flint. After one look, however, the dwarf snorted derisively and walked back to his couch.

Tanis laughed ruefully. "We might have expected it. I wonder if the great Phudge remembers where the 'big secret room' is?"

"Of course not." Raistlin sat up, opening his strange, golden eyes and peering at them through half-closed lids. "That is why he has never returned for the treasure. However, there is one among us who knows where the dragon's lair is located." Everyone followed the mage's gaze.

Bupu glared back at them defiantly. "You right. I know," she said, sulking. "I know secret place. I go there, find pretty rocks. But don't tell Highbulp!"

"Will you tell us?" Tanis asked. Bupu looked at Raistlin. He nodded.

"I tell," she mumbled. "Give map."

Raistlin, seeing the others engrossed in looking at the map, beckoned to his brother.

"Is the plan still the same?" the mage whispered.

"Yes." Caramon frowned. "And I don't like it. I should go with you."

"Nonsense," Raistlin hissed. "You would only be in my way!" Then he added more gently, "I will be in no danger, I assure you." He laid his hand on his twin's arm and drew him close. "Besides"—the mage glanced around—"there is something you must do for me, my brother. Something you must bring me from the dragon's lair."

Raistlin's touch was unusually hot, his eyes burned. Caramon uneasily started to pull back, seeing something in his brother he hadn't seen since the Towers of High Sorcery, but Raistlin's hand clutched at him.

"What is it?" Caramon asked reluctantly.

"A spellbook!" Raistlin whispered.

"So this is why you wanted to come to Xak Tsaroth!" said Caramon. "You knew this spellbook would be here."

"I read about it, years ago. I knew it had been in Xak Tsaroth prior to the Cataclysm, all of the Order knew it, but we assumed it had been destroyed with the city. When I found out Xak Tsaroth had escaped destruction, I realized there might be a chance the book had survived!"

"How do you know it's in the dragon's lair?"

"I don't. I am merely surmising. To magic-users, this book

is Xak Tsaroth's greatest treasure. You may be certain that if the dragon found it, she is using it!"

"And you want me to get it for you," Caramon said slowly. "What does it look like?"

"Like my spellbook, of course, except the bone-white parchment is bound in night-blue leather with runes of silver stamped on the front. It will feel deathly cold to the touch."

"What do the runes say?"

"You do not want to know . . ." Raistlin whispered.

"Whose book was it?" Caramon asked suspiciously.

Raistlin fell silent, his golden eyes abstracted as if he were searching inwardly, trying to remember something forgotten. "You have never heard of him, my brother," he said finally, in a whisper that forced Caramon to lean closer. "Yet he was one of the greatest of my order. His name was Fistandantilus."

"The way you describe the spellbook—" Caramon hesitated, fearing what Raistlin would reply. He swallowed and started over. "This Fistandantilus—did he wear the Black Robes?" He could not meet his brother's piercing gaze.

"Ask me no more!" Raistlin hissed. "You are as bad as the others! How can any of you understand me!" Seeing his twin's look of pain, the mage sighed. "Trust me, Caramon. It is not a particularly powerful spellbook, one of the mage's early books, in fact. One he had when he was very young, very young indeed," Raistlin murmured, staring far off. Then he blinked and said more briskly, "But it will be valuable to me, nonetheless. You must get it! You must—" He started to cough.

"Sure, Raist," Caramon promised, soothing his brother. "Don't get worked up. I'll find it."

"Good Caramon. Excellent Caramon," Raistlin whispered when he could speak. He sank back into the corner and closed his eyes. "Now let me rest. I must be ready."

Caramon stood up, looked at his brother a moment, then he turned around and nearly fell over Bupu who was standing behind him, gazing up at him suspiciously with wide eyes.

"What was all that about?" Sturm asked gruffly as Caramon returned to the group.

"Oh, nothing," the big man mumbled, flushing guiltily. Sturm cast an alarmed glance at Tanis.

"What is it, Caramon?" Tanis asked, putting the rolled map in his belt and facing the warrior. "Anything wrong?"

"N-no—" Caramon stuttered. "It's nothing. I—uh—tried to get Raistlin to let me go with him. He said I'd just be in the way."

Tanis studied Caramon. He knew the big man was telling the truth, but Tanis also knew the warrior wasn't telling all the truth. Caramon would cheerfully shed the last drop of his blood for any member of the company, but Tanis suspected he would betray them all at Raistlin's command.

The giant looked at Tanis, silently begging him to ask no more questions.

"He's right, you know, Caramon," Tanis said finally, clapping the big man on the arm. "Raistlin won't be in danger. Bupu will be with him. She'll bring him back here to hide. He's just got to conjure up some of his fancy pyrotechnics, create a diversion to draw the dragon away from her lair. He'll be long gone by the time she gets there."

"Sure, I know that," said Caramon, forcing a chuckle. "You need me anyway."

"We do," Tanis said seriously. "Now is everyone ready?"

Silently, grimly, they stood up. Raistlin rose and came forward, hood over his face, hands folded in his robes. There was an aura around the mage, indefinable, yet frightening—the aura of power derived and created from within. Tanis cleared his throat.

"We'll give you a five hundred count," Tanis said to Raistlin. "Then we'll start. The 'secret place' marked on the map is a trap door located in a building not far from here, according to your little friend. It leads beneath the city to a tunnel that comes up under the dragon's lair, near where we saw her today. Create your diversion in the plaza, then come back here. We'll meet here, give the Highbulp his treasure, and lie low until night. When it's dark, we'll escape."

"I understand," Raistlin said calmly.

I wish I did, Tanis thought bitterly. I wish I understood what was going on in that mind of yours, mage. But the half-elf said nothing.

"We go now?" asked Bupu, looking at Tanis anxiously.

"We go now," Tanis said.

Raistlin crept from the shadowy alley and moved swiftly down the street to the south. He saw no signs of life. It was as if all the gully dwarves had been swallowed up by the mist. He found this thought disturbing and kept to the shadows. The frail mage could move silently if there was need. He only hoped he could control his coughing. The pain and congestion in his chest had eased when he drank the herbal mixture whose recipe had been given him by Par-Salian—a kind of apology from the great sorcerer for the trauma the young mage had endured. But the mixture's effect would soon wear off.

Bupu peered out from behind his robes, her beady black eyes squinting down the street leading east to the Great Plaza. "No one," she said and tugged on the mage's robe. "We go now."

No one—thought Raistlin, worried. It didn't make sense. Where were the crowds of gully dwarves? He had the feeling something had gone wrong, but there wasn't time to turn back—Tanis and the others were on their way to the secret tunnel entrance. The mage smiled bitterly. What a fool's quest this was turning out to be. They would probably all die in this wretched city.

Bupu tugged on his robe again. Shrugging, he cast his hood over his head and, together, he and the gully dwarf flitted down the mist-shrouded street.

Two armor-clad figures detached themselves from a dark doorway and slunk quickly after Raistlin and Bupu.

"This is the place," Tanis said softly. Opening a rotting door, he peered in. "It's dark in here. We'll need a light."

There was a sound of flint striking metal and then a flare of light as Caramon lit one of the torches they had borrowed from the Highbulp. The warrior handed one to Tanis and lit one for himself and Riverwind. Tanis stepped inside the building and immediately found himself up to his ankles in water. Holding the torch aloft, he saw water pouring in steady streams down the walls of the dismal room. It swirled around the center of the floor, then ran out through cracks around the edges. Tanis sloshed to the center and held his torch close to the water.

"There it is. I can see it," he said as the others waded into the room. He pointed to a trap door in the floor. An iron pull-ring was barely visible in its center.

"Caramon?" Tanis stood back.

"Bah!" Flint snorted. "If a gully dwarf can open this, I can open it. Stand aside." The dwarf elbowed everyone back, plunged his hand into the water, and heaved. There was a moment's silence. Flint grunted, his face turned red. He stopped, straightened up with a gasp, then reached down and tried again. There wasn't a creak. The door remained shut.

Tanis put his hand on the dwarf's shoulder. "Flint, Bupu says she only goes down during the dry season. You're trying to lift half of Newsea along with the door."

"Well"—the dwarf puffed for breath—"why didn't you say so? Let the big ox try his luck."

Caramon stepped forward. He reached down into the water and gave a heave. His shoulder muscles bulged, and veins in his neck stood out. There was a sucking sound, then the suction was released so suddenly that the big warrior nearly fell over backward. Water drained from the room as Caramon eased the wooden plank door over. Tanis held his torch down to see. A four-foot-square shaft gaped in the floor; a narrow iron ladder descended into the shaft.

"What's the count?" Tanis asked, his throat dry.

"Four hundred and three," answered Sturm's deep voice. "Four hundred and four."

The companions stood around the trap door, shivering in the chill air, hearing nothing but the sound of water pouring down the shaft.

"Four hundred and fifty-one," noted the knight calmly.

Tanis scratched his beard. Caramon coughed twice, as though reminding them of his absent brother. Flint fidgeted and dropped his axe in the water. Tas absent-mindedly chewed on the end of his topknot. Goldmoon, pale but composed, drew near Riverwind, the nondescript brown staff in her hand. He put his arm around her. Nothing was worse than waiting.

"Five hundred," said Sturm finally.

"About time!" Tasslehoff swung himself down onto the ladder. Tanis went next, holding his torch to light the way for

Goldmoon, who came after him. The others followed, climbing slowly down into an access shaft of the city sewage system. The shaft ran about twenty feet straight down, then opened up into a five-foot-wide tunnel that ran north and south.

"Check the depth of the water," Tanis warned the kender as Tas was about to let go of the ladder. The kender, hanging onto the last rung with one hand, lowered his hoopak staff into the dark, swirling water below him. The staff sank about half-way.

"Two feet," said Tas cheerfully. He dropped in with a splash, the water hitting him around the thighs. He looked up at Tanis inquiringly.

"That way," Tanis pointed. "South."

Holding his staff in the air, Tasslehoff let the current sweep him along.

"Where's that diversion?" Sturm asked, his voice echoing.

Tanis had been wondering that himself. "We probably won't be able to hear anything down here." He hoped that was true.

"Raist'll come through. Don't worry," Caramon said grimly.

"Tanis!" Tasslehoff fell back into the half-elf. "There's something down here! I felt it go by my feet."

"Just keep moving," Tanis muttered, "and hope it isn't hungry—"

They waded on in silence, the torchlight flickering off the walls, creating illusions in the mind's eye. More than once, Tanis saw something reach out for him, only to realize it was the shadow cast by Caramon's helm or Tas's hoopak.

The tunnel ran straight south for about two hundred feet, then turned east. The companions stopped. Down the eastern arm of the sewer glimmered a column of dim light, filtering from above. This—according to Bupu—marked the dragon's lair.

"Douse the torches!" Tanis hissed, plunging his torch in the water. Touching the slimy wall, Tanis followed the kender—Tas's red outline showing up vividly to his elven eyes—through the tunnel. Behind him he heard Flint complaining about the effects of water on his rheumatism.

"Shhhh," Tanis whispered as they drew near the light. Trying to be silent in spite of clanking armor, they soon stood by a slender ladder that ran up to an iron grating.

"No one ever bothers to lock floor gratings." Tas pulled Tanis close to whisper in his ear. "But I'm sure I can open it, if it is."

Tanis nodded. He didn't add that Bupu had been able to open it as well. The art of picking locks was as much a matter of pride to the kender as Sturm's moustaches were to the knight. They all stood watching, knee-deep in water, as Tas skimmed up the ladder.

"I still don't hear anything outside," Sturm muttered.

"Shhhh!" Caramon growled harshly.

The grating had a lock, a simple one that Tas opened in moments. Then he silently lifted the grating and peered out. Sudden darkness descended on him, darkness so thick and impenetrable it seemed to hit him like a lead weight, nearly making him lose his hold on the grating. Hurriedly he put the grating back into place without making a sound, then slid down the ladder, bumping into Tanis.

"Tas?" the half-elf grabbed him. "Is that you? I can't see. What's going on?"

"I don't know. It just got dark all of a sudden."

"What do you mean, you can't see?" Sturm whispered to Tanis. "What about your elf-talent?"

"Gone," Tanis said grimly, "just as in Darken Wood—and out by the well. . . ."

No one spoke as they stood huddled in the tunnel. All they could hear was the sound of their own breathing and water dripping from the walls.

The dragon was up there—waiting for them.

21

The sacrifice.
The twice-dead city.

Despair blacker than the darkness blinded Tanis. It was my plan, the only way we had a chance to get out of here alive, he thought. It was sound, it should have worked! What went wrong? Raistlin—could he have betrayed us? No! Tanis clenched his fist. No, damn it. The mage was distant, unlikable, impossible to understand, yes, but he was loyal to them, Tanis would swear it. Where was Raistlin? Dead, perhaps. Not that it mattered. They would all be dead.

"Tanis"—the half-elf felt a firm grasp on his arm and recognized Sturm's deep voice—"I know what you're thinking. We have no choice. We're running out of time. This is our only chance to get the Disks. We won't get another."

"I'm going to look," Tanis said. He climbed past the kender and peered through the grate. It was dark, magically dark. Tanis put his head in his hand and tried to think. Sturm was

239

right: time was running out. Yet how could he trust the knight's judgement? Sturm wanted to fight the dragon! Tanis crawled back down the ladder. "We're going," he said. Suddenly all he wanted to do was get this over with, then they could go home. Home to Solace. "No, Tas." He grabbed hold of the kender and dragged him back down the ladder. "The fighters go first—Sturm and Caramon. Then the rest."

But the knight was already shoving past him eagerly, his sword clanking against his thigh.

"We're always last!" Tasslehoff sniffed, shoving the dwarf along. Flint climbed the ladder slowly, his knees creaking. "Hurry up!" Tas said. "I hope nothing happens before we get there. I've never talked to a dragon."

"I'll bet the dragon's never talked to a kender either!" The dwarf snorted. "You realize, you hare-brain, that we're probably going to die. Tanis knows, I could tell by his voice."

Tas paused, clinging to the ladder while Sturm slowly pushed on the grating. "You know, Flint," the kender said seriously, "my people don't fear death. In a way, we look forward to it, the last big adventure. But I think I'd feel badly about leaving this life. I'd miss my things"—he patted his pouches—"and my maps, and you and Tanis. Unless," he added brightly, "we all go to the same place when we die."

Flint had a sudden vision of the happy-go-lucky kender lying cold and dead. He felt a lump of pain in his chest and was thankful for the concealing darkness. Clearing his throat, he said huskily, "If you think I'm going to share my afterlife with a bunch of kender, you're crazier than Raistlin. Come on!"

Sturm carefully lifted the grating and shoved it to one side. It scraped over the floor, causing him to grit his teeth. He heaved himself up easily. Turning, he bent down to help Caramon who was having trouble squeezing his body and his clanking arsenal through the shaft.

"In the name of Istar, be quiet!" Sturm hissed.

"I'm trying," Caramon muttered, finally climbing over the edge. Sturm gave his hand to Goldmoon. Last came Tas, delighted that nobody had done anything exciting in his absence.

"We've got to have light," Sturm said.

"Light?" replied a voice as cold and dark as winter midnight. "Yes, let us have light."

The darkness fled instantly. The companions saw they were in a huge domed chamber that soared hundreds of feet into the air. Cold gray light filtered into the room through a crack in the ceiling, shining on a large altar in the center of the circular room. On the floor surrounding the altar were masses of jewels, coins, and other treasures of the dead city. The jewels did not gleam. The gold did not glitter. The dim light illuminated nothing, nothing except a black dragon perched on top of the pedestal like some huge beast of prey.

"Feeling betrayed?" the dragon asked in conversational tones.

"The mage betrayed us! Where is he? Serving you?" Sturm cried fiercely, drawing his sword and taking a step forward.

"Stand back, foul Knight of Solamnia. Stand back or your magic-user will use his magic no more!" The dragon snaked her great neck down and stared at them with gleaming red eyes. Then, slowly and delicately, she lifted one clawed foot. Lying beneath it, on the pedestal, was Raistlin.

"Raist!" Caramon roared and lunged for the altar.

"Stop, fool!" the dragon hissed. She rested one pointed claw lightly on the mage's abdomen. With a great effort, Raistlin moved his head to look at his brother with his strange golden eyes. He made a weak gesture and Caramon halted. Tanis saw something move on the floor beneath the altar. It was Bupu, huddled among the riches, too afraid even to whimper. The Staff of Magius lay next to her.

"Move one step closer and I will impale this shriveled human upon the altar with my claw."

Caramon's face flushed a deep, ugly red. "Let him go!" he shouted. "Your fight is with me."

"My fight is with none of you," the dragon said, lazily moving its wings. Raistlin flinched as the dragon's clawed foot shifted slightly, teasingly, digging her claw into his flesh. The mage's metallic skin glistened with sweat. He drew a deep, ragged breath. "Don't even twitch, mage," the dragon sneered. "We speak the same language, remember? One word of a spell and your friends' carcasses will be used to feed the gully dwarves!"

241

Raistlin's eyes closed as in exhaustion. But Tanis could see the mage's hands clench and unclench, and he knew Raistlin was preparing one final spell. It would be his last—by the time he cast it the dragon would kill him. But it might give Riverwind a chance to reach the Disks and get out alive with Goldmoon. Tanis edged toward the Plainsman.

"As I was saying," the dragon continued smoothly. "I do not choose to fight any of you. How you have escaped my wrath so far, I do not understand. Still, you are here. And you return to me that which was stolen. Yes, Lady of Que-shu, I see you hold the blue crystal staff. Bring it to me."

Tanis hissed one word to Goldmoon—"Stall!" But, looking at her cool marble face, he wondered if she heard him or if she even heard the dragon. She seemed to be listening to other words, other voices.

"Obey me." The dragon lowered her head menacingly. "Obey me or the mage dies. And after him—the knight. And then the half-elf. And so on—one after the other, until you, Lady of Que-shu, are the last survivor. Then you will bring me the staff and you will beg me to be merciful."

Goldmoon bowed her head in submission. Gently pushing Riverwind away with her hand, she turned to Tanis and clasped the half-elf in a loving embrace. "Farewell, my friend," she said loudly, laying her cheek against his. Her voice dropped to a whisper. "I know what I must do. I am going to take the staff to the dragon and—"

"No!" Tanis said fiercely. "It won't matter. The dragon intends to kill us anyway."

"Listen to me!" Goldmoon's nails dug into Tanis's arm. "Stay with Riverwind, Tanis. Do not let him try to stop me."

"And if I tried to stop you?" Tanis asked gently, holding Goldmoon close in his arms.

"You won't," she said with a sweet, sad smile. "You know that each of us has a destiny to fulfill, as the Forestmaster said. Riverwind will need you. Farewell, my friend."

Goldmoon stepped back, her clear blue eyes on Riverwind as though she would memorize every detail to keep with her throughout eternity. Realizing she was saying good-bye, he started to go to her.

"Riverwind," Tanis said softly. "Trust her. She trusted you, all those years. She waited while you fought the battles. Now it is you who must wait. This is her battle."

Riverwind trembled, then stood still. Tanis could see the veins swell in his neck, his jaw muscles clench. The half-elf gripped the Plainsman's arm. The tall man didn't even look at him. His eyes were on Goldmoon.

"What is this delay?" the dragon asked. "I grow bored. Come forward."

Goldmoon turned away from Riverwind. She walked past Flint and Tasslehoff. The dwarf bowed his head. Tas watched wide-eyed and solemn. Somehow this wasn't as exciting as he had imagined. For the first time in his life, the kender felt small and helpless and alone. It was a horrible, unpleasant feeling, and he thought death might be preferable.

Goldmoon stopped near Caramon, put her hand on his arm. "Don't worry," she said to the big warrior, who was staring at his brother in agony, "he'll be all right." Caramon choked and nodded. And then Goldmoon neared Sturm. Suddenly, as if the horror of the dragon was too overwhelming, she slumped forward. The knight caught her and held her.

"Come with me, Sturm," Goldmoon whispered as he put his arm around her. "You must vow to do as I command, no matter what happens. Vow on your honor as a knight of Solamnia."

Sturm hesitated. Goldmoon's eyes, calm and clear, met his. "Vow," she demanded, "or I go alone."

"I vow, lady," he said reverently. "I will obey."

Goldmoon sighed thankfully. "Walk with me. Make no threatening gesture."

Together the barbarian woman of the Plains and the knight walked toward the dragon.

Raistlin lay beneath the dragon's claw, his eyes closed, preparing himself mentally for the spell that would be his last. But the words to the spell would not form out of the turmoil in his mind. He fought to regain control.

I am wasting myself—and for what? Raistlin wondered bitterly. To get these fools out of the mess they got themselves into. They will not attack for fear of hurting me—even though they fear and despise me. It makes no sense—just as my sacrifice makes no sense. Why am I dying for them when I deserve to live more than they?

It is not for them you do this, a voice answered him. Raistlin started, trying to concentrate, to catch hold of the voice. It was a real voice, a familiar voice, but he couldn't remember whose it was or where he had heard it. All he knew was that it spoke to him in moments of great stress. The closer to death he came, the louder was the voice.

It is not for them that you make this sacrifice, the voice repeated. *It is because you cannot bear defeat! Nothing has ever defeated you, not even death itself. . . .*

Raistlin drew a deep breath and relaxed. He did not understand the words completely, just as he could not remember the voice. But now the spell came easily to his mind. "*Astol arakhkh um—*" he murmured, feeling the magic begin to course through his frail body. Then another voice broke his concentration and this voice was a living voice speaking to his mind. He opened his eyes, turned his head slowly, and stared into the chamber at his companions.

The voice came from the woman—barbarian princess of a dead tribe. Raistlin looked at Goldmoon as she walked toward him, leaning on Sturm's arm. The words in her mind had touched Raistlin's mind. He regarded the woman coldly, detachedly. His distorted vision had forever killed any physical desire the mage might have felt when he looked upon human flesh. He could not see the beauty that so captivated Tanis and his brother. His hourglass eyes saw her withering and dying. He felt no closeness, no compassion for her. He knew she pitied him—and he hated her for that—but she feared him as well. So why, then, was she speaking to him?

She was telling him to wait.

Raistlin understood. She knew what he intended and she was telling him it wasn't necessary. She had been chosen. She was the one who was going to make the sacrifice.

He watched Goldmoon with his strange golden eyes as she drew nearer and nearer, her own eyes on the dragon. He saw Sturm moving solemnly beside her, looking as ancient and noble as old Huma himself. What a perfect cat's paw Sturm made, the ideal participant in Goldmoon's sacrifice. But why had Riverwind allowed her to go? Couldn't he see this coming? Raistlin glanced quickly at Riverwind. Ah, of course! The half-elf stood by his side, looking pained and grieved, dropping words of wisdom like blood, no doubt. The barbarian was becoming as gullible as Caramon. Raistlin flicked his eyes back to Goldmoon.

She stood before the dragon now, her face pale with resolve. Next to her, Sturm appeared grave and tortured, gnawed by inner conflict. Goldmoon had probably extracted some vow of strict obedience which the knight was honorbound to fulfill. Raistlin's lip curled in a sneer.

The dragon spoke and the mage tensed, ready for action. "Lay the staff down with the other remnants of mankind's folly," the dragon commanded Goldmoon, inclining her shining, scaled head toward the pile of treasure below the altar.

Goldmoon, overcome with dragonfear, did not move. She could do nothing but stare at the monstrous creature, trembling. Sturm, next to her, searched the treasure trove with his eyes, looking for the Disks of Mishakal, fighting to control his fear of the dragon. Sturm had not known he could be this frightened of anything. He repeated the code, "Honor is Life," over and over, and he knew it was pride alone that kept him from running away.

Goldmoon saw Sturm's hand shake, she saw the knight's face glistening with sweat. Dear goddess, she cried in her soul, grant me courage! Then Sturm nudged her. She had to say something, she realized. She had been silent too long.

"What will you give us in return for the miraculous staff?" Goldmoon asked, forcing herself to speak calmly, though her throat was parched and her tongue felt swollen.

The dragon laughed—shrill, ugly laughter. "What will I give you?" The dragon snaked her head to stare at Goldmoon. "Nothing! Nothing at all. I do not deal with thieves. Still—" The dragon reared its head back, its red eyes closed to slits. Playfully she dug her claw into Raistlin's flesh; the mage flinched, but he bore the pain without a murmur. The dragon removed the claw and held it just high enough so that they could all see the blood drip from it. "It is not inconceivable that Lord Verminaard—the Dragon Highmaster—may view favorably the fact that you surrender the staff. He may even be inclined to mercy—he is a cleric and they have strange values. But know this, Lady of Que-shu, Lord Verminaard does not need your friends. Give up the staff now and they will be spared. Force me to take it—and they will die. The mage first of all!"

Goldmoon, her spirit seemingly broken, slumped in defeat. Sturm moved close to her, appearing to console her.

"I have found the Disks," he whispered harshly. He grasped her arm, feeling her shivering with fear. "Are you resolved on this course of action, my lady?" he asked softly.

Goldmoon bowed her head. She was deathly pale but composed and calm. Tendrils of her fine silver-golden hair had escaped from the binding and fell around her face, hiding her expression from the dragon. Though she appeared defeated, she looked up at Sturm and smiled. There was both peace and sorrow in her smile, much like the smile on the marble goddess. She did not speak but Sturm had his answer. He bowed in submission.

"May my courage be equal to yours, lady" he said. "I will not fail you."

"Farewell, knight. Tell Riverwind—" Goldmoon faltered, blinking her eyes as tears filled them. Fearing her resolve might yet break, she swallowed her words and turned to face the dragon as the voice of Mishakal filled her being, answering her prayer. *Present the staff boldly!* Goldmoon, imbued with an inner strength, raised the blue crystal staff.

"We do not choose to surrender!" Goldmoon shouted, her voice echoing throughout the chamber. Moving swiftly, before the startled dragon could react, Chieftain's Daughter swung her staff one last time, striking the clawed foot poised above Raistlin.

The staff made a low ringing sound as it struck the dragon—then it shattered. A burst of pure, radiant blue light beamed from the broken staff. The light grew brighter, spreading out in concentric waves, engulfing the dragon.

Khisanth screamed in rage. The dragon was injured, terribly, mortally. She lashed out with her tail, flung her head about, and fought to escape the burning blue flame. She wanted nothing except to kill those that dared inflict such pain, but the intense blue fire relentlessly consumed her—as it consumed Goldmoon.

The Chieftain's Daughter had not dropped the staff when it shattered. She held on to the fragmented end, watching as the light grew, keeping it as close to the dragon as she could. When the blue light touched her hands she felt intense, burning pain. Staggering, she fell to her knees, still clutching the staff. She heard the dragon shrieking and roaring above her, then she could hear nothing but the ringing of the staff. The pain grew so horrible it was no longer a part of her, and she was overcome with a great weariness. I will sleep, she thought. I will sleep and when I waken, I will be where I truly belong. . . .

Sturm saw the blue light slowly destroy the dragon, then it spread along the staff to Goldmoon. He heard the ringing sound grow louder and louder until it drowned out even the screams of the dying dragon. Sturm took a step toward Goldmoon, thinking to wrench the splintered staff from her hand and drag her clear of the deadly blue flame . . . but even as he approached, he knew he could not save her.

Half-blinded by the light and deafened by the sound, the knight realized that it would take all his strength and courage to fulfill his oath—to retrieve the Disks. He tore his gaze from Goldmoon, whose face was twisted in agony and whose flesh was withering in the fire. Gritting his teeth against the pain in his head, he staggered toward the treasure pile where he had seen the Disks—hundreds of thin sheets of platinum bound together by a single ring through the top. Reaching down, he lifted them, amazed at their lightness. Then his heart almost stopped beating when a bloody hand reached up from the pile of treasure and grasped his wrist.

"Help me!"

He could not hear the voice so much as sense the thought. Grasping Raistlin's hand, he pulled the mage to his feet. Blood was visible through the red of Raistlin's robe, but he did not appear to be seriously injured—at least he could stand. But could he walk? Sturm needed help. He wondered where the others were; he couldn't see them in the brilliance. Suddenly Caramon loomed up by his side, his armor gleaming in the blue flame.

Raistlin clutched at him. "Help me find the spellbook!" he hissed.

"Who cares about that?" Caramon roared, reaching for his brother. "I'll get you out of here!"

Raistlin's mouth twisted so in fury and frustration that he could not speak. He dropped to his knees and began to search frantically through the pile of treasure. Caramon tried to draw him away, but Raistlin shoved him back with his frail hand.

And still the ringing sound pierced their ears. Sturm felt tears of pain trickle down his cheeks. Suddenly something crashed to the floor in front of the knight. The chamber ceiling was collapsing! The entire building shook around them, the ringing sound causing the pillars to tremble and the walls to crack.

Then the ringing died—and with it the dragon. Khisanth had vanished, leaving behind nothing but a pile of smoldering ash.

Sturm gasped in relief but not for long. As soon as the ringing sound ended, he could hear the sounds of the palace caving in, the cracking of the ceiling and the thuds and explosive crashes as huge stone slabs struck the floor. Then, out of the dust and noise, Tanis appeared before him. Blood trickled from a cut on the half-elf's cheek. Sturm grabbed his friend and pulled him to the altar as another chunk of ceiling plummeted near them.

"The whole city is collapsing!" Sturm yelled. "How do we get out?"

Tanis shook his head. "The only way I know is back the way we came, through that tunnel," he shouted. He ducked as another piece of ceiling crashed onto the empty altar.

"That'll be a death trap! There must be another way!"

"We'll find it," Tanis said firmly. He peered through the billowing dust. "Where are the others?" he asked. Then, turning, he saw Raistlin and Caramon. Tanis stared in horror and disgust at the mage scavenging among the treasure. Then he saw a small figure tugging Raistlin's sleeve. Bupu! Tanis made a lunge for her, nearly scaring the gully dwarf witless. She shrank back against Raistlin with a startled scream.

"We've got to get out of here!" Tanis roared. He grabbed hold of Raistlin's robes and dragged the slender young man to his feet. "Stop looting and get that gully dwarf of yours to show us the way out, or so help me, you'll die by my hands!"

Raistlin's thin lips parted in a ghastly smile as Tanis flung him back against the altar. Bupu shrieked. "Come! We go! I know way!"

"Raist," Caramon begged, "you can't find it! You'll die if we don't get out of here!"

"Very well," the mage snarled. He lifted the Staff of Magius from the altar and stood up, reaching out his arm for his brother's aid. "Bupu, show us the way," he commanded.

"Raistlin, light your staff so we can follow you." Tanis ordered. "I'm going to find the others."

"Over there," Caramon said grimly. "You're going to need help with the Plainsman."

Tanis flung his arm over his face as more stone fell, then jumped across the rubble. He found Riverwind collapsed where Goldmoon had been standing, Flint and Tasslehoff trying to get the Plainsman to his feet. There was nothing there now except a large area of blackened stone. Goldmoon had been totally consumed in the flames.

"Is he alive?" Tanis shouted.

"Yes!" Tas answered, his voice carrying shrilly above the noise. "But he won't move!"

"I'll talk to him," Tanis said. "Follow the others. We'll be there in a moment. Go on!"

Tasslehoff hesitated, but Flint, after a glance at Tanis's face, put his hand on the kender's arm. Snuffling, Tas turned and began running through the rubble with the dwarf.

Tanis knelt beside Riverwind, then the half-elf glanced up as Sturm appeared out of the gloom. "Go on," Tanis said. "You're in command now."

Sturm hesitated. A column toppled over near them, showering them in rock dust. Tanis flung his body across Riverwind's. "Go on!" he yelled at Sturm. "I'm holding you responsible!" Sturm drew a breath, laid a hand on Tanis's shoulder, then ran toward the light from Raistlin's staff.

The knight found the others huddled in a narrow hallway. The arched ceiling above them seemed to be holding together, but Sturm could hear thudding sounds above. The ground shook beneath their feet and little rivulets of water were beginning to seep through new cracks in the walls.

"Where's Tanis?" Caramon asked.

"He'll be along," Sturm said harshly. "We'll wait . . . a few moments at least." He did not mention that he would wait until waiting had dissolved into death.

There was a shattering crack. Water began to gush through the wall, flooding the floor. Sturm was about to order the others out when a figure emerged from the collapsing doorway. It was Riverwind, carrying Tanis's inert body in his arms.

"What happened? " Sturm leaped forward, his throat constricting. "He's not—"

"He stayed with me," Riverwind said softly. "I told him to leave me. I wanted to die—there with her. Then—a slab of stone. He never saw it—"

"I'll carry him," Caramon said.

"No!" Riverwind glared at the big warrior. His arms gripped Tanis's body tighter. "I will carry him. We must go."

"Yes! This way! We go now!" urged the gully dwarf. She led them out of the city that was dying a second time. They emerged from the dragon's lair into the plaza, which was rapidly being submerged as Newsea poured into the crumbling cavern. The companions waded across, holding onto each other to keep from being swept away in the vicious current. Howling gully dwarves swarmed everywhere in a state of wild confusion, some getting caught in the current, others climbing up into the top stories of shaking buildings, still others dashing down the streets.

Sturm could think of only one way out. "Go east!" he shouted, gesturing down the broad street that led to the waterfall. He looked anxiously at Riverwind. The dazed Plainsman seemed oblivious to the commotion around him. Tanis was unconscious—maybe dead. Fear chilled Sturm's blood, but he forcibly suppressed all emotions. The knight ran ahead, catching up with the twins.

"Our only chance is the lift!" he yelled.

Caramon nodded slowly. "It will mean a fight."

"Yes, damn it!" said Sturm in exasperation, envisioning all of the draconians trying to leave this stricken city. "It *will* mean a fight! You got any better ideas?"

Caramon shook his head.

At a corner, Sturm waited to herd his limping, exhausted band in the right direction. Peering through the dust and mist, he could see the lift ahead of them. It was, as he had foreseen, surrounded by a dark, writhing mass of draconians. Fortunately, they were all intent on escape. They had to strike quickly, Sturm knew, to catch the creatures off guard. Timing was critical. He caught hold of the kender as Tas scurried past.

"Tas!" he yelled. "We're going up the lift!"

Tasslehoff nodded to show he understood, then made a face to imitate a draconian and slashed his hand across his throat.

"When we get near," Sturm shouted—"sneak around to where you can see the pot descending. When it starts to come down, signal me. We'll attack when it reaches the ground."

Tasslehoff's topknot bobbed.

"Tell Flint!" Sturm finished, his voice nearly gone from shouting. Tas nodded again and raced off to find the dwarf. Sturm straightened his aching back with a sigh and continued on down the street. He could see about twenty or twenty-five draconians gathered in the courtyard, watching for the pot that would carry them to safety to begin its descent. Sturm imagined the confusion up on the top—draconians whipping and bullying the panic-stricken gully dwarves, forcing them into the lift. He hoped the confusion would last.

Sturm saw the brothers in the shadows at the edge of the courtyard. He joined them, glancing up nervously as a stone slab crashed down behind him. As Riverwind staggered out of the mist and dust, Sturm started to help him, but the Plainsman looked at the knight as if he had never seen him before in his life.

"Bring Tanis over here," Sturm said. "You can lay him down and rest a moment. We're going up in the lift and we'll have a fight on our hands. Wait here. When we signal—"

"Do what you must," Riverwind interrupted coldly. He laid Tanis's body gently on the ground and slumped down beside him, burying his face in his hands.

Sturm hesitated. He started to kneel down by Tanis as Flint came to stand by his side.

"Go on. I'll check on him," the dwarf offered.

Sturm nodded thankfully. He saw Tasslehoff skitter across the courtyard and into a doorway. Looking toward the lift, he saw the draconians yelling and cursing into the mist as if they could hurry the pot's descent.

Flint poked Sturm in the ribs. "How are we going to fight all of them?" he shouted.

"We're not. You're going to stay here with Riverwind and Tanis," Sturm said. "Caramon and I can handle this," he added, wishing he believed it himself.

"And I," whispered the mage. "I still have my spells." The knight did not answer. He distrusted magic and he distrusted Raistlin. Still, he had no choice—Caramon would not go into battle without his brother by his side. Tugging at his moustaches, Sturm restlessly loosened his sword. Caramon flexed his arms, clenching and unclenching his huge hands. Raistlin, his eyes closed, was lost in concentration. Bupu, hidden in a niche in the wall behind him, watched everything with wide, frightened eyes.

The pot swung into view, gully dwarves hanging from its sides. As Sturm hoped, the draconians on the ground began to fight among themselves, none wanting to be left behind. Their panic increased as great cracks ran through the pavement toward them. Water rose through the cracks. The city of Xak Tsaroth would soon be lying at the bottom of Newsea.

As the pot touched ground, the gully dwarves scurried over the sides and fled. The draconians clambered in, hitting and shoving each other.

"Now!" the knight yelled.

"Get out of my way!" the mage hissed. Pulling a handful of sand from one of his pouches, he sprinkled it on the ground and whispered, *"Ast tasark sinuralan krynaw,"* moving his right hand in an arc in the direction of the draconians. First one, then a few more blinked their eyes and slumped to the ground in sleep, but others remained standing, glancing around in alarm. The mage ducked back into the doorway and, seeing nothing, the draconians turned back to the lift, stepping on the bodies of their sleeping comrades in their frantic rush. Raistlin leaned against the wall, closing his eyes wearily.

"How many?" he asked.

"Only about six." Caramon drew his sword from its sheath.

"Just get in the damn pot!" Sturm yelled. "We'll come back for Tanis when the fight's ended."

Under cover of the mist, the two warriors—swords drawn—covered the distance to the draconians within a few heartbeats,

Raistlin stumbling behind. Sturm shouted his battle cry. At the sound, the draconians spun around in alarm.

And Riverwind raised his head.

The sound of battle penetrated Riverwind's fog of despair. The Plainsman saw Goldmoon before him, dying in the blue flame. The dead expression left his face, replaced by a ferocity so bestial and terrifying that Bupu, still hiding in the doorway, screamed in alarm. Riverwind leaped to his feet. He didn't even draw his sword but charged forward, empty-handed. He tore into the ranks of the scrambling draconians like a starving panther and began to kill. He killed with his bare hands, twisting, choking, gouging. Draconians stabbed at him with their swords; soon his leather tunic was soaked with blood. Yet he never stopped moving among them, never stopped killing. His face was that of a madman. The draconians in Riverwind's path saw death in his eyes, and they also saw that their weapons had no effect. One broke and ran and, soon, another.

Sturm, finishing an opponent, looked up grimly, prepared to find six more coming at him. Instead he saw the enemy fleeing for their lives into the mist. Riverwind, covered with blood, collapsed onto the ground.

"The lift!" The mage pointed. It was hovering about two feet off the ground and starting to move upward. There were gully dwarves in the top pot coming down.

"Stop it!" Sturm yelled. Tasslehoff raced from his hiding place and leaped for the edge. He clung, his feet dangling, trying desperately to keep the empty pot from rising. "Caramon! Hang onto it!" Sturm ordered the warrior. "I'll get Tanis!"

"I can hold it, but not for long." The big man grunted, grasping onto the edge and digging his feet into the ground. He dragged the lift to a halt. Tasslehoff climbed inside, hoping his small body might add ballast.

Sturm ran back swiftly to Tanis. Flint was beside him, his axe in his hands.

"He's alive!" the dwarf called as the knight approached.

Sturm paused a moment to thank some god, somewhere, then he and Flint lifted the unconscious half-elf and carried him to the pot. They placed him inside, then returned for

Riverwind. It took four of them to get Riverwind's bloody body into the lift. Tas tried without much success to stanch the wounds with one of his handkerchiefs.

"Hurry!" Caramon gasped. Despite all his efforts, the pot was rising slowly.

"Get in!" Sturm ordered Raistlin.

The mage glanced at him coldly and ran back into the mist. Within moments, he reappeared, carrying Bupu in his arms. The knight grabbed the trembling gully dwarf and flung her into the lift. Bupu, whimpering, crouched on the bottom, still clutching her bag to her chest. Raistlin climbed over the side. The pot continued to rise; Caramon's arms were nearly pulled out of their sockets.

"Go on," Sturm ordered Caramon, the knight being the last to leave the field of battle as usual. Caramon knew better than to argue. He heaved himself up, nearly tipping the pot over. Flint and Raistlin dragged him in. Without Caramon holding it, the pot lunged upward rapidly. Sturm caught hold of it with both hands and clung to the side as it rose into the air. After two or three tries, he managed to swing a leg over the edge and climbed in with Caramon's help.

The knight knelt down beside Tanis and was relieved beyond expression to see the half-elf stir and moan. Sturm grasped the half-elf and held him close. "You have no idea how glad I am you're back!" the knight said, his voice husky.

"Riverwind—" Tanis murmured groggily.

"He's here. He saved your life. He saved all our lives." Sturm talked rapidly, almost incoherently. "We're in the lift, going up. The city's destroyed. Where are you hurt?"

"Broken ribs, feels like." Wincing in pain, Tanis looked over at Riverwind, still conscious, despite his wounds. "Poor man," Tanis said softly. "Goldmoon. I saw her die, Sturm. There was nothing I could do."

Sturm helped the half-elf rise to his feet. "We have the Disks," the knight said firmly. "It was what she wanted, what she fought for. They're in my pack. Are you sure you can stand?"

"Yes," Tanis said. He drew a ragged, painful breath. "We have the Disks, whatever good that will do us."

They were interrupted by the shrill screams as the second pot, gully dwarves flying like banners, went past them. The gully dwarves shook their fists and cursed the companions. Bupu laughed, then she stood up, looking at Raistlin in concern. The mage leaned wearily against the side of the pot, his lips moving silently, calling to mind another spell.

Sturm peered up through the mist. "I wonder how many will be at the top?" he asked.

Tanis, too, glanced up. "Most have fled, I hope," he said. He caught his breath sharply and clutched at his ribs.

There was a sudden lurch. The pot fell about a foot, stopped with a jolt, then slowly started to rise again. The companions looked at each other in alarm.

"The mechanism—"

"It's either starting to collapse or the draconians have recognized us and are trying to destroy it," Tanis said.

"There's nothing we can do," Sturm said in bitter frustration. He stared down at the pack containing the Disks, which lay at his feet. "Except pray to these gods—"

The pot lurched and dropped again. For a moment it hung, suspended, swaying in the mist-shrouded air. Then it started up, moving slowly, shuddering. The companions could see the edge of the rock ledge and the opening above them. The pot rose inch by creaking inch, each of those inside mentally supporting every link of the chain that was carrying them up to—

"Draconians!" cried Tas shrilly, pointing up.

Two draconians stared down at them. As the pot crept closer and closer, Tanis saw the draconians crouch, ready to jump.

"They're going to leap down here! The pot won't hold!" Flint rumbled. "We'll crash!"

"That may be their intent," Tanis said. "They have wings."

"Stand back," Raistlin said, staggering to his feet.

"Raist, don't!" His brother caught hold of him. "You're too weak."

"I have strength for one more spell," the mage whispered. "But it may not work. If they see I am magi, they may be able to resist my magic."

"Hide behind Caramon's shield," Tanis said swiftly. The big man thrust his body and his shield in front of his brother.

The mist swirled around them, concealing them from draconian eyes but also preventing them from seeing the draconians.

The pot rose, inch by inch, the chain creaking and lurching upward. Raistlin stood poised behind Caramon's shield, his strange eyes staring, waiting for the mists to part.

Cool air touched Tanis's cheek. A breeze swirled the mists apart, just for an instant. The draconians were so close they could have almost touched them! The draconians saw them at the same time. One spread its wings and floated down toward the pot, sword in hand, shrieking in triumph.

Raistlin spoke. Caramon moved his shield and the mage spread his thin fingers. A ball of white shot from his hands, hitting the draconian squarely in the chest. The ball exploded, covering the creature in sticky webbing. Its cry of triumph changed to a horrifying shriek as the webbing tangled its wings. It plummeted into the mist, its body striking the edge of the iron pot as it fell. The pot began to rock and sway.

"There's still one more!" Raistlin gasped, sinking to his knees. "Hold me up, Caramon, help me stand. The mage began to cough violently, blood trickling from his mouth.

"Raist!" his brother pleaded, dropping his shield and catching his fainting twin. "Stop! There's nothing you can do. You'll kill yourself!"

A look of command was enough. The warrior supported his brother as the mage began to speak again the eerie-sounding language of magic.

The remaining draconian hesitated, still hearing the yells of its fallen companion. It knew the human was a magic-user. It also knew that it could probably resist the magic. But this human facing it was like no human magic-user it had ever encountered. The human's body seemed weak practically to the point of death, but a strong aura of power surrounded him.

The mage raised his hand, pointing at the creature. The draconian cast one last, vicious glance at the companions, then turned and fled. Raistlin, unconscious, sank into his brother's arms as the pot completed its journey to the surface.

22

Bupu's Gift. An Ominous Sight.

ust as they pulled Riverwind out of the lift, a sharp tremor shook the floor of the Hall of the Ancestors. The companions, dragging Riverwind with them, scrambled back as the floor cracked. The floor gave way and tumbled down, carrying the great wheel and the iron pots down into the mist below.

"This whole place is caving in!" Caramon shouted in alarm, holding his brother in his arms.

"Run! Back to the Temple of Mishakal." Tanis gasped with pain.

"Trusting in the gods again, huh?" Flint said. Tanis could not answer.

Sturm took hold of Riverwind's arms and started to lift him, but the Plainsman shook his head and shoved him away. "My wounds are not serious. I can manage. Leave me." He remained slumped on the shattered floor. Tanis glanced questioningly at Sturm. The knight shrugged. The Solamnic Knights considered suicide noble and honorable. The elves considered it blasphemy.

The half-elf took hold of the Plainsman's long dark hair and jerked his head back so that the startled man was forced to look into Tanis's eyes. "Go ahead. Lie down and die!" Tanis said through clenched teeth. "Shame your chieftain! She at least had the courage to fight!"

Riverwind's eyes smoldered. He caught hold of Tanis's wrist and flung the half-elf away from him with such force that Tanis staggered into the wall, groaning in agony. The Plainsman stood up, staring at Tanis with hatred. Then he turned and stumbled down the shaking corridor, his head bent.

Sturm helped Tanis to his feet, the half-elf dizzy from the pain. They followed the others as fast as they could. The floor tilted crazily. When Sturm slipped, they crashed against a wall. A sarcophagus slid out into the hallway, spilling its grisly contents. A skull rolled over by Tanis's feet, startling the half-elf who fell to his knees. He feared he might faint from the pain.

"Go," he tried to say to Sturm, but he couldn't talk. The knight picked him up and together they staggered on through the dust-choked corridor. At the foot of the stairs called the Paths of the Dead, they found Tasslehoff waiting.

"The others?" Sturm gasped, coughing in the dust.

"They've already gone up to the temple," Tasslehoff said. "Caramon told me to wait here for you. Flint says the temple's safe, dwarven stonework, you know. Raistlin's conscious. He said it was safe, too. Something about being held in the palm of the goddess. Riverwind's there. He glared at me. I think he could have killed me! But he made it up the stairs—"

"All right!" Tanis said to stop the prattling. "Enough! Put me down, Sturm. I've got to rest a minute or I'll pass out. Take Tas and I'll meet you upstairs. Go on, damn it!"

Sturm grabbed Tasslehoff by the collar and dragged him upstairs. Tanis sank back. Sweat chilled his body; every breath was agony. Suddenly the remainder of the floor in the Hall of the Ancestors collapsed with a loud snapping noise. The Temple of Mishakal trembled and shook. Tanis staggered to his feet, then he paused a moment. Faintly, behind him, he could now hear the low, thundering rumble of water surging. Newsea had claimed Xak Tsaroth. The city that was dead was now buried.

Tanis emerged slowly from the stairwell into the circular room at the top. The climb had been a nightmare, each new step a miracle. The chamber was blessedly quiet, the only sound the harsh breathing of his friends who had made it that far and collapsed. He, too, could go no farther.

The half-elf glanced around to make certain the others were all right. Sturm had set down the pack containing the Disks and was slumped against a wall. Raistlin lay on a bench, his eyes closed, his breathing quick and shallow. Of course, Caramon sat beside him, his face dark with anxiety. Tasslehoff sat at the bottom of the pedestal, staring up at the top. Flint leaned against the doors, too tired to grumble.

"Where's Riverwind?" Tanis asked. He saw Caramon and Sturm exchange glances, then lower their eyes. Tanis staggered up, anger defeating his pain. Sturm rose and blocked his path.

"It's his decision, Tanis. It is the way of his people as it is the way of mine."

Tanis shoved the knight aside and walked toward the double doors. Flint did not move.

"Get out of my way," the half-elf said, his voice shaking. Flint looked up; the lines of grief and sorrow etched by a hundred years softened the dwarf's scowling expression. Tanis saw in Flint's eyes the accumulated wisdom that had drawn an unhappy half-human, half-elven boy into a strange and lasting friendship with a dwarf.

"Sit down, lad," Flint said in a gentle voice, as if he, too, remembered their origins. "If your elven head cannot understand, then listen to your human heart for once."

Tanis shut his eyes, tears stinging his lids. Then he heard a great cry from inside the temple—Riverwind. Tanis thrust the dwarf aside and pushed open the huge golden doors. Striding rapidly, ignoring his pain, he threw open the second set of doors and entered the chamber of Mishakal. Once again he felt peace and tranquillity flood over him, but now the feelings only added to his anger over what had happened.

"I cannot believe in you!" Tanis cried. "What kind of gods are you, that you demand a human sacrifice? You are the same gods who brought the Cataclysm down on man. All right—so you're powerful! Now leave us alone! We don't need you!" The half-elf wept. Through his tears, he could see that Riverwind, sword in hand, knelt before the statue. Tanis stumbled forward, hoping to prevent the act of self-destruction. Tanis rounded the base of the statue and stopped, stunned. For a minute he refused to believe his own sense of sight; perhaps grief and pain were playing tricks on his mind. He lifted his eyes to the statue's beautiful, calm face and steadied his reeling, confused senses. Then he looked again.

Goldmoon lay there, sound asleep, her breast rising and falling with the rhythm of her quiet breathing. Her silver-gold hair had come loose from its braid and drifted around her face in the gentle wind that filled the chamber with the fragrance of spring. The staff was once again part of the marble statue, but Tanis saw that Goldmoon wore around her throat the necklace that had once adorned the statue.

"I am a true cleric now," Goldmoon said softly. "I am a disciple of Mishakal and, though I have much to learn, I have the power of my faith. Above all else, I am a healer. I bring the gift of healing back into the land."

Reaching out her hand, Goldmoon touched Tanis on the forehead, whispering a prayer to Mishakal. The half-elf felt peace and strength flow through his body, cleansing his spirit and healing his wounds.

"We've got a cleric, now," Flint said, "and that'll come in handy. But from what we hear, this Lord Verminaard's a cleric, too, and a powerful one at that. We may have found the ancient gods of good, but he found the ancient gods of evil a lot sooner. I don't see how these Disks are going to help much against hordes of dragons."

"You are right," Goldmoon said softly. "I am not a warrior. I am a healer. I do not have the power to unite the peoples of our world to fight this evil and restore the balance. My duty is to *find* the person who has the strength and the wisdom for this task. I am to give the Disks of Mishakal to that person."

The companions were silent for long moments. Then . . .

"We must leave here, Tanis," Raistlin hissed from out of the shadows of the Temple where he stood, staring out the door into the courtyard. "Listen."

Horns. They could all hear the shrill braying of many, many horns, carried on the north wind.

"The armies," said Tanis softly. "War has begun."

The companions fled Xak Tsaroth into the twilight. They traveled west, toward the mountains. The air was cold with the bite of early winter. Dead leaves, blown by chill winds, flew past their faces. They decided to head for Solace, planning to stock up on supplies and gather what information they could before determining where to go in their search for a leader. Tanis could foresee arguments along those lines. Already Sturm was talking of Solamnia. Goldmoon mentioned Haven, while Tanis himself was thinking the Disks of Mishakal would be safest in the elven kingdom.

Discussing vague plans, they traveled on well into the night. They saw no draconians and supposed that those escaping Xak Tsaroth had traveled north to join up with the armies of this Lord Verminaard, Dragon Highmaster. The silver moon rose, then the red. The companions climbed high, the sound of the horns driving them on past the point of exhaustion. They made camp on the summit of the mountain. After eating a cheerless supper, not daring to light a fire, they set the watch, then slept.

Raistlin woke in the cold gray hour before dawn. He had heard something. Had he been dreaming? No, there it was again—the sound of someone crying. Goldmoon, the mage thought irritably, and started to lie back down. Then he saw Bupu, curled in a ball of misery, blubbering into a blanket.

Raistlin glanced around. The others were asleep except for Flint standing watch on the other side of camp. The dwarf had apparently heard nothing, and he wasn't looking in Raistlin's direction. The mage stood up and padded softly over. Kneeling down beside the gully dwarf, he laid his hand on her shoulder.

"What is it, little one?"

Bupu rolled over to face him. Her eyes were red, her nose swollen. Tears streaked down her dirty face. She snuffled and wiped her hand across her nose. "I don't want to leave you. I want to go with you," she said brokenly, "but—oh—I will miss my people!" Sobbing, she buried her face in her hands.

A look of infinite tenderness touched Raistlin's face, a look no one in his world would ever see. He reached out and stroked Bupu's coarse hair, knowing what it felt like to be weak and miserable, an object of ridicule and pity.

"Bupu," he said, "you have been a good and true friend to me. You saved my life and the lives of those I care about. Now you will do one last thing for me, little one. Go back. I must travel roads that will be dark and dangerous before the end of my long journey. I cannot ask you to go with me."

Bupu lifted her head, her eyes brightening. Then a shadow fell across her face. "But you will be unhappy without me."

"No," Raistlin said, smiling, "my happiness will lie in knowing you are back with your people."

"You sure?" Bupu asked anxiously.

"I am sure," Raistlin answered.

"Then I go." Bupu stood up. "But first, you take gift." She began to rummage around in her bag.

"No, little one," Raistlin began, remembering the dead lizard, "that's not necessary—" The words caught in his throat as he watched Bupu pull from her bag—a book! He stared in amazement, seeing the pale light of the chill morning illuminate silver runes on a night-blue leather binding.

Raistlin reached out a trembling hand. "The spellbook of Fistandantilus!" he breathed.

"You like?" Bupu said shyly.

"Yes, little one!" Raistlin took the precious object in his hands and held it lovingly, stroking the leather. "Where—"

"I take from dragon," Bupu said, "when blue light shine. I glad you like. Now, I go. Find Highbulp Phudge I, the great." She slung her bag over her shoulder. Then she stopped and turned. "That cough, you sure you not want lizard cure?"

"No, thank you, little one," Raistlin said, rising.

Bupu looked at him sadly, then—greatly daring—she caught his hand in hers and kissed it swiftly. She turned away, her head bowed, sobbing bitterly.

Raistlin stepped forward. He laid his hand on her head. If I have any power at all, Great One, he said inside himself, power that has not yet been revealed to me, grant that this little one goes through her life in safety and happiness.

"Farewell, Bupu," he said softly.

She stared at him with wide, adoring eyes, then turned and ran off as fast as her floppy shoes would carry her.

"What was all that about?" Flint said, stumping over from the other side of the camp. "Oh," he added, seeing Bupu running off. "So you got rid of your pet gully dwarf."

Raistlin did not answer, but simply stared at Flint with a malevolence that made the dwarf shiver and walk hurriedly away.

The mage held the spellbook in his hands, admiring it. He longed to open it and revel in its treasures, but he knew that long weeks of study lay ahead of him before he could even read the new spells, much less acquire them. And with the spells would come more power! He sighed in ecstasy and hugged the book to his thin chest. Then he slipped it swiftly into his pack with his own spellbook. The others would be waking soon—let them wonder how he got the book.

Raistlin stood up, glancing out to the west, to his homeland, where the sky was brightening with the early morning sun. Suddenly he stiffened. Then, dropping his pack, he ran across the camp and knelt down beside the half-elf.

"Tanis!" Raistlin hissed. "Wake up!"

Tanis woke and grabbed his dagger. "What—"

Raistlin pointed to the west.

Tanis blinked, trying to focus his sleep-scummed eyes. The view from the top of the mountain where they were camped was magnificent. He could see the tall trees give way to the grassy Plains. And beyond the Plains, snaking up into the sky—

"No!" Tanis choked. He gripped the mage. "No, it can't be!"

"Yes," Raistlin whispered. "Solace is burning."

BOOK 2

I

Night of the Dragons.

ika wrung the rag out in the pail and watched, dully, as the water turned black. She threw the rag down on the bar and started to lift the bucket to carry it back to the kitchen to draw more water. Then she thought, why bother! Picking up the rag, she began to mop the tables again. When she thought Otik wasn't watching, she wiped her eyes with her apron.

But Otik was watching. His pudgy hands took hold of Tika's shoulders and gently turned her around. Tika gave a choking sob and laid her head on his shoulder.

"I'm sorry," Tika sobbed, "but I can't get this clean!"

Otik knew, of course, that this wasn't the real reason the girl was weeping, but it came close. He patted her back gently. "I know, I know, child. Don't cry. I understand."

"It's this damn soot!" Tika wailed. "It covers everything

with black and every day I scrub it up and the next day it's back. They keep burning and burning!"

"Don't worry about it, Tika," Otik said, stroking her hair. "Be thankful the Inn's in one piece—"

"Be thankful!" Tika pushed away from him, her face flushed. "No! I wish it had burned like everything else in Solace, then *they* wouldn't come in here! I wish it had burned! I wish it had burned!" Tika sank down at the table, sobbing uncontrollably. Otik hovered around her.

"I know, my dear, I know," he repeated, smoothing the puffy sleeves of the blouse Tika had taken such pride in keeping clean and white. Now it was dingy and covered with soot, like everything in the ravaged town.

The attack on Solace had come without warning. Even when the first pitiable refugees began to trickle into the town from the north, telling horror stories of huge, winged monsters, Hederick, the High Theocrat, assured the people of Solace that they were safe, their town would be spared. And the people believed him because they wanted to believe him.

And then came the night of the dragons.

The Inn was crowded that night, one of the few places people could go and not be reminded of the storm clouds hanging low in the northern skies. The fire burned brightly, the ale was rich, the spiced potatoes were delicious. Yet, even here, the outside world intruded: everyone talked loudly and fearfully of war.

Hederick's words soothed their fearful hearts.

"We are not like these reckless fools to the north who made the mistake of defying the might of the Dragon Highlords," he called out, standing on a chair to be heard. "Lord Verminaard has personally assured the Council of Highseekers in Haven that he wants only peace. He seeks permission to move his armies through our town so that he may conquer the elflands to the south. And I say more power to him!"

Hederick paused for scattered cheering and applause.

"We have tolerated the elves in Qualinesti too long. I say, let this Verminaard drive them back to Silvanost or wherever they came from! In fact"—Hederick warmed to his subject— "some of you young men might consider joining the armies of this great lord. And he is a great lord! I have met him! He is a true cleric! I have seen the miracles he has performed! We will enter a new age under his leadership! We will drive the elves, dwarves, and other foreigners from our land and—"

There came a low, dull, roaring sound, like the gathering of the waters of a mighty ocean. Silence fell abruptly. Everyone listened, puzzled, trying to figure out what might make such a noise. Hederick, aware that he had lost his audience, glanced around in irritation. The roaring sound grew louder and louder, coming closer. Suddenly the Inn was plunged into thick, smothering darkness. A few people screamed. Most ran for the windows, trying to peer out the few clear panes scattered among the colored glass.

"Go down and find out what's going on," someone said.

"It's so blasted dark I can't see the stairs," someone else muttered.

And then it was no longer dark.

Flames exploded outside the Inn. A wave of heat hit the building with force enough to shatter windows, showering those inside with glass. The mighty vallenwood tree—which no storm on Krynn had ever stirred—began to sway and rock from the blast. The Inn tilted. Tables scooted sideways; benches slid down the floor to slam up against the wall. Hederick lost his balance and tumbled off his chair. Hot coals spewed from the fireplace as oil lamps from the ceiling and candles from the tables started small fires.

A high-pitched shriek rose above the noise and confusion—the scream of some living creature—a scream filled with hatred and cruelty. The roaring noise passed over the Inn. There was a rush of wind, then the darkness lifted as a wall of flame sprang up to the south.

Tika dropped a tray of mugs to the floor as she grabbed desperately at the bar for support. People around her shouted and screamed, some in pain, some with terror.

Solace was burning.

A lurid orange glow lit the room. Clouds of black smoke rolled in through the broken windows. Smells of blazing wood filled Tika's nostrils, along with a more horrible smell, the smell of burned flesh. Tika choked and looked up to see small flames licking the great limbs of the vallenwood that held up the ceiling. Sounds of varnish sizzling and popping in the heat mingled with the screams of the injured.

"Douse those fires!" Otik was yelling wildly.

"The kitchen!" The cook screamed as she flew out of the swinging doors, her clothes smoldering, a solid wall of flame behind her. Tika grabbed a pitcher of ale from the bar and tossed it on the cook's dress and held her still to drench her clothes. Rhea sank into a chair, weeping hysterically.

"Get out! The whole place'll go up!" someone shouted.

Hederick, pushing past the injured, was one of the first to reach the door. He ran onto the Inn's front landing, then stopped, stunned, and gripped the rail for support. Staring northward, he saw the woods blazing and, by the ghastly light of the flames, he could see hundreds of marching creatures, the lurid firelight reflecting off their leathery wings. Draconian ground troops. He watched, horrified, as the front ranks poured into the city of Solace, knowing there must be thousands more behind them. And above them flew creatures out of the stories of children.

Dragons.

Five red dragons wheeled overhead in the flame-lit sky. First one, then another, dove down, incinerating parts of the small town with its fiery breath, casting the thick, magical darkness. It was impossible to fight them—warriors could not see well enough to aim their arrows or strike with their swords.

The rest of the night blurred in Tika's memory. She kept telling herself she must leave the burning Inn, yet the Inn was her home, she felt safe there, and so she stayed though the heat from the flaming kitchen grew so intense it hurt her lungs to breathe. Just when the flames spread to the common room, the kitchen crashed to the ground. Otik and the barmaids flung buckets of ale on the flames in the common room until, finally, the fire was extinguished.

Once the fire was out, Tika turned her attention to the wounded. Otik collapsed in a corner, shaking and sobbing. Tika sent one of the other barmaids to tend to him, while she began treating the injured. She worked for hours, resolutely refusing to look out of the windows, blocking from her mind the awful sounds of death and destruction outside.

Suddenly it occurred to her that there was no end to the wounded, that more people were lying on the floor than had been in the Inn when it was attacked. Dazed, she looked up to see people straggling in. Wives helped their husbands. Husbands carried their wives. Mothers carried dying children.

"What's going on?" Tika asked a Seeker guard who staggered in, clutching his arm where an arrow had penetrated it. Others pushed behind him. "What's happening? Why are these people coming here?"

The guard looked at her with dull, pain-filled eyes. "This is the only building," he mumbled. "All burning. All . . ."

"No!" Tika went limp with shock and her knees trembled. At that moment, the guard fainted in her arms and she was forced to pull herself together. The last thing she saw as she dragged him inside was Hederick, standing on the porch, staring out over the flaming town with glazed eyes. Tears streamed unheeded down his soot-streaked face.

"There's been a mistake," he whimpered, wringing his hands. "There's been a mistake made somewhere."

That had been a week ago. As it turned out, the Inn was not the only building left standing. The draconians knew which buildings were essential to their needs and destroyed all those that were not. The Inn, Theros Ironfeld's blacksmith shop, and the general store were saved. The blacksmith shop had always been on the ground—because of the inadvisability of having the hot forge located in a tree—but the others had to be lowered to the ground because the draconians found it difficult to get into the trees.

Lord Verminaard ordered the dragons to lower the buildings. After a space had been scorched clear, one of the huge red monsters stuck his claws into the Inn and lifted it. The draconians cheered as the dragon dropped it, not gently, onto the blackened grass. Fewmaster Toede, in charge of the town, ordered Otik to repair the Inn immediately. The draconians had one great weakness, a thirst for strong drink. Three days after the town was taken, the Inn reopened.

"I'm all right now," Tika told Otik. She sat up and dried her eyes, wiping her nose with her apron. "I haven't cried once, since that night," she said, more to herself than to him. Her lips tightened into a thin line. "And I'll never cry again!" she swore, rising from the table.

Otik, not understanding but thankful that Tika had regained her composure before the patrons arrived, bustled back behind the bar. "Nearly opening time," he said, trying to sound cheerful. "Maybe we'll have a good crowd today."

"How can you take their money!" Tika flared.

Otik, fearing another outburst, looked at her pleadingly. "Their money is as good as anyone else's. Better than most these days," he said.

"Humpf!" Tika snorted. Her thick red curls quivered as she stalked angrily across the floor. Otik, knowing her temper, stepped backward. It didn't help. He was caught. She jabbed her finger into his fat stomach. "How can you laugh at their crude jokes and cater to their whims?" she demanded. "I hate the stench of them! I hate their leers and their cold, scaly hands touching mine! Someday I'll—"

"Tika, please!" Otik begged. "Have some regard for me. I'm too old to be carried off to the slave mines! And you, they'd take you tomorrow if you didn't work here. Please behave—there's a good girl!"

Tika bit her lip in anger and frustration. She knew Otik was right. She risked more than being sent off in the slave caravans that passed through town almost daily—an angered draconian killed swiftly and without mercy. Just as she was thinking this, the door banged open and six draconian guards swaggered in. One of the them pulled the CLOSED sign off the door and tossed it into a corner.

"You're open," the creature said, dropping into a chair.

"Yes, certainly." Otik grinned weakly. "Tika . . ."

"I see them," Tika said dully.

2

The Stranger. Captured!

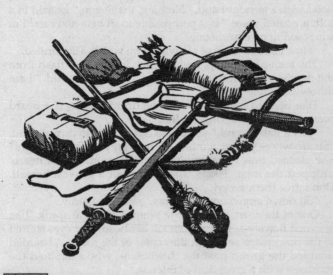

The crowd at the Inn that night was sparse. The patrons were now draconians, though occasionally Solace residents came in for a drink. They generally did not stay long, finding the company unpleasant and memories of former times hard to bear.

Tonight there was a group of hobgoblins who kept wary eyes on the draconians and three crudely dressed humans from the north. Originally impressed into Lord Verminaard's service, they now fought for the sheer pleasure of killing and looting. A few Solace citizens sat huddled in a corner. Hederick, the Theocrat, was not in his nightly spot. Lord Verminaard had rewarded the High Theocrat's service by placing him among the first to be sent to the slave mines.

Near dusk, a stranger entered the Inn, taking a table in a dark corner near the door. Tika couldn't tell much about him—he was heavily cloaked and wore a hood pulled low over his head. He seemed fatigued, sinking down into his chair as though his legs would not support him.

"What will you have?" Tika asked the stranger.

The man lowered his head, pulling down one side of his hood with a slender hand. "Nothing, thank you," he said in a soft, accented voice. "Is it permissible to sit here and rest? I'm supposed to meet someone."

"How about a glass of ale while you wait?" Tika smiled.

The man glanced up, and she saw brown eyes flash from the depths of his hood. "Very well," the stranger said. "I am thirsty. Bring me your ale."

Tika headed for the bar. As she drew the ale, she heard more customers entering the Inn.

"Just a half second," she called out, unable to turn around. "Sit anywhere you've a mind. I'll be with you soon as I can!" She glanced over her shoulder at the newcomers and nearly dropped the mug. Tika gasped, then got a grip on herself. Don't give them away!

"Sit down anywhere, *strangers*," she said loudly.

One of the men, a big fellow, seemed about to speak. Tika frowned fiercely at him and shook her head. Her eyes shifted to the draconians seated in the center of the room. A bearded man led the group past the draconians, who examined the strangers with a great deal of interest.

They saw four men and a woman, a dwarf, and a kender. The men were dressed in mud-stained cloaks and boots. One was unusually tall, another unusually big. The woman was cloaked in furs and walked with her hand through the arm of the tall man. All of them seemed downcast and tired. One of the men coughed and leaned heavily upon a strange-looking staff. They crossed the room and sat down at a table in the far corner.

"More refugee scum," sneered a draconian. "The humans look healthy, though, and all know dwarves are hard workers. Wonder why they haven't been shipped out?"

"They will be, soon as the Fewmaster sees them."

"Perhaps we should take care of the matter now," said a third, scowling in the direction of the eight strangers.

"Naw, I'm off duty. They won't go far."

The others laughed and returned to their drinking. A number of empty glasses already sat before each of them.

Tika carried the ale to the brown-eyed stranger, set it before him hurriedly, then bustled back to the newcomers.

"What'll you have?" she asked coldly.

The tall, bearded man answered in a low, husky voice. "Ale and food," he said. "And wine for him," he nodded at the man who was coughing almost continually.

The frail man shook his head. "Hot water," he whispered.

Tika nodded and left. Out of habit, she started back toward where the old kitchen had been. Then, remembering it was gone, she whipped around and headed for the makeshift kitchen that had been built by goblins under draconian supervision. Once inside, she astounded the cook by grabbing the entire skillet of fried spiced potatoes and carrying it back out into the common room.

"Ale all around and a mug of hot water!" she called to Dezra behind the bar. Tika blessed her stars that Otik had gone home early. "Itrum, take that table." She motioned to the hobgoblins as she hurried back to the newcomers. She slammed the skillet down, glancing at the draconians. Seeing them absorbed in their drinking, she suddenly flung her arms around the big man and gave him a kiss that made him flush.

"Oh, Caramon," she whispered swiftly. "I knew you'd come back for me! Take me with you! Please, please!"

"Now, there, there," Caramon said, patting her awkwardly on the back and looking pleadingly at Tanis. The half-elf swiftly intervened, his eyes on the draconians.

"Tika, calm down," he told her. "We've got an audience."

"Right," she said briskly and stood up, smoothing her apron. Handing plates around, she began to ladle out the spiced potatoes as Dezra brought the ale and hot water.

"Tell us what happened to Solace," Tanis said, his voice choked.

Quickly Tika whispered the story as she filled everyone's plate, giving Caramon a double portion. The companions listened in grim silence.

"And so," Tika concluded, "every week, the slave caravans leave for Pax Tharkas, except now they've taken almost everyone—leaving only the skilled, like Theros Ironfeld, behind.

I fear for him." She lowered her voice. "He swore to me last night that he would work for them no more. It all started with that captive party of elves—"

"Elves? What are elves doing here?" Tanis asked, speaking too loudly in his astonishment. The draconians turned to stare at him; the hooded stranger in the corner raised his head. Tanis hunched down and waited until the draconians turned their attention to their drinks. Then he started to ask Tika more about the elves. At that moment, a draconian yelled for ale.

Tika sighed. "I better go." She set the skillet down. "I'll leave that here. Finish them off."

The companions ate listlessly, the food tasting like ashes. Raistlin mixed his strange herbal brew and drank it down; his cough improved almost immediately. Caramon watched Tika as he ate, his expression thoughtful. He could still feel the warmth of her body as she had embraced him and the softness of her lips. Pleasant sensations flowed through him, and he wondered if the stories he had heard about Tika were true. The thought both saddened him and made him angry.

One of the draconians raised its voice. "We may not be men like you're accustomed to, sweetie," it said drunkenly, flinging its scaled arm around Tika's waist. "But that doesn't mean we can't find ways of making you happy."

Caramon rumbled, deep in his chest. Sturm, overhearing, glowered and put his hand on his sword. Catching hold of the knight's arm, Tanis said urgently, "Both of you, stop it! We're in an occupied town! Be sensible. This is no time for chivalry! You, too, Caramon! Tika can handle herself."

Sure enough, Tika slipped deftly out of the draconian's grip and flounced angrily into the kitchen.

"Well, what do we do now?" Flint grumbled. "We came back to Solace for supplies and find nothing but draconians. My house is little more than a cinder. Tanis doesn't even have a vallenwood tree, much less a home. All we've got are platinum Disks of some ancient goddess and a sick mage with a few new spells." He ignored Raistlin's glower. "We can't eat the Disks and the magician hasn't learned to conjure up food, so even if we knew where to go, we'd starve before we got there!"

"Should we still go to Haven?" Goldmoon asked, looking

up at Tanis. "What if it is as bad as this? How do we know the Highseeker Council is even in existence?"

"I don't have the answers," Tanis said, sighing. He rubbed his eyes with his hand. "But I think we should try to reach Qualinesti."

Tasslehoff, bored by the conversation, yawned and leaned back in his chair. It didn't matter to him where they went. Examining the Inn with intense interest, he wanted to get up and look at where the kitchen had burned, but Tanis had warned him before they entered to stay out of trouble. The kender contented himself with studying the other customers.

He immediately noticed the hooded and cloaked stranger in the front of the Inn watching them intently as the conversation among the companions grew heated. Tanis raised his voice, and the word "Qualinesti" rang out again. The stranger set down his mug of ale with a thud. Tas was just about to call Tanis's attention to this when Tika came out of the kitchen and slammed food down in front of the draconians, skillfully avoiding their clawed hands. Then she walked back over to the group.

"Could I have some more potatoes?" Caramon asked.

"Of course." Tika smiled at him and picked up the skillet to return to the kitchen. Caramon felt Raistlin's eyes on him. He flushed and began to play with his fork.

"In Qualinesti—" Tanis reiterated, his voice rising as he contested a point with Sturm who wanted to go north.

Tas saw the stranger in the corner rise and start walking toward them. "Tanis, company," the kender said softly.

The conversation ceased. Their eyes on their tankards, all of them could feel and hear the approach of the stranger. Tanis cursed himself for not noticing him sooner.

The draconians, however, had noticed the stranger. Just as he reached the creatures' table, one of the draconians stuck out its clawed foot. The stranger tripped over it, stumbling headlong into a nearby table. The creatures laughed loudly. Then a draconian caught a glimpse of the stranger's face.

"Elf!" the draconian hissed, pulling off the hood to reveal the almond-shaped eyes, slanted ears, and delicate, masculine features of an elflord.

"Let me pass," the elf said, backing up, his hands raised. "I was only going to exchange a word of greeting with these travelers."

"You'll exchange a word of greeting with the Fewmaster, elf," the draconian snarled. Jumping up and grabbing the stranger's cloak collar, the creature shoved the elf back up against the bar. The other two draconians laughed loudly.

Tika, on her way back to the kitchen with the skillet, stalked over toward the draconians. "Stop this!" she cried, taking hold of one of the draconians by the arm. "Leave him alone. He's a paying customer. Same as you."

"Go about your business, girl!" The draconian shoved Tika aside, then grabbed the elf with a clawed hand and hit him, twice, across the face. The blows drew blood. When the draconian let go, the elf staggered, shook his head groggily.

"Ah, kill him," shouted one of the humans from the north. "Make him screech, like the others!"

"I'll cut his slanty eyes out of his head, that's what I'll do!" The draconian drew his sword.

"This has gone far enough!" Sturm rushed forward, the others behind him, though all feared there was little hope of saving the elf—they were too far from him. But help was closer. With a shrill cry of rage, Tika Waylan brought her heavy iron skillet down on the draconian's head.

There was a loud clunking sound. The draconian stared stupidly at Tika for an instant, then slithered to the floor. The elf jumped forward, drawing a knife as the other two draconians leaped for Tika. Sturm reached her side and clubbed one of the draconians with his sword. Caramon caught the other up in his great arms and tossed it over the bar.

"Riverwind! Don't let them out the door!" Tanis cried, seeing the hobgoblins leap up. The Plainsman caught one hobgoblin as it put its hand on the doorknob, but another escaped his grasp. They could hear it shouting for the guard.

Tika, still wielding her skillet, thunked a hobgoblin over the head. But another hobgoblin, seeing Caramon charge over, leaped out of the window.

Goldmoon rose to her feet. "Use your magic!" she said to Raistlin, grabbing him by the arm. "Do something!"

The mage looked at the woman coldly. "It is hopeless," he whispered. "I will not waste my strength."

Goldmoon glared at him in fury, but he had returned to his drink. Biting her lip, she ran over to Riverwind, the pouch with the precious Disks of Mishakal in her arms. She could hear horns blowing wildly in the streets.

"We've got to get out of here!" Tanis said, but at that moment one of the human fighters wrapped his arms around Tanis's neck, dragging him to the floor. Tasslehoff, with a wild shout, leaped onto the bar and began flinging mugs at the half-elf's attacker, narrowly missing Tanis in the process.

Flint stood in the midst of the chaos, staring at the elven stranger. "I know you!" he yelled suddenly. "Tanis, isn't this—"

A mug hit the dwarf in the head, knocking him cold.

"Oops," said Tas.

Tanis throttled the northerner and left him unconscious under a table. He grabbed Tas off the bar, set the kender on the floor, and knelt down beside Flint who was groaning and trying to sit up.

"Tanis, that elf—" Flint blinked groggily, then asked "What hit me?"

"That big guy, under the table!" Tas said pointing.

Tanis stood up and looked at the elf Flint indicated. "Gilthanas?"

The elf stared at him. "Tanthalas," he said coldly. "I would never have recognized you. That beard—"

Horns blew again, this time closer.

"Great Reorx!" The dwarf groaned, staggering to his feet. "We've got to get out of here! Come on! Out the back!"

"There is no back!" Tika cried wildly, still hanging onto the skillet.

"No," said a voice at the door. "There is no back. You are my prisoners."

A blaze of torchlight flared into the room. The companions shielded their eyes, making out the forms of hobgoblins behind a squat figure in the doorway. The companions could hear the sounds of flapping feet outside, then what seemed like a hundred goblins stared into the windows and peered in through the door. The hobgoblins inside the bar that were still alive or conscious picked themselves up and drew their weapons, regarding the companions hungrily.

"Sturm, don't be a fool!" Tanis cried, catching hold of the knight as he prepared to charge into the seething mass of goblins slowly forming a ring of steel around them. "We surrender," the half-elf called out.

Sturm glared at the half-elf in anger, and for a moment Tanis thought he might disobey.

"Please, Sturm," Tanis said quietly. "Trust me. This is not our time to die."

Sturm hesitated, glanced around at the goblins crowding inside the Inn. They stood back, fearful of his sword and his skill, but he knew they would charge in a rush if he made the slightest move. "It is not our time to die." What odd words. Why had Tanis said them? Did a man ever have a "time to die"? If so, Sturm realized, this wasn't it—not if he could help it. There was no glory dying in an inn, trampled by stinking, flapping goblin feet.

Seeing the knight put his weapon away, the figure at the door decided it was safe to enter, surrounded as he was by a hundred or so loyal troops. The companions saw the gray, mottled skin and red, squinting pig eyes of Fewmaster Toede.

Tasslehoff gulped and moved quickly to stand beside Tanis. "Surely he won't recognize us," Tas whispered. "It was dusk when they stopped us, asking about the staff."

Apparently Toede did not recognize them. A lot had happened in a week's time and the Fewmaster had important things stuffed in a mind already overloaded. His red eyes focused on the knight's emblems beneath Sturm's cloak. "More refugee scum from Solamnia," Toede remarked.

"Yes," Tanis lied quickly. He doubted if Toede knew of the destruction of Xak Tsaroth. He thought it highly unlikely that this fewmaster would know anything about the Disks of Mishakal. But Lord Verminaard knew of the Disks and he would soon learn of the dragon's death. Even a gully dwarf could add that one up. No one must know they came out of the east. "We have journeyed long days from the north. We did not intend to cause trouble. These draconians started it—"

"Yes, yes," Toede said impatiently. "I've heard this before." His squinty eyes suddenly narrowed. "Hey, you!" he shouted, pointing at Raistlin. "What are you doing, skulking back there? Fetch him, lads!" The Fewmaster took a nervous step behind the door, watching Raistlin warily. Several goblins charged back, overturning benches and tables to reach the frail young man. Caramon rumbled deep in his chest. Tanis gestured to the warrior, warning him to remain calm.

"On yer feet!" one of the goblins snarled, prodding at Raistlin with a spear.

Raistlin stood slowly and carefully gathered his pouches. As he reached for his staff, the goblin grabbed hold of the mage's thin shoulder.

"Touch me not!" Raistlin hissed, drawing back. "I am magi!"

The goblin hesitated and glanced back at Toede.

"Take him!" yelled the Fewmaster, moving behind a very large goblin. "Bring him here with the others. If every man wearing red robes was a magician, this country'd be overrun with rabbits! If he won't come peaceably, stick him!"

"Maybe I'll stick him anyway," the goblin croaked. The creature held the tip of its spear up to the mage's throat, gurgling with laughter.

Again Tanis held back Caramon. "Your brother can take care of himself," he whispered swiftly.

Raistlin raised his hands, fingers spread, as though to surrender. Suddenly he spoke the words, "*Kalith karan, tobaniskar!*" and pointed his fingers at the goblin. Small, brightly glowing darts made of pure white light beamed from the mage's fingertips, streaked through the air, and embedded themselves deep in the goblin's chest. The creature fell over with a shriek and lay writhing on the floor.

As the smell of burning flesh and hair filled the room, other goblins sprang forward, howling in rage.

"Don't kill him, you fools!" Toede yelled. The Fewmaster had backed clear out the door, keeping the big goblin in front of him as cover. "Lord Verminaard pays a handsome bounty for magic-users. But"—Toede was inspired—"the Lord does not pay a bounty for live kenders, only their tongues! Do that again, magician, and the kender dies!"

"What is the kender to me?" Raistlin snarled.

There was a long heartbeat of silence in the room. Tanis felt cold sweat chill him. Raistlin could certainly take care of himself! Damn the mage!

That was certainly not the answer Toede had expected either, and it left him not quite knowing what to do—

especially since these big warriors still had their weapons. He looked almost pleadingly at Raistlin. The magician appeared to shrug.

"I will come peacefully," Raistlin whispered, his golden eyes gleaming. "Just do not touch me."

"No, of course not," Toede muttered. "Bring him."

The goblins, casting uneasy glances in the direction of the Fewmaster, allowed the mage to stand beside his brother.

"Is that everyone?" demanded Toede irritably. "Then take their weapons and their packs."

Tanis, hoping to avoid more trouble, pulled his bow from his shoulder and laid it and his quiver on the soot-blackened floor of the Inn. Tasslehoff quickly laid down his hoopak; the dwarf—grumbling—added his battle-axe. The others followed Tanis's lead, except Sturm, who stood, his arms folded across his chest, and—

"Please, let me keep my pack," Goldmoon said. "I have no weapons in it, nothing of value to you. I swear!"

The companions turned to face her—each remembering the precious Disks she carried. A strained, tense silence fell. Riverwind stepped in front of Goldmoon. He had laid his bow down, but he still wore his sword, as did the knight.

Suddenly Raistlin intervened. The mage had laid down his staff, his pouches of spell components, and the precious bag that contained his spellbooks. He was not worried about these—spells of protection had been laid on the books; anyone other than their owner attempting to read them would go insane; and the Staff of Magius was quite capable of taking care of itself. Raistlin held out his hands toward Goldmoon.

"Give them the pack," he said gently. "Otherwise they will kill us."

"Listen to him, my dear," called out Toede hastily. "He's an intelligent man."

"He's a traitor!" cried Goldmoon, clutching the pack.

"Give them the pack," Raistlin repeated hypnotically.

Goldmoon felt herself weakening, felt his strange power breaking her. "No!" She choked. "This is our hope—"

"It will be all right," Raistlin whispered, staring intently into her clear blue eyes. "Remember the staff? Remember when I touched it?"

Goldmoon blinked. "Yes," she murmured. "It shocked you—"

"Hush," Raistlin warned swiftly. "Give them the pouch. Do not worry. All will be well. The gods protect their own."

Goldmoon stared at the mage, then nodded reluctantly. Raistlin reached out his thin hands to take the pouch from her. Fewmaster Toede stared at it greedily, wondering what was in it. He would find out, but not in front of all these goblins.

Finally there was only one person left who had not obeyed the command. Sturm stood unmoving, his face pale, his eyes glittering feverishly. He held his father's ancient, two-handed sword tightly. Suddenly Sturm turned, shocked to feel Raistlin's burning fingers on his arm.

"I will insure its safety," the mage whispered.

"How?" the knight asked, withdrawing from Raistlin's touch as from a poisonous snake.

"I do not explain my ways to you," Raistlin hissed. "Trust me or not, as you choose."

Sturm hesitated.

"This is ridiculous!" shrieked Toede. "Kill the knight! Kill them if they cause more trouble. I'm losing sleep!"

"Very well!" Sturm said in a strangled voice. Walking over, he reverently laid the sword down on the pile of weapons. Its ancient silver scabbard, decorated with the kingfisher and rose, gleamed in the light.

"Ah, truly a beautiful weapon," Toede said. He had a sudden vision of himself walking into audience with Lord Verminaard, the sword of a Solamnic knight hanging at his side. "Perhaps I should take that into custody myself. Bring it—"

Before he could finish, Raistlin stepped forward swiftly and knelt beside the pile of weapons. A bright flash of light sprang from the mage's hand. Raistlin closed his eyes and began to murmur strange words, holding his outstretched hands above the weapons and packs.

"Stop him!" yelled Toede. But none dared.

Finally Raistlin ceased speaking and his head slumped forward. His brother hurried to help.

Raistlin stood. "Know this!" the mage said, his golden eyes staring around the common room. "I have cast a spell upon our belongings. Anyone who touches them will be slowly devoured by the great worm, Catyrpelius, who will rise from the Abyss and suck the blood from your veins until you are nothing more than a dried husk."

"The great worm Catyrpelius!" breathed Tasslehoff, his eyes shining. "That's incredible. I've never heard of—"

Tanis clapped his hand over the kender's mouth.

The goblins backed away from the pile of weapons, which seemed to almost glow with a green aura.

"Get those weapons, somebody!" ordered Toede in a rage.

"You get 'em," muttered a goblin.

No one moved. Toede was at a loss. Although he was not particularly imaginative, a vivid picture of the great worm, Catyrpelius, reared up in his mind. "Very well," he muttered,"take the prisoners away! Load them into the cages. And bring those weapons, too, or you'll wish that worm what's-its-name was sucking your blood!" Toede stomped off angrily.

The goblins began to shove their prisoners toward the door, prodding them in the back with their swords. None, however, touched Raistlin.

"That's a wonderful spell, Raist," Caramon said in a low voice. "How effective is it? Could it—"

"It's about as effective as your wit!" Raistlin whispered and held up his right hand. As Caramon saw the tell-tale black marks of flashpowder, he smiled grimly in sudden understanding.

Tanis was the last to leave the Inn. He cast a final look around. A single light swung from the ceiling. Tables were overturned, chairs broken. The beams of the ceiling were blackened from the fires, in some cases burned through completely. The windows were covered with greasy black soot.

"I almost wish I had died before I saw this."

The last thing he heard as he left were two hobgoblin captains arguing heatedly about who was going to move the enchanted weapons.

3

The slave caravan.
A strange old magician.

he companions spent a chill, sleepless night, penned up in an iron-barred cage on wheels in the Solace Town Square. Three cages were chained to one of the posts driven into the ground around the clearing. The wooden posts were black from flame and heat, the bases scorched and splintered. No living thing grew in the clearing; even the rocks were black and melted.

When day dawned, they could see other prisoners in the other cages. The last slave caravan leaving Solace for Pax Tharkas, it was to be personally led by the Fewmaster himself, Toede having decided to take this opportunity to impress Lord Verminaard who was in residence at Pax Tharkas.

Caramon tried once, during the cover of night, to bend the bars of the cage and had to give up.

A cold mist arose in the early morning hours, hiding the ravaged town from the companions. Tanis glanced over at Goldmoon and Riverwind. Now I understand them, Tanis thought. Now I know the cold emptiness inside that hurts worse than any sword thrust. My home is gone.

He glanced over at Gilthanas, huddled in a corner. The elf had spoken to no one that night, excusing himself by begging that his head hurt and he was tired. But Tanis, who had kept watch all through the night, saw that Gilthanas did not sleep or even make a pretense of sleeping. He gnawed his lower lip and stared out into the darkness. The sight reminded Tanis that he had—if he chose to claim it—another place he could call home: Qualinesti.

No, Tanis thought, leaning against the bars, Qualinesti was never home. It was simply a place I lived. . . .

Fewmaster Toede emerged from the mist, rubbing his fat hands together and grinning widely as he regarded the slave caravan with pride. There may be a promotion here. A fine catch, considering pickings were drying up in this burned-out shell of a town. Lord Verminaard should be pleased, especially with this last batch. That large warrior, particularly—an excellent specimen. He could probably do the work of three men in the mines. The tall barbarian would do nicely, too. Probably have to kill the knight, though, the Solamnics were notoriously uncooperative. But Lord Verminaard will certainly enjoy the two females—very different, but both lovely. Toede himself had always been attracted to the red-haired barmaid, with her alluring green eyes, the low-cut white blouse purposefully revealing just enough of her lightly freckled skin to tantalize a man with thoughts of what lay beyond.

The Fewmaster's reveries were interrupted by the sound of clashing steel and hoarse shouts floating eerily through the mist. The shouts grew louder and louder. Soon almost everyone in the slave caravan was awake and peering through the fog, trying to see.

Toede cast an uneasy glance at the prisoners and wished he'd kept a few more guards handy. The goblins, seeing the prisoners stir, jumped to their feet and trained their bows and arrows on the wagons.

"What is this?" Toede grumbled aloud. "Can't those fools even take one prisoner without all this turmoil?"

Suddenly a cry bellowed above the noise. It was the cry of a man in torment and pain, but whose rage surpassed all else.

Gilthanas stood up, his face pale.

"I know that voice," he said. "Theros Ironfeld. I feared this. He's been helping elves escape ever since the slaughter. This Lord Verminaard has sworn to exterminate the elves"— Gilthanas watched Tanis's reaction—"or didn't you know?"

"No!" Tanis said, shocked. "I didn't know. How could I?"

Gilthanas fell silent, studying Tanis for long moments. "Forgive me," he said at last. "It appears I have misjudged you. I thought perhaps that was why you had grown the beard."

"Never!" Tanis leaped up. "How dare you accuse me—"

"Tanis," cautioned Sturm.

The half-elf turned to see the goblin guards crowding forward, their arrows trained at his heart. Raising his hands, he stepped back to his place just as a squadron of hobgoblins dragged a tall, powerfully built man into sight.

"I heard Theros had been betrayed," Gilthanas said softly. "I returned to warn him. But for him, I never would have escaped Solace alive. I was supposed to meet him in the Inn last night. When he did not come, I was afraid—"

Fewmaster Toede threw open the door to the companions' cage, yelling and gesturing for the hobgoblins to hurry their prisoner forward. The goblins kept the other prisoners covered while the hobgoblins threw Theros into the cage.

Fewmaster Toede slammed the door shut quickly. "That's it!" he yelled. "Hitch up the beasts. We're moving out."

Squads of goblins drove huge elk into the clearing and began hitching them to wagons. Their yelling and the confusion registered only in the back of Tanis's mind. For the moment, his shocked attention was on the smith.

Theros Ironfeld lay unconscious on the straw-covered floor of the cage. Where his strong right arm should have been was a mangled stump. His arm had been hacked off, apparently by some blunt weapon, just below the shoulder. Blood poured from the terrible wound and pooled on the floor of the cage.

"Let that be a lesson to all those who help elves!" The Few-master peered in the cage, his red pig eyes squinching in their pouches of fat. "He won't be forging anything ever again, unless it be a new arm! I, eh—" A huge elk lumbered into the Fewmaster, forcing him to scramble for his life.

Toede turned on the creature leading the elk. "Sestun! You oaf!" Toede knocked the smaller creature to the ground.

Tasslehoff stared down at the creature, thinking it was a very short goblin. Then he saw it was a gully dwarf dressed in a goblin's armor.The gully dwarf picked himself up, shoved his oversized helm back, and glared after the Fewmaster, who was waddling up to the front of the caravan. Scowling, the gully dwarf began kicking mud in his direction. This apparently relieved his soul, for he soon quit and returned to prodding the slow elk into line.

"My faithful friend," Gilthanas murmured, bending over Theros and taking the smith's strong, black hand in his. "You have paid for your loyalty with your life."

Theros looked at him with vacant eyes, clearly not hearing the elf's voice. Gilthanas tried to stanch the dreadful wound, but blood continued to pump onto the floor of the cart. The smithy's life was emptying before their eyes.

"No," said Goldmoon, coming to kneel beside the smith. "He need not die. I am a healer."

"Lady," Gilthanas said impatiently, "there exists no healer on Krynn who could help this man. He has lost more blood than the dwarf has in his whole body! His lifebeat is so faint I can barely feel it. The kindest thing to do is let him die in peace without any of your barbarian rituals!"

Goldmoon ignored him. Placing her hand upon Theros's forehead, she closed her eyes.

"Mishakal," she prayed, "beloved goddess of healing, grace this man with your blessing. If his destiny be not fulfilled, heal him, that he may live and serve the cause of truth."

Gilthanas began to remonstrate once more, reaching out to pull Goldmoon away. Then he stopped and stared in amazement. Blood ceased to drain from the smith's wound and, even as the elf watched, the flesh began to close over it. Warmth returned to the smith's dusky black skin, his breathing grew peaceful and easy, and he appeared to drift into a healthful, relaxed sleep. There were gasps and murmurs of astonishment from the other prisoners in the nearby cages. Tanis glanced around fearfully to see if any of the goblins or draconians had noticed, but apparently they were all preoccupied with hitching the recalcitrant elk to the wagons. Gilthanas subsided back into his corner, his eyes on Goldmoon, his expression thoughtful.

"Tasslehoff, pile up some of that straw," Tanis instructed. "Caramon, you and Sturm help me move him to a corner."

"Here." Riverwind offered his cloak. "Take this to cover him from the chill."

Goldmoon made certain Theros was comfortable, then returned to her place beside Riverwind. Her face radiated a peace and calm serenity that made it seem as if the reptilian creatures on the outside of the cage were the true prisoners.

It was nearly noon before the caravan got under way. Goblins came by and threw some food into the cages, hunks of meat and bread. No one, not even Caramon, could eat the rancid, stinking meat and they threw it back out. But they devoured the bread hungrily, having eaten nothing since last nightfall. Soon Toede had everything in order and, riding by on his shaggy pony, gave the orders to move out. The gully dwarf, Sestun, trotted after Toede. Seeing the hunk of meat lying in the mud and filth outside the cage, the gully dwarf stopped, grabbed it eagerly, and crammed it into his mouth.

Each wheeled cage was pulled by four elk. Two hobgoblins sat high on crude wooden platforms, one holding the reins of the elk, the other a whip and a sword. Toede took his place at the front of the line, followed by about fifty draconians dressed in armor and heavily armed. Another troop of about twice as many hobgoblins fell into line behind the cages.

After a great deal of confusion and swearing, the caravan finally lurched forward. Some of the remaining residents of Solace stared at them as they drove off. If they knew anyone among the prisoners, they made no sound or gesture of farewell. The faces, both inside and outside the cages, were the faces of those who no longer can feel pain. Like Tika, they had vowed never to cry again.

The caravan traveled south from Solace, down the old road through Gateway Pass. The hobgoblins and draconians grumbled about traveling in the heat of the day, but they cheered up and moved faster once they marched into the shade of the Pass's high canyon walls. Although the prisoners were chilled in the canyon, they had their own reasons for being grateful—they no longer had to look upon their ravaged homeland.

It was evening by the time they left the canyon's winding roads and reached Gateway. The prisoners strained against the bars for some glimpse of the thriving market town. But now only two low stone walls, melted and blackened, marked where the town might have once stood. No living creature stirred. The prisoners sank back in misery.

Once more out in the open country, the draconians announced their preference for traveling by night, out of the sun's light. Consequently, the caravan made only brief stops until dawn. Sleep was impossible in the filthy cages jolting and jouncing over every rut in the road. The prisoners suffered from thirst and hunger. Those who managed to gag down the food the draconians tossed them soon vomited it back up. They were given only small cups of water two or three times a day.

Goldmoon remained near the injured smithy. Although Theros Ironfeld was no longer at the point of death, he was still very ill. He developed a high fever and, in his delirium, he raved about the sacking of Solace. Theros spoke of draconians whose bodies, when dead, turned into pools of acid, burning the flesh of their victims; and of draconians whose bones exploded after death, destroying everything within a wide radius. Tanis listened to the smith relive horror after horror until he felt sick. For the first time, Tanis realized the enormity of the situation. How could they hope to fight dragons whose breath could kill, whose magic exceeded that of all but the most powerful magic-users who had ever lived? How could they defeat vast armies of these draconians when even the corpses of the creatures had the power to kill?

All we have, Tanis thought bitterly, are the Disks of Mishakal—and what good are they? He had examined the Disks during their journey from Xak Tsaroth to Solace. He had been able to read little of what was written, however.

Although Goldmoon had been able to understand those words that pertained to the healing arts, she could decipher little more.

"All will be made clear to the leader of the people," she said with steadfast faith. "My calling now is to find him."

Tanis wished he could share her faith, but as they traveled through the ravaged countryside, he began to doubt that any leader could defeat the might of this Lord Verminaard.

These doubts merely compounded the half-elf's other problems. Raistlin, bereft of his medicine, coughed until he was nearly in as bad a state as Theros, and Goldmoon had two patients on her hands. Fortunately, Tika helped the Plainswoman tend the mage. Tika, whose father had been a magician of sorts, held anyone who could work magic in awe.

In fact, it had been Tika's father who inadvertently introduced Raistlin to his calling. Raistlin's father took the twin boys and his stepdaughter, Kitiara, to the local Summer's End festival where the children watched the Wonderful Waylan perform his illusions. Eight-year-old Caramon was soon bored and readily agreed to accompany his teenage half-sister to the event that attracted her—the swordplay. Raistlin, thin and frail even then, had no use for such active sports. He spent the entire day watching Waylan the Illusionist. When the family returned home that evening, Raistlin astounded them by being able to duplicate flawlessly every trick. The next day, his father took the boy to study with one of the great masters of the magic arts.

Tika had always admired Raistlin and she had been impressed by the stories she heard about his mysterious journey to the fabled Towers of High Sorcery. Now she helped care for the mage out of respect and her own innate need to help those weaker than herself. She also tended him (she admitted privately to herself) because her deeds won a smile of gratitude and approval from Raistlin's handsome twin brother.

Tanis wasn't certain which to worry about most, the worsening condition of the mage or the growing romance between the older, experienced soldier and the young and—Tanis believed, despite gossip to the contrary—inexperienced, vulnerable barmaid.

He had another problem as well. Sturm, humiliated at being taken prisoner and hauled through the countryside like an animal to slaughter, lapsed into a deep depression from which Tanis thought he might never escape. Sturm either sat all day, staring out between the bars, or—perhaps worse—he lapsed into periods of deep sleep from which he could not be wakened.

Finally Tanis had to cope with his own inner turmoil, physically manifested by the elf sitting in the corner of the cage. Every time he looked at Gilthanas, Tanis's memories of his home in Qualinesti haunted him. As they neared his homeland, the memories he had thought long buried and forgotten crept into his mind, their touch every bit as chilling as the touch of the undead in Darken Wood.

Gilthanas, childhood friend—more than friend, brother. Raised in the same household and close to the same age, the two had played and fought and laughed together. When Gilthanas's little sister grew old enough, the boys allowed the captivating blonde child to join them. One of the threesome's greatest delights was teasing the older brother, Porthios, a strong and serious youth who took on the responsibilities and sorrows of his people at an early age. Gilthanas, Laurana, and Porthios were the children of the Speaker of the Suns, the ruler of the elves of Qualinesti, a position Porthios would inherit at his father's death.

Some in the elven kingdom thought it odd that the Speaker would take into his house the bastard son of his dead brother's wife after she had been raped by a human warrior. She had died of grief only months after the birth of her half-breed child. But the Speaker, who had strong views on responsibility, took in the child without hesitation. It was only in later years, as he watched with growing unease the developing relationship between his beloved daughter and the bastard half-elf, that he began to regret his decision. The situation confused Tanis as well. Being half-human, the young man acquired a maturity the slower developing elfmaid could not understand. Tanis saw the unhappiness their union must bring down upon the family he loved. He also was beset by the inner turmoil that would torment him in later life: the constant battle between the elvish and the human within him. At the age of eighty—about twenty in human years—Tanis left Qualinost. The Speaker was not sorry to see Tanis leave. He tried to hide his feelings from the young half-elf, but both of them knew it.

Gilthanas had not been so tactful. He and Tanis had exchanged bitter words over Laurana. It was years before the sting of those words faded, and Tanis wondered if he had ever truly forgotten or forgiven. Clearly, Gilthanas had done neither.

The journey for these two was very long. Tanis made a few attempts at desultory conversation and became immediately aware that Gilthanas had changed. The young elflord had always been open and honest, fun-loving and light-hearted. He did not envy his older brother the responsibilities inherent in his role as heir to the throne. Gilthanas was a scholar, a dabbler in the magic arts, though he never took them as seriously as Raistlin. He was an excellent warrior, though he disliked fighting, as do all elves. He was deeply devoted to his family, especially his sister. But now he sat silent and moody, an unusual characteristic in elves. The only time he showed any interest in anything was when Caramon had begun plotting an escape. Gilthanas told him sharply to forget it, he would ruin everything. When pressed to elaborate, the elf fell silent, muttering only something about "overwhelming odds."

By sunrise of the third day, the draconian army was flagging from the night's long march and looking forward to a rest. The companions had spent another sleepless night and looked forward to nothing but another chill and dismal day. But the cages suddenly rolled to a stop. Tanis glanced up, puzzled at the change in routine. The other prisoners roused themselves and looked out the cage bars. They saw an old man, dressed in long robes that once might have been white and a battered, pointed hat. He appeared to be talking to a tree.

"I say, did you hear me?" The old man shook a worn walking stick at the oak. "I said move and I meant it! I was sitting on that rock"—he pointed to a boulder—"enjoying the rising sun on my old bones when you had the nerve to cast a shadow over it and chill me! Move this instant, I say!"

The tree did not respond. It also did not move.

"I won't take any more of your insolence!" The old man began to beat on the tree with his stick. "Move or I'll, I'll—"

"Someone shut that loony in a cage!" Fewmaster Toede shouted, galloping back from the front of the caravan.

"Get your hands off me!" the old man shrieked at the draconians who ran up and accosted him. He beat on them feebly with his staff until they took it away from him. "Arrest the tree!" he insisted. "Obstructing sunlight! That's the charge!"

The draconians threw the old man roughly into the companions' cage. Tripping over his robes, he fell to the floor.

"Are you all right, Old One?" Riverwind asked as he assisted the old man to a seat.

Goldmoon left Theros's side. "Yes, Old One," she said softly. "Are you hurt? I am a cleric of—"

"Mishakal!" he said, peering at the amulet around her neck. "How very interesting. My, my." He stared at her in astonishment. "You don't look three hundred years old!"

Goldmoon blinked, uncertain how to react. "How did you know? Did you recognize—? I'm not three hundred—" She was growing confused.

"Of course, you're not. I'm sorry, my dear." The old man patted her hand. "Never bring up a lady's age in public. Forgive me. It won't happen again. Our little secret," he said in a piercing whisper. Tas and Tika started to giggle. The old man looked around. "Kind of you to stop and offer me a lift. The road to Qualinost is long."

"We're not going to Qualinost," Gilthanas said sharply. "We're prisoners, going to the slave mines of Pax Tharkas."

"Oh?" the old man glanced around vaguely. "Is there another group due by here soon, then? I could have sworn this was the one."

"What is your name, Old One?" Tika asked.

"My name?" The old man hesitated, frowning. "Fizban? Yes, that's it. Fizban."

"Fizban!" Tasslehoff repeated as the cage lurched to a start again. "That's not a name!"

"Isn't it?" the old man asked wistfully. "That's too bad. I was rather fond of it."

"I think it's a splendid name," Tika said, glaring at Tas. The kender subsided into a corner, his eyes on the pouches slung over the old man's shoulder.

Suddenly Raistlin began to cough and they all turned their attention to him. His coughing spasms had been growing worse and worse. He was exhausted and in obvious pain; his skin burned to the touch. Goldmoon was unable to help him. Whatever was burning the mage up inside, the cleric could not heal. Caramon knelt beside him, wiping away the bloody saliva that flecked his brother's lips.

"He's got to have that stuff he drinks!" Caramon looked up in anguish. "I've never seen him this bad. If they won't listen to reason"—the big man scowled—"I'll break their heads! I don't care how many there are!"

"We'll talk to them when we stop for the night," Tanis promised, though he could guess the Fewmaster's answer.

"Excuse me," the old man said. "May I?" Fizban sat down beside Raistlin. He laid his hand on the mage's head and sternly spoke a few words.

Caramon, listening closely, heard "Fistandan . . ." and "not the time . . ." Certainly it wasn't a healing prayer, such as Goldmoon had tried, but the big man saw that his brother responded! The response was astonishing, however. Raistlin's eyes fluttered and opened. He looked up at the old man with a wild expression of terror and grasped Fizban's wrist in his thin, frail hand. For an instant it seemed Raistlin knew the old man, then Fizban passed his hand over the mage's eyes. The look of terror subsided, replaced by confusion.

"Hullo," Fizban beamed at him. "Name's—uh—Fizban." He shot a stern glance at Tasslehoff, daring the kender to laugh.

"You are . . . magi!" Raistlin whispered. His cough was gone.

"Why, yes, I suppose I am."

"I am magi!" Raistlin said, struggling to sit up.

"No kidding!" Fizban seemed immensely tickled. "Small world, Krynn. I'll have to teach you a few of my spells. I have one . . . a fireball . . . let's see, how did that go?"

The old man rambled on long past the time the caravan stopped at the rising of the sun.

4

Rescued! Fizban's magic.

Raistlin suffered in body, Sturm suffered in mind, but perhaps the one who experienced the keenest suffering during the companions' four-day imprisonment was Tasslehoff.

The cruelest form of torture one can inflict on a kender is to lock him up. Of course, it is also widely believed that the cruelest form of torture one can inflict on any other species is to lock them up with a kender. After three days of Tasslehoff's incessant chatter, pranks, and practical jokes, the companions would have willingly traded the kender for a peaceful hour of being stretched on the rack—at least that's what Flint said. Finally, after even Goldmoon lost her temper and nearly slapped him, Tanis sent Tasslehoff to the back of the cart. His legs hanging over the edge, the kender pressed his face against the iron bars and thought he would die of misery. He had never been so bored in his entire life.

Things got interesting with the discovery of Fizban, but the old man's amusement value wore thin when Tanis made Tas return the old magician's pouches. And so, driven to the point of desperation, Tasslehoff latched onto a new diversion.

Sestun, the gully dwarf.

The companions generally regarded Sestun with amused pity. The gully dwarf was the object of Toede's ridicule and mistreatment. He ran the Fewmaster's errands all night long, carrying messages from Toede at the front of the caravan to the hobgoblin captain at the rear, lugging food up to the Fewmaster from the supply cart, feeding and watering the Fewmaster's pony, and any other nasty jobs the Fewmaster could devise. Toede knocked him flat at least three times a day, the draconians tormented him, and the hobgoblins stole his food. Even the elk kicked at him whenever he trotted past. The gully dwarf bore it all with such a grimly defiant spirit that it won him the sympathy of the companions.

Sestun began to stay near the companions when not busy. Tanis, eager for information about Pax Tharkas, asked him about his homeland and how he came to work for the Fewmaster. The story took over a day for Sestun to relate and another day for the companions to piece together, since he started in the middle and plunged headlong into the beginning.

What it amounted to, eventually, wasn't much help. Sestun was among a large group of gully dwarves living in the hills around Pax Tharkas when Lord Verminaard and his draconians captured the iron mines which he needed to make steel weapons for his troops.

"Big fire—all day, all night. Bad smell." Sestun wrinkled his nose. "Pound rock. All day, all night. I get good job in kitchen"—his face brightened a moment—"fix hot soup. Very hot." His face fell. "Spill soup. Hot soup heat up armor real fast. Lord Verminaard sleep on back for week." He sighed. "I go with Fewmaster. Me volunteer."

"Maybe we can shut the mines down," Caramon suggested.

"That's a thought," Tanis mused. "How many draconians does Lord Verminaard have guarding the mines?"

"Two!" Sestun said, holding up ten grubby fingers.

Tanis sighed, remembering where they had heard that before.

Sestun looked at him hopefully. "There be only two dragons, too."

"Two dragons!" Tanis said incredulously.

"Not more than two."

Caramon groaned and settled back. The warrior had been giving dragon fighting serious thought ever since Xak Tsaroth. He and Sturm had reviewed every tale about Huma, the only known dragon fighter the knight could remember. Unfortunately, no one had ever taken the legends of Huma seriously before (except the Solamnic Knights, for which they were ridiculed), so much of Huma's tale had been distorted by time or forgotten.

"A knight of truth and power, who called down the gods themselves and forged the mighty Dragonlance," Caramon murmured now, glancing at Sturm, who lay asleep on the straw-covered floor of their prison.

"Dragonlance?" muttered Fizban, waking with a snort. "Dragonlance? Who said anything about the Dragonlance?"

"My brother," Raistlin whispered, smiling bitterly. "Quoting the Canticle. It seems he and the knight have taken a fancy to children's stories that have come to haunt them."

"Good story, Huma and the Dragonlance," said the old man, stroking his beard.

"Story—that's all it is." Caramon yawned and scratched his chest. "Who knows if it's real or if the Dragonlance was real or if even Huma was real?"

"We know the dragons are real," Raistlin murmured.

"Huma was real," Fizban said softly. "And so was the Dragonlance." The old man's face grew sad.

"Was it?" Caramon sat up. "Can you describe it?"

"Of course!" Fizban sniffed disdainfully.

Everyone was listening now. Fizban was, in fact, a bit disconcerted by his audience for his stories.

"It was a weapon similar to—no, it wasn't. Actually it was—no, it wasn't that either. It was closer to . . . almost a . . . rather it was, sort of a—lance, that's it! A lance!" He nodded earnestly. "And it was quite good against dragons."

"I'm taking a nap," Caramon grumbled.

Tanis smiled and shook his head. Sitting back against the bars, he wearily closed his eyes. Soon everyone except Raistlin and Tasslehoff fell into a fitful sleep. The kender, wide awake and bored, looked at Raistlin hopefully. Sometimes, if Raistlin was in a good mood, he would tell stories about magic-users of old. But the mage, wrapped in his red robes, was staring curiously at Fizban. The old man sat on a bench, snoring gently, his head bobbing up and down as the cart jounced over the road. Raistlin's golden eyes narrowed to gleaming slits as though he had been struck by a new and disturbing thought. After a moment, he pulled his hood up over his head and leaned back, his face lost in the shadows.

Tasslehoff sighed. Then, glancing around, he saw Sestun walking near the cage. The kender brightened. Here, he knew, was an appreciative audience for his stories.

Tasslehoff, calling him over, began to relate one of his own personal favorites. The two moons sank. The prisoners slept. The hobgoblins trailed along behind, half-asleep, talking about making camp soon. Fewmaster Toede rode up ahead, dreaming about promotion. Behind the Fewmaster, the draconians muttered among themselves in their harsh language, casting baleful glances at Toede when he wasn't looking.

Tasslehoff sat, swinging his legs over the side of the cage, talking to Sestun. The kender noticed without seeming to that Gilthanas was only pretending to sleep. Tas saw the elf's eyes open and glance quickly around when he thought no one was watching. This intrigued Tas immensely. It seemed almost as if Gilthanas was watching or waiting for something. The kender lost the thread of his story.

"And so I . . . uh . . . grabbed a rock from my pouch, threw it and—thunk—hit the wizard right on the head," Tas finished hurriedly. "The demon grabbed the wizard by the foot and dragged him down into the depths of the Abyss."

"But first demon thank you," prompted Sestun who had heard this story—with variations—twice before. "You forgot."

"Did I?" Tas asked, keeping an eye on Gilthanas. "Well, yes, the demon thanked me and took away the magic ring he'd given me. If it wasn't dark, you could see the outline the ring burned on my finger."

"Sun uping. Morning soon. I see then," the gully dwarf said eagerly.

It was still dark, but a faint light in the east hinted that soon the sun would be rising on the fourth day of their journey.

Suddenly Tas heard a bird call in the woods. Several answered it. What odd-sounding birds, Tas thought. Never heard their like before. But then he'd never been this far south before. He knew where they were from one of his many maps. They had passed over the only bridge across the White-rage River and were heading south toward Pax Tharkas, which was marked on the kender's map as the site of the famed Thadarkan iron mines. The land began to rise, and thick forests of aspens appeared to the west. The draconians and hobgoblins kept eyeing the forests, and their pace picked up. Concealed within these woods was Qualinesti, the ancient elvenhome.

Another bird called, much nearer now. Then the hair rose on Tasslehoff's neck as the same bird call sounded from right behind him. The kender turned to see Gilthanas on his feet, his fingers to his lips, an eerie whistle splitting the air.

"Tanis!" Tas yelled, but the half-elf was already awake. So was everyone in the cart.

Fizban sat up, yawned, and glanced around. "Oh, good," he said mildly, "the elves are here."

"What elves, where?" Tanis sat up.

There was a sudden whirring sound like a covey of quail taking flight. A cry rang out from the supply wagon in front of them, then there was a splintering sound as the wagon, now driverless, lurched into a rut and tipped over. The driver of their cage wagon pulled sharply on the reins, stopping the elk before they ran into the wrecked supply wagon. The cage tipped precariously, sending the prisoners sprawling. The driver got the elk going again and guided them around the wreckage.

Suddenly the driver of the cage screamed and clutched at his neck where the companions saw the feathered shaft of an arrow silhouetted against the dimly lit morning sky. The driver's body tumbled from the seat. The other guard stood up, sword raised, then he, too, toppled forward with an arrow in his chest. The elk, feeling the reins go slack, slowed until the cage rolled to a halt. Cries and screams echoed up and down the caravan as arrows whizzed through the air.

The companions fell for cover face first on the floor of the cage.

"What is it? What's going on?" Tanis asked Gilthanas.

But the elf, ignoring him, peered through the dawn gloom into the forest. "Porthios!" he called.

"Tanis, what's happening?" Sturm sat up, speaking his first words in four days.

"Porthios is Gilthanas's brother. I take it this is a rescue," Tanis said. An arrow zipped past and lodged in the wooden side of the cart, narrowly missing the knight.

"It won't be much of a rescue if we end up dead!" Sturm dropped to the floor. "I thought elves were expert marksmen!"

"Keep low." Gilthanas ordered. "The arrows are only to cover our escape. This is a strike-and-run raid. My people are not capable of attacking a large body directly. We must be ready to run for the woods."

"And how do we get out of these cages?" Sturm demanded.

"We cannot do everything for you!" Gilthanas replied coldly. "There are magic-users—"

"I cannot work without my spell components!" Raistlin hissed from beneath a bench. "Keep down, Old One," he said to Fizban who, head raised, was looking around with interest.

"Perhaps I can help," the old magician said, his eyes brightening. "Now, let me think—"

"What in the name of the Abyss is going on?" roared a voice out of the darkness. Fewmaster Toede appeared, galloping on his pony. "Why have we stopped?"

"We under attack!" Sestun cried, crawling out from under the cage where he'd taken cover.

"Attack? *Blyxtshok!* Get this cart moving!" Toede shouted. An arrow thunked into the Fewmaster's saddle. Toede's red eyes flew open and he stared fearfully into the woods. "We're under attack! Elves! Trying to free the prisoners!"

"Driver and guard dead!" Sestun shouted, flattening himself against the cage as another arrow just missed him. "What me do?"

An arrow zipped over Toede's head. Ducking, he had to clutch his pony's neck to keep himself from falling off. "I'll get another driver," he said hastily. "You stay here. Guard these prisoners with your life! I'll hold you responsible if they escape."

The Fewmaster stuck his spurs into his pony and the fear-crazed animal leaped forward. "My guard! Hobgoblins! To

301

me!" the Fewmaster yelled as he galloped to the rear of the line. His shouts echoed back. "Hundreds of elves! We're surrounded. Charge to the north! I must report this to Lord Verminaard." Toede reined in at the sight of a draconian captain. "You draconians tend to the prisoners!" He spurred his horse on, still shouting, and one hundred hobgoblins charged after their valiant leader away from the battle. Soon, they were completely out of sight.

"Well, that takes care of the hobgoblins," Sturm said, his face relaxing in a smile. "Now all we have left to worry about is fifty or so draconians. I don't suppose, by the way, that there are hundreds of elves out there?"

Gilthanas shook his head. "More like twenty."

Tika, lying flat on the floor, cautiously raised her head and looked south. In the pale morning light, she could see the hulking forms of the draconians about a mile ahead, leaping into the cover on either side of the road as the elven archers moved down to fire into their ranks. She touched Tanis's arm, pointing.

"We've got to get out of this cage," Tanis said, looking back. "The draconians won't bother taking us to Pax Tharkas now that the Fewmaster's gone. They'll just butcher us in these cages. Caramon?"

"I'll try," the fighter rumbled. He stood and gripped the bars of the cage in his huge hands. Closing his eyes, he took a deep breath and tried to force the bars apart. His face reddened, the muscles in his arms bunched, the knuckles on his big hands turned white. It was useless. Gasping for breath, Caramon flattened himself on the floor.

"Sestun!" Tasslehoff cried. "Your axe! Break the lock!"

The gully dwarf's eyes opened wide. He stared at the companions, then he glanced down the trail the Fewmaster had taken. His face twisted in an agony of indecision.

"Sestun—" Tasslehoff began. An arrow zinged past the kender. The draconians behind them were moving forward, firing into the cages. Tas flattened himself on the floor. "Sestun," he began again, "help free us and you can come with us!"

A look of firm resolve hardened Sestun's features. He reached for his axe, which he wore strapped onto his back.

The companions watched in nail-biting frustration as Sestun felt all around his shoulders for the axe, which was located squarely in the middle of his back. Finally, one hand discovered the handle and he pulled the axe out. The blade glinted in the gray light of dawn.

Flint saw it and groaned. "That axe is older than I am! It must date back to the Cataclysm! He probably couldn't cut through a kender's brain, let alone that lock!"

"Hush!" Tanis instructed, although his own hopes sank at the sight of the gully dwarf's weapon. It wasn't even a battle-axe, just a small, battered, rusty wood-cutting axe the gully dwarf had apparently picked up somewhere, thinking it was a weapon. Sestun tucked the axe between his knees and spat on his hands.

Arrows thunked and clattered around the bars of the cage. One struck Caramon's shield. Another pinned Tika's blouse to the side of the cage, grazing her arm. Tika couldn't remember being more terrified in her life—not even the night dragons struck Solace. She wanted to scream, she wanted Caramon to put her arm around her. But Caramon didn't dare move.

Tika caught sight of Goldmoon, shielding the injured Theros with her body, her face pale but calm. Tika pressed her lips together and drew a deep breath. Grimly she yanked the arrow out of the wood and tossed it to the floor, ignoring the stinging pain in her arm. Looking south, she saw that the draconians, momentarily confused by the sudden attack and the disappearance of Toede, were organized now, on their feet and running toward the cages. Their arrows filled the air. Their chest armor gleamed in the dim gray light of morning, so did the bright steel of their longswords, which they carried clamped in their jaws as they ran.

"Draconians, closing in," she reported to Tanis, trying to keep her voice from shaking.

"Hurry, Sestun!" Tanis shouted.

The gully dwarf gripped the axe, swung it with all his might, and missed the lock, striking the iron bars a blow that nearly jarred the axe from his hands. Shrugging apologetically, he swung again. This time he struck the lock.

"He didn't even dent it," Sturm reported.

"Tanis," Tika quavered, pointing. Several draconians were

within ten feet of them, pinned down for a few moments by the elven archers, but all hope of rescue seemed lost.

Sestun struck the lock again.

"He chipped it," Sturm said in exasperation. "At this rate we'll be out in about three days! What are those elves doing, anyway? Why don't they quit skulking about and attack!"

"We don't have enough men to attack a force this size!" Gilthanas returned angrily, crouching next to the knight. "They'll get to us when they can! We are at the front of the line. See, others are escaping."

The elf pointed to the two wagons behind them. The elves had broken the locks and the prisoners were dashing madly for the woods as the elves covered them, darting out from the trees to let fly their deadly barrage of arrows. But once the prisoners were safe, the elves retreated into the trees.

The draconians had no intention of going into the elven woods after them. Their eyes were on the last prison cage and the wagon containing the prisoners' possessions. The companions could hear the shouts of the draconian captains. The meaning was clear: "Kill the prisoners. Divide the spoils."

Everyone could see that the draconians would reach them long before the elves did. Tanis swore in frustration. Everything seemed futile. He felt a stirring at his side. The old magician, Fizban, was getting to his feet.

"No, Old One!" Raistlin grasped at Fizban's robes. "Keep under cover!"

An arrow zipped through the air and stuck in the old man's bent and battered hat. Fizban, muttering to himself, did not seem to notice. He presented a wonderful target in the gray light. Draconian arrows flew around him like wasps, and seemed to have as little effect, although he did appear mildly annoyed when one stuck into a pouch he happened to have his hand in at the moment.

"Get down!" Caramon roared. "You're drawing their fire!"

Fizban did kneel down for a moment, but it was only to talk to Raistlin. "Say there, my boy," he said as an arrow flew past right where he'd been standing. "Have you got a bit of bat guano on you? I'm out."

"No, Old One," Raistlin whispered frantically. "Get down!"

"No? Pity. Well, I guess I'll have to wing it." The old magician stood up, planted his feet firmly on the floor, and rolled up the sleeves of his robes. He shut his eyes, pointed at the cage door, and began to mumble strange words.

"What spell is he casting?" Tanis asked Raistlin. "Can you understand?"

The young mage listened intently, his brow furrowed. Suddenly Raistlin's eyes opened wide. "NO!" he shrieked, trying to pull on the old magician's robe to break his concentration. But it was too late. Fizban said the final word and pointed his finger at the lock on the back door of the cage.

"Take cover!" Raistlin threw himself beneath a bench. Sestun, seeing the old magician point at the cage door—and at him on the other side of it—fell flat on his face. Three draconians, reaching the cage door, their weapons dripping with their saliva, skidded to a halt, staring up in alarm.

"What is it?" Tanis yelled.

"Fireball!" Raistlin gasped, and at that moment a gigantic ball of yellow-orange fire shot from the old magician's fingertips and struck the cage door with an explosive boom. Tanis buried his face in his hands as flames billowed and crackled around him. A wave of heat washed over him, searing his lungs. He heard the draconians scream in pain and smelled burning reptile flesh. Then smoke flew down his throat.

"The floor's on fire!" Caramon yelled.

Tanis opened his eyes and staggered to his feet. He expected to see the old magician nothing but a mound of black ash like the bodies of the draconians lying behind the wagon. But Fizban stood staring at the iron door, stroking his singed beard in dismay. The door was still shut.

"That really should have worked," he said.

"What about the lock?" Tanis yelled, trying to see through the smoke. The iron bars of the cell door already glowed red hot.

"It didn't budge!" Sturm shouted. He tried to approach the cage door to kick it open, but the heat radiating from the bars made it impossible. "The lock may be hot enough to break!" He choked in the smoke.

"Sestun!" Tasslehoff's shrill voice rose above the crackling flames. "Try again! Hurry!"

The gully dwarf staggered to his feet, swung the axe, missed, swung again, and hit the lock. The superheated metal shattered, the lock gave way, and the cage door swung open.

"Tanis, help us!" Goldmoon cried as she and Riverwind struggled to pull the injured Theros from his smoking pallet.

"Sturm, the others!" Tanis yelled, then coughed in the smoke. He staggered to the front of the wagon, as the rest jumped out, Sturm grabbing hold of Fizban, who was still staring sadly at the door.

"Come on, Old One!" he yelled, his gentle actions belying his harsh words as he took Fizban's arm. Caramon, Raistlin, and Tika caught Fizban as he jumped from the flaming wreckage. Tanis and Riverwind lifted Theros by the shoulders and dragged him out, Goldmoon stumbled after them. She and Sturm jumped from the cart just as the ceiling collapsed.

"Caramon! Get our weapons from the supply wagon!" Tanis shouted. "Go with him, Sturm. Flint and Tasslehoff, get the packs. Raistlin—"

"I will, get my pack," the mage said, choking in the smoke. "And my staff. No one else may touch them."

"All right," Tanis said, thinking quickly. "Gilthanas—"

"I am not yours to order around, Tanthalas," the elf snapped and ran off into the woods without looking back.

Before Tanis could answer, Sturm and Caramon ran back. Caramon's knuckles were split and bleeding. There had been two draconians looting the supply wagon.

"Get moving!" Sturm shouted. "More coming! Where's your elf friend?" he asked Tanis suspiciously.

"He's gone ahead into the woods," Tanis said. "Just remember, he and his people saved us."

"Did they?" Sturm said, his eyes narrow. "It seems that between the elves and the old man, we came closer to getting killed than with just about anything short of the dragon!"

At that moment, six draconians rushed out from the smoke, skidding to a halt at the sight of the warriors.

"Run for the woods!" Tanis yelled, bending down to help Riverwind lift Theros. They carried the smith to cover while Caramon and Sturm stood, side by side, covering their retreat. Both noticed immediately that the creatures they faced were unlike the draconians they had fought before. Their armor and coloring were different, and they carried bows and longswords, the latter dripping with some sort of awful icor. Both men remembered stories about draconians that turned to acid and those whose bones exploded.

Caramon charged forward, bellowing like an enraged animal, his sword slashing in an arc. Two draconians fell before they knew what was attacking. Sturm saluted the other four with his sword and swept off the head of one in the return stroke. He jumped at the others, but they stopped just out of his range, grinning, apparently waiting for something.

Sturm and Caramon watched uneasily, wondering what was going on. Then they knew. The bodies of the slain draconians near them began to melt into the road. The flesh boiled and ran like lard in a skillet. A yellowish vapor formed over them, mixing with the thinning smoke from the smoldering cage. Both men gagged as the yellow vapor rose around them. They grew dizzy and knew they were being poisoned.

"Come on! Get back!" Tanis yelled from the woods.

The two stumbled back, fleeing through a rainstorm of arrows as a force of forty or fifty draconians swept around the cage, screeching in anger. The draconians started after them, then fell back when a clear voice called out, *"Hai! Ulsain!"* and ten elves, led by Gilthanas, ran from the woods.

"Quen talas uvenelei!" Gilthanas shouted. Caramon and Sturm staggered past him, the elves covering their retreat, then the elves fell back.

"Follow me," Gilthanas told the companions, switching to High Common. At a sign from Gilthanas, four of the elven warriors picked up Theros and carried him into the woods.

Tanis looked back at the cage. The draconians had come to a halt, eyeing the woods warily.

"Hurry!" Gilthanas urged. "My men will cover you."

Elven voices rose out of the woods, taunting the approaching draconians, trying to lure them into arrow range. The companions looked at each other hesitantly.

"I do not want to enter Elvenwood," Riverwind said harshly.

"It is all right," Tanis said, putting his hand on Riverwind's arm. "You have my pledge." Riverwind stared at him for a moment, then plunged into the woods, the others walking by

his side. Last to come were Caramon and Raistlin, helping
Fizban. The old man glanced back at the cage, now nothing
more than a pile of ashes and twisted iron.

"Wonderful spell. And did anyone say a word of thanks?"
he asked wistfully.

The elves led them swiftly through the wilderness. Without
their guidance, the party would have been hopelessly lost.
Behind them, the sounds of battle turned half-hearted.

"The draconians know better than to follow us into the
woods," Gilthanas said, smiling grimly. Tanis, seeing armed
elven warriors hidden among the leaves of the trees, had little
fear of pursuit. Soon all sounds of fighting were lost.

A thick carpeting of dead leaves covered the ground. Bare
tree limbs creaked in the chill wind of early morning. After
spending days riding cramped in the cage, the companions
moved slowly and stiffly, glad for the exercise that warmed
their blood. Gilthanas led them into a wide glade as the morning sun lit the woods with a pale light.

The glade was crowded with freed prisoners. Tasslehoff
glanced eagerly around the group, then shook his head sadly.

"I wonder what happened to Sestun," he said to Tanis. "I
thought I saw him run off."

"Don't worry." The half-elf patted him on the shoulder.
"He'll be all right. The elves have no love for gully dwarves,
but they wouldn't kill him."

Tasslehoff shook his head. It wasn't the elves he was worried about.

Entering the clearing, the companions saw an unusually
tall and powerfully built elf speaking to the group of refugees.
His voice was cold, his demeanor serious and stern.

"You are free to go, if any are free to go in this land. We
have heard rumors that the lands south of Pax Tharkas are not
under the control of the Dragon Highlord. I suggest, therefore,
that you head southeast. Move as far and as fast as you can
this day. We have food and supplies for your journey, all that
we can spare. We can do little else for you."

The refugees from Solace, stunned by their sudden freedom, stared around bleakly and helplessly. They had been
farmers on the outskirts of Solace, forced to watch while their

homes burned and their crops were stolen to feed the Dragon Highlord's army. Most of them had never been farther from Solace than Haven. Dragons and elves were creatures of legend. Now children's stories had come to haunt them.

Goldmoon's clear blue eyes glinted. She knew how they felt. "How can you be so cruel?" she called out angrily to the tall elf. "Look at these people. They have never been out of Solace in their lives and you tell them calmly to walk through a land overrun by enemy forces—"

"What would you have me do, human?" the elf interrupted her. "Lead them south myself? It is enough that we have freed them. My people have their own problems. I cannot be concerned with those of humans." He shifted his eyes to the group of refugees. "I warn you. Time is wasting. Be on your way!"

Goldmoon turned to Tanis, seeking support, but he just shook his head, his face dark and shadowed.

One of the men, giving the elves a haggard glance, stumbled off on the trail that meandered south through the wilderness. The other men shouldered crude weapons, women caught up their children, and the families straggled off.

Goldmoon strode forward to confront the elf. "How can you care so little for—"

"For humans?" The elf stared at her coldly. "It was humans who brought the Cataclysm upon us. They were the ones who sought the gods, demanding in their pride the power that was granted Huma in humility. It was humans who caused the gods to turn their faces from us—"

"They haven't!" Goldmoon shouted. "The gods are among us!"

Porthios's eyes flared with anger. He started to turn away when Gilthanas stepped up to his brother and spoke to him swiftly in the elven language.

"What do they say?" Riverwind asked Tanis suspiciously.

"Gilthanas is telling how Goldmoon healed Theros," Tanis said slowly. It had been many, many years since he had heard or spoken more than a few words in the elven tongue. He had forgotten how beautiful the language was, so beautiful it seemed to cut his soul and leave him wounded and bleeding inside. He watched as Porthios's eyes widened in disbelief.

Then Gilthanas pointed at Tanis. Both the brothers turned to face him, their expressive elven features hardening. Riverwind flicked a glance at Tanis, saw the half-elf standing pale but composed under this scrutiny.

"You return to the land of your birth, do you not?" Riverwind asked. "It does not seem you are welcome."

"Yes," Tanis said grimly, aware of what the Plainsman was thinking. He knew Riverwind was not prying into personal affairs out of curiosity. In many ways, they were in more danger now than they had been with the Fewmaster.

"They will take us to Qualinost," Tanis said slowly, the words apparently causing him deep pain. "I have not been there for many years. As Flint will tell you, I was not forced out, but few were sorry to see me leave. As you once said to me, Riverwind—to humans I am half-elven. To elves, I was half-man."

"Then let us leave and travel south with the others," Riverwind said.

"You would never get out of here alive," Flint murmured.

Tanis nodded. "Look around," he said.

Riverwind glanced around him and saw the elven warriors moving like shadows among the trees, their brown clothing blending in with the wilderness that was their home. As the two elves ended their conversation, Porthios turned his gaze from Tanis back to Goldmoon.

"I have heard strange tales from my brother that bear investigation. I extend to you, therefore, what the elves have extended to no humans in years—our hospitality. You will be our honored guests. Please follow me."

Porthios gestured. Nearly two dozen elven warriors emerged from the woods, surrounding the companions.

"Honored prisoners is more like it. This is going to be rough on you, my lad," Flint said to Tanis in a low, gentle voice.

"I know, old friend." Tanis rested his hand on the dwarf's shoulder. "I know."

5

The Speaker of the Suns.

have never imagined such beauty existed," Goldmoon said softly. The day's march had been difficult, but the reward at the end was beyond their dreams. The companions stood on a high cliff over the fabled city of Qualinost.

Four slender spires rose from the city's corners like glistening spindles, their brilliant white stone marbled with shining silver. Graceful arches, swooping from spire to spire, soared through the air. Crafted by ancient dwarven metalsmiths, they were strong enough to hold the weight of an army, yet they appeared so delicate that a bird lighting on them might overthrow the balance. These glistening arches were the city's only boundaries; there was no wall around Qualinost. The elven city opened its arms lovingly to the wilderness.

The buildings of Qualinost enhanced nature, rather than concealing it. The houses and shops were carved from rose-colored quartz. Tall and slender as aspen trees, they vaulted upward in impossible spirals from quartz-lined avenues. In the center stood a great tower of burnished gold, catching the sunlight and throwing it back in whirling, sparkling patterns that gave the tower life. Looking down upon the city, it seemed that peace and beauty unchanged from ages past must dwell in Qualinost, if it dwelled anywhere in Krynn.

"Rest here," Gilthanas told them, leaving them in a grove of aspen trees. "The journey has been long, and for that I apologize. I know you are weary and you hunger—"

Caramon looked up hopefully.

"But I must beg your indulgence a few moments longer. Please excuse me." Gilthanas bowed, then walked to stand by his brother. Sighing, Caramon began rummaging through his pack for the fifth time, hoping perhaps he had overlooked a morsel. Raistlin read his spellbook, his lips repeating the difficult words, trying to grasp their meaning, to find the correct inflection and phrasing that would make his blood burn and so tell him the spell was his at last.

The others looked around, marveling at the beauty of the city beneath them and the aura of ancient tranquillity that lay over it. Even Riverwind seemed touched; his face softened and he held Goldmoon close. For a brief instant, their caress and their sorrows eased and they found comfort in each other's nearness. Tika sat apart, watching them wistfully. Tasslehoff was trying to map their way from Gateway into Qualinost, although Tanis had told him four times that the way was secret and the elves would never permit him to carry off a map. The old magician, Fizban, was asleep. Sturm and Flint watched Tanis in concern—Flint because he alone had any idea of what the half-elf was suffering; Sturm because he knew what it was like returning to a home that didn't want you.

The knight laid his hand on Tanis's arm. "Coming home isn't easy, my friend, is it?" he asked.

"No," Tanis answered softly. "I thought I had left this behind long ago, but now I know I never truly left at all. Qualinesti is part of me, no matter how much I want to deny it."

"Hush, Gilthanas," Flint warned.

The elf came over to Tanis. "Runners were sent ahead and now they have returned," he said in elven. "My father has asked to see you—all of you—at once, in the Tower of the Sun. I cannot permit time for refreshment. In this we seem crude and impolite—"

"Gilthanas," Tanis interrupted in Common. "My friends and I have been through unimagined peril. We have traveled roads where—literally—the dead walked. We won't faint from hunger"—he glanced at Caramon—"some of us won't, at any rate."

The warrior, hearing Tanis, sighed and tightened his belt.

"Thank you," Gilthanas said stiffly. "I am glad you understand. Now, please follow as swiftly as you can."

The companions gathered their things hastily and woke Fizban. Rising to his feet, he fell over a tree root. "Big lummox!" he snapped, striking it with his staff. "There—did you see it? Tried to trip me!" he said to Raistlin.

The mage slipped his precious book back into its pouch. "Yes, Old One." Raistlin smiled, assisting Fizban to his feet. The old magician leaned on the young one's shoulder as they walked after the others. Tanis watched them, wondering. The old magician was obviously a dotard. Yet Tanis remembered Raistlin's look of stark terror when he woke and found Fizban leaning over him. What had the mage seen? What did he know about this old man? Tanis reminded himself to ask. Now, however, he had other, more pressing matters on his mind. Walking forward, he caught up with the elf.

"Tell me, Gilthanas," Tanis said in elven, the unfamiliar words haltingly coming back to him. "What's going on? I have a right to know."

"Have you?" Gilthanas asked harshly, glancing at Tanis from the corners of his almond-shaped eyes. "Do you care what happens to elves anymore? You can barely speak our language!"

"Of course, I care," Tanis said angrily. "You are my people, too!"

"Then why do you flaunt your human heritage?" Gilthanas gestured to Tanis's bearded face. "I would think you would be ashamed—" He stopped, biting his lip, his face flushing.

Tanis nodded grimly. "Yes, I was ashamed, and that's why I left. But if I was ashamed—who made me so?"

"Forgive me, Tanthalas," Gilthanas said, shaking his head. "What I said was cruel and, truly, I did not mean it. It's just that . . . if you only understood the danger we face!"

"Tell me!" Tanis practically shouted in his frustration. "I want to understand!"

"We are leaving Qualinesti," Gilthanas said.

Tanis stopped and stared at the elf. "Leaving Qualinesti?" he repeated, switching to Common in his shock. The companions heard him and cast quick glances at each other. The old magician's face darkened as he tugged at his beard.

"You can't mean it!" Tanis said softly. "Leaving Qualinesti! Why? Surely things aren't this bad—"

"They are worse," Gilthanas said sadly. "Look around you, Tanthalas. You see Qualinost in its final days."

They entered the first streets of the city. Tanis, at first glance, saw everything exactly as he had left it fifty years ago. Neither the streets of crushed gleaming rock nor the aspen trees they ran among had changed; the clean streets sparkled brightly in the sunshine; the aspens had grown perhaps, perhaps not. Their leaves glimmered in the late morning light, the gold and silver-inlaid branches rustled and sang. The houses along the streets had not changed. Decorated with quartz, they shimmered in the sunlight, creating small rainbows of color everywhere the eye looked. All seemed as the elves loved it—beautiful, orderly, unchanging. . . .

No, that was wrong, Tanis realized. The song of the trees was now sad and lamenting, not the peaceful, joyful song Tanis remembered. Qualinost *had* changed and the change was change itself. He tried to grasp hold of it, to understand it, even as he felt his soul shrivel with loss. The change was not in the buildings, not in the trees, or the sun shining through the leaves. The change was in the air. It crackled with tension, as before a storm. And, as Tanis walked the streets of Qualinost, he saw things he had never before seen in his homeland. He saw haste. He saw hurry. He saw indecision. He saw panic, desperation, and despair.

Women, meeting friends, embraced and wept, then parted and hurried on separate ways. Children sat forlorn, not understanding, knowing only that play was out of place. Men gathered in groups, hands on their swords, keeping watchful eyes on their families. Here and there, fires burned as the elves destroyed what they loved and could not carry with them, rather than let the coming darkness consume it.

Tanis had grieved over the destruction of Solace, but the sight of what was happening in Qualinost entered his soul like the blade of a dull knife. He had not realized it meant so much to him. He had known, deep in his heart, that even if he never returned, Qualinesti would always be there. But no, he was losing even that. Qualinesti would perish.

Tanis heard a strange sound and turned around to see the old magician weeping.

"What plans have you made? Where will you go? Can you escape?" Tanis asked Gilthanas bleakly.

"You will find out the answers to those questions and more, too soon, too soon," Gilthanas murmured.

The Tower of the Sun rose high above the other buildings in Qualinost. Sunlight reflecting off the golden surface gave the illusion of whirling movement. The companions entered the Tower in silence, awestruck by the beauty and majesty of the ancient building. Only Raistlin glanced around, unimpressed. To his eyes, there existed no beauty, only death.

Gilthanas led the companions to a small alcove. "This room is just off the main chamber," he said. "My father is meeting with the Heads of Household to plan the evacuation. My brother has gone to tell him of our arrival. When the business is finished, we will be summoned." At his gesture, elves entered, bearing pitchers and basins of cool water. "Please, refresh yourselves as time permits."

The companions drank, then washed the dust of the journey from their faces and hands. Sturm removed his cloak and carefully polished his armor as best he could with one of Tasslehoff's handkerchiefs. Goldmoon brushed out her shining hair, kept her cloak fastened around her neck. She and Tanis had decided the medallion she wore should remain hidden until the time seemed proper to reveal it; some would recognize it. Fizban tried, without much success, to straighten his bent and shapeless hat. Caramon looked around for something to eat. Gilthanas stood apart from them all, his face pale and drawn.

Within moments, Porthios appeared in the arched doorway. "You are called," he said sternly.

The companions entered the chamber of the Speaker of the Suns. No human had seen the inside of this building for hundreds of years. No kender had ever seen it. The last dwarves who saw it were the ones present at its construction, hundreds of years before.

"Ah, now this is craftsmanship," Flint said softly, tears misting his eyes.

The chamber was round and seemed immensely larger than the slender Tower could possibly encompass. Built entirely of white marble, there were no support beams, no columns. The room soared upwards hundreds of feet to form a dome at the very top of the tower where a beautiful mosaic made of inlaid, glittering tile portrayed the blue sky and the sun on one half; the silver moon, the red moon, and the stars on the other half, the halves separated by a rainbow.

There were no lights in the chamber. Cunningly built windows and mirrors focused sunlight into the room, no matter where the sun was located in the sky. The streams of sunlight converged in the center of the chamber illuminating a rostrum.

There were no seats in the Tower. The elves stood—men and women together; only those designated as Heads of Household had the right to be in this meeting. There were more women present than Tanis ever remembered seeing; many dressed in deep purple, the color of mourning. Elves marry for life and if the spouse dies do not remarry. Thus the widow has the status of Head of Household until her death.

The companions were led to the front of the chamber. The elves made room for them in respectful silence but gave them strange, forbidding looks—particularly the dwarf, the kender, and the two barbarians, who seemed grotesque in their outlandish furs. There were astonished murmurs at the sight of the proud and noble Knight of Solamnia. And there were scattered mutterings over the appearance of Raistlin in his red robes. Elven magic-users wore the white robes of good, not the red robes proclaiming neutrality. That, the elves believed, was just one step removed from black. As the crowd settled down, the Speaker of the Suns came forward to the rostrum.

It had been many years since Tanis had seen the Speaker, his adopted father, as it were. And here, too, he saw change. The man was still tall, taller even than his son Porthios. He was dressed in the yellow, shimmering robes of his office. His face was stern and unyielding, his manner austere. He was the Speaker of the Suns, called the Speaker; he had been called the Speaker for well over a century. Those who knew his name never pronounced it—including his children. But Tanis saw in his hair touches of silver, which had not been there before, and there were lines of care and sorrow in the face, which had previously seemed untouched by time.

Porthios joined his brother as the companions, led by the elves, entered. The Speaker extended his arms and called them by name. They walked forward into their father's embrace.

"My sons," the Speaker said brokenly, and Tanis was startled at this show of emotion. "I never thought to see either of you in this life again. Tell me of the raid—" he said, turning to Gilthanas.

"In time, Speaker," said Gilthanas. "First, I bid you, greet our guests."

"Yes, I am sorry." The Speaker passed a trembling hand over his face and it seemed to Tanis that he aged even as he stood before them. "Forgive me, guests. I bid you welcome, you who have entered this kingdom no one has entered for many years."

Gilthanas spoke a few words and the Speaker stared shrewdly at Tanis, then beckoned the half-elf forward. His words were cool, his manner polite, if strained. "Is it indeed you, Tanthalas, son of my brother's wife? The years have been long, and all have wondered about your fate. We welcome you back to your homeland, though I fear you come only to see its final days. My daughter, in particular, will be glad to see you. She has missed her childhood playmate."

Gilthanas stiffened at this, his face darkening as he looked at Tanis. The half-elf felt his own face flush. He bowed low before the Speaker, unable to say a word.

"I welcome the rest of you and hope to learn more of you later. We shall not keep you long, but it is right that you learn

317

in this room what is happening in the world. Then you will be allowed to rest and refresh yourselves. Now, my son—" The Speaker turned to Gilthanas, obviously thankful to end the formalities. "The raid on Pax Tharkas?"

Gilthanas stepped forward, his head bowed. "I have failed, Speaker of the Suns."

A murmur passed among the elves like the wind among the aspens. The Speaker's face bore no expression. He simply sighed and stared unseeing out a tall window. "Tell your story," he said quietly.

Gilthanas swallowed, then spoke, his voice so low many in the back of the room leaned forward to hear.

"I traveled south with my warriors in secrecy, as was planned. All went well. We found a group of human resistance fighters, refugees from Gateway, who joined us, adding to our numbers. Then, by the cruelest mischance, we stumbled into the advance patrols of the dragonarmy. We fought valiantly, elves and humans together, but for naught. I was struck on the head and remember nothing more. When I awoke, I was lying in a ravine, surrounded by the bodies of my comrades. Apparently, the foul dragonmen shoved the wounded over the cliff, leaving us for dead." Gilthanas paused, clearing his throat. "Druids in the woods tended my injuries. From them, I learned that many of my warriors were still alive and had been taken prisoner. Leaving the druids to bury the dead, I followed the tracks of the dragonarmy and eventually came to Solace."

Gilthanas stopped. His face glistened with sweat and his hands twitched nervously. He cleared his throat again, tried to speak and failed. His father watched him with growing concern.

Gilthanas spoke. "Solace is destroyed."

There was a gasp from the audience.

"The mighty vallenwoods have been cut and burned, few now stand."

The elves wailed and cried out in dismay and anger. The Speaker held up his hand for order. "This is grievous news," he said sternly. "We mourn the passing of trees old even to us. But continue—what of our people?"

"I found my men tied to stakes in the center of the town square along with the humans who had helped us," Gilthanas said, his voice breaking. "They were surrounded by draconian guards. I hoped to be able to free them at night. Then—" His voice failed completely and he bowed his head as his older brother came over and laid a hand on his shoulder. Gilthanas straightened. "A red dragon appeared in the sky—"

Sounds of shock and dismay came from the assembled elves. The Speaker shook his head in sorrow.

"Yes, Speaker," Gilthanas said and his voice was loud, unnaturally loud and jarring. "It is true. These monsters have returned to Krynn. The red dragon circled above Solace and all who saw him fled in terror. He flew lower and lower and then landed in the town square. His great gleaming red reptile body filled the clearing, his wings spread destruction, his tail toppled trees. Yellow fangs glistened, green saliva dripped from his massive jaws, his huge talons tore the ground . . . and riding upon his back was a human male.

"Powerfully built, he was dressed in the black robes of a cleric of the Queen of Darkness. A black and gold cape fluttered around him. His face was hidden by a hideous horned mask fashioned in black and gold to resemble the face of a dragon. The dragonmen fell to their knees in worship as the dragon landed. The goblins and hobgoblins and foul humans who fight with the dragonmen cowered in terror; many ran away. Only the example of my people gave me the courage to stay."

Now that he was speaking, Gilthanas seemed eager to tell the story. "Some of the humans tied to stakes went into a frenzy of terror, screaming piteously. But my warriors remained calm and defiant, although all were affected alike by the dragonfear the monster generates. The dragonrider did not seem to find this pleasing. He glared at them, and then spoke in a voice that came from the depths of the Abyss. His words still burn in my mind.

"'I am Verminaard, Dragon Highlord of the North. I have fought to free this land and these people from the false beliefs spread by those who call themselves Seekers. Many have come to work for me, pleased to further the great cause of the Dragon Highlords. I have shown them mercy and graced them with the blessings my goddess has granted me. Spells of healing I possess, as do no others in this land, and therefore you know that I am the representative of the true gods.

But you humans who stand before me now have defied me. You chose to fight me and therefore your punishment will serve as an example to any others who choose folly over wisdom.'

"Then he turned to the elves and said, 'Be it known by this act that I, Verminaard, will destroy your race utterly as decreed by my goddess. Humans can be taught to see the errors of their ways, but elves—never!' The man's voice rose until it raged louder than the winds. 'Let this be your final warning— all who watch! Ember, destroy!'

"And, with that, the great dragon breathed out fire upon all those tied to the stakes. They writhed helplessly, burning to death in terrible agony. . . ."

There was no sound at all in the chamber. The shock and horror were too great for words.

"A madness swept over me," Gilthanas continued, his eyes burning feverishly, almost a reflection of what he had seen. "I started to rush forward, to die with my people, when a great hand grasped me and dragged me backward. It was Theros Ironfeld, 'Now is not the time to die, elf,' he told me. "Now is the time for revenge.' I . . . I collapsed then, and he took me back to his house, in peril of his own life. And he would have paid for his kindness to elves with his life, had not this woman healed him!"

Gilthanas pointed to Goldmoon, who stood at the back of the group, her face shrouded by her fur cape. The Speaker turned to stare at her, as did the other elves in the chamber, their murmurings dark and ominous.

"Theros is the man brought here today, Speaker," Porthios said. "The man with but one arm. Our healers say he will live. But they say it is only by a miracle that his life was spared, so dreadful were his wounds."

"Come forward, woman of the Plains," the Speaker commanded sternly. Goldmoon took a step toward the rostrum, Riverwind at her side. Two elven guards moved swiftly to block him. He glared at them but stood where he was.

The Chieftain's Daughter moved forward, holding her head proudly. As she removed her hood, the sun shone on the silver-gold hair cascading down her back. The elves marveled at her beauty.

"You claim to have healed this man—Theros Ironfeld?" The Speaker asked her with disdain.

"I claim nothing," Goldmoon answered coolly. "Your son saw me heal him. Do you doubt his words?"

"No, but he was overwrought, sick and confused. He may have mistaken witchcraft for healing."

"Look on this," Goldmoon said gently and untied her cape, letting it fall away from her neck. The medallion sparkled in the sunlight.

The Speaker left the rostrum and came forward, his eyes widening in disbelief. Then his face became distorted with rage. "Blasphemy!" he shouted. Reaching out, he started to rip the medallion from Goldmoon's throat.

There was a flash of blue light. The Speaker crumbled to the floor with a cry of pain. As the elves shouted out in alarm, drawing their swords, the companions drew theirs. Elven warriors rushed to surround them.

"Stop this nonsense!" said the old magician in a strong, stern voice. Fizban tottered up to the rostrum, calmly pushing aside the sword blades as if they were slender branches of an aspen tree. The elves stared in astonishment, seemingly unable to stop him. Muttering to himself, Fizban came up to the Speaker, who was lying stunned on the floor. The old man helped the elf to his feet.

"Now then, you asked for that, you know," Fizban scolded, brushing the Speaker's robes as the elf gaped at him.

"Who are you?" the Speaker gasped.

"Mmmm. What was that name?" The old magician glanced around at Tasslehoff.

"Fizban," the kender said helpfully.

"Yes, Fizban. That's who I am." The magician stroked his white beard. "Now, Solostaran, I suggest you call off your guards and tell everyone to settle down. I, for one, would like to hear the story of this young woman's adventures, and you, for one, would do well to listen. It wouldn't hurt you to apologize, either."

As Fizban shook his finger at the Speaker, his battered hat tilted forward, covering his eyes. "Help! I've gone blind!" Raistlin, with a distrustful glance at the elven guards, hurried forward. He took the old man's arm and straightened his hat.

"Ah, thank the true gods," the magician said, blinking and shuffling across the floor. The Speaker watched the old magician, a puzzled expression on his face. Then, as if in a dream, he turned to face Goldmoon.

"I do apologize, lady of the Plains," he said softly. "It has been over three hundred years since the elven clerics vanished, three hundred years since the symbol of Mishakal was seen in this land. My heart bled to see the amulet profaned, as I thought. Forgive me. We have been in despair so long I failed to see the arrival of hope. Please, if you are not weary, tell us your story."

Goldmoon related the story of the medallion, telling of Riverwind and the stoning, the meeting of the companions at the Inn, and their journey to Xak Tsaroth. She told of the destruction of the dragon and of how she received the medallion of Mishakal. But she didn't mention the Disks.

The sun's rays lengthened as she spoke, changing color as twilight approached. When her story ended, the Speaker was silent for long moments.

"I must consider all of this and what it means to us," he said finally. He turned to the companions. "You are exhausted. I see some of you stand by courage alone. Indeed"—he smiled, looking at Fizban who leaned against a pillar, snoring softly—"some of you are asleep on your feet. My daughter, Laurana, will guide you to a place where you can forget your fears. We will hold a banquet in your honor tonight, for you bring us hope. May the peace of the true gods go with you."

The elves parted, and out of their midst came an elfmaiden who walked forward to stand beside the Speaker. At sight of her, Caramon's mouth sagged open. Riverwind's eyes widened. Even Raistlin stared, his eyes seeing beauty at last, for no hint of decay touched the young elfmaiden. Her hair was honey pouring from a pitcher; it spilled over her arms and down her back, past her waist, touching her wrists as she stood with her arms at her sides. Her skin was smooth and woodland brown. She had the delicate, refined features of the elves, but these were combined with full, pouting lips and large liquid eyes that changed color like leaves in flickering sunshine.

"On my honor as a knight," Sturm said with a catch in his voice, "I've never seen any woman so lovely."

"Nor will you in this world," Tanis murmured.

All the companions glanced at Tanis sharply as he spoke, but the half-elf did not notice. His eyes were on the elfmaid. Sturm raised his eyebrows, exchanged looks with Caramon who nudged his brother. Flint shook his head and sighed a sigh that seemed to come from his toes.

"Now much is made clear," Goldmoon said to Riverwind.

"It hasn't been made clear to me," Tasslehoff said. "Do you know what's going on, Tika?"

All Tika knew was that, looking at Laurana, she felt suddenly dumpy and half-dressed, freckled and red-headed. She tugged her blouse up higher over her full bosom, wishing it didn't reveal quite so much or that she had less to reveal.

"Tell me what's going on," Tasslehoff whispered, seeing the knowing looks exchanged by the others.

"I don't know!" Tika snapped. "Just that Caramon's making a fool of himself. Look at the big ox. You'd think he'd never seen a woman before."

"She is pretty," Tas said. "Different from you, Tika. She's slender and she walks like a tree bending in the wind and—"

"Oh, shut up!" Tika snapped furiously, giving Tas a shove that nearly knocked him down.

Tasslehoff gave her a wounded glance, then walked over to stand beside Tanis, determined to keep near the half-elf until he figured out what was going on.

"I welcome you to Qualinost, honored guests," Laurana said shyly, in a voice that was like a clear stream rippling among the trees. "Please follow me. The way is not far, and there is food and drink and rest at the end."

Moving with childlike grace, she walked among the companions who parted for her as the elves had done, all of them staring at her admiringly. Laurana lowered her eyes in maidenly modesty and self-consciousness, her cheeks flushing. She looked up only once, and that was as she passed Tanis—a fleeting glance, that only Tanis saw. His face grew troubled, his eyes darkened.

The companions left the Tower of the Sun, waking Fizban as they departed.

6

Tanis and Laurana.

aurana led them to a sun-dappled grove of aspens in the very center of the city. Here, though surrounded by buildings and streets, they seemed to be in the heart of a forest. Only the murmurings of a nearby brook broke the stillness. Laurana, gesturing toward fruit trees among the aspens, told the companions to pick and eat their fill. Elfmaids brought in baskets of fresh, fragrant bread. The companions washed in the brook, then returned to relax on soft moss beds to revel in the silent peacefulness around them.

All except Tanis. Refusing food, the half-elf wandered around the grove, absorbed in his own thoughts. Tasslehoff watched him closely, eaten alive by curiosity.

Laurana was a perfect, charming hostess. She made certain everyone was seated and comfortable, speaking a few words to each of them.

"Flint Fireforge, isn't it?" she said. The dwarf flushed with pleasure. "I still have some of the wonderful toys you made me. We have missed you, these many years."

So flustered he couldn't talk, Flint plopped down on the grass and gulped down a huge mug of water.

"You are Tika?" Laurana asked, stopping by the barmaid.

"Tika Waylan," the girl said huskily.

"Tika, what a pretty name. And what beautiful hair you have," Laurana said, reaching out to touch the bouncy red curls admiringly.

"Do you think so?" Tika said, blushing, seeing Caramon's eyes on her.

"Of course! It is the color of flame. You must have a spirit to match. I heard how you saved my brother's life in the Inn, Tika. I am deeply indebted to you."

"Thank you," Tika answered softly. "Your hair is real pretty, too."

Laurana smiled and moved on. Tasslehoff noticed, however, that her eyes constantly strayed to Tanis. When the half-elf suddenly threw down an apple and disappeared into the trees, Laurana excused herself hurriedly and followed.

"Ah, now I'll find out what's going on!" Tas said to himself. Glancing around, he slipped after Tanis.

Tas crept along the winding trail among the trees and suddenly came upon the half-elf standing beside the foaming stream alone, tossing dead leaves into the water. Seeing movement to his left, Tas quickly crouched down into a clump of bushes as Laurana emerged from another trail.

"*Tanthalas Quisif nan-Pah!*" she called.

As Tanis turned at the sound of his elven name, she flung her arms around his neck, kissing him. "Ugh," she said teasingly, pulling back. "Shave off that horrible beard. It itches! And you don't look like Tanthalas anymore."

Tanis put his hands to her waist and gently pushed her away. "Laurana—" he began.

"No, don't be mad about the beard. I'll learn to like it, if you insist," Laurana pleaded, pouting. "Kiss me back. No? Then I'll kiss you until you cannot help yourself." She kissed him again until finally Tanis broke free of her grip.

"Stop it, Laurana," he said harshly, turning away.

"Why, what's the matter?" she asked, catching hold of his hand. "You've been gone so many years. And now you're back. Don't be cold and gloomy. You are my betrothed, remember? It is proper for a girl to kiss her betrothed."

"That was a long time ago," Tanis said. "We were children, then, playing a game, nothing more. It was romantic, a secret to share. You know what would have happened if your father had found out. Gilthanas did find out, didn't he?"

"Of course! I told him," Laurana said, hanging her head, looking up at Tanis through her long eyelashes. "I tell Gilthanas everything, you know that. I didn't think he'd react like that! I know what he said to you. He told me later. He felt badly."

"I'll bet he did." Tanis gripped her wrists, holding her hands still. "What he said was true, Laurana! I am a bastard half-breed. Your father would have every right to kill me! How could I bring disgrace down on him, after what he did for my mother and me? That was one reason I left—that and to find out who I am and where I belong."

"You are Tanthalas, my beloved, and you belong here!" Laurana cried. She broke free of his grip and caught his hands in her own. "Look! You wear my ring still. I know why you left. It was because you were afraid to love me, but you don't need to be, not anymore. Everything's changed. Father has so much to worry about, he won't mind. Besides, you're a hero now. Please, let us be married. Isn't that why you came back?"

"Laurana," Tanis spoke gently but firmly—"my returning was an accident—"

"No!" she cried, pushing him away. "I don't believe you."

"You must have heard Gilthanas's story. If Porthios had not rescued us, we would have been in Pax Tharkas now!"

"He made it up! He didn't want to tell me the truth. You came back because you love me. I won't listen to anything else."

"I didn't want to tell you, but I see that I must," Tanis said, exasperated. "Laurana, I'm in love with someone else—a human woman. Her name is Kitiara. That doesn't mean I don't love you, too. I do—" Tanis faltered.

Laurana stared at him, all color drained from her face.

"I do love you, Laurana. But, you see, I can't marry you, because I love her, too. My heart is divided, just like my blood." He took off the ring of golden ivy leaves and handed it to her.

"I release you from any promises you made to me, Laurana. And I ask you to release me."

Laurana took the ring, unable to speak. She looked at Tanis pleadingly, then, seeing only pity in his face, shrieked and flung the ring away from her. It fell at Tas's feet. He picked it up and slipped it into a pouch.

"Laurana," Tanis said sorrowfully, taking her in his arms as she sobbed wildly. "I'm so sorry. I never meant—"

At this point, Tasslehoff slipped out of the brush and made his way back up the trail.

"Well," said the kender to himself, sighing in satisfaction— "now at least I know what's going on."

Tanis awoke suddenly to find Gilthanas standing over him. "Laurana?" he asked, getting to his feet.

"She is all right," Gilthanas said quietly. "Her maidens brought her home. She told me what you said. I just want you to know I understand. It was what I feared all along. The human half of you cries to other humans. I tried to tell her, hoping she wouldn't get hurt. She will listen to me now. Thank you, Tanthalas. I know it cannot have been easy."

"It wasn't," Tanis said, swallowing. "I'm going to be honest, Gilthanas—I love her, I really do. It's just that—"

"Please, say no more. Let us leave it as it is and perhaps, if we cannot be friends, we can at least respect each other." Gilthanas's face was drawn and pale in the setting sun. "You and your friends must prepare yourselves. When the silver moon rises, there will be a feast, and then the High Council meeting. Now is the time when decisions must be made."

He left. Tanis stared after him a moment, then, sighing, went to wake the others.

7

Farewell. The companions' decision.

he feast held in Qualinost reminded Goldmoon of her mother's funeral banquet. Like the feast, the funeral was supposed to be a joyous occasion—after all, Tearsong had become a goddess. But the people found it difficult to accept the death of this beautiful woman. And so the Que-shu mourned her passing with a grief that approached blasphemy.

Tearsong's funeral banquet was the most elaborate to be given in the memory of the Que-shu. Her grieving husband had spared no expense. Like the banquet in Qualinost on this night, there was a great deal of food which few could eat. There were half-hearted attempts at conversation when no one wanted to talk. Occasionally someone, overcome with sorrow, was forced to leave the table.

So vivid was this memory that Goldmoon could eat little;

the food was ash in her mouth. Riverwind regarded her with concern. His hand found hers beneath the table and she gripped it hard, smiling as his strength flowed into her body.

The elven feast was held in the courtyard just south of the great golden tower. There were no walls about the platform of crystal and marble which sat atop the highest hill in Qualinost, offering an unobstructed view of the glittering city below, the dark forest beyond, and even the deep purple edge of the Tharkadan Mountains far to the south. But the beauty was lost on those in attendance, or made more poignant by the knowledge that soon it would be gone forever. Goldmoon sat at the right hand of the Speaker. He tried to make polite conversation, but eventually his worries and concerns overwhelmed him and he fell silent.

To the Speaker's left sat his daughter, Laurana. She made no pretense at eating, just sat with her head bowed, her long hair flowing around her face. When she did look up, it was to gaze at Tanis, her heart in her eyes.

The half-elf, very much aware of the heart-broken stare as well as of Gilthanas eyeing him coldly, ate his food without appetite, his eyes fixed on his plate. Sturm, next to him, was drawing up in his mind plans for the defense of Qualinesti.

Flint felt strange and out of place as dwarves always feel among elves. He didn't like elven food anyway and refused everything. Raistlin nibbled at his food absently, his golden eyes studying Fizban. Tika, feeling awkward and out of place among the graceful elven women, couldn't eat a morsel. Caramon decided he knew why elves were so slender: the food consisted of fruits and vegetables, cooked in delicate sauces, served with bread and cheeses and a very light, spicy wine. After starving for four days in the cage, the food did nothing to satisfy the big warrior's hunger.

The only two in the entire city of Qualinost to enjoy the feast were Tasslehoff and Fizban. The old magician carried on a one-sided argument with an aspen, while Tasslehoff simply enjoyed everything, discovering later—to his surprise—that two golden spoons, a silver knife, and a butter dish made of a seashell had wandered into one of his pouches.

The red moon was not visible. Solinari, a slim band of silver in the sky, began to wane. As the first stars appeared,

the Speaker of the Suns nodded sadly at his son. Gilthanas
rose and moved to stand next to his father's chair.

Gilthanas began to sing. The elven words flowed into a
melody delicate and beautiful. As he sang, Gilthanas held a
small crystal lamp in both hands, the candlelight within illuminating his marble features. Tanis, listening to the song,
closed his eyes; his head sank into his hands.

"What is it? What do the words mean?" Sturm asked softly.
Tanis raised his head. His voice breaking, he whispered:

The Sun
The splendid eye
Of all our heavens
Dives from the day,

And leaves
The dozing sky,
Spangled with fireflies,
Deepening in gray.

The elves about the table stood quietly now, taking up their
own lamps as they joined in the song. Their voices blended,
weaving a haunting song of infinite sadness.

Now Sleep,
Our oldest friend,
Lulls in the trees
And calls
Us in.

The Leaves
Give off cold fire,
They blaze into ash
At the end of the year.

And birds
Coast on the winds,
And wheel to the North
When Autumn ends.

The day grows dark,
The seasons bare,
But we
Await the sun's
Green fire upon
The trees.

Points of flickering lantern light spread from the courtyard like ripples in a still, calm pond, through the streets, into the forests and beyond. And, with each lamp lit, another voice was raised in song, until the surrounding forest itself seemed to sing with despair.

The wind
Dives through the days.
By season, by moon
Great kingdoms arise.

The breath
Of firefly, of bird,
Of trees, of mankind
Fades in a word.

Now Sleep,
Our oldest friend,
Lulls in the trees
And calls
Us in.

The Age,
The thousand lives
Of men and their stories
Go to their graves.

But We,
The people long
In poem and glory
Fade from the song.

Gilthanas's voice died away. With a gentle breath, he blew

out the flame of his lamp. One by one, as they had started, the others around the table ended the song and blew out their candles. All through Qualinost, the voices hushed and the flames were extinguished until it seemed that silence and darkness swept over the land. At the very end, only the distant mountains returned the final chords of the song, like the whispering of leaves falling to the ground.

The Speaker stood.

"And now," he said heavily, "it is time for the meeting of the High Council. It will be held in the Hall of the Sky. Tanthalas, if you will lead your companions there."

The Hall of the Sky, they discovered, was a huge square, lit by torches. The giant dome of the heavens, glittering with stars, arched above it. But it was dark to the north where lightning played on the horizon. The Speaker motioned to Tanis to bring the companions to stand near him, then the entire population of Qualinost gathered around them. There was no need to call for silence. Even the wind hushed as the Speaker began.

"Here you see our situation." He gestured at something on the ground. The companions saw a gigantic map beneath their feet. Tasslehoff, standing in the middle of the Plains of Abanasinia, drew in a deep breath. He couldn't remember ever seeing anything so wonderful.

"There's Solace!" he cried in excitement, pointing.

"Yes, Kenderkin," the Speaker replied. "And that is where the dragonarmies mass. In Solace"—he touched the spot on the map with a staff—"and in Haven. Lord Verminaard has made no secret of his plans to invade Qualinesti. He waits only to gather his forces and secure his supply routes. We cannot hope to stand against such a horde."

"Surely Qualinost is easily defended," Sturm spoke up. "There is no direct route overland. We crossed bridges over ravines that no army in existence could get through if the bridges were cut. Why do you not stand up to them?"

"If it were only an army, we could defend Qualinesti," the Speaker answered. "But what can we do against dragons?" The Speaker spread his hands helplessly. "Nothing! According to legends, it was only with the Dragonlance that the mighty Huma defeated them. There are none now—at least that we know of—who remember the secret of that great weapon."

Fizban started to speak, but Raistlin hushed him.

"No," the Speaker continued, "we must abandon this city and these woods. We plan to go west, into the unknown lands there, hoping to find a new home for our people—or perhaps even return to Silvanesti, the most ancient elvenhome. Until a week ago, our plans were advancing well. It will take three days of forced marching for the Dragon Highlord to move his men into attack position, and spies will inform us when the army leaves Solace. We will have time to escape into the west. But then we learned of a third dragonarmy at Pax Tharkas, less than a day's journey from us. Unless that army is stopped, we are doomed."

"And you know a way to stop that army?" Tanis asked.

"Yes." The Speaker looked at his youngest son. "As you know, men from Gateway and Solace and surrounding communities are being held prisoner in the fortress of Pax Tharkas, working as slaves for the Dragon Highlord. Verminaard is clever. Lest his slaves revolt, he keeps the women and children of these men hostages, ransom for the men's behavior. It is our belief that, were these captives freed, the men would turn on their masters and destroy them. It was to have been Gilthanas's mission to free the hostages and lead the revolt. He would have taken the humans south into the mountains, drawing off this third army in pursuit, allowing us time to escape."

"And what of the humans then?" Riverwind asked harshly. "It seems to me you throw them to the dragonarmies as a desperate man throws hunks of meat to pursuing wolves."

"Lord Verminaard will not keep them alive much longer, we fear. The ore is nearly gone. He is gleaning every last little bit, then the slaves' usefulness to him will end. There are valleys in the mountains, caves where the humans can live and fend off the dragonarmies. They can easily hold the mountain passes against them, especially now that winter is setting in. Admittedly, some may die, but that is a price that must be paid. If you had the choice, man of the Plains, would you rather die in slavery or die fighting?"

Riverwind, not answering, stared down at the map darkly.

"Gilthanas's mission failed," Tanis said, "and now you want us to try and lead the revolt?"

"Yes, Tanthalas," the Speaker replied. "Gilthanas knows a way into Pax Tharkas—the Sla-Mori. He can lead you into the fortress. You not only have a chance to free your own kind, but you offer the elves a chance to escape"—the Speaker's voice hardened—"a chance to live that many elves were not given when humans brought the Cataclysm down upon us!"

Riverwind glanced up, scowling. Even Sturm's expression darkened. The Speaker drew a deep breath, then sighed. "Please forgive me," he said. "I do not mean to flog you with whips from the past. We are not uncaring about the humans' plight. I send my son, Gilthanas, with you willingly, knowing that—if we part—we may never see each other again. I make this sacrifice, so that my people—and yours—may live."

"We must have time to consider," Tanis said, though he knew what his decision must be. The Speaker nodded and elven warriors cleared a path through the crowd, leading the companions to a grove of trees. Here, they left them alone.

Tanis's friends stood before him, their solemn faces masks of light and shadow beneath the stars. All this time, he thought, I have fought to keep us together. Now I see that we must separate. We cannot risk taking the Disks into Pax Tharkas, and Goldmoon will not leave them behind.

"I will go to Pax Tharkas," Tanis said softly. "But I believe it is time now that we separate, my friends. Before you speak, let me say this. I would send Tika, Goldmoon, Riverwind, Caramon and Raistlin, and you, Fizban, with the elves in hopes that you may carry the Disks to safety. The Disks are too precious to risk on a raid into Pax Tharkas."

"That may be, Half-Elf," Raistlin whispered from the depths of his cowl, "but it is not among the Qualinesti elves that Goldmoon will find the one she seeks."

"How do you know?" Tanis asked, startled.

"He doesn't know anything, Tanis," Sturm interrupted bitterly. "More talk—"

"Raistlin?" Tanis repeated, ignoring Sturm.

"You heard the knight!" the mage hissed. "I know nothing!"

Tanis sighed, letting it go, and glanced around. "You named me your leader—"

"Aye, we did, lad," said Flint suddenly. "But this decision

is coming from your head, not your heart. Deep inside, you don't really believe we should split up."

"Well, I'm not staying with these elves," Tika said, folding her arms across her chest. "I'm going with you, Tanis. I plan to become a swordswoman, like Kitiara."

Tanis winced. Hearing Kitiara's name was like a physical blow.

"I will not hide with elves," Riverwind said, "especially if it means leaving my kind behind to fight for me."

"He and I are one," Goldmoon said, putting her hand on his arm. "Besides," she said more softly, "somehow I know that what the mage says is true—the leader is not among the elves. They want to flee the world, not fight for it."

"We're all going, Tanis," Flint said firmly.

The half-elf looked helplessly around at the group, then he smiled and shook his head. "You're right. I didn't truly believe we should separate. It's the sensible, logical thing to do, of course, which is why we won't do it."

"Now maybe we can get some sleep." Fizban yawned.

"Wait a minute, Old One," Tanis said sternly. "You are not one of us. You're definitely going with the elves."

"Am I?" the old mage asked softly as his eyes lost their vague, unfocused look. He stared at Tanis with such a penetrating—almost menacing—gaze that the half-elf involuntarily took a step back, suddenly sensing an almost palpable aura of power surrounding the old man. His voice was soft and intense. "I go where I choose in this world, and I choose to go with you, Tanis Half-Elven."

Raistlin glanced at Tanis as if to say, *Now you understand!* Tanis, irresolute, returned the glance. He regretted putting off discussing this with Raistlin, but wondered how they could confer now, knowing the old man would not leave.

"I speak you this, Raistlin," Tanis said suddenly, using Camptalk, a corrupted form of Common developed among the racially mixed mercenaries of Krynn. The twins had done a bit of mercenary work in their time, as had most of the companions, in order to eat. Tanis knew Raistlin would understand. He was fairly certain the old man wouldn't.

"We talk if want," Raistlin answered in the same language, "but little know I."

"You fear. Why?"

Raistlin's strange eyes stared far away as he answered slowly. "I know not, Tanis. But—you right. There power be, within Old One. I feel great power. I fear." His eyes gleamed. "And I hunger!" The mage sighed and seemed to return from wherever it was he had been. "But he right. Try to stop him? Very much danger."

"As if there wasn't enough already," Tanis said bitterly, switching back to Common. "We take our own in with us in the form of a doddering old magician."

"Others there are, as dangerous, perhaps," Raistlin said, with a meaningful look at his brother. The mage returned to Common. "I am weary. I must sleep. Are you staying, brother?"

"Yes," Caramon answered, exchanging glances with Sturm. "We're going to talk with Tanis."

Raistlin nodded and gave his arm to Fizban. The old mage and the young one left, the old mage lashing out at a tree with his staff, accusing it of trying to sneak up on him.

"As if one crazed mage wasn't bad enough," Flint muttered. "I'm going to bed."

One by one the others left until Tanis stood with Caramon and Sturm. Wearily, Tanis turned to face them. He had a feeling he knew what this was going to be about. Caramon's face was flushed and he stared at his feet. Sturm stroked his moustaches and regarded Tanis thoughtfully.

"Well?" Tanis asked.

"Gilthanas," Sturm answered.

Tanis frowned and scratched his beard. "That's my business, not yours," he said shortly.

"It is *our* business, Tanis," Sturm persisted, "if he's leading us into Pax Tharkas. We don't want to pry, but it's obvious there's a score to settle between you two. I've seen his eyes when he looks at you, Tanis, and, if I were you, I wouldn't go anywhere without a friend at my back."

Caramon looked at Tanis earnestly, his brow furrowed. "I know he's an elf and all," the big man said slowly. "But, like Sturm says, he gets a funny look in his eyes sometimes. Don't you know the way to this Sla-Mori? Can't we find it ourselves? I don't trust him. Neither do Sturm and Raist."

"Listen, Tanis," Sturm said, seeing the half-elf's face darken with anger. "If Gilthanas was in such danger in Solace as he claimed, why was he casually sitting in the Inn? And then there's his story about his warriors 'accidentally' running into a whole damn army! Tanis, don't shake your head so quickly. He may not be evil, just misguided. What if Verminaard's got some hold over him? Perhaps the Dragon Highlord convinced him he'd spare his people if—in return—he betrays us! Maybe that's why he was in Solace, waiting for us."

"That's ridiculous!" Tanis snapped. "How would he know we were coming?"

"We didn't exactly keep our journey from Xak Tsaroth to Solace secret," Sturm returned coldly. "We saw draconians all along the way and those that escaped Xak Tsaroth must have realized we came for the Disks. Verminaard probably knows our descriptions better than he knows his own mother."

"No! I don't believe it!" Tanis said angrily, glaring at Sturm and Caramon. "You two are wrong! I'll stake my life on it. I grew up with Gilthanas, I know him! Yes, there *is* a score to settle between us, but we have discussed it and the matter is closed. I'll believe he's turned traitor to his people the day I believe you or Caramon turn traitor. And no, I don't know the way to Pax Tharkas. I've never been there. And one more thing," Tanis shouted, now in a fury, "if there's people I don't trust in this group, it's that brother of yours and that old man!" He stared accusingly at Caramon.

The big man grew pale and lowered his eyes. He began to turn away. Tanis came to his senses, suddenly realizing what he had said. "I'm sorry, Caramon." He put his hand on the warrior's arm. "I didn't mean that. Raistlin's saved our lives more than once on this insane journey. It's just that I can't believe Gilthanas is a traitor!"

"We know, Tanis," Sturm said quietly. "And we trust your judgment. But—it's too dark a night to walk with your eyes closed, as my people say."

Tanis sighed and nodded. He put his other hand on Sturm's arm. The knight clasped him and the three men stood in silence, then they left the grove and walked back to the Hall of the Sky. They could still hear the Speaker talking with his warriors.

"What does Sla-Mori mean?" Caramon asked.

"Secret Way," Tanis answered.

Tanis woke with a start, his hand on the dagger at his belt. A dark shape crouched over him in the night, blotting out the stars overhead. Reaching up quickly, he grabbed hold of and yanked the person down across his body, putting his dagger to the exposed throat.

"Tanthalas!" There was a small scream at the sight of the steel flashing in the starlight.

"Laurana!" Tanis gasped.

Her body pressed against his. He could feel her trembling and, now that he was fully awake, he could see the long hair flowing loosely about her shoulders. She was dressed only in a flimsy nightdress. Her cloak had fallen off in the brief struggle.

Acting on impulse, Laurana had risen from her bed and slipped out into the night, throwing a cloak around her to protect her from the cold. Now she lay across Tanis's chest, too frightened to move. This was a side of Tanis she had never known existed. She realized suddenly that if she had been an enemy, she would be dead now—her throat slit.

"Laurana . . ." Tanis repeated, thrusting the dagger back into his belt with a shaking hand. He pushed her away and sat up, angry at himself for frightening her and angry at her for awakening something deep within him. For an instant, when she lay on top of him, he was acutely conscious only of the smell of her hair, the warmth of her slender body, the play of the muscles in her thighs, the softness of her small breasts. Laurana had been a girl when he left. He returned to find a woman—a very beautiful, desirable woman

"What in the name of the Abyss are you doing here at this time of night?"

"Tanthalas," she said, choking, pulling her cape around her tightly. "I came to ask you to change your mind. Let your friends go to free the humans in Pax Tharkas. You must come with us! Don't throw your life away. My father is desperate. He doesn't believe this will work—I know he doesn't. But he hasn't any choice! He's already mourning Gilthanas as if he were dead. I'm going to lose my brother. I can't lose you, too!" She began to sob. Tanis glanced around hastily. There were almost certainly elven guards around. If the elves caught him in this compromising situation . . .

"Laurana," he said, gripping her shoulders and shaking her. "You're not a child anymore. You've got to grow up and grow up fast. I wouldn't let my friends face danger without me! I know the risks we're taking; I'm not blind! But if we can free the humans from Verminaard and give you and your people time to escape, it's a chance we have to take! There comes a time, Laurana, when you've got to risk your life for something you believe in—something that means more than life itself. Do you understand?"

She looked up at him through a mass of golden hair. Her sobs stopped and she ceased to tremble. She stared at him very intently.

"Do you understand, Laurana?" he repeated.

"Yes, Tanthalas," she answered softly. "I understand."

"Good!" He sighed. "Now go back to bed. Quickly. You've put me in danger. If Gilthanas saw us like this—"

Laurana stood up and walked swiftly from the grove, flitting along the streets and buildings like the wind among the aspens. Sneaking past the guards to get back inside her father's dwelling was simple—she and Gilthanas had been doing it since childhood. Returning quietly to her room, she stood outside her father's and mother's door for a moment, listening. There was light inside. She could hear parchment rustling, smell an acrid odor. Her father was burning papers. She heard her mother's soft murmur, calling her father to bed. Laurana closed her eyes for a moment in silent agony, then her lips tightened in firm resolve, and she ran down the dark, chill hallway to her bedchamber.

8

Doubts. Ambush!
A new friend.

he elves woke the companions before dawn. Storm clouds lowered on the northern horizon, reaching like grasping fingers toward Qualinesti. Gilthanas arrived after breakfast, dressed in a tunic of blue cloth and a suit of chain mail.

"We have supplies," he said, gesturing toward the warriors who held packs in their hands. "We can also provide weapons or armament, if you have need."

"Tika needs armor and shield and sword," said Caramon.

"We will provide what we can," Gilthanas said, "though I doubt if we have a full set of armor small enough."

"How is Theros Ironfeld this morning?" Goldmoon asked.

"He rests comfortably, cleric of Mishakal." Gilthanas bowed respectfully to Goldmoon. "My people will, of course, take him with them when we leave. You may bid him farewell."

Elves soon returned with armor of every make and description for Tika and a lightweight shortsword, favored by the elven women. Tika's eyes glowed when she saw the helm and shield. Both were of elvish design, tooled and decorated with jewels.

Gilthanas took the helm and shield from the elf. "I have yet to thank you for saving my life in the Inn," he said to Tika. "Accept these. They are my mother's ceremonial armor, dating back to the time of the Kinslayer Wars. These would have gone to my sister, but Laurana and I both believe you are the proper owner."

"How beautiful," Tika murmured, blushing. She accepted the helm, then looked at the rest of the armor in confusion. "I don't know what goes where," she confessed.

"I'll help!" Caramon offered eagerly.

"I'll handle this," Goldmoon said firmly. Picking up the armor, she led Tika into a grove of trees.

"What does she know about armor?" Caramon grumbled.

Riverwind looked at the warrior and smiled, the rare, infrequent smile that softened his stern face. "You forget," he said—"she is Chieftain's Daughter. It was her duty, in her father's absence, to lead the tribe to war. She knows a great deal about armor, warrior—and even more about the heart that beats beneath it."

Caramon flushed. Nervously, he picked up a pack of supplies and glanced inside. "What's this junk?" he asked.

"*Quith-pa,*" said Gilthanas. "Iron rations, in your language. It will last us for many weeks, if need be."

"It looks like dried fruit!" Caramon said in disgust.

"That's what it is," Tanis replied, grinning.

Caramon groaned.

Dawn was just beginning to tinge the wispy storm clouds with a pale, chill light when Gilthanas led the party out of Qualinesti. Tanis kept his eyes straight ahead, refusing to look back. He wished that his final trip here could have been happier. He had not seen Laurana all morning and, though he felt relieved to have avoided a tearful farewell, he secretly wondered why she hadn't come to bid him good-bye.

The trail moved south, descending gradually but constantly. It had been thick and overgrown with brush, but the party of warriors Gilthanas led before had cleared it as they moved, so that walking was relatively easy. Caramon walked beside Tika, resplendent in her mismatched armor, instructing her on the use of her sword. Unfortunately, the teacher was having a bad time of it.

Goldmoon had slit Tika's red barmaid skirt up to her thighs for easier movement. Bits of fluffy white from Tika's fur-trimmed undergarments peeped enticingly through the slits. Her legs were visible as she walked, and the girl's legs were just as Caramon had always imagined—round and well-formed. Thus Caramon found it rather difficult to concentrate on his lesson. Absorbed in his pupil, he did not notice that his brother had disappeared.

"Where's the young mage?" Gilthanas asked harshly.

"Maybe something's happened to him," Caramon said worriedly, cursing himself for forgetting his brother. The warrior drew his sword and started back along the trail.

"Nonsense!" Gilthanas stopped him. "What could have happened to him? There is no enemy for miles. He must have gone off somewhere—for some purpose."

"What are you saying?" Caramon asked, glowering.

"Maybe he left to—"

"To collect what I need for the making of my magic, elf," Raistlin whispered, emerging from the brush. "And to replenish the herbs that heal my cough."

"Raist!" Caramon nearly hugged him in his relief. "You shouldn't go off by yourself—it's dangerous."

"My spell components are secret," Raistlin whispered irritably, shoving his brother away. Leaning on the Staff of Magius, the mage rejoined Fizban in the line.

Gilthanas cast a sharp glance at Tanis, who shrugged and shook his head. As the group continued on, the trail became steeper and steeper, leading down from the aspenwoods to the pines of the lowlands. It joined up with a clear brook that soon became a raging stream as they traveled farther south.

When they stopped for a hasty lunch, Fizban came over and hunkered down beside Tanis. "Someone's following us," he said in a penetrating whisper.

"What?" Tanis asked, his head snapping up to stare at the old man incredulously.

"Yes, indeed," the old mage nodded solemnly. "I've seen it—darting in and out among the trees."

Sturm saw Tanis's look of concern. "What's the matter?"

"The Old One says someone's following us."

"Bah!" Gilthanas threw down his last bit of quith-pa in disgust and stood up. "That's insane. Let us go now. The Sla-Mori is still many miles and we must be there by sundown."

"I'll take rear guard," Sturm said to Tanis softly.

They walked through the ragged pines for several more hours. The sun slanted down in the sky, lengthening shadows across the trail, when the group came suddenly to a clearing.

"Hsst!" Tanis warned, falling back in alarm.

Caramon, instantly alert, drew his sword, motioning for Sturm and his brother with his free hand.

"What is it?" piped Tasslehoff. "I can't see!"

"Shhh!" Tanis glared at the kender, and Tas clapped his own hand over his own mouth to save Tanis the trouble.

The clearing was the site of a recent bloody fight. Bodies of men and hobgoblins lay scattered about in the obscene postures of brutal death. The companions looked about fearfully and listened for long minutes but could hear nothing above the roar of the water.

"No enemy for miles!" Sturm glared at Gilthanas and started to step out into the clearing.

"Wait!" Tanis said. "I thought I saw something move!"

"Maybe one of them's still alive," Sturm said coolly and walked forward. The rest followed more slowly. A low moaning sound came from beneath two hobgoblin bodies. The warriors walked toward the carnage, swords level.

"Caramon . . ." Tanis gestured.

The big warrior shoved the bodies to one side. Beneath was a moaning figure.

"Human," Caramon reported. "And covered with blood. Unconscious, I think."

The rest came up to look at the man on the ground. Goldmoon started to kneel down, but Caramon stopped her.

"No, lady," he said gently. "It would be senseless to heal him if we just have to kill him again. Remember—humans fought for the Dragon Highlord in Solace."

The group gathered round to examine the man. He wore chain mail that was of good quality, if rather tarnished. His clothes were rich, though the cloth had worn thin in places. He appeared to be in his late thirties. His hair was thick and black, his chin firm, and his features regular. The stranger opened his eyes and stared up at the companions blearily.

"Thank the gods of the Seekers!" he said hoarsely. "My friends—are they all dead?"

"Worry about yourself first," Sturm said sternly. "Tell us who your friends were—the humans or the hobgoblins?"

"The humans—fighters against the dragonmen." The man broke off, his eyes widening. "Gilthanas?"

"Eben," Gilthanas said in quiet surprise. "How did you survive the battle at the ravine?"

"How did you, for that matter?" The man named Eben tried to stagger to his feet. Caramon reached out a hand to help him when suddenly Eben pointed. "Look out! Drac—"

Caramon whipped around, letting Eben fall back with a groan. The others turned to see twelve draconians standing at the edge of the clearing, weapons drawn.

"All strangers in the land are to be taken to the Dragon Highlord for questioning," one called out. "We charge you to come with us peacefully."

"No one was supposed to know about this path to Sla-Mori," Sturm whispered to Tanis with a meaningful glance at Gilthanas. "According to the elf, that is!"

"We do not take orders from Lord Verminaard!" Tanis yelled, ignoring Sturm.

"You will, soon enough," the draconian said and waved its arm. The creatures surged forward to attack.

Fizban, standing near the edge of the woods, pulled something from his pouch and began to mumble a few words.

"Not Fireball!" Raistlin hissed, grabbing the old mage's arm. "You'll incinerate everyone out there!"

"Oh, really? I suppose you're right." The old mage sighed in disappointment, then brightened. "Wait, I'll think of something else."

"Just stay here, under cover!" Raistlin ordered. "I'm going to my brother."

"Now, what was that web spell?" The old man pondered.

Tika, her new sword drawn and ready, trembled with fear and excitement. One draconian rushed her and she swung a tremendous blow. The blade missed the draconian by a mile, Caramon's head by inches. Pulling Tika behind him, he knocked the draconian down with the flat of his sword. Before it could rise, he stepped on its throat, breaking its neck.

"Get behind me," he said to Tika, then glanced down at the sword she was still waving around wildly. "On second thought," Caramon amended nervously, "run over to those trees with the old man and Goldmoon. There's a good girl."

"I will not!" Tika said indignantly. "I'll show him," she muttered, her sweaty palms slipping on the hilt of the sword. Two more draconians charged Caramon, but his brother was beside him now—the two combining magic and steel to destroy their enemy. Tika knew she would only get in their way, and she feared Raistlin's anger more than she feared draconians. She looked around to see if anyone needed her help. Sturm and Tanis fought side by side. Gilthanas made an unlikely team with Flint, while Tasslehoff, his hoopak planted solidly in the ground, sent a deadly barrage of rocks whizzing onto the field. Goldmoon stood beneath the trees, Riverwind near her. The old magician had pulled out a spellbook and was flipping through its pages.

"Web . . . web . . . how did that go?" he mumbled.

"Aaarrrgghh!" A screech behind Tika nearly caused her to swallow her tongue. Whirling around, she dropped her sword in alarm as a draconian, laughing horribly, launched itself into the air straight at her. Panic-stricken, Tika gripped her shield in both hands and struck the draconian in its hideous, reptilian face. The impact nearly jarred the shield from her hands, but it knocked the creature onto its back, unconscious. Tika picked up her sword and, grimacing in disgust, stabbed the creature through the heart. Its body immediately turned to stone, encasing her sword. Tika yanked at it, but it remained stuck fast.

"Tika, to your left!" yelled Tasslehoff shrilly.

Tika stumbled around and saw another draconian. Swinging her shield, she blocked its sword thrust. Then, with a strength born of terror, she hit at the creature again and again with her shield, knowing only that she had to kill the thing. She kept bashing until she felt a hand on her arm. Whipping around, her blood-stained shield ready, she saw Caramon.

"It's all right!" the big warrior said soothingly. "It's all over, Tika. They're all dead. You did fine, just fine."

Tika blinked. For a moment she didn't recognize the warrior. Then, with a shudder, she lowered her shield.

"I wasn't very good with the sword," she said, starting to tremble in reaction to her fear and the memory of the horrible creature lunging at her.

Caramon saw her start to shake. He reached out and clasped her in his arms, stroking the sweat-damp red curls.

"You were braver than many men I've seen—experienced warriors," the big man said in a deep voice.

Tika looked up into Caramon's eyes. Her terror melted away, replaced by exultation. She pressed against Caramon. The feel of his hard muscles, the smell of sweat mingled with leather, increased her excitement. Tika flung her arms around his neck and kissed him with such violence her teeth bit into his lip. She tasted blood in her mouth.

Caramon, astonished, felt the tingle of pain, an odd contrast to the softness of her lips, and was overwhelmed with desire. He wanted this woman more than any other woman—and there had been many—in his life. He forgot where he was, who was around him. His brain and his blood were on fire, and he ached with the pain of his passion. Crushing Tika to his chest, he held her and kissed her with bruising intensity.

The pain of his embrace was delicious to Tika. She longed for the pain to grow and envelop her, but at the same time, she felt suddenly cold and afraid. Remembering stories told by the other barmaids of the terrible, wonderful things that happened between men and women, she began to panic.

Caramon completely lost all sense of reality. He caught Tika up in his arms with a wild idea of carrying her into the woods, when he felt a cold, familiar hand on his shoulder.

The big man stared at his brother and regained his senses with a gasp. He gently set Tika on her feet. Dizzy and disoriented, she opened her eyes to see Raistlin standing beside his brother, regarding her with his strange, glittering stare.

Tika's face burned. She backed away, stumbled over the body of the draconian, then picked up her shield and ran.

Caramon swallowed, cleared his throat, and started to say something, but Raistlin simply glanced at him in disgust and walked back to rejoin Fizban. Caramon, trembling like a new-born colt, sighed shakily and walked over to where Sturm, Tanis, and Gilthanas stood, talking to Eben.

"No, I'm fine," the man assured them. "I just felt a little faint when I saw those creatures, that's all. You really have a cleric among you? That's wonderful, but don't waste her healing powers on me. Just a scratch. It's more their blood than mine. My party and I were tracking these draconians through the woods when we were attacked by at least forty hobgoblins."

"And you alone live to tell the tale," Gilthanas said.

"Yes," Eben replied, returning the elf's suspicious gaze. "I am an expert swordsman, as you know. I killed these"—he gestured to the bodies of six hobgoblins who lay around him—"then fell to the overwhelming numbers. The rest must have assumed I was dead and left me. But, enough of my heroics. You fellows are pretty good with swords yourselves. Where are you headed?"

"Some place called the Sla—" began Caramon, but Gilthanas cut him off.

"Our journey is secret," Gilthanas said. Then he added in a tentative voice. "We could use an expert swordsman."

"As long as you're fighting draconians, your fight is my fight," Eben said cheerfully. He pulled his pack out from under the body of a hobgoblin and slung it over his shoulder.

"My name's Eben Shatterstone. I come from Gateway. You've probably heard of my family," he said. "We had one of the most impressive mansions west of—"

"That's it!" cried Fizban. "I remembered!"

Suddenly the air was filled with strands of sticky, floating cobweb.

The sun set just as the group reached an open plain edged by tall mountain peaks. Rivaling the mountains for dominance of the land before it was the gigantic fortress known as Pax Tharkas, which guarded the pass between the mountains. The companions stared at it in awed silence.

Tika's eyes widened at the sight of the massive twin towers soaring into the sky. "I've never seen anything so big! Who built it? They must have been powerful men."

"It was not men," said Flint sadly. The dwarf's beard quivered as he looked at Pax Tharkas with a wistful expression. "It was elves and dwarves working together. Once, long ago, when times were peaceful."

"The dwarf speaks truly," Gilthanas said. "Long ago Kith-Kanan broke his father's heart and left the ancient home of Silvanesti. He and his people came to the beautiful woods given them by the Emperor of Ergoth following the scribing of the Swordsheath Scroll that ended the Kinslayer Wars. Elves have lived in Qualinesti for long centuries since Kith-Kanan's death. His greatest achievement, however, was the building of Pax Tharkas. Standing between elven and dwarven kingdoms, it was constructed by both in a spirit of friendship since lost on Krynn. It grieves me to see it now, the bastion of a mighty war machine."

Even as Gilthanas spoke, the companions saw the huge gate that stood at the front of Pax Tharkas swing open. An army—long rows of draconians, hobgoblins, and goblins—marched out into the plains. The sound of braying horns echoed back from the mountaintops. Watching them from above was a great red dragon. The companions cowered among the scrub brush and trees. Though the dragon was too far away to see them, the dragonfear touched them even from this distance.

"They march on Qualinesti," Gilthanas said, his voice breaking. "We must get inside and free the prisoners. Then Verminaard will be forced to call the army back."

"You're going inside Pax Tharkas!" Eben gasped.

"Yes," Gilthanas answered reluctantly, apparently regretting he had said so much.

"Whew!" Eben blew out a deep breath. "You people have guts, I'll give you that. So—how do we get in there? Wait until the army leaves? There will probably be only a couple of guards at the front gate. We could handle them easily, couldn't we, big man?" He nudged Caramon.

"Sure," Caramon grinned.

"That is not the plan," Gilthanas said coldly. The elf pointed to a narrow vale leading into the mountains, just visible in the rapidly fading light. "There is our way. We will cross in the cover of darkness."

He stood up and started off. Tanis hurried forward to catch up with him. "What do you know of this Eben?" the half-elf asked in elven, glancing back to where the man was chatting with Tika.

Gilthanas shrugged. "He was with the band of humans who fought with us at the ravine. Those who survived were taken to Solace and died there. I suppose he could have escaped. I did, after all," Gilthanas said, glancing sideways at Tanis. "He comes from Gateway where his father and father before him were wealthy merchants. The others told me, when he was out of hearing, that his family lost their money and he has since earned his living by his sword."

"I figured as much," Tanis said. "His clothes are rich, but they've seen better days. You made the right decision, bringing him along."

"I dared not leave him behind," Gilthanas answered grimly. "One of us should keep an eye on him."

"Yes." Tanis fell silent.

"And on me, too, you're thinking," Gilthanas said in a tight voice. "I know what the others say—the knight especially. But, I swear to you, Tanis, I'm not a traitor! I want one thing!" The elf's eyes gleamed feverishly in the dying light. "I want to destroy this Verminaard. If you could have seen him as his dragon destroyed my people! I'd gladly sacrifice my life—" Gilthanas stopped abruptly.

"And our lives as well?" Tanis asked.

As Gilthanas turned to face him, his almond-shaped eyes regarding Tanis without emotion. "If you must know, Tanthalas, your life means that—" He snapped his fingers. "But the lives of my people are everything to me. That is all I care for now." He walked on ahead as Sturm caught up with them.

"Tanis," he said. "The old man was right. We are being followed."

9

Suspicions grow. The Sla-Mori.

he narrow trail climbed steeply up from the plains
into a wooded valley in the foothills. Evening's shadows gathered close around them as they followed the
stream up into the mountain. They had traveled only a short
distance, however, when Gilthanas left the trail and disappeared into the brush. The companions stopped, looking at
each other doubtfully.

"This is madness," Eben whispered to Tanis. "Trolls live in
this valley—who do you think made that trail?" The dark-
haired man took Tanis's arm with a cool familiarity the half-
elf found disconcerting. "Admittedly, I'm the new kid in
town, so to speak, and the gods know you don't have any
reason to trust me, but how much do you know about this
Gilthanas?"

"I know—" Tanis began, but Eben ignored him.

"There were some of us who didn't believe that draconian army stumbled onto us by accident, if you take my meaning. My boys and I had been hiding in the hills, fighting the dragonarmies ever since they hit Gateway. Last week, these elves showed up out of nowhere. They told us they were going to raid one of the Dragon Highlord's fortresses and would we like to come along and help? We said, sure, why not—anything to stick a bone in the Dragon High Man's craw.

"As we hiked, we began to get really nervous. There were draconian tracks all over the place! But it didn't bother the elves. Gilthanas said the tracks were old. That night we made camp and posted a watch. It didn't do us a lot of good, just gave us about twenty seconds warning before the draconians hit. And"—Eben glanced around and moved even closer—"while we were trying to wake up, grab our weapons, and fight those foul creatures, I heard the elves calling out, as if someone was lost. And who do you suppose they were calling for?"

Eben regarded Tanis intently. The half-elf frowned and shook his head, irritated at the dramatics.

"Gilthanas!" Eben hissed. "He was gone! They shouted and shouted for him—their leader!" The man shrugged. "Whether he ever showed up or not, I don't know. I was captured. They took us to Solace, where I got away. Anyway, I'd think twice about following that elf. He may have had good reason to be gone when the draconians attacked, but—"

"I've known Gilthanas a long time," Tanis interrupted gruffly, more disturbed than he wanted to admit.

"Sure. Just thought you should know," Eben said, smiling sympathetically. He clapped Tanis on the back and dropped back to stand by Tika.

Tanis didn't have to look around to know Caramon and Sturm had heard every word. Neither said anything, however, and before Tanis could talk to them, Gilthanas appeared suddenly, slipping out from among the trees.

"It is not much farther," the elf said. "The brush thins up ahead and the walking is easier."

"I say we just go in the front gate," Eben said.

"I agree," Caramon said. The big man glanced at his brother who sat limply beneath a tree. Goldmoon was pale with fatigue. Even Tasslehoff's head hung wearily.

"We could camp here tonight and go in by the front gates at dawn," Sturm suggested.

"We stick to the original plan," Tanis said sharply. "We make camp once we reach the Sla-Mori."

Then Flint spoke up. "You can go ring the bell at the gate and ask Lord Verminaard to let you in if you want, Sturm Brightblade. I'm sure he'd oblige. C'mon, Tanis." The dwarf stumped off down the trail.

"At least," Tanis said to Sturm in a low voice, "maybe this will throw off our pursuer."

"Whoever or whatever it is," Sturm answered. "It's woodscrafty, I'll say that for it. Every time I caught a glimpse and started back for a closer look, it vanished. I thought about ambushing it, but there wasn't time."

The group emerged from the brush thankfully, arriving at the base of a gigantic granite cliff. Gilthanas walked along the cliff face for several hundred feet, his hand feeling for something on the rock. Suddenly he stopped.

"We are here," he whispered. Reaching into his tunic, he removed a small gem that began to glow a soft, muted yellow. Running his hand over the rock wall, the elf found what he was searching for, a small niche in the granite. He placed the gem in the niche and began reciting ancient words and tracing unseen symbols in the night air.

"Very impressive," whispered Fizban. "I didn't know he was one of us," he said to Raistlin.

"A dabbler, nothing more," the mage replied. Leaning wearily on his staff, he watched Gilthanas intently, however.

Suddenly and silently, a huge block of stone separated from the cliff face and began moving slowly to one side. The companions backed up as a blast of chill, dank air flowed from the gaping hole in the rock.

"What's in there? " Caramon asked suspiciously.

"I do not know what is in there now," Gilthanas replied. "I have never entered. I know of this place only through the lore of my people."

"All right," Caramon growled. "What *used* to be in there?"

Gilthanas paused, then said. "This was the burial chamber of Kith-Kanan."

"More spooks," Flint grumbled, peering into the darkness.

"Send the mage in first, so he can warn them we're coming."

"Throw the dwarf in," Raistlin returned. "They are accustomed to living in dark, dank caves."

"You speak of the mountain dwarves!" Flint said, his beard bristling. "It has been long years since the hill dwarves lived below ground in the kingdom of Thorbardin."

"Only because you were cast out!" Raistlin hissed.

"Stop it, both of you!" Tanis said in exasperation. "Raistlin, what do you sense about this place?"

"Evil. Great evil," the mage replied.

"But I sense great goodness, too," Fizban spoke unexpectedly. "The elves are not truly forgotten within, though evil things have come to rule in their stead."

"This is crazy!" Eben shouted. The noise echoed uncannily among the rocks and the others whirled, startled, staring at him in alarm. "I'm sorry," he said, dropping his voice. "But I can't believe you people are going in there! It doesn't take a magician to tell there's evil inside that hole. *I* can feel it! Go back around to the front," he urged. "Sure, there'll be one or two guards, but that's nothing compared to whatever lurks in that darkness beyond!"

"He's got a point, Tanis," Caramon said. "You can't fight the dead. We learned that in Darken Wood."

"This is the only way!" Gilthanas said angrily. "If you are such cowards—"

"There's a difference between caution and cowardice, Gilthanas," Tanis said, his voice steady and calm. The half-elf thought a moment. "We might be able to take on the guards at the front gate, but not before they could alert others. I say we enter and at least explore this way. Flint, you lead. Raistlin, we'll need your light."

"*Shirak*," spoke the mage softly, and the crystal on his staff began to glow. He and Flint plunged into the cave, followed closely by the rest. The tunnel they entered was obviously ancient, but whether it was natural or artifact was impossible to tell.

"What about our pursuer?" Sturm asked in a low voice. "Do we leave the entrance open?"

"A trap," Tanis agreed softly. "Leave it open just a crack, Gilthanas, enough so that whoever's tracking us knows we came in here and can follow, but not enough so that it looks like a trap."

Gilthanas drew forth the gem, placed it in a niche on the inner side of the entrance, and spoke a few words. The stone began to slide silently back into place. At the last moment, when it was about seven or eight inches from closing, Gilthanas swiftly removed the gemstone. The stone shuddered to a halt, and the knight, the elf, and the half-elf joined the companions in the entrance to the Sla-Mori.

"There is a great deal of dust," Raistlin reported, coughing—"but no tracks, at least in this part of the cave."

"About one hundred and twenty feet farther on, there's a crossroads," Flint added. "We found footprints there, but we could not make out what they were. They don't look like draconians or hobgoblins and they don't come this direction. The mage says the evil flows from the road to the right."

"We will camp here for the night," Tanis said, "near the entry. We'll post double watch—one by the door, one down the corridor. Sturm, you and Caramon first. Gilthanas and I, Eben and Riverwind, Flint and Tasslehoff."

"And me," said Tika stoutly, though she couldn't ever remember being so tired in her life. "I'll take my turn."

Tanis was glad the darkness hid his smile. "Very well," he said. "You watch with Flint and Tasslehoff."

"Good!" Tika replied. Opening her pack, she shook out a blanket and lay down, conscious all the while of Caramon's eyes on her. She noticed Eben watching her, too. She didn't mind that. She was accustomed to men staring at her admiringly and Eben was handsomer even than Caramon. Certainly he was wittier and more charming than the big warrior. Still, just the memory of Caramon's arms around her made her shiver with delightful fear. She firmly put the memory from her mind and tried to get comfortable. The chain mail was cold and it pinched her through her blouse. Yet she noticed the others didn't take theirs off. Besides, she was tired enough to sleep dressed in a full suit of plate armor. The last thing Tika remembered as she drifted off was telling herself she was thankful she wasn't alone with Caramon.

Goldmoon saw the warrior's eyes linger on Tika. Whispering something to Riverwind—who nodded, smiling—she left him and walked over to Caramon. Touching him on the arm, she drew him away from the others into the shadow of the corridor.

"Tanis tells me you have an older sister," she stated.

"Yes," Caramon answered, startled. "Kitiara. Though she's my half-sister."

Goldmoon smiled and laid her hand gently on Caramon's arm. "I'm going to talk to you like an older sister."

Caramon grinned. "Not like Kitiara, you won't, Lady of Que-shu. Kit taught me the meaning of every swear word I'd ever heard, plus a few I hadn't. She taught me to use a sword and fight with honor in the tournaments, but she also taught me how to kick a man in the groin when the judges weren't watching. No, lady, you're not much like my older sister."

Goldmoon's eyes opened wide, startled by this portrayal of a woman she guessed the half-elf loved. "But I thought she and Tanis, I mean they . . ."

Caramon winked. "They certainly did!" he said.

Goldmoon drew a deep breath. She hadn't meant the conversation to wander off, but it did lead to her subject. "In a way, that's what I wanted to speak to you about. Only this has to do with Tika."

"Tika?" Caramon flushed. "She's a big girl. Begging your pardon, I don't see that what we do is any of your concern."

"She is a *girl*, Caramon," Goldmoon said gently. "Don't you understand?"

Caramon looked blank. He knew Tika was a girl. What did Goldmoon mean? Then he blinked in sudden understanding and groaned. "No, she isn't—"

"Yes." Goldmoon sighed. "She is. She's never been with a man before. She told me, while we were in the grove putting on her armor. She's frightened, Caramon. She's heard a lot of stories. Don't rush her. She desperately wants approval from you, and she might do anything to win it. But don't let her use that as a reason to do something she'll regret later. If you truly love her, time will prove it and enhance the moment's sweetness."

"I guess you know that, huh?" Caramon said, looking at Goldmoon.

"Yes," she said softly her eyes going to Riverwind. "We have waited long, and sometimes the pain is unbearable. But the laws of my people are strict. I don't suppose it would matter now," she spoke in a whisper, more to herself than Caramon, "since we are the only two left. But, in a way, that makes it even more important. When our vows are spoken, we will lie together as man and wife. Not until then."

"I understand. Thanks for telling me about Tika," Caramon said. He patted Goldmoon awkwardly on the shoulder and returned to his post.

The night passed quietly, with no sign of their pursuer. When the watches changed, Tanis discussed Eben's story with Gilthanas and received an unsatisfactory answer. Yes, what the man said was true. Gilthanas had been gone when the draconians attacked. He had been trying to convince the druids to help. He'd returned when he heard the sounds of battle and that's when he'd been struck on the head. He told Tanis all this in a low, bitter voice.

The companions woke when morning's pale light crept through the door. After a quick breakfast, they gathered their things and walked down the corridor into the Sla-Mori.

Arriving at the crossroads, they examined both directions, left and right. Riverwind knelt to study the tracks, then rose, his expression puzzled.

"They are human," he said, "but they are not human. There are animal tracks as well—probably rats. The dwarf was right. I see no sign of draconians or goblins. What is odd, however, is that the animal tracks end right here where the paths cross. They do not go into the right-hand corridor. The other strange tracks do not go to the left."

"Well, which way do *we* go?" Tanis asked.

"I say we don't go either way!" Eben stated. "The entrance is still open. Let's turn back."

"Turning back is no longer an option," Tanis said coldly. "I would give you leave to go yourself, only—"

"Only you don't trust me," Eben finished. "I don't blame you, Tanis Half-Elven. All right, I said I'd help and I meant it. Which way—left or right?"

"The evil comes from the right," Raistlin whispered.

"Gilthanas?" Tanis asked. "Do you have any idea where we are?"

"No, Tanthalas," the elf answered. "Legend says that there were many entrances from Sla-Mori into Pax Tharkas, all secret. Only the elven priests were allowed down here, to honor the dead. One way is as good as another."

"Or as bad," whispered Tasslehoff to Tika. She gulped and crept over to stand near Caramon.

"We'll go left," Tanis said—"since Raistlin feels uneasy about the right."

Walking by the light of the mage's staff, the companions followed the dusty, rock-strewn tunnel for several hundred feet, then reached an ancient stone wall rent by a huge hole through which only darkness was visible. Raistlin's small light showed faintly the distant walls of a great hall.

The warriors entered first, flanking the mage, who held his staff high. The gigantic hall must once have been splendid, but now it had fallen into such decay that its faded splendor seemed pathetic and horrible. Two rows of seven columns ran the length of the hall, though some lay shattered on the floor. Part of the far wall was caved in, evidence of the destructive force of the Cataclysm. At the very back of the room stood two double bronze doors.

As Raistlin advanced, the others spread out, swords drawn. Suddenly Caramon, in the front of the hall, gave a strangled cry. The mage hurried to shine his light where Caramon pointed with a trembling hand.

Before them was a massive throne, ornately carved of granite. Two huge marble statues flanked the throne, their sightless eyes staring forward into the darkness. The throne they guarded was not empty. Upon it sat the skeletal remains of what had once been a male—of what race, none could say, death being the great equalizer. The figure was dressed in regal robes that, even though faded and decayed, still gave evidence of their richness. A cloak covered the gaunt shoulders. A crown gleamed on the fleshless skull. The bone hands, fingers lying gracefully in death, rested on a sheathed sword.

Gilthanas fell to his knees. "Kith-Kanan," he said in a whisper. "We stand in the Hall of the Ancients, his burial tomb. None have seen this sight since the elven clerics vanished in the Cataclysm."

Tanis stared at the throne until, slowly, overcome by feelings he did not understand, the half-elf sank to his knees. *"Fealan thalos, Im murquanethi. Sai Kith-Kananoth Murtari*

357

Larion," he murmured in tribute to the greatest of the elven kings.

"What a beautiful sword," Tasslehoff said, his shrill voice breaking the reverent silence. Tanis glared at him sternly. "I'm not going to take it!" the kender protested, looking wounded. "I just mentioned it, as an item of interest."

Tanis rose to his feet. "Don't touch it," he said sternly to the kender, then went to explore other parts of the room.

As Tas walked closer to examine the sword, Raistlin went with him. The mage began to murmur, "*Tsaran korilath ith hakon,*" and moved his thin hand swiftly above the sword in a prescribed pattern. The sword began to give off a faint red glow. Raistlin smiled and said softly, "It is enchanted."

Tas gasped. "Good enchantment? Or bad?"

"I have no way of knowing," the mage whispered. "But since it has lain undisturbed for so long, I certainly would not venture to touch it!"

He turned away, leaving Tas to wonder if he dared disobey Tanis and risk being turned into something icky.

While the kender was wrestling with temptation, the rest searched the walls for secret entrances. Flint helped by giving them learned and lengthy descriptions of dwarven-built hidden doorways. Gilthanas walked to the far end from Kith-Kanan's throne, where the two huge bronze double doors stood. One, bearing a relief map of Pax Tharkas, was slightly ajar. Calling for light, he and Raistlin studied the map.

Caramon gave the skeletal figure of the long dead king a final backward glance and joined Sturm and Flint in searching the walls for secret doors. Finally Flint called, "Tasslehoff, you worthless kender, this is your specialty. At least you're always bragging about how you found the door that had been lost for one hundred years which led to the great jewel of the some-thing-or-other."

"It was in a place like this, too," Tas said, his interest in the sword forgotten. Skipping over to help, he came to a sudden stop.

"What's that?" he asked, cocking his head.

"What's what?" Flint said absently, slapping the walls.

"A scraping sound," the kender said, puzzled. "It's coming from those doors."

Tanis looked up, having learned, long ago, to respect Tasslehoff's hearing. He walked toward the doors where Gilthanas and Raistlin were intent upon the map. Suddenly Raistlin took a step backward. Foul-smelling air wafted into the room through the open door. Now everyone could hear the scraping sound and a soft, squishing noise.

"Shut the door!" Raistlin whispered urgently.

"Caramon!" Tanis cried. "Sturm!" The two were already running for the door, along with Eben. All of them leaned against it, but they were flung backward as the bronze doors flew open, banging against the walls with a hollow booming sound. A monster slithered into the hall.

"Help us, Mishakal!" Goldmoon breathed the goddess's name as she sank back against the wall. The thing entered the room swiftly despite its great bulk. The scraping sound they had heard was caused by its gigantic, bloated body sliding along the floor.

"A slug!" Tas said, running up to examine it with interest. "But look at the size of that thing! How do you suppose it got so big? I wonder what it eats—"

"Us, you ninny!" Flint shouted, grabbing the kender and flinging him to the ground just as the huge slug spat out a stream of saliva. Its eyes, perched atop slender, rotating stalks on top of its head, were not of much use, nor did it need them. The slug could find and devour rats in the darkness by sense of smell alone. Now it detected much larger prey, and it shot its paralyzing saliva in the general direction of the living flesh it craved.

The deadly liquid missed as the kender and the dwarf rolled out of the way. Sturm and Caramon charged in, slashing at the monster with their swords. Caramon's sword didn't even penetrate the thick, rubbery hide. Sturm's two-handed blade bit, causing the slug to rear back in pain. Tanis charged forward as the slug's head swiveled toward the knight.

"Tanthalas!"

The scream pierced Tanis's concentration and he halted, turning back to stare in amazement at the entrance to the hall.

"Laurana!"

At that moment, the slug, sensing the half-elf, spat the corrosive liquid at him. The saliva struck his sword, causing the

359

metal to fizz and smoke, then dissolve in his hand. The burning liquid ran down his arm, searing his flesh. Tanis, screaming in agony, fell to his knees.

"Tanthalas!" Laurana cried again, running to him.

"Stop her!" Tanis gasped, doubled over in pain, clutching a hand and sword-arm suddenly blackened and useless.

The slug, sensing success, slithered forward, dragging its pulsating gray body through the door. Goldmoon cast a fearful glance at the huge monster, then ran to Tanis. Riverwind stood over them, protectively.

"Get away!" Tanis said through clenched teeth.

Goldmoon grasped his injured hand in her own, praying to the goddess. Riverwind fit an arrow to his bow and shot at the slug. The arrow struck the creature in the neck, doing little damage, but distracting its attention from Tanis.

The half-elf saw Goldmoon's hand touch his, but he could feel nothing but pain. Then the pain eased and feeling returned to his hand. Smiling at Goldmoon, he marveled at her healing powers, even as he lifted his head to see what was happening.

The others were attacking the creature with renewed fury, attempting to distract it from Tanis, but they might as well have been plunging their weapons into a thick, rubbery wall.

Tanis rose to his feet shakily. His hand was healed, but his sword lay on the ground, a molten lump of metal. Weaponless except for his longbow, he fell back, pulling Goldmoon with him as the slug slid into the room.

Raistlin ran to Fizban's side. "Now is the time for the casting of the fireball, Old One," he panted.

"It is?" Fizban's face filled with delight. "Wonderful! How does it go?"

"Don't you remember!" Raistlin practically shrieked, dragging the mage behind a pillar as the slug spat another glob of burning saliva onto the floor.

"I used to . . . let me see." Fizban's brow furrowed in concentration. "Can't you do it?"

"I have not gained the power yet, Old One! That spell is still beyond my strength!" Raistlin closed his eyes and began to concentrate on those spells he did know.

"Fall back! Get out of here!" Tanis shouted, shielding

Laurana and Goldmoon as best he could while he fumbled for his longbow and his arrows.

"It'll just come after us!" Sturm yelled, thrusting his blade home once again. But all he and Caramon accomplished was to enrage the monster further.

Suddenly Raistlin held up his hands. *"Kalith karan, tobaniskar!"* he cried, and flaming darts sprang from his fingers, striking the creature in the head. The slug reared in silent agony and shook its head, but returned to the hunt. Suddenly it lunged straight forward, sensing victims at the end of the room where Tanis sought to protect Goldmoon and Laurana. Maddened by pain, driven wild by the smell of blood, the slug attacked with unbelievable speed. Tanis's arrow bounced off the leathery hide and the monster dove for him, its mouth gaping open. The half-elf dropped the useless bow and staggered backward, nearly stumbling over the steps leading to the throne of Kith-Kanan.

"Behind the throne!" he yelled, preparing to hold the monster's attention while Goldmoon and Laurana ran for cover. His hand reached out, grabbing for a huge rock, anything to hurl at the creature!—when his fingers closed over the metal hilt of a sword.

Tanis nearly dropped the weapon in amazement. The metal was so cold it burned his hand. The blade gleamed brightly in the wavering light of the mage's staff. There wasn't time to question, however. Tanis drove the point into the slug's gaping maw just as the creature swooped in for the kill.

"Run!" Tanis yelled. Grasping Laurana's hand, he dragged her toward the hole. Pushing her through, he turned around, preparing to help keep the slug at bay while the others escaped. But the slug's appetite had died. Writhing in misery, it slowly turned and slithered back toward its lair. Clear, sticky liquid dribbled from its wounds.

The companions crowded into the tunnel, stopping for a moment to calm their hearts and breathe deeply. Raistlin, wheezing, leaned on his brother. Tanis glanced around. "Where's Tasslehoff?" he asked in frustration. Whirling around to go back into the hall, he nearly fell over the kender.

"I brought you the scabbard," Tas said, holding it up. "For the sword."

"Back down the tunnel," Tanis said firmly, stopping everyone's questions.

Reaching the crossroads and sinking down on the dusty floor to rest, Tanis turned to the elfmaid. "What in the name of the Abyss are you doing here, Laurana? Has something happened in Qualinost?"

"Nothing happened," Laurana said, shaking from the encounter with the slug. "I . . . I . . . just came."

"Then you're going right back!" Gilthanas yelled angrily, grabbing Laurana. She broke away from his grasp.

"I'm not either going back," she said petulantly. "I'm coming with you and Tanis and . . . the rest."

"Laurana, this is madness," Tanis snapped. "We're not going on an outing. This isn't a game. You saw what happened in there—we were nearly killed!"

"I know, Tanthalas," Laurana said pleadingly. Her voice quivered and broke. "You told me that there comes a time when you've got to risk your life for something you believe in. I'm the one who followed you."

"You could have been killed—" Gilthanas began.

"But I wasn't!" Laurana cried defiantly. "I have been trained as a warrior—all elven women are, in memory of the time when we fought beside our men to save our homeland."

"It's not serious training—" Tanis began angrily.

"I followed you, didn't I?" Laurana demanded, casting a glance at Sturm. "Skillfully?" she asked the knight.

"Yes," he admitted. "Still, that doesn't mean—"

Raistlin interrupted him. "We are losing time," the mage whispered. "And I for one do not want to spend any longer than I must in this dank and musty tunnel." He was wheezing, barely able to breathe. "The girl has made her decision. We can spare no one to return with her, nor do we dare trust her to leave on her own. She might be captured and reveal our plans. We must take her."

Tanis glared at the mage, hating him for his cold, unfeeling logic, and for being right. The half-elf stood up, yanking Laurana to her feet. He came very close to hating her, too, without quite understanding why, knowing simply that she was making a difficult task much harder.

"You are on your own," he told her quietly, as the rest stood up and gathered their things. "I can't hang around, protecting you. Neither can Gilthanas. You have behaved like a spoiled brat. I told you once before—you'd better grow up. Now, if you don't, you're going to die and probably get all the rest of us killed right along with you!"

"I'm sorry, Tanthalas," Laurana said, avoiding his angry gaze. "But I couldn't lose you, not again. I love you." Her lips tightened and she said softly, "I'll make you proud of me."

Tanis turned and walked away. Catching sight of Caramon's grinning face and hearing Tika giggle, he flushed. Ignoring them, he approached Sturm and Gilthanas. "It seems we must take the right-hand corridor after all, whether or not Raistlin's feelings about evil are correct." He buckled on his new sword belt and scabbard, noticing, as he did so, Raistlin's eyes lingering on the weapon.

"What is it now?" he asked irritably.

"The sword is enchanted," Raistlin said softly, coughing. "How did you get it?"

Tanis started. He stared at the blade, moving his hand as though it might turn into a snake. He frowned, trying to remember. "I was near the body of the elven king, searching for something to throw at the slug, when, suddenly, the sword was in my hand. It had been taken out of the sheath and—" Tanis paused, swallowing.

"Yes?" Raistlin pursued, his eyes glittering eagerly.

"*He* gave it to me," Tanis said softly. "I remember, his hand touched mine. He pulled it from its sheath."

"Who?" asked Gilthanas. "None of us were near there."

"Kith-Kanan. . . ."

10

The Royal Guard.
The Chain Room.

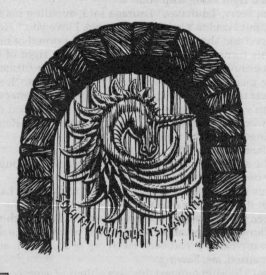

Perhaps it was just imagination, but the darkness seemed thicker as they walked down the other tunnel and the air grew colder. No one needed the dwarf to tell them that this was not normal in a cave, where the temperature supposedly stayed constant. They reached a branch in the tunnel, but no one felt inclined to go left, which might lead them back to the Hall of the Ancients—and the wounded slug.

"The elf almost got us killed by the slug," Eben said accusingly. "I wonder what's in store for us down here?"

No one answered. By now, everyone was experiencing the sense of growing evil Raistlin had warned of. Their footsteps slowed, and it was only through force of group will that they continued on. Laurana felt fear convulse her limbs and she clung to the wall for support. She longed for Tanis to comfort her and protect her, as he had done when they were younger and facing imaginary foes, but he walked at the head of the line with her brother. Each had his own fear to contend with. At that moment, Laurana decided that she would die before she asked for their help. It occurred to her, then, that she was really serious when she said she wanted to make Tanis proud of her. Shoving herself away from the side of the crumbling tunnel, she gritted her teeth and moved forward.

The tunnel came to an abrupt end. Crumbled stone and rubble lay beneath a hole in the rock wall. The sense of malevolent evil flowing from the darkness beyond the hole could almost be felt, wafting across the flesh like the touch of unseen fingers. The companions stopped, none of them—not even the nerveless kender—daring to enter.

"It's not that I'm afraid," Tas confided in a whisper to Flint. "Its just that I'd rather be somewhere else."

The silence became oppressive. Each could hear his own heart beat and the breathing of the others. The light jittered and wavered in the mage's shaking hand.

"Well, we can't stay here forever," Eben said hoarsely. "Let the elf go in. He's the one who brought us here!"

"I'll go," Gilthanas answered. "But I'll need light."

"None may touch the staff but I," Raistlin hissed. He paused, then added reluctantly, "I'll go with you."

"Raist—" Caramon began, but his brother stared at him coldly. "I'll go, too," the big man muttered.

"No," Tanis said. "You stay here and guard the others. Gilthanas, Raistlin, and I will go."

Gilthanas entered the hole in the wall, followed by the mage and Tanis, the half-elf assisting Raistlin. The light revealed a narrow chamber, vanishing into darkness beyond the staff's reach. On either side were rows of large stone doors, each held in place by huge iron hinges, spiked directly into the rock wall. Raistlin held the staff high, shining it down the shadowy chamber. Each knew that the evil was centered here.

"There's carving on the doors," Tanis murmured. The staff's light threw the stone figures into high relief.

Gilthanas stared at it. "The Royal Crest!" he said in a strangled voice.

"What does that mean?" Tanis asked, feeling the elf's fear infect him like a plague.

"These are the crypts of the Royal Guard," Gilthanas whispered. "They are pledged to continue their duties, even in death, and guard the king—so the legends speak."

"And so the legends come to life!" Raistlin breathed, gripping Tanis's arm. Tanis heard the sound of huge stone blocks shifting, of rusting iron hinges creaking. Turning his head, he saw each of the stone doors begin to swing wide! The hallway filled with a cold so severe that Tanis felt his fingers go numb. Things moved behind the stone doors.

"The Royal Guard! They made the tracks!" Raistlin whispered frantically. "Human and not human. There is no escape!" he said, grasping Tanis tighter. "Unlike the spectres of Darken Wood, these have but one thought—to destroy all who commit the sacrilege of disturbing the king's rest!"

"We've got to try!" Tanis said, unclenching the mage's biting fingers from his arm. He stumbled backward and reached the entryway, only to find it blocked by two figures.

"Get back!" Tanis gasped. "Run! Who, Fizban? No, you crazy old man! We've got to run! The dead guards—"

"Oh, calm down," the old man muttered. "Young people. Alarmists." He turned around and helped someone else enter. It was Goldmoon, her hair gleaming in the light.

"It's all right, Tanis," she called softly. "Look!" She drew aside her cape: the medallion she wore glowed blue. "Fizban said they would let us pass, Tanis, if they saw the medallion. And when he said that—it began to glow!"

"No!" Tanis started to order her back, but Fizban tapped him on the chest with a long, bony finger.

"You're a good man, Tanis Half-Elven," the old mage said softly, "but you worry too much. Now just relax and let us send these poor souls back to their sleep. Bring the others along, will you?"

Tanis, too startled for words, fell back as Goldmoon and Fizban walked past, Riverwind following. As Tanis watched, they walked slowly between the rows of gaping stone doors. Behind each stone door, movement ceased as she passed. Even at that distance, he could feel the sense of malevolent evil slip away.

As the others came to the crumbling entryway and he helped them through, he answered their whispered questions with a shrug. Laurana didn't say a word to him as she entered; her hand was cold to the touch and he could see, to his astonishment, blood on her lip. Knowing she must have bitten it to keep from screaming, Tanis, remorseful, started to say something to her. But the elfmaid held her head high and refused to look at him.

The others ran after Goldmoon hurriedly, but Tasslehoff, pausing to peek into one of the crypts, saw a tall figure dressed in resplendent armor lying on a stone bier. Skeletal hands grasped the hilt of a longsword lying across the body. Tas looked up at the Royal Crest curiously, sounding out the words.

"*Sothi Nuinqua Tsalarioth*," said Tanis, coming up behind the kender.

"What does it mean?" Tas asked.

"Faithful beyond Death," Tanis said softly.

At the west end of the crypts, they found a set of bronze double doors. Goldmoon pushed it open easily and led them into a triangular passage that opened into a large hall. Inside this room, the only difficulty they faced was in trying to get the dwarf out of it. The hall was perfectly intact, the only room in the Sla-Mori they had encountered so far that had survived the Cataclysm without damage. And the reason for that, Flint explained to anyone who would listen, was the wonderful dwarven construction—particularly the twenty-three columns supporting the ceiling.

The only way out was two identical bronze doors at the far end of the chamber, leading west. Flint, tearing himself away from the columns, examined each and grumbled that he hadn't any idea what was behind them or where they led. After a brief discussion, Tanis decided to take the door to his right.

The door opened onto a clean, narrow passageway that led them, after about thirty feet, to another single bronze door. This door, however, was locked. Caramon pushed, tugged, pried—all to no avail.

"It's no use," the big man grunted. "It won't budge."

Flint watched Caramon for several minutes, then finally stumped forward. Examining the door, he snorted and shook his head. "It's a false door!"

"Looks real to me!" Caramon said, staring at the door suspiciously. "It's even got hinges!"

"Of course, it does," Flint snorted. "We don't build false doors to look false—even a gully dwarf knows that."

"So we're at a dead end!" Eben said grimly.

"Stand back," Raistlin whispered, carefully leaning his staff against a wall. He placed both hands on the door, touching it only with the tips of his fingers, then said, *"Khetsaram pakliol!"* There was a flare of orange light, but not from the door—it came from the wall!

"Move!" Raistlin grabbed his brother and jerked him back, just as the entire wall, bronze door and all, began to pivot.

"Quickly, before it shuts," Tanis said, and everyone hurried through the door, Caramon catching his brother as Raistlin staggered.

"Are you all right?" Caramon asked, as the wall slammed shut behind them.

"Yes, the weakness will pass," Raistlin whispered. "That is the first spell I have cast from the spellbook of Fistandantilus. The spell of opening worked, but I did not believe it would drain me like this."

The door led them into another passageway that ran straight west for about forty feet, took a sharp turn to the south, then east, then continued south again. Here the way was blocked by another single bronze door.

Raistlin shook his head. "I can only use the spell once. It is gone from my memory."

"A fireball would open the door," said Fizban. "I think I remember that spell now—"

"No, Old One," Tanis said hastily. "It would fry all of us in this narrow passage. Tas—"

Reaching the door, the kender pushed on it. "Drat, it's open," he said, disappointed not to have to pick a lock. He peered inside. "Just another room."

They entered cautiously, Raistlin illuminating the chamber with the staff's light. The room was perfectly round, about one hundred feet in diameter. Directly across from them, to the south, stood a bronze door and in the center of the room—

"A crooked column," Tas said, giggling. "Look, Flint. The dwarves built a crooked column!"

"If they did, they had a good reason," the dwarf snapped, shoving the kender aside to examine the tall, thin column. It definitely slanted.

"Hmmmm," said Flint, puzzled. Then—"It isn't a column at all, you doorknob!" Flint exploded. "It's a great, huge chain! Look, you can see here it's hooked to an iron bracket on the floor."

"Then we are in the Chain Room!" Gilthanas said in excitement. "This is the famed defense mechanism of Pax Tharkas. We must be almost in the fortress."

The companions gathered around, staring at the monstrous chain in wonder. Each link was as long as Caramon was tall and as thick around as the trunk of an oak.

"What does the mechanism do?" asked Tasslehoff, longing to climb up the great chain. "Where does this lead?"

"The chain leads to the mechanism itself," Gilthanas answered. "As to how it works, you must ask the dwarf for I am unfamiliar with engineering. But if this chain is released from its moorings"—he pointed to the iron bracket in the floor—"massive blocks of granite drop down behind the gates of the fortress. Then no force on Krynn can open them."

Leaving the kender to peer up into the shadowy darkness, trying in vain to get a glimpse of the wondrous mechanism, Gilthanas joined the others in searching the room.

"Look at this!" he finally cried, pointing to a faint door-shaped line in the stones on the north wall. "A secret door! This must be the entrance!"

"There's the catch." Tasslehoff, turning from the chain, pointed to a chipped piece of stone at the bottom. "The dwarves slipped up," he said, grinning at Flint. "This is a false door that looks false."

"And therefore not to be trusted," Flint said flatly.

"Bah, dwarves have bad days like everyone else," Eben said, bending down to try the catch.

"Don't open it!" Raistlin said suddenly.

"Why not?" asked Sturm. "Because you want to alert someone before we find the way into Pax Tharkas?"

"If I had wanted to betray you, knight, I could have done so a thousand times before this!" Raistlin hissed, staring at the secret door. "I sense a power behind that door greater than any I have felt since—" He stopped, shuddering.

"Since when?" his brother prompted gently.

"The Towers of High Sorcery!" Raistlin whispered. "I warn you, do not open that door!"

"See where the south door leads," Tanis told the dwarf.

Flint stumped over to the bronze door on the south wall and shoved it open. "Near as I can tell, it leads down another passage exactly like all the others," he reported glumly

"The way to Pax Tharkas is through a secret door," Gilthanas repeated. Before anyone could stop him, he reached down and pulled out the chipped stone. The door shivered and began to swing silently inward.

"You will regret this!" Raistlin choked.

The door slid aside to reveal a large room, nearly filled with yellow, brick-like objects. Through a thick layer of dust, a faint yellowish color was visible.

"A treasure room!" Eben cried. "We've found the treasure of Kith-Kanan!"

"All in gold," Sturm said coldly. "Worthless, these days, since steel's the only thing of any value. . . ." His voice trailed off, his eyes widened in horror.

"What is it?" shouted Caramon, drawing his sword.

"I don't know!" Sturm said, more as a gasp than words.

"I do!" Raistlin breathed as the thing took shape before his eyes. "It is the spirit of a dark elf! I warned you not to open that door."

"Do something!" Eben said, stumbling backward.

"Put up your weapons, fools!" Raistlin said in a piercing whisper. "You cannot fight her! Her touch is death, and if she wails while we are within these walls, we are doomed. Her keening voice alone kills. Run, run all of you! Quickly! Through the south door!"

Even as they fell back, the darkness in the treasure room took shape, coalescing into the coldly beautiful, distorted features of a female drow—an evil elf of ages past, whose punishment for crimes unspeakable had been execution. Then the powerful elven magic-users chained her spirit, forcing her to guard forever the king's treasure. At the sight of these living beings, she stretched out her hands, craving the warmth of flesh, and opened her mouth to scream out her grief and her hatred of all living things.

The companions turned and fled, stumbling over each other in their haste to escape through the bronze door. Caramon fell over his brother, knocking the staff from Raistlin's hand. The staff clattered on the floor, its light still glowing, for only dragonfire can destroy the magic crystal. But now its light flared out over the floor, plunging the rest of the room into darkness.

Seeing her prey escaping, the spirit flitted into the Chain Room, her grasping hand brushing Eben's cheek. He screamed at the chilling, burning touch and collapsed. Sturm caught him and dragged him through the door just as Raistlin grabbed his staff and he and Caramon lunged through.

"Is that everyone?" Tanis asked, reluctant to close the door. Then he heard a low, moaning sound, so frightful that he felt his heart stop beating for a moment. Fear seized him. He couldn't breathe. The cry ceased, and his heart gave a great, painful leap. The spirit sucked in its breath to scream again.

"No time to look!" Raistlin gasped. "Shut the door, brother!"

Caramon threw all his weight on the bronze door. It slammed shut with a boom that echoed through the hall.

"That won't stop her!" Eben cried, panic-stricken.

"No," said Raistlin softly. "Her magic is powerful, more powerful than mine. I can cast a spell on the door, but it will weaken me greatly. I suggest you run while you can. If it fails, perhaps I can stall her."

"Riverwind, take the others on ahead," Tanis ordered. "Sturm and I'll stay with Raistlin and Caramon."

The others crept down the dark corridor, looking back to watch in horrible fascination. Raistlin ignored them and handed the staff to his brother. The light from the glowing crystal flashed out at the unfamiliar touch.

The mage put his hands on the door, pressing both palms flat against it. Closing his eyes, he forced himself to forget everything except the magic. "*Kalis-an budrunin—*" His concentration broke as he felt a terrible chill.

The dark elf! She had recognized his spell and was trying to break him! Images of his battle with another dark elf in the

Towers of High Sorcery came back to his mind. He struggled to blot out the evil memory of the battle that wrecked his body and came close to destroying his mind, but he felt himself losing control. He had forgotten the words! The door trembled. The elf was coming through!

Then from somewhere inside the mage came a strength he had discovered within himself only twice before—in the Tower and on the altar of the black dragon in Xak Tsaroth. The familiar voice that he could hear clearly in his mind yet never identify, spoke to him, repeating the words of the spell. Raistlin shouted them aloud in a strong, clear voice that was not his own. *"Kalis-an budrunin kara-emarath!"*

From the other side of the door came a wail of disappointment, failure. The door held. The mage collapsed.

Caramon handed the staff to Eben as he picked up his brother in his arms and followed the others as they groped their way along the dark passage. Another secret door opened easily to Flint's hand, leading to a series of short, debris-filled tunnels. Trembling with fear, the companions wearily made their way past these obstacles. Finally they emerged into a large, open room filled from ceiling to floor with stacks of wooden crates. Riverwind lit a torch on the wall. The crates were nailed shut. Some bore the label SOLACE, some GATEWAY.

"This is it. We're inside the fortress." Gilthanas said, grimly victorious. "We stand in the cellar of Pax Tharkas."

"Thank the true gods!" Tanis sighed and sank onto the floor, the others slumping down beside him. It was then they noticed that Fizban and Tasslehoff were missing.

II

Lost. The plan. Betrayed!

asslehoff could never afterward clearly recall those last, few, panicked moments in the Chain Room. He remembered saying, "A dark elf? Where?" and standing on his tiptoes, trying desperately to see, when suddenly the glowing staff fell on the floor. He heard Tanis shouting, and—above that—a kind of a moaning sound that made the kender lose all sense of where he was or what he was doing. Then strong hands grabbed him around the waist, lifting him up into the air.

"Climb!" shouted a voice beneath him.

Tasslehoff stretched out his hands, felt the cool metal of the chain, and began to climb. He heard a door boom, far below, and the chilling wail of the dark elf again. It didn't sound deadly this time, more like a cry of rage and anger. Tas hoped this meant his friends had escaped.

"I wonder how I'll find them again," he asked himself softly, feeling discouraged for a moment. Then he heard Fizban muttering to himself and cheered up. He wasn't alone.

Thick, heavy darkness wrapped around the kender. Climbing by feel alone, he was growing extremely tired when he felt cool air brush his right cheek. He sensed, rather than saw, that he must be coming to the place where the chain and the mechanism linked up (Tas was rather proud of that pun). If only he could see! Then he remembered. He was, after all, with a magician.

"We could use a light," Tas called out.

"A fight? Where?" Fizban nearly lost his grip on the chain.

"Not fight! Light!" Tas said patiently, clinging to a link. "I think we're near the top of this thing and we really ought to have a look around."

"Oh, certainly. Let's see, light . . ." Tas heard the magician fumbling in his pouches. Apparently he found what he was searching for, because he soon gave a little crow of triumph, spoke a few words, and a small puffball of bluish-yellow flame appeared, hovering near the magician's hat.

The glowing puffball whizzed up, danced around Tasslehoff as if to inspect the kender, then returned to the proud magician. Tas was enchanted. He had all sorts of questions regarding the wonderful flaming puffball, but his arms were getting shaky and the old magician was nearly done in. He knew they had better find some way to get off this chain.

Looking up, he saw that they were, as he had guessed, at the top part of the fortress. The chain ran up over a huge wooden cogwheel mounted on an iron axle anchored in solid stone. The links of the chain fit over teeth big as tree trunks, then the chain stretched out across the wide shaft, disappearing into a tunnel to the kender's right.

"We can climb onto that gear and crawl along the chain into the tunnel," the kender said, pointing. "Can you send the light up here?"

"Light, to the wheel," Fizban instructed.

The light wavered in the air for a moment, then danced back and forth in a decidedly nay-saying manner.

Fizban frowned. "Light—to the wheel!" he repeated firmly.

The puffball flame darted around to hide behind the magician's hat. Fizban, making a wild grab for it, nearly fell, and flung both arms around the chain. The puffball light danced in the air behind him as if enjoying the game.

"Uh, I guess we've got enough light, after all," Tas said.

"No discipline in the younger generation," Fizban grumbled. "His father—now there was a puffball . . ." The old magician's voice died away as he began to climb again, the puffball flame hovering near the tip of his battered hat.

Tas soon reached the first tooth on the wheel. Discovering the teeth were rough hewn and easy to climb, Tas crawled from one to another until he reached the top. Fizban, his robes hiked up around his thighs, followed with amazing agility.

"Could you ask the light to shine in the tunnel?" Tas asked.

"Light—to the tunnel," Fizban ordered, his bony legs wrapped around a link in the chain.

The puffball appeared to consider the command. Slowly it skittered to the edge of the tunnel, and then stopped.

"Inside the tunnel!" the magician commanded.

The puffball flame refused.

"I think it's afraid of the dark," Fizban said apologetically.

"My goodness, how remarkable!" the kender said in astonishment. "Well," he thought for a moment, "if it will stay where it is, I think I can see enough to make my way across the chain. It looks like it's only about fifteen feet or so to the tunnel." With nothing below but several hundred feet of darkness and air, never mind the stone floor at the bottom, Tas thought.

"Someone should come up here and grease this thing," Fizban said, examining the axle critically. "That's all you get today, shoddy workmanship."

"I'm really rather glad they didn't," Tas said mildly, crawling forward onto the chain. About halfway across the gap, the kender considered what it would be like to fall from this height, tumbling down and down and down, then hitting the stone floor at the bottom. He wondered what it would feel like to splatter all over the floor. . . .

"Get a move on!" Fizban shouted, crawling out onto the chain after the kender.

Tas crawled forward quickly to the tunnel entrance where the puffball flame waited, then jumped off the chain onto the stone floor about five feet below him. The puffball flame darted in after him, and finally Fizban reached the tunnel entrance, too. At the last moment, he fell, but Tas caught hold of his robes and dragged the old man to safety.

They were sitting on the floor resting when suddenly the old man's head snapped up.

"My staff," he said.

"What about it?" Tas yawned, wondering what time it was.

The old man struggled to his feet. "Left it down below," he mumbled, heading for the chain.

"Wait! You can't go back!" Tasslehoff jumped up in alarm.

"Who says?" asked the old man petulantly, his beard bristling.

"I m-mean . . ." Tas stuttered, "it would be too dangerous. But I know you how feel—my hoopak's down there."

"Hmmmm," Fizban said, sitting back down disconsolately.

"Was it magic?" Tas asked after a moment.

"I was never quite certain," Fizban said wistfully.

"Well," said Tas practically, "maybe after we've finished the adventure we can go back and get it. Now let's try to find some place to rest."

He glanced around the tunnel. It was about seven feet from floor to ceiling. The huge chain ran along the top with numerous smaller chains attached, stretching across the tunnel floor into a vast dark pit beyond. Tas, staring down into it, could vaguely make out the shape of gigantic boulders.

"What time do you suppose it is?" Tas asked.

"Lunch time," said the old man. "And we might as well rest right here. It's as safe a place as any." He plopped back down. Pulling out a handful of quith-pa, he began to chew on it noisily. The puffball flame wandered over and settled on the brim of the magician's hat.

Tas sat down next to the mage and began to nibble on his own bit of dried fruit. Then he sniffed. There was suddenly a very peculiar smell, like someone burning old socks. Looking up, he sighed and tugged on the magician's robe.

"Uh, Fizban," he said. "Your hat's on fire."

"Flint," Tanis said sternly, "for the last time—I feel as badly as you do about losing Tas, but we cannot go back! He's with Fizban and, knowing those two, they'll both manage to get out of whatever predicament they're in."

"If they don't bring the whole fortress down around our ears," Sturm muttered.

The dwarf wiped his hand across his eyes, glared at Tanis, then whirled on his heel and stumped back to a corner where he hurled himself onto the floor, sulking.

Tanis sat back down. He knew how Flint felt. It seemed odd—there'd been so many times he could happily have strangled the kender, but now that he was gone, Tanis missed him—and for exactly the same reasons. There was an innate, unfailing cheerfulness about Tasslehoff that made him an invaluable companion. No danger ever frightened a kender and, therefore, Tas never gave up. He was never at a loss for something to do in an emergency. It might not always be the right thing, but at least he was ready to act. Tanis smiled sadly. I only hope this emergency doesn't prove to be his last, he thought.

The companions rested for an hour, eating quith-pa and drinking fresh water from a deep well they discovered. Raistlin regained consciousness but could eat nothing. He sipped water, then lay limply back. Caramon broke the news to him about Fizban hesitantly, fearing his brother might take the old mage's disappearance badly. But Raistlin simply shrugged, closed his eyes, and sank into a deep sleep.

After Tanis felt his strength return, he rose and walked toward Gilthanas, noting that the elf was intently studying a map. Passing Laurana, who sat alone, he smiled at her. She refused to acknowledge it. Tanis sighed. Already he regretted speaking harshly to her back in the Sla-Mori. He had to admit that she had handled herself remarkably well under terrifying circumstances. She had done what she was told to quickly and without question. Tanis supposed he would have to apologize, but first he needed to talk to Gilthanas.

"What's the plan?" he asked, sitting down on a crate.

"Yes, where are we?" Sturm asked. Soon almost everyone was crowded around the map except Raistlin who appeared to sleep, though Tanis thought he saw a slit of gold shining through the mage's supposedly closed eyelids.

Gilthanas spread his map flat.

"Here is the fortress of Pax Tharkas and the surrounding mine area," he said, then he pointed. "We are in the cellars here on the lowest level. Down this hallway, about fifty feet from here, are the rooms where the women are imprisoned. This is a guard room, across from the women, and this"—he tapped the map gently—"is the lair of one of the red dragons, the one Lord Verminaard called Ember. The dragon is so big, of course, that the lair extends up above ground level, communicating with Lord Verminaard's chambers on the first floor, up through the gallery on the second floor, and out into the open sky.

Gilthanas smiled bitterly. "On the first floor, behind Verminaard's chambers, is the prison where the children are kept. The Dragon Highlord is wise. He keeps the hostages separated, knowing that the women would never consider leaving without their children, and the men would not leave without their families. The children are guarded by a second red dragon in this room. The men—about three hundred of them—work in mines out in the mountain caves. There are several hundred gully dwarves working the mines as well."

"You seem to know a lot about Pax Tharkas," Eben said.

Gilthanas glanced up quickly. "What do you insinuate?"

"I'm not insinuating anything," Eben answered. "It's just that you know a lot about this place for never having been here! And wasn't it interesting that we kept running into creatures who damn near killed us back in the Sla-Mori."

"Eben," Tanis spoke very quietly, "we've had enough of your suspicions. I don't believe any of us is a traitor. As Raistlin said, the traitor could have betrayed any of us long before this. What's the point of coming this far?"

"To bring me and the Disks to Lord Verminaard," Goldmoon said softly. "He knows I am here, Tanis. He and I are linked by our faith."

"That's ridiculous!" Sturm snorted.

"No, it isn't," Goldmoon said. "Remember, there are two constellations missing. One was the Queen of Darkness. From what little I have been able to understand in the Disks of Mishakal, the Queen was also one of the ancient gods. The gods of good are matched by the gods of evil, with the gods of neutrality striving to keep the balance. Verminaard worships the Queen of Darkness as I worship Mishakal: that is what Mishakal meant when she said we were to restore the balance.

The promise of good that I bring is the one thing he fears and he is exerting all his will to find me. The longer I stay here . . ." Her voice died.

"All the more reason to quit bickering," Tanis stated, switching his gaze to Eben.

The fighter shrugged. "Enough said. I'm with you."

"What is your plan, Gilthanas?" Tanis asked, noticing with irritation that Sturm and Caramon and Eben exchanged quick glances, three humans sticking together against the elves, he caught himself thinking. But perhaps I'm just as bad, believing in Gilthanas because he's an elf.

Gilthanas saw the exchange of glances, too. For a moment he stared at them with an intense, unblinking gaze, then began to speak in a measured tone, considering his words, as if reluctant to reveal any more than was absolutely necessary.

"Every evening, ten to twelve women are allowed to leave their cells and take food to the men in the mines. Thus the Highlord lets the men see that he is keeping his side of the bargain. The women are allowed to visit the children once a day for the same reason. My warriors and I planned to disguise ourselves as women, go out to the men in the mines, tell them of the plan to free the hostages, and alert them to be ready to strike. Beyond that we had not thought, particularly in regard to freeing the children. Our spies indicated something strange about the dragon guarding the children, but we could not determine what."

"What sp—?" Caramon started to ask, caught Tanis's eye, and thought better of his question. Instead he asked, "When will we strike? And what about the dragon, Ember?"

"We strike tomorrow morning. Lord Verminaard and Ember will most certainly join the army tomorrow as it reaches the outskirts of Qualinesti. He has been preparing for this invasion a long time. I do not believe he will miss it."

The group discussed the plan for several minutes, adding to it, refining it, generally agreeing that it appeared viable. They gathered their things as Caramon woke his brother. Sturm and Eben pushed open the door leading to the hallway. It appeared empty, although they could hear faint sounds of harsh, drunken laughter from a room directly across from them. Draconians. Silently, the companions slipped into the dark and dingy corridor.

Tasslehoff stood in the middle of what he had named the Mechanism Room, staring around the tunnel lighted dimly by the puffball. The kender was beginning to feel discouraged. It was a feeling he didn't get often and likened to the time he'd eaten an entire green tomato pie acquired from a neighbor. To this day, discouragement and green tomato pie both made him want to throw up.

"There's got to be some way out of here," said the kender. "Surely they inspect the mechanism occasionally, or come up to admire it, or give tours, or something!"

He and Fizban had spent an hour walking up and down the tunnel, crawling in and out among the myriad chains. They found nothing. It was cold and barren and covered with dust.

"Speaking of light," said the old magician suddenly, though they hadn't been. "Look there."

Tasslehoff looked. A thin sliver of light was visible through a crack in the bottom of the wall, near the entrance to the narrow tunnel. They could hear voices, and the light grew brighter as if torches were being lit in a room below them.

"Maybe that's a way out," the old man said.

Running lightly down the tunnel, Tas knelt down and peered through the crack. "Come here!"

The two looked down into a large room, furnished with every possible luxury. All that was beautiful, graceful, delicate, or valuable in the lands under Verminaard's control had been brought to decorate the private chambers of the Dragon Highlord. An ornate throne stood at one end of the room. Rare and priceless silver mirrors hung on the walls, arranged so cunningly that no matter where a trembling captive turned, the only image he saw was the grotesque, horned helm of the Dragon Highlord glowering at him.

"That must be him!" Tas whispered to Fizban. "That must be Lord Verminaard!" The kender sucked in his breath in awe. "That must be his dragon—Ember. The one Gilthanas told us about, that killed all the elves in Solace."

Ember, or Pyros (his true name being a secret known only to draconians, or to other dragons—never to common mortals) was an ancient and enormous red dragon. Pyros had been given to Lord Verminaard ostensibly as a reward from the Queen of Darkness to her cleric. In reality, Pyros was sent to keep a watchful eye on Verminaard, who had developed a strange, paranoid fear regarding discovery of the true gods. All the Dragon Highlords on Krynn possessed dragons, however, though perhaps not as strong and intelligent. For Pyros had another, more important mission that was secret even to the Dragon Highlord himself, a mission assigned to him by the Queen of Darkness and known only to her and her evil dragons.

Pyros's mission was to search this part of Ansalon for one man, a man of many names. The Queen of Darkness called him Everman. The dragons called him Green Gemstone Man. His human name was Berem. And it was because of this unceasing search for the human, Berem, that Pyros was present in Verminaard's chamber this afternoon when he would have much preferred to be napping in his lair.

Pyros had received word that Fewmaster Toede was bringing in two prisoners for interrogation. There was always the possibility this Berem might be one of them. Therefore, the dragon was always present during interrogations, though he often appeared vastly bored. The only time interrogations became interesting—as far as Pyros was concerned—was when Verminaard ordered a prisoner to "feed the dragon."

Pyros was stretched out along one side of the enormous throne room, completely filling it. His huge wings were folded at his sides, his flanks heaved with every breath he took like some great gnomish engine. Dozing, he snorted and shifted slightly. A rare vase toppled to the floor with a crash. Verminaard looked up from his desk where he was studying a map of Qualinesti.

"Transform yourself before you wreck the place," he snarled.

Pyros opened one eye, regarded Verminaard coldly for a moment, then grudgingly rumbled a brief word of magic.

The gigantic red dragon began to shimmer like a mirage, the monstrous dragon shape condensing into the shape of a human male, slight of build with dark black hair, a thin face, and slanting red eyes. Dressed in crimson robes, Pyros the man walked to a desk near Verminaard's throne. Sitting down, he folded his hands and stared at Verminaard's broad, muscled back with undisguised loathing.

There was a scratch at the door.

"Enter," Verminaard commanded absently.

A draconian guard threw open the door, admitting Fewmaster Toede and his prisoners, then withdrew, swinging the great bronze and gold doors shut. Verminaard kept the Fewmaster waiting several long minutes while he continued to study his battle plan. Then, favoring Toede with a condescending gaze, he walked over and ascended the steps to his throne. It was elaborately carved to resemble the gaping jaws of a dragon.

Verminaard was an imposing figure. Tall and powerfully built, he wore dark night-blue dragonscale armor trimmed in gold. The hideous mask of a Dragon Highlord concealed his face. Moving with a grace remarkable in such a large man, he leaned back comfortably, his leather-encased hand absently caressing a black, gold-trimmed mace by his side.

Verminaard regarded Toede and his two captives irritably, knowing full well that Toede had dredged up these two in an effort to redeem himself from the disastrous loss of the cleric. When Verminaard discovered from his draconians that a woman matching the description of the cleric had been among those prisoners taken from Solace and that she had been allowed to escape, his fury was terrifying. Toede had nearly paid for his mistake with his life, but the hobgoblin was exceptionally skilled at whining and groveling. Knowing this, Verminaard had considered refusing to admit Toede at all today, but he had a strange, nagging sensation that all was not well in his realm.

It's that blasted cleric! Verminaard thought. He could sense her power coming nearer and nearer, making him nervous and uneasy. He intently studied the two prisoners Toede led into the room. Then, seeing that neither of them matched the descriptions of those who had raided Xak Tsaroth, Verminaard scowled behind the mask.

Pyros reacted differently to the sight of the prisoners. The transformed dragon half-rose to his feet while his thin hands clenched the ebony desktop with such ferocity he left the impressions of his fingers in the wood. Shaking with excitement, it took a great effort of will to force himself to sit back down, outwardly calm. Only his eyes, burning with a devouring flame, gave a hint of his inner elation as he stared at the prisoners.

One of the prisoners was a gully dwarf, Sestun, in fact. He was chained hand and foot (Toede was taking no chances) and could barely walk. Stumbling forward, he dropped to his knees before the Dragon Highlord, terror-stricken. The other prisoner—the one Pyros watched—was a human male, dressed in rags, who stood staring at the floor.

"Why have you bothered me with these wretches, Fewmaster?" Verminaard snarled.

Toede, reduced to a quivering mass, gulped and immediately launched into his speech. "This prisoner"—he hobgoblin kicked Sestun—"was the one who freed the slaves from Solace, and this prisoner"—he indicated the man, who lifted his head, a confused and puzzled expression on his face—"was found wandering around Gateway which, as you know, has been declared off limits to all nonmilitary personnel."

"So why bring them to me?" asked Lord Verminaard irritably. "Throw them into the mines with the rest of the rabble."

Toede stammered. "I thought the human m-m-might b-be a s-spy. . . ."

The Dragon Highlord studied the human intently. He was tall, about fifty human years old. His hair was white and his clean-shaven face brown and weathered, streaked with lines of age. He was dressed like a beggar, which is probably what he was, Verminaard thought in disgust. There was certainly nothing unusual about him, except for his eyes which were bright and young. His hands, too, were those of a man in his prime. Probably elven blood. . . .

"The man is feeble-minded," Verminaard said finally. "Look at him—gaping like a landed fish."

"I b-b-believe he's, uh, deaf and dumb, my lord," Toede said, sweating.

Verminaard wrinkled his nose. Not even the dragonhelm could keep away the foul odor of perspiring hobgoblin.

"So you have captured a gully dwarf and a spy who can neither hear nor speak," Verminaard said caustically. "Well done, Toede. Perhaps now you can go out and pick me a bouquet of flowers."

383

"If that is your lordship's pleasure," Toede replied solemnly, bowing.

Verminaard began to laugh beneath his helm, amused in spite of himself. Toede was such an entertaining little creature, a pity he couldn't be taught to bathe. Verminaard waved his hand. "Remove them—and yourself."

"What shall I do with the prisoners, my lord?"

"Have the gully dwarf feed Ember tonight. And take your spy to the mines. Keep a watch on him though—he looks deadly!" The Dragon Highlord laughed.

Pyros ground his teeth and cursed Verminaard for a fool.

Toede bowed again. "Come on, you," he snarled, yanking on the manacles, and the man stumbled after him. "You, too!" He prodded Sestun with his foot. It was useless. The gully dwarf, hearing he was to feed the dragon, had fainted. A draconian was called to remove him.

Verminaard left his throne and walked over to his desk. He gathered up his maps in a great roll. "Send the wyvern with dispatches," he ordered Pyros. "We fly tomorrow morning to destroy Qualinesti. Be ready when I call."

When the bronze and golden doors had closed behind the Dragon Highlord, Pyros, still in human form, rose from the desk and began to pace feverishly back and forth across the room. There came a scratching at the door.

"Lord Verminaard has gone to his chambers!" Pyros called out, irritated at the interruption.

The door opened a crack.

"It is you I wish to see, royal one," whispered a draconian.

"Enter," Pyros said. "But be swift."

"The traitor has been successful, royal one," the draconian said softly. "He was able to slip away only for a moment, lest they suspect. But he has brought the cleric—"

"To the Abyss with the cleric!" Pyros snarled. "This news is of interest only to Verminaard. Take it to him. No, wait." The dragon paused.

"As you instructed, I came to you first," the draconian said apologetically, preparing to make a hasty departure.

"Don't go," the dragon ordered, raising a hand. "This news is of value to me after all. Not the cleric. There is much more at stake. . . . I must meet with our treacherous friend. Bring him to me tonight, in my lair. Do not inform Lord Verminaard—not yet. He might meddle." Pyros was thinking rapidly now, his plans coming together. "Verminaard has Qualinesti to keep him occupied."

As the draconian bowed and left the throne room, Pyros began pacing once again, back and forth, back and forth, rubbing his hands together, smiling.

12

The parable of the gem.
Traitor revealed. Tas's dilemma.

top that, you bold man!" Caramon simpered, slapping Eben's hand as the fighter slyly slid his hand up Caramon's skirt.

The women in the room laughed so heartily at the antics of the two warriors that Tanis glanced nervously at the cell door, afraid of arousing the suspicion of the guards.

Maritta saw his worried gaze. "Don't worry about the guards!" she said with a shrug. "There are only two down here on this level and they're drunk half the time, especially now that the army's moved out." She looked up from her sewing at the women and shook her head. "It does my heart good to hear them laugh, poor things," she said softly. "They've had little enough to laugh about these past days."

Thirty-four women were crowded into one cell—Maritta said there were sixty women living in another nearby—under conditions so shocking that even the hardened campaigners were appalled. Rude straw mats covered the floor. The women had no possessions beyond a few clothes. They were allowed outdoors for a brief exercise period each morning. The rest of the time they were forced to sew draconian uniforms. Though they had been imprisoned only a few weeks, their faces were pale and wan, their bodies thin and gaunt from the lack of nourishing food.

Tanis relaxed. Though he had known Maritta only a few hours, he already relied on her judgment. She was the one who had calmed the terrified women when the companions burst into their cell. She was the one who listened to their plan and agreed that it had possibilities.

"Our menfolk will go along with you," she told Tanis. "It's the Highseekers who'll give you trouble."

"The Council of Highseekers?" Tanis asked in astonishment. "They're here? Prisoners?"

Maritta nodded, frowning. "That was their payment for believing in that black cleric. But they won't want to leave, and why should they? They're not forced to work in the mines—the Dragon Highlord sees to that! But we're with you." She glanced around at the others, who nodded firmly. "On one condition—that you'll not put the children in danger."

"I can't guarantee that," Tanis said. "I don't mean to sound harsh, but we may have to fight a dragon to reach them and—"

"Fight a dragon? Flamestrike?" Maritta looked at him in amazement. "Pah! There's no need to fight the pitiful critter. In fact, were you to hurt her, you'd have half the children ready to tear you apart, they're that fond of her."

"Of a dragon?" Goldmoon asked. "What's she done, cast a spell on them?"

"No. I doubt Flamestrike could cast a spell on anything anymore." Maritta smiled sadly. "The poor critter's more than half-mad. Her own children were killed in some great war or other and now she's got it in her head that our children are *her* children. I don't know where his lordship dug her up, but it was a sorry thing to do and I hope he pays for it someday!" She snapped a thread viciously.

"T'won't be difficult to free the children," she added, seeing Tanis's worried look. "Flamestrike always sleeps late of a morning. We feed the children their breakfast, take them out for their exercise, and she never stirs. She'll never know they're gone till she wakes, poor thing."

The women, filled with hope for the first time, began modifying old clothes to fit the men. Things went smoothly until it came time to fit them.

"Shave!" Sturm roared in such fury that the women scurried away from the knight in alarm. Sturm had taken a dim view of the disguise idea, anyway, but had agreed to go along with it. It seemed the best way to cross the wide-open courtyard between the fortress and the mines. But, he announced, he would rather die a hundred deaths at the hands of the Dragon Highlord than shave his moustaches. He only calmed down when Tanis suggested covering his face with a scarf.

Just when that was settled, another crisis arose. Riverwind stated flatly that he would not dress up as a woman and no amount of arguing could convince him otherwise. Goldmoon finally took Tanis aside to explain that, in their tribe, any warrior who committed a cowardly act in battle was forced to wear women's clothes until he redeemed himself. Tanis was baffled by this one. But Maritta had wondered how they would manage to outfit the tall man anyway.

After much discussion, it was decided Riverwind would bundle up in a long cloak and walk hunched over, leaning on a staff like an old woman. Things went smoothly after this, for a time at least.

Laurana walked over to a corner of the room where Tanis was wrapping a scarf around his own face.

"Why don't *you* shave?" Laurana asked, staring at Tanis's beard. "Or do you truly enjoy flaunting your human side as Gilthanas says?"

"I don't flaunt it," Tanis replied evenly. "I just got tired of trying to deny it, that's all." He drew a deep breath. "Laurana, I'm sorry I spoke to you as I did back in the Sla-Mori. I had no right—"

"You had every right," Laurana interrupted. "What I did was the act of a lovesick little girl. I foolishly endangered your lives." Her voice faltered, then she regained control. "It will not happen again. I will prove I can be of value to the group."

Exactly how she meant to do this, she wasn't certain.

Although she talked glibly about being skilled in fighting, she had never killed so much as a rabbit. She was so frightened now that she was forced to clasp her hands behind her back to keep Tanis from seeing how she trembled. She was afraid that if she let herself, she would give way to her weakness and seek comfort in his arms, so she left him and went over to help Gilthanas with his disguise.

Tanis told himself he was glad Laurana was showing some signs of maturity at last. He steadfastly refused to admit that his soul stood breathless whenever he looked into her large, luminous eyes.

The afternoon passed swiftly and soon it was evening and time for the women to take dinner to the mines. The companions waited for the guards in tense silence, laughter forgotten. There had, after all, been one last crisis. Raistlin, coughing until he was exhausted, said he was too weak to accompany them. When his brother offered to stay behind with him, Raistlin glared at him irritably and told him not to be a fool.

"You do not need me this night," the mage whispered. "Leave me alone. I must sleep."

"I don't like leaving him here—" Gilthanas began, but before he could continue, they heard the sound of clawed feet outside the cell, and another sound of pots rattling. The cell door swung open and two draconian guards, both smelling strongly of stale wine, stepped inside. One of them reeled a bit as it peered, bleary-eyed, at the women.

"Get moving," it said harshly.

As the "women" filed out, they saw six gully dwarves standing in the corridor, lugging large pots of some sort of nameless stew. Caramon sniffed hungrily, then wrinkled his nose in disgust. The draconians slammed the cell door shut behind them. Glancing back, Caramon saw his twin, shrouded in blankets, lying in a dark, shadowy corner.

Fizban clapped his hands. "Well done, my boy!" said the old magician in excitement as part of the wall in the Mechanism Room swung open.

"Thanks," Tas replied modestly. "Actually, *finding* the secret door was more difficult than opening it. I don't know how you managed. I thought I'd looked everywhere."

He started to crawl through the door, then stopped as a thought occurred to him. "Fizban, is there any way you can tell that light of yours to stay behind? At least until we see if anyone's in here? Otherwise, I'm going to make an awfully good target and we're not far from Verminaard's chambers."

"I'm afraid not." Fizban shook his head. "It doesn't like to be left alone in dark places."

Tasslehoff nodded—he had expected the answer. Well, there was no use worrying about it. If the milk's spilled, the cat will drink it, as his mother used to say. Fortunately, the narrow hallway he crawled into appeared empty. The flame hovered near his shoulder. He helped Fizban through, then explored his surroundings. They were in a small hallway that ended abruptly not forty feet away in a flight of stairs descending into darkness. Double bronze doors in the east wall provided the only other exit.

"Now," muttered Tas, "we're above the throne room. Those stairs probably lead down to it. I suppose there's a million draconians guarding it! So that's out." He put his ear to the door. "No sound. Let's look around." Pushing gently, he easily opened the double doors. Pausing to listen, Tas entered cautiously, followed closely by Fizban and the puffball flame.

"Some sort of art gallery," he said, glancing around a giant room where paintings, covered with dust and grime, hung on the walls. High slit windows in the walls gave Tas a glimpse of the stars and the tops of high mountains. With a good idea of where he was now, he drew a crude map in his head.

"If my calculations are correct, the throne room is to the west and the dragon's lair is to the west of that. At least that's where he went when Verminaard left this afternoon. The dragon must have some way to fly out of this building, so the lair should open up into the sky, which means a shaft of some sort, and maybe another crack where we can see what's going on."

So involved was Tas with his plans that he was not paying any attention to Fizban. The old magician was moving purposefully around the room, studying each painting as if searching for one in particular.

"Ah, here it is," Fizban murmured, then turned and whispered, "Tasslehoff!"

The kender lifted his head and saw the painting suddenly begin to glow with a soft light. "Look at that!" Tasslehoff said, entranced. "Why, it's a painting of dragons—red dragons like Ember, attacking Pax Tharkas and . . ."

The kender's voice died. Men—Knights of Solamnia— mounted on other dragons were fighting back! The dragons the Knights rode were beautiful dragons—gold and silver dragons—and the men carried bright weapons that gleamed with a shining radiance. Suddenly Tasslehoff understood! There were *good* dragons in the world, if they could be found, who would help fight the evil dragons, and there was—

"The Dragonlance!" he murmured.

The old magician nodded to himself. "Yes, little one," he whispered. "You understand. You see the answer. And you will remember. But not now. Not now." Reaching out, he ruffled the kender's hair with his gnarled hand.

"Dragons. What was I saying?" Tas couldn't remember. And what was he doing here anyhow, staring at a painting so covered with dust he couldn't make it out. The kender shook his head. Fizban must be rubbing off on him. "Oh, yes. The dragon's lair. If my calculations are correct, it's over here." He walked away.

The old magician shuffled along behind, smiling.

The companions' journey to the mines proved uneventful. They saw only a few draconian guards, and they appeared half-asleep with boredom. No one paid any attention to the women going by. They passed the glowing forge, continually fed by a scrambling mass of exhausted gully dwarves.

Hurrying past that dismal sight quickly, the companions entered the mines where draconian guards locked the men in huge cave rooms at night, then returned to keep an eye on the gully dwarves. Guard duty over the men was a waste of time, anyway, Verminaard figured—the humans weren't going anyplace.

And, for a while, it looked to Tanis as if this might prove horribly true. The men *weren't* going anyplace. They stared at Goldmoon, unconvinced, as she spoke. After all, she was a barbarian, her accent was strange, her dress even stranger. She told what seemed a children's tale of a dragon dying in a blue flame she herself survived. And all she had to show for it was a collection of shining platinum disks.

Hederick, the Solace Theocrat, was loud in his denunciation of the Que-shu woman as a witch and a charlatan and a blasphemer. He reminded them of the scene in the Inn, exhibiting his scarred hand as evidence. Not that the men paid a great deal of attention to Hederick. The Seeker gods, after all, had not kept the dragons from Solace.

Many of them, in fact, were interested in the prospect of escape. Nearly all bore some mark of ill-treatment—whip lashes, bruised faces. They were poorly fed, forced to live in conditions of filth and squalor, and everyone knew that when the iron beneath the hills was gone, their usefulness to Lord Verminaard would end. But the Highseekers—still the governing body, even in prison—opposed such a reckless plan.

Arguments started. The men shouted back and forth. Tanis hastily posted Caramon, Flint, Eben, Sturm, and Gilthanas at the doors, fearing the guards would hear the disturbance and return. The half-elf hadn't expected this—the arguing might last for days! Goldmoon sat despondently before the men, looking as though she might cry. She had been so imbued with her newfound convictions, and so eager to bring her knowledge to the world, that she was cast into despair when her beliefs were doubted.

"These humans are fools!" Laurana said softly, coming up to stand beside Tanis.

"No," replied Tanis, sighing. "If they were fools, it would be easier. We promise them nothing tangible and ask them to risk the only thing they have left—their lives. And for what? To flee into the hills, fighting a running battle all the way. At least here they are alive—for the time being."

"But how can life be worth anything, living like this?" Laurana asked.

"That's a very good question, young woman," said a feeble voice. They turned to see Maritta kneeling beside a man lying on a crude cot in a corner of the cell. Wasted with illness and deprivation, his age was indeterminable. He struggled to sit up, stretching out a thin, pale hand to Tanis and Laurana. His breath rattled in his chest. Maritta tried to hush him, but he stared at her irritably. "I know I'm dying, woman! It doesn't mean I have to be bored to death first. Bring that barbarian woman over to me."

Tanis looked at Maritta questioningly. She rose and came over, drawing him to one side. "He is Elistan," she said as if Tanis should know the name. When Tanis didn't respond, she clarified. "Elistan—one of the Highseekers from Haven. He was much loved and respected by the people, the only one who spoke out against this Lord Verminaard. But no one listened—not wanting to hear, of course."

"You speak of him in the past tense," Tanis said. "He isn't dead yet."

"No, but it won't be long." Maritta wiped away a tear. "I've seen the wasting sickness before. My own father died of it. There's something inside of him, eating him alive. These last few days he has been half mad with the pain, but that's gone now. The end is very near."

"Maybe not." Tanis smiled. "Goldmoon is a cleric. She can heal him."

"Perhaps, perhaps not," Maritta said skeptically. "I wouldn't want to chance it. We shouldn't excite Elistan with false hope. Let him die in peace."

"Goldmoon," Tanis said as the Chieftain's Daughter came near. "This man wants to meet you." Ignoring Maritta, the half-elf led Goldmoon over to Elistan. Goldmoon's face, hard and cold with disappointment and frustration, softened as she saw the man's pitiful condition.

Elistan looked up at her. "Young woman," he said sternly, though his voice was weak, "you claim to bring word from ancient gods. If it truly was we humans who turned from them, not the gods who turned from us as we've always thought, then why have they waited so long to make their presence known?"

Goldmoon knelt down beside the dying man in silence, thinking how to phrase her answer. Finally, she said, "Imagine you are walking through a wood, carrying your most precious possession—a rare and beautiful gem. Suddenly you are attacked by a vicious beast. You drop the gem and run away. When you realize the gem is lost, you are afraid to go back into the woods and search for it. Then someone comes along with another gem. Deep in your heart, you know it is not as valuable as the one you lost, but you are still too frightened to go back to look for the other. Now, does this mean the gem has left the forest, or is it still lying there, shining brightly beneath the leaves, waiting for you to return?"

Elistan closed his eyes, sighing, his face filled with anguish. "Of course, the gem waits for *our* return. What fools we have been! I wish I had time to learn of your gods," he said, reaching out his hand.

Goldmoon caught her breath, her face drained until she was nearly as pale as the dying man on the cot. "You will be given time," she said softly, taking his hand in hers.

Tanis, absorbed in the drama before him, started in alarm when he felt a touch on his arm. He turned around, his hand on his sword, to find Sturm and Caramon standing behind him.

"What is it?" he asked swiftly. "The guards?"

"Not yet," Sturm said harshly. "But we can expect them any minute. Both Eben and Gilthanas are gone."

Night deepened over Pax Tharkas.

Back in his lair, the red dragon, Pyros, had no room to pace, a habit he had fallen into in his human form. He barely had room to spread his wings in this chamber, though it was the largest in the fortress and had even been expanded to accommodate him. But the ground-floor chamber was so narrow, all the dragon could do was turn his great body around.

Forcing himself to relax, the dragon laid down upon the floor and waited, his eyes on the door. He didn't notice two heads peeking over the railing of a balcony on the third level far above him.

There was a scratch on the door. Pyros raised his head in eager anticipation, then dropped it again with a snarl as two goblins appeared, dragging between them a wretched specimen.

"Gully dwarf!" Pyros sneered, speaking Common to underlings. "Verminaard's taken leave of his senses if he thinks I'd eat gully dwarf. Toss him in a corner and get out!" he snarled at the goblins who hastened to do as instructed. Sestun cowered in the corner, whimpering.

"Shut up!" Pyros ordered irritably. "Perhaps I should just flame you and stop that blubbering—"

There came another sound at the door, a soft knocking the dragon recognized. His eyes burned red. "Enter!"

A figure came into the lair of the dragon. Dressed in a long cloak, a hood covered its face.

"I have come as you commanded, Ember," the figure said softly.

"Yes," Pyros replied, his talons scratching the floor. "Remove the hood. I would see the faces of those I deal with."

The man cast his hood back. Up above the dragon, on the third level, came a strangled, choking gasp. Pyros stared up at the darkened balcony. He considered flying up to investigate, but the figure interrupted his thought.

"I have only limited time, royal one. I must return before they suspect. And I should report to Lord Verminaard—"

"In due course," Pyros snapped irritably. "What are these fools that you accompany plotting?"

"They plan to free the slaves and lead them in revolt, forcing Verminaard to recall the army marching on Qualinesti."

"That's all?"

"Yes, royal one. Now I must warn the Dragon Highlord."

"Bah! What does that matter? It will be I who deal with the slaves if they revolt. Unless they have plans for me?"

"No, royal one. They fear you a great deal, as all must," the figure added. "They will wait until you and Lord Verminaard have flown to Qualinesti. Then they will free the children and escape into the mountains before you return."

"That seems to be a plan equal to their intelligence. Do not worry about Verminaard. I will see he learns of this when I am ready for him to learn of it. Much greater matters are brewing. Much greater. Now listen closely. A prisoner was brought in today by that imbecile Toede—" Pyros paused, his eyes glowing. His voice dropped to a hissing whisper. "It is *he!* The one we seek!"

The figure stared in astonishment. "Are you certain?"

"Of course!" Pyros snarled viciously. "I see this man in my dreams! He is here, within my grasp! When all of Krynn is searching for him, I have found him!"

"You will inform Her Dark Majesty?"

"No. I dare not trust a messenger. I must deliver this man in person, but I cannot leave now. Verminaard cannot deal with Qualinesti alone. Even if the war is just a ruse, we must keep up appearances, and the world will be better for the absence of elves anyway. I will take the Everman to the Queen when time permits."

"So why tell me?" the figure asked, an edge in his voice.

"Because you must keep him safe!" Pyros shifted his great bulk into a more comfortable position. His plans were coming together rapidly now. "It is a measure of Her Dark Majesty's power that the cleric of Mishakal and the man of the green gemstone arrive together within my reach! I will allow Verminaard the pleasure of dealing with the cleric and her friends tomorrow. In fact"—Pyros's eyes gleamed—"this may work out quite well! We can remove the Green Gemstone Man in the confusion and Verminaard will know nothing! When the slaves attack, you must find the Green Gemstone Man. Bring him back here and hide him in the lower chambers. When the humans have all been destroyed, and the army has wiped out Qualinesti, I will deliver him to my Dark Queen."

"I understand." The figure bowed again. "And my reward?"

"Will be all you deserve. Now leave me."

The man cast the hood up over his head and withdrew. Pyros folded his wings and, curling his great body around with the huge tail up over his snout, he lay staring into the darkness. The only sound that could be heard was Sestun's pitiful weeping.

"Are you all right?" Fizban asked Tasslehoff gently as they sat crouched by the balcony, afraid to move. It was pitch dark, Fizban having overturned a vase on the highly indignant puff-ball flame.

"Yes," Tas said dully. "I'm sorry I choked like that. I couldn't help myself. Even though I expected it—sort of—it's still hard to realize someone you know could betray you. Do you think the dragon heard me?"

"I couldn't say." Fizban sighed. "The question is, what do we do now?"

"I don't know," Tas said miserably. "I'm not supposed to be the one that thinks. I just come along for the fun. We can't warn Tanis and the others, because we don't know where they are. And if we start wandering around looking for them, we might get caught and only make things worse!" He put his chin in his hand. "You know," he said with unusual somberness, "I asked my father once why kenders were little, why we weren't big like humans and elves. I really wanted to be big," he said softly and for a moment he was quiet.

"What did your father say?" asked Fizban gently.

"He said kenders were small because we were meant to do small things. 'If you look at all the big things in the world closely,' he said, 'you'll see that they're really made up of small things all joined together.' That big dragon down there comes to nothing but tiny drops of blood, maybe. It's the small things that make the difference."

"Very wise, your father."

"Yes." Tas brushed his hand across his eyes. "I haven't seen him in a long time." The kender's pointed chin jutted forward, his lips tightened. His father, if he had seen him, would not have known this small, resolute person for his son.

"We'll leave the big things to the others," Tas announced finally. "They've got Tanis and Sturm and Goldmoon. They'll manage. We'll do the small thing, even if it doesn't seem very important. We're going to rescue Sestun."

13

Questions. No answers. Fizban's hat.

I heard something, Tanis, and I went to investigate," Eben said, his mouth set in a firm line. "I looked outside the cell door I was guarding and I saw a draconian crouched there, listening. I crept out and got it in a choke hold, then a second one jumped me. I knifed it, then took off after the first. I caught it and knocked it out, then decided I'd better get back here."

The companions had returned to the cells to find both Gilthanas and Eben waiting for them. Tanis had Maritta keep the women busy in a far corner while he questioned the two about their absence. Eben's story appeared true—Tanis had seen the bodies of the draconians as he returned to the prison—and Eben had certainly been in a fight. His clothes were torn, blood trickled from a cut on his cheek.

Tika got a relatively clean cloth from one of the women and

began washing the cut. "He saved our lives, Tanis," she snapped. "I'd think you'd be grateful, instead of glaring at him as if he'd stabbed your best friend."

"No, Tika," Eben said gently. "Tanis has a right to ask. It did look suspicious, I admit. But I have nothing to hide." Catching hold of her hand, he kissed her fingertips. Tika flushed and dipped the cloth in water, raising it to his cheek again. Caramon, watching, scowled.

"What about you, Gilthanas?" the warrior asked abruptly. "Why did you leave?"

"Do not question me," the elf said sullenly. "You don't want to know."

"Know what?" Tanis said sternly. "Why did you leave?"

"Leave him alone!" Laurana cried, going to her brother's side.

Gilthanas's almond-eyes flashed as he glanced at them; his face was drawn and pale.

"This is important, Laurana," Tanis said. "Where did you go, Gilthanas?"

"Remember—I warned you." Gilthanas's eyes shifted to Raistlin. "I returned to see if our mage was really as exhausted as he said. He must not have been. He was gone."

Caramon stood up, his fists clenched, his face distorted with anger. Sturm grabbed hold of him and shoved him backwards as Riverwind stepped in front of Gilthanas.

"All have a right to speak and all have a right to respond in their own defense," the Plainsman said in his deep voice. "The elf has spoken. Let us hear from your brother."

"Why should I speak?" Raistlin whispered harshly, his voice soft and lethal with hatred. "None of you trusts me, so why should you believe me? I refuse to answer, and you may think as you choose. If you believe I am a traitor—kill me now! I will not stop you—" He began to cough.

"You'll have to kill me, too," Caramon said in a choked voice. He led his brother back to his bed.

Tanis felt sick.

"Double watches all night. No, not you, Eben. Sturm, you and Flint first, Riverwind and I'll take second." Tanis slumped down on the floor, his head on his arms. We've been betrayed, he thought. One of those three is a traitor and has been all along. The guards might come at any moment. Or perhaps Verminaard was more subtle, some trap to catch us all. . . .

Then Tanis saw it all with sickening clarity. Of course! Verminaard would use the revolt as an excuse to kill the hostages and the cleric. He could always get more slaves, who would have a horrible example before their eyes of what happened to those who disobeyed him. This plan—Gilthanas's plan—played right into his hands!

We should abandon it, Tanis thought wildly, then he forced himself to calm down. No, the people were too excited. Following Elistan's miraculous healing and his announced determination to study these ancient gods, the people had hope. They believed that the gods had truly come back to them. But Tanis had seen the other Highseekers look at Elistan jealously. He knew that, though they made a show of supporting the new leader, given time they would try and subvert him. Perhaps, even now, they were moving among the people, spreading doubt.

If we backed out now, they'd never trust us again, Tanis thought. We must go ahead—no matter how great the risk. Besides, perhaps he was wrong. Maybe there was no traitor. Hoping, he fell into a fitful sleep.

The night passed in silence.

Dawn filtered through the gaping hole in the tower of the fortress. Tas blinked, then sat up, rubbing his eyes, wondering for a moment where he was. I'm in a big room, he thought, staring up at a high ceiling that had a hole cut in it to allow the dragon access to the outside. There are two other doors, besides the one Fizban and I came through last night.

Fizban! The dragon!

Tas groaned, remembering. He hadn't meant to fall asleep! He and Fizban had only been waiting until the dragon slept to rescue Sestun. Now it was morning! Perhaps it was too late! Fearfully the kender crept to the balcony and peered over the edge. No! He sighed in relief. The dragon was asleep. Sestun slept, too, worn out with fear.

Now was their chance! Tasslehoff crawled back to the mage.

"Old One!" he whispered. "Wake up!" He shook him.

"What? Who? Fire?" The mage sat up, peering around blearily. "Where? Run for the exits!"

"No, not a fire." Tas sighed. "It's morning. Here's your hat—" He handed it to the magician who was groping around, searching for it. "What happened to the puffball light?"

"Humpf!" Fizban sniffed. "I sent it back. Kept me awake, shining in my eyes."

"We were supposed to stay awake, remember?" Tas said in exasperation. "Rescue Sestun from the dragon?"

"How were we going to do that?" Fizban asked eagerly.

"You were the one with the plan!"

"I was? Dear, dear." The old magician blinked. "Was it a good one?"

"You didn't tell me!" Tas nearly shouted, then he calmed down. "All you said was that we had to rescue Sestun before breakfast, because gully dwarf might start looking more appetizing to a dragon who hadn't eaten in twelve hours."

"Makes sense," Fizban conceded. "Are you sure I said it?"

"Look," said Tasslehoff patiently, "all we really need is a long rope to throw down to him. Can't you magic that up?"

"Rope!" Fizban glared at him. "As if I'd stoop so low! That is an insult to one of my skill. Help me stand."

Tas helped the mage stand. "I didn't mean to insult you," the kender said, "and I know there's nothing fancy about rope and you are very skilled. . . . It's just that—oh, all right!" Tas gestured toward the balcony. "Go ahead. I just hope we all survive," he muttered under his breath.

"I won't let you down, or Sestun either, for that matter," Fizban promised, beaming. The two peeked over the balcony. Everything was as before. Sestun lay in a corner. The dragon slept soundly. Fizban closed his eyes. Concentrating, he murmured eerie words, then stretched his thin hand through the railing of the balcony and began to make a lifting motion.

Tasslehoff, watching, felt his heart fly up in his throat. "Stop!" he gurgled. "You've got the wrong one!"

Fizban's eyes flew open to see the red dragon, Pyros, slowly rising off the floor, his body still curled in sleep. "Oh, dear!" the magician gasped and, quickly saying different words, he reversed the spell, lowering the dragon to the ground. "Missed my aim," the mage said. "Now I'm zeroed in. Let's try again."

Tas heard the eerie words again. This time Sestun began to rise off the floor and, breath by breath, came level with the balcony. Fizban's face grew red with exertion.

"He's almost here! Keep going!" Tas said, hopping up and down in excitement. Guided by Fizban's hand, Sestun sailed peacefully over the balcony. He came to rest on the dusty floor, still asleep.

"Sestun!" Tas whispered, putting his hand over the gully dwarf's mouth so that he wouldn't yell. "Sestun! It's me, Tasslehoff. Wake up."

The gully dwarf opened his eyes. His first thought was that Verminaard had decided to feed him to a vicious kender instead of the dragon. Then the gully dwarf recognized his friend and went limp with relief.

"You're safe, but don't say a word," the kender warned. "The dragon can still hear us—" He was interrupted by a loud booming from below. The gully dwarf sat up in alarm.

"Shhh," said Tas, "probably just the door into the dragon's lair." He hurried back to the balcony where Fizban was peering through the railing. "What is it?"

"The Dragon Highlord," Fizban pointed to the second level where Verminaard stood on a ledge overlooking the dragon.

"Ember, awaken!" Verminaard yelled down at the sleeping dragon. "I have received reports of intruders! That cleric is here, inciting the slaves to rebellion!"

Pyros stirred and slowly opened his eyes, awakening from a disturbing dream in which he'd seen a gully dwarf fly. Shaking his giant head to clear away the sleep, he heard Verminaard ranting about clerics. He yawned. So the Dragon Highlord had found out the cleric was in the fortress. Pyros supposed he'd have to deal with this now, after all.

"Do not trouble yourself, my lord—" Pyros began, then stopped abruptly, staring at something very strange.

"Trouble myself!" Verminaard fumed. "Why I—" He stopped, too. The object at which both stared was drifting down through the air, gently as a feather.

Fizban's hat.

Tanis woke everyone in the darkest hour before dawn.

"Well," said Sturm, "do we go ahead?"

"We have no choice," Tanis said grimly, looking at the group. "If one of you has betrayed us, then he must live with the knowledge that he has brought about the deaths of innocents. Verminaard will kill not only us, but the hostages as well. I pray that there is no traitor, and so I'm going ahead with our plans."

No one said anything, but each glanced sideways at the others, suspicion gnawing at all of them.

When the women were awake, Tanis went over the plan again.

"My friends and I will sneak up to the children's room with Maritta, disguised as the women who usually bring the children breakfast. We'll lead them to the courtyard," Tanis said quietly. "You must go about your business as you do every morning. When you are allowed into the exercise area, get the children and start moving immediately toward the mines. Your menfolk will handle the guards there and you can escape safely into the mountains to the south. Do you understand?"

The women nodded silently as they heard the sound of the guards approaching.

"This is it," Tanis said softly. "Back to your work."

The women scattered. Tanis beckoned to Tika and Laurana. "If we have been betrayed, you will both be in great danger, since you'll be guarding the women—" he began.

"We'll all be in great danger," Laurana amended coldly. She hadn't slept all night. She knew that if she released the tight bands she had wrapped around her soul, fear would overwhelm her.

Tanis saw none of this inner turmoil. He thought she appeared unusually pale and exceptionally beautiful this morning. A long-time campaigner himself, his preoccupation made him forget the terrors of a first battle.

Clearing his throat, he said huskily, "Tika, take my advice. Keep your sword in your scabbard. You're less dangerous that way." Tika giggled and nodded nervously. "Go say good-bye to Caramon," Tanis told her.

Tika blushed crimson and, giving Tanis and Laurana a meaningful look, ran off.

Tanis gazed at Laurana steadily for a moment, and—for the first time—saw that her jaw muscles were clenched so tightly the tendons in her neck were stretched. He reached out to hold her, but she was stiff and cold as a draconian's corpse.

"You don't have to do this," Tanis said, releasing her. "This isn't your fight. Go to the mines with the other women."

Laurana shook her head, waiting to speak until she was certain her voice was under control. "Tika is not trained for fighting. I am. No matter if it was 'ceremonial.' " She smiled bitterly at Tanis's look of discomfiture. "I will do my part, Tanis." His human name came awkwardly to her lips. "Otherwise, you might think I am a traitor."

"Laurana, please believe me!" Tanis sighed. "I don't think Gilthanas is a traitor any more than you do! It's just—damn it, there are so many lives at stake, Laurana! Can't you realize?"

Feeling his hands on her arms shake, she looked up at him and saw the anguish and the fear in his own face, mirroring the fear she felt inside. Only his was not fear for himself, it was fear for others. She drew a deep breath. "I am sorry, Tanis," she said. "You are right. Look. The guards are here. It is time to go."

She turned and walked away without looking back. It didn't occur to her until it was too late that Tanis might have been silently asking for comfort himself.

Maritta and Goldmoon led the companions up a flight of narrow stairs to the first level. The draconian guards didn't accompany them, saying something about "special duty." Tanis asked Maritta if that was usual and she shook her head, her face worried. They had no choice but to go on. Six gully dwarves trailed after them, carrying heavy pots of what smelled like oatmeal. They paid little attention to the women until Caramon stumbled over his skirt climbing the stairs and fell to his knees, uttering a very unladylike oath. The gully dwarves' eyes opened wide.

"Don't even squeak!" Flint said, whirling around to face them, a knife flashing in his hand.

The gully dwarves cowered against the wall, shaking their heads frantically, the pots clattering.

The companions reached the top of the stairs and stopped.

"We cross this hall to the door—" Maritta pointed. "Oh,

no!" She grasped Tanis's arm. "There's a guard at the door. It's never guarded!"

"Hush, it could be coincidence," Tanis said reassuringly, although he knew it wasn't. "Just keep on as we planned." Maritta nodded fearfully and walked across the hall.

"Guards!" Tanis turned to Sturm. "Be ready. Remember—quick and deadly. No noise!"

According to Gilthanas's map, the playroom was separated from the children's sleeping quarters by two rooms. The first was a storeroom which Maritta reported was lined with shelves containing toys and clothing and other items. A tunnel ran through this room to the second—the room that housed the dragon, Flamestrike.

"Poor thing," Maritta had said when discussing the plan with Tanis. "She is as much a prisoner as we are. The Dragon Highlord never allows her out. I think they're afraid she'll wander off. They've even built a tunnel through the storeroom, too small for her to fit through. Not that she wants to get out, but I think she might like to watch the children play."

Tanis regarded Maritta dubiously, wondering if they might encounter a dragon very different from the mad, feeble creature she described.

Beyond the dragon's lair was the room where the children slept. This was the room they would have to enter, to wake the children and lead them outdoors. The playroom connected directly with the courtyard through a huge door locked with a great oaken beam.

"More to keep the dragon in than us," Maritta stated.

It must be just about dawning, Tanis thought, as they emerged from the stairwell and turned toward the playroom. The torchlight cast their shadows ahead of them. Pax Tharkas was quiet, deathly quiet. Too quiet—for a fortress preparing for war. Four draconian guards stood huddled together talking at the doorway to the playroom. Their conversation broke off as they saw the women approach.

Goldmoon and Maritta walked in front, Goldmoon's hood was drawn back, her hair glimmering in the torchlight. Directly behind Goldmoon came Riverwind. Bent over a staff, the Plainsman was practically walking on his knees. Caramon and Raistlin followed, the mage staying close to his brother, then Eben and Gilthanas. All the traitors together, as Raistlin had sarcastically observed. Flint brought up the rear, turning occasionally to glower at the panic-stricken gully dwarves.

"You're early this morning," a draconian growled.

The women clustered like chickens in a half-circle around the guards and stood, waiting patiently to be allowed inside.

"It smells of thunder," Maritta said sharply. "I want the children to have their exercise before the storm hits. And what are you doing here? This door is never guarded. You'll frighten the children."

One of the draconians made some comment in their harsh language and two of the others grinned, showing rows of pointed teeth. The spokesman only snarled.

"Lord Verminaard's command. He and Ember are gone this morning to finish the elves. We're ordered to search you before you enter." The draconian's eyes fastened onto Goldmoon hungrily. "That's going to be a pleasure, I'd say."

"For you maybe," muttered another guard, staring at Sturm in disgust. "I've never seen an uglier female in my life than—ugh—" The creature slumped over, a dagger thrust deep into its ribs. The other three draconians died within seconds. Caramon wrapped his hands around the neck of one. Eben hit his in the stomach and Flint lobbed off its head with an axe as it fell. Tanis stabbed the leader through the heart with his sword. He started to let go of the weapon, expecting it to remain stuck in the creature's stony corpse. To his amazement, his new sword slid out of the stone carcass as easily as if it had been nothing more than goblin flesh.

He had no time to ponder this strange occurrence. The gully dwarves, catching sight of the flash of steel, dropped their pots and ran wildly down the corridor.

"Never mind them!" Tanis snapped at Flint. "Into the playroom. Hurry!" Stepping over the bodies, he flung the door open.

"If anyone finds these bodies, it'll be all over," Caramon said.

"It was over before we began!" Sturm muttered angrily. "We've been betrayed, so it's just a matter of time."

"Keep moving!" Tanis said sharply, shutting the door behind them.

"Be very quiet," Maritta whispered. "Flamestrike generally sleeps soundly. If she does waken, act like women. She'll never recognize you. She's blind in one eye."

The chill dawn light filtered in through tiny windows high above the floor, shining on a grim, cheerless playroom. A few well-used toys lay scattered about. There was no furniture. Caramon walked over to inspect the huge wooden beam barring the double doors that led to the courtyard outside.

"I can manage," he said. The big man appeared to lift the beam effortlessly, then set it against the wall and shoved on the door. "Not locked from the outside," he reported. "I guess they didn't expect us to get this far."

Or perhaps Lord Verminaard wants us out there, Tanis thought. He wondered if what the draconian said was true. Had the Dragon Highlord and the dragon really gone? Or were they—angrily he wrenched his mind back. It doesn't matter, he told himself. We have no choice. We must go on.

"Flint, stay here," he said. "If anyone comes, warn us first, then fight."

Flint nodded and took a position just inside the door leading to the corridor, first opening it a crack to see. The draconian bodies had turned to dust on the floor.

Maritta took a torch from the wall. Lighting it, she led the companions through a dark archway into the tunnel leading to the dragon's lair.

"Fizban! Your hat!" Tas risked whispering. Too late. The old magician made a grab for it but missed.

"Spies!" yelled Verminaard in a rage, pointing up to the balcony. "Capture them, Ember! I want them alive!"

Alive? the dragon repeated to himself. No, that could not be! Pyros recalled the strange sound he had heard last night and he knew without a doubt that these spies had overheard him talking about the Green Gemstone Man! Only a privileged few knew that dread secret, the great secret, the secret that would conquer the world for the Queen of Darkness. These spies must die, and the secret die with them.

Pyros spread his wings and launched himself into the air, using his powerful back legs to propel himself from the floor with tremendous speed.

This is it! thought Tasslehoff. Now we've done it. There's no escape this time.

Just as he resigned himself to being cooked by a dragon, he heard the magician shout a single word of command and a thick, unnatural darkness almost knocked the kender over.

"Run!" panted Fizban, grabbing the kender's hand and dragging Tas to his feet.

"Sestun—"

"I've got him! Run!"

Tasslehoff ran. They flew out the door and into the gallery, then he had no idea where he was going. He just kept hold of the old man and ran. Behind him he could hear the sound of the dragon whooshing up out of his lair and he heard the dragon's voice.

"So you are a magic-user, are you, spy?" Pyros shouted. "We can't have you running around in the dark. You might get lost. Let me light your way!"

Tasslehoff heard a great intake of breath into a giant body, then flames crackled and burned around him. The darkness vanished, driven away by the fire's flaring light, but, to his amazement, Tas wasn't touched by the flame. He looked at Fizban—hatless—running next to him. They were in the gallery still, heading for the double doors.

The kender twisted his head. Behind him loomed the dragon, more horrible than anything he had imagined, more terrifying than the black dragon in Xak Tsaroth. The dragon breathed on them again and once more Tas was enveloped by flame. The paintings on the walls blazed, furniture burned, curtains flared like torches, smoke filled the room. But none of it touched him and Sestun and Fizban. Tasslehoff looked at the mage in admiration, truly impressed.

"How long can you keep this up?" he shouted to Fizban as they wheeled around a corner, the double bronze doors in sight.

The old man's eyes were wide and staring. "I have no idea!" he gasped. "I didn't know I could do it at all!"

Another blast of flame exploded around them. This time, Tasslehoff felt the heat and glanced at Fizban in alarm. The mage nodded. "I'm losing it!" he cried.

"Hang on," Tasslehoff panted. "We're almost to the door! He can't get through it."

The three pushed through the bronze double doors that led from the gallery back into the hallway just as Fizban's magic spell wore off. Before them was the secret door, still open, that led to the Mechanism Room. Tasslehoff flung the bronze doors shut and stopped a moment to catch his breath.

But just as he was about to say, "We made it!" one of the dragon's huge clawed feet broke through the stone wall, right above the kender's head!

Sestun, giving a shriek, headed for the stairs.

"No!" Tasslehoff grabbed him. "That leads to Verminaard's quarters!"

"Back to the Mechanism Room!" Fizban cried. They dashed through the secret door just as the stone wall gave way with a tremendous crash. But they could not shut the door.

"I have a lot to learn about dragons, apparently," Tas muttered. "I wonder if there are any good books on the subject—"

"So I have run you rats into your hole and now you are trapped," boomed Pyros's voice from outside. "You have nowhere to go and stone walls do not stop me."

There was a terrible grinding and grating sound. The walls of the Mechanism Room trembled, then began to crack.

"It was a nice try," Tas said ruefully. "That last spell was a doozy. Almost worth getting killed by a dragon to see."

"Killed!" Fizban seemed to wake up. "By a dragon? I should say not! I've never been so insulted. There must be a way out—" His eyes began to gleam. "Down the chain!"

"The chain?" repeated Tas, thinking he must have misunderstood, what with the walls cracking around him and the dragon roaring and all.

"We'll crawl down the chain! Come on!" Cackling with delight, the old mage turned and ran down the tunnel.

Sestun looked dubiously at Tasslehoff, but just then the dragon's huge claw appeared through the wall. The kender and the gully dwarf turned and ran after the old magician.

By the time they reached the great wheel, Fizban had already crawled along the chain leading from the tunnel and reached the first tree-trunk tooth of the wheel itself. Tucking his robes up around his thighs, he dropped down from the tooth onto the first rung of the huge chain. The kender and gully dwarf swung onto the chain after him. Tas was just beginning to think they might get out of this alive after all, especially if the dark elf at the bottom of the chain had taken the day off, when Pyros burst suddenly into the shaft where the great chain hung.

Sections of the stone tunnel caved in around them, falling to the ground with a hollow booming thud. The walls shuddered, and the chain started to tremble. Above them hovered the dragon. He did not speak but simply stared at them with his red eyes. Then he drew in a huge breath that seemed to suck in the air of the whole valley. Tas started instinctively to close his eyes, then opened them wide. He'd never seen a dragon breathe fire and he wasn't going to miss seeing it now—especially as it would probably be his last chance.

Flames billowed out from the dragon's nose and mouth. The blast from the heat alone nearly knocked Tasslehoff off the chain. But, once again, the fire burned all around him and did not touch him. Fizban cackled with delight.

"Quite clever, old man," said the dragon angrily. "But I, too, am a magic-user and I feel you weakening. I hope your cleverness amuses you—all the way down!"

Flames flared out again, but this time the dragon's fire was not aimed at the trembling figures clinging to the chain. The flames struck the chain itself and the iron links began to glow red hot at the first touch of the dragonfire. Pyros breathed again and the links burned white hot. The dragon breathed a third time. The links melted. The massive chain gave a great shudder and broke, plunging into the darkness below.

Pyros watched it as it plummeted down. Then, satisfied that the spies would not live to tell their tale, he flew back to his lair where he could hear Verminaard shouting for him.

In the darkness left behind by the dragon, the great cogwheel—free of the chain that had held it in place for centuries—gave a groan and began to turn.

Matafleur. The magic sword. White feathers.

ight from Maritta's torch illuminated a large, barren windowless room. There was no furniture. The only objects in the chill, stone chamber were a huge basin of water, a bucket filled with what smelled like rotted meat, and a dragon.

Tanis caught his breath. He had thought the black dragon in Xak Tsaroth formidable. He was truly awed at the massive size of this red dragon. Her lair was enormous, probably over one hundred feet in diameter, and the dragon stretched the length of it, the tip of her long tail lying against the far wall. For a moment the companions stood stunned, with ghastly visions of the giant head rising up and searing them with the burning flame breathed by the red dragons, the flames that had destroyed Solace.

Maritta did not appear worried, however. She advanced

steadily into the room and, after a moment's hesitation, the companions hurried after her. As they drew closer to the creature, they could see that Maritta had been right—the dragon was clearly in pitiful condition. The great head that lay on the cold stone floor was lined and wrinkled with age, the brilliant red skin grayish and mottled. She breathed noisily through her mouth, her jaws parted to reveal the once sword-sharp teeth, now yellowed and broken. Long scars ran along her sides; her leathery wings were dry and cracked.

Now Tanis could understand Maritta's attitude. Clearly, the dragon had been ill-used, and he caught himself feeling pity, relaxing his guard. He realized how dangerous this was when the dragon—awakened by the torchlight—stirred in her sleep. Her talons were as sharp and her fire as destructive as any other red dragon in Krynn, Tanis reminded himself sharply.

The dragon's eyes opened, slits of glistening red in the torchlight. The companions halted, hands on their weapons.

"Is it time for breakfast already, Maritta?" Matafleur (Flamestrike being her name to common mortals) said in a sleepy, husky voice.

"Yes, we're just a bit early today, dearie," Maritta said soothingly. "But there's a storm brewing and I want the children to have their exercise before it breaks. Go back to sleep. I'll see they don't wake you on their way out."

"I don't mind." The dragon yawned and opened her eyes a bit farther. Now Tanis could see that one of them had a milky covering; she was blind in that eye.

"I hope we don't have to fight her, Tanis," Sturm whispered. "It'd be like fighting someone's grandmother."

Tanis forced his expression to harden. "She's a deadly grandmother, Sturm. Just remember that."

"The little ones had a restful night," the dragon murmured, apparently drifting off to sleep again. "See that they don't get wet if it does storm, Maritta. Especially little Erik. He had a cold last week." Her eyes closed.

Turning, Maritta beckoned the others on, putting her finger to her lips. Sturm and Tanis came last, their weapons and armor muffled by numerous cloaks and skirts. Tanis was about thirty feet from the dragon's head when the noise started.

At first he thought it was his imagination, that his nervousness was making him hear a buzzing sound in his head. But the sound grew louder and louder and Sturm turned, staring at him in alarm. The buzzing sound increased until it was like a thousand swarming locusts. Now the others were looking back, too—all of them staring at him! Tanis looked at his friends helplessly, an almost comic look of confusion on his face.

The dragon snorted and stirred in irritation, shaking her head as though the noise hurt her ears.

Suddenly Raistlin broke from the group and ran back to Tanis. "The sword!" he hissed. He grabbed the half-elf's cloak and threw it back to reveal the blade.

Tanis stared down at the sword in its antique scabbard. The mage was right. The blade hummed as if in the highest state of alarm. Now that Raistlin called his attention to it, the half-elf could actually feel the vibrations.

"Magic," the mage said softly, studying it with interest.

"Can you stop it?" yelled Tanis over the weird noise.

"No," said Raistlin. "I remember now. This is Wyrmslayer, the famed magical sword of Kith-Kanan. It is reacting to the presence of the dragon."

"This is an abysmal time to remember!" Tanis said in fury.

"Or a very convenient time," snarled Sturm.

The dragon slowly raised her head, her eyes blinking, a thin stream of smoke drifting from a nostril. She focused her bleary red eyes on Tanis, pain and irritation in her gaze.

"Who have you brought, Maritta?" Matafleur's voice was filled with menace. "I hear a sound I have not heard in centuries, I smell the foul smell of steel! These are not the women! These are warriors!"

"Don't hurt her!" Maritta wailed.

"I may not have any choice!" Tanis said viciously, drawing Wyrmslayer from its sheath. "Riverwind and Goldmoon, get Maritta out of here!" The blade began to shine with a brilliant white light as the buzzing grew louder and angrier. Matafleur shrank back. The light of the sword pierced her good eye painfully; the terrible sound went through her head like a spear. Whimpering, she huddled away from Tanis.

"Run, get the children!" Tanis yelled, realizing that they didn't need to fight—at least not yet. Holding the shining sword high in the air, he moved forward cautiously, driving the pitiful dragon back against the wall.

Maritta, after one fearful glance at Tanis, led Goldmoon to the children's room. About one hundred children were wide-eyed with alarm over the strange sounds outside their chamber. Their faces relaxed at the sight of Maritta and Goldmoon and a few of the littler ones actually giggled when Caramon came rushing in, his skirts flapping around his armored legs. But at the sight of warriors and their drawn weapons, the children sobered immediately.

"What is it, Maritta?" asked the oldest girl. "What's happening? Is it fighting again?"

"We hope there'll be no fighting, dear one," Maritta said softly. "But I'll not lie to you—it may come to that. Now I want you to gather your things, particularly your warm cloaks, and come with us. The older of you carry the wee ones, as you do when we go outdoors for exercise."

Sturm expected confusion and wailing and demands for explanations. But the children quickly did as they were told, wrapping themselves in warm clothing and helping to dress the younger ones. They were quiet and calm, if a bit pale. These were children of war, Sturm remembered.

"I want you to move very swiftly through the dragon's lair and out into the playroom. When we get there, the big man"—Sturm gestured to Caramon—"will lead you out into the courtyard. Your mothers are waiting for you there. When you get outside, look immediately for your mother and go to her. Does everyone understand?" He glanced dubiously at the smaller children, but the girl at the front of the line nodded.

"We understand, sir," she said.

"All right," Sturm turned. "Caramon?"

The warrior, flushing in embarrassment as one hundred pairs of eyes turned to look at him, led the way back into the dragon's lair. Goldmoon scooped up a toddler in her arms, Maritta picked up another one. The older boys and girls carried little ones on their backs. They hurried out the door in orderly fashion, without saying a word until they saw Tanis, the gleaming sword, and the terrified dragon.

"Hey, you! Don't hurt our dragon!" one little boy yelled. Leaving his place in line, the child ran up to Tanis, his fists raised, his face twisted into a snarl.

"Dougl!" cried the oldest girl, shocked. "Get back in line this instant!" But some of the children were crying now.

Tanis, the sword still raised—knowing that this was the only thing keeping the dragon at bay—shouted, "Get them out of here!"

"Children, please!" Chieftain's Daughter, her voice stern and commanding, brought order to the chaos. "Tanis will not hurt the dragon if he does not have to. He is a gentle man. You must leave now. Your mothers need you."

There was an edge of fear in Goldmoon's voice, a feeling of urgency that influenced even the youngest child. They got back into line quickly.

"Good-bye, Flamestrike," several of the children called out, wistfully, waving their hands as they followed Caramon. Dougl gave Tanis one final threatening glance, then he returned to line, wiping his eyes with grubby fists.

"No!" shrieked Matafleur in a heartbroken voice. "No! Don't fight my children. Please! It is me you want! Fight me! Don't harm my children!"

Tanis realized the dragon was back in her past, reliving whatever terrible event had deprived her of her children.

Sturm stayed near Tanis. "She's going to kill you when the children are out of danger, you know."

"Yes," said Tanis grimly. Already the dragon's eyes—even the bad eye, were flaring red. Saliva dripped from the great, gaping mouth, and her talons scratched the floor.

"Not my children!" she said with rage.

"I'm with you—" Sturm began, drawing his sword.

"Leave us, knight," Raistlin whispered softly from the shadows. "Your weapon is useless. *I* will stay with Tanis."

The half-elf glanced at the mage in astonishment. Raistlin's strange, golden eyes met his, knowing what he was thinking: do I trust him? Raistlin gave him no help, almost as if he were goading him to refusal.

"Get out," Tanis said to Sturm.

"What?" he yelled. "Are you crazy? You're trusting this—"

"Get out!" Tanis repeated. At that moment, he heard Flint yelling loudly. "Go, Sturm, they need you out there!"

The knight stood a moment, irresolute, but he could not in honor ignore a direct order from one he considered his commander. Casting a baleful glance at Raistlin, Sturm turned on his heel and entered the tunnel.

"There is little magic I can work against a red dragon," Raistlin whispered swiftly.

"Can you buy us time?" Tanis asked.

Raistlin smiled the smile of one who knows death is so near it is past fearing. "I can," he whispered. "Move back near the tunnel. When you hear me start to speak, run."

Tanis began backing up, still holding the sword high. But the dragon no longer feared its magic. She knew only that her children were gone and she must kill those responsible. She lunged directly at the warrior with the sword as he began to run toward the tunnel. Then darkness descended upon her, a darkness so deep Matafleur thought for a horrible moment she had lost the sight of the other eye. She heard whispered words of magic and knew the robed human had cast a spell.

"I'll burn them!" she howled, sniffing the smell of steel through the tunnel. "They will not escape!" But just as she sucked in a great breath, she heard another sound—the sound of her children. "No," she realized in frustration. "I dare not. My children! I might harm my children. . . ." Her head drooped down on the cold stone floor.

Tanis and Raistlin ran down the tunnel, the half-elf dragging the weakened mage with him. Behind them they heard a pitiful, heartbroken moan.

"Not my children! Please, fight me! Don't hurt my children!"

Tanis emerged from the tunnel into the playroom, blinking in the bright light as Caramon swung the huge doors open to the rising sun. The children raced out the door into the courtyard. Through the door, Tanis could see Tika and Laurana, standing with their swords drawn, looking their way anxiously. A draconian lay crumbling on the floor of the playroom, Flint's battle-axe stuck in its back.

"Outside, all of you!" Tanis shouted. Flint, retrieving his battle-axe, joined the half-elf as the last to leave the playroom. As they did so, they heard a terrifying roar, the roar of a dragon, but a very different dragon than the pitiful Matafleur. Pyros had discovered the spies. The stone walls began to tremble—the dragon was rising from his lair.

"Ember!" Tanis swore bitterly. "He hasn't gone!"

The dwarf shook his head. "I'll bet my beard," he said gloomily, "that Tasslehoff's involved."

The broken chain plummeted to the stone floor of the Chain Room in the Sla-Mori, three little figures falling with it.

Tasslehoff, clinging uselessly to the chain, tumbled through the darkness and thought, this is how it feels to die. It was an interesting sensation and he was sorry he couldn't experience it longer. Above him, he could hear Sestun shrieking in terror. Below, he heard the old mage muttering to himself, probably trying one last spell. Then Fizban raised his voice: *"Pveatherf—"* The word was cut off with a scream. There was the sound of a bone-crushing thud as the old magician crashed to the floor. Tasslehoff grieved, even though he knew he was next. The stone floor was approaching. Within a very few seconds he too would be dead. . . .

Then it was snowing.

At least that was what the kender thought. Then he realized with a shock that he was surrounded by millions and millions of feathers—like an explosion of chickens! He sank into a deep, vast pile of white feathers, Sestun tumbling in after him.

"Poor Fizban," Tas said, blinking tears from his eyes as he floundered in an ocean of white chicken feathers. "His last spell must have been *featherfall* like Raistlin uses. Wouldn't you know it? He just got the feathers."

Above him, the cogwheel turned faster and faster, the freed chain rushing through it as if rejoicing in its release from bondage.

Outdoors in the courtyard chaos reigned.

"Over here!" Tanis yelled, bursting out of the door, knowing they were doomed but refusing to give in. The companions gathered around him, weapons drawn, looking at him anxiously. "Run to the mines! Run for shelter! Verminaard and the red dragon didn't leave. It is a trap. They'll be on us any moment."

The others, their faces grim, nodded. All of them knew it was hopeless—they must cover about two hundred yards of flat, wide-open surface to reach safety.

They tried to herd the women and children along as swiftly

as possible, but not very successfully. All the mothers and children needed to be sorted out. Then Tanis, looking over at the mines, swore aloud in added frustration.

The men of the mines, seeing their families free, quickly overpowered the guards and began running toward the courtyard! That wasn't the plan! What was Elistan thinking about? Within moments there would be eight hundred frantic people milling around out in the open without a scrap of shelter! He had to get them to head back south to the mountains.

"Where's Eben?" he called to Sturm.

"Last I saw him, he was running for the mines. I couldn't figure out why—"

The knight and half-elf gasped in sudden realization.

"Of course," said Tanis softly, his voice lost in the commotion. "It all fits."

As Eben ran for the mines, his one thought was to obey Pyros's command. Somehow, in the midst of this furor, he had to find the Green Gemstone Man. He knew what Verminaard and Pyros were going to do to these poor wretches. Eben felt a moment's pity—he was not, after all, cruel and vicious. He had simply seen, long ago, which side was bound to win, and he determined, for once, to be on a winning side.

When his family's fortune was wiped out, Eben was left with only one thing to sell—himself. He was intelligent, handy with a sword, and as loyal as money could buy. It was on a journey to the north, looking for possible buyers, that Eben met Verminaard. Eben had been impressed with Verminaard's power and had wormed his way into the evil cleric's favor. But more importantly, he had managed to make himself useful to Pyros. The dragon found Eben charming, intelligent, resourceful, and—after a few tests—trustworthy.

Eben was sent home to Gateway just before the dragon-armies struck. He conveniently "escaped" and started his resistance group. Stumbling upon Gilthanas's party of elves the first time they tried to sneak into Pax Tharkas was a stroke of luck that further improved Eben's relationship with both Pyros and Verminaard. When the cleric actually fell into Eben's hands, he couldn't believe his luck. It must go to show how much the Dark Queen favored him, he supposed.

He prayed that the Dark Queen continue to favor him. Finding the Green Gemstone Man in this confusion was going to take divine intervention. Hundreds of men were milling about uncertainly. Eben saw a chance to do Verminaard another favor. "Tanis wants you men to meet in the courtyard," he cried. "Join your families."

"No! That isn't the plan!" Elistan cried, trying to stop them. But he was too late. The men, seeing their families free, surged forward. Several hundred gully dwarves added to the confusion, rushing gleefully out of the mines to join the fun, thinking, perhaps, it was a holiday.

Eben scanned the crowd anxiously for the Green Gemstone Man, then decided to look inside the prison cells. Sure enough, he found the man sitting alone, staring vaguely around the empty cell. Eben swiftly knelt beside him, racking his brain to come up with the man's name. It was something odd, old-fashioned. . . .

"Berem," Eben said after a moment. "Berem?"

The man looked up, interest lighting his face for the first time in many weeks. He was not, as Toede had assumed, deaf and dumb. He was, instead, a man obsessed, totally absorbed in his own secret quest. He was human, however, and the sound of a human voice speaking his name was inordinately comforting.

"Berem," said Eben again, licking his lips nervously. Now that he had him, he wasn't sure what to do with him. He knew the first thing those poor wretches outside would do when the dragon struck would be to head for the safety of the mines. He had to get Berem out of here before Tanis caught them. But where? He could take the man inside Pax Tharkas as Pyros had ordered, but Eben didn't like that idea. Verminaard would certainly find them and, his suspicions aroused, would ask questions Eben couldn't answer.

No, there was only one place Eben could take him and be safe—outside the walls of Pax Tharkas. They could lie low in the wilderness until the confusion died, then sneak back inside the fortress at night. His decision made, Eben took Berem's arm and helped the man rise to his feet.

"There's going to be fighting," he said. "I'm going to take you away, keep you safe until it is over. I am your friend. Do you understand?"

The man regarded him with a look of penetrating wisdom and intelligence. It was not the ageless look of the elves but of a human who has lived in torment for countless years. Berem gave a small sigh and nodded.

Verminaard strode from his chamber in a fury, yanking at his leather, armored gloves. A draconian trotted behind, carrying the Highlord's mace, Nightbringer. Other draconians milled around, acting on the orders Verminaard gave as he stepped into the corridor, returning to Pyros's lair.

"No, you fools, don't recall the army! This will take but a moment of my time. Qualinesti will be in flames by nightfall. Ember!" he shouted, throwing open the doors that led to the dragon's lair. He stepped out onto the ledge. Peering upward toward the balcony he could see smoke and flame and, in the distance, hear the dragon's roar.

"Ember!" There was no answer. "How long does it take to capture a handful of spies?" he demanded furiously. Turning, he nearly fell over a draconian captain.

"Will you be using the dragon saddle, my lord?"

"No, there isn't time. Besides, I use that only for combat and there will be no one to fight out there, simply a few hundred slaves to burn."

"But the slaves have overcome the guards at the mine and are rejoining their families in the courtyard."

"How strong are your forces?"

"Not nearly strong enough, my lord," the draconian captain said, its eyes glinting. The captain had never thought it wise to deplete the garrison. "We are forty or fifty, perhaps, to over three hundred men and an equal number of women. The women will undoubtedly fight alongside the men, your lordship, and if they ever get organized and escape into the mountains—"

"Bah! Ember!" Verminaard called. He heard, in another part of the fortress, a heavy, metallic thud. Then he heard another sound, the great wheel—unused in centuries—creaking with protest at being forced into labor. Verminaard was wondering what these odd sounds portended, when Pyros flew down into his lair.

The Dragon Highlord ran to the ledge as Pyros dropped past him. Verminaard climbed swiftly and skillfully onto the dragon's back. Though separated by mutual distrust, the two fought well together. Their hatred for the petty races they strove to conquer, combined with their desire for power, joined them in a bond much stronger than either cared to admit.

"Fly!" Verminaard roared, and Pyros rose into the air.

"It is useless, my friend," Tanis said quietly to Sturm, laying his hand on the knight's shoulder as Sturm frantically called for order. "You're only wasting your breath. Save it for fighting."

"There'll be no fighting." Sturm coughed, hoarse from shouting. "We'll die, trapped like rats. Why won't these fools listen?"

He and Tanis stood at the northern end of the courtyard, about twenty feet from the front gates of Pax Tharkas. Looking south, they could see the mountains and hope. Behind them were the great gates of the fortress that would, at any moment, open to admit the vast draconian army, and within these walls, somewhere, were Verminaard and the red dragon.

In vain, Elistan sought to calm the people and urge them to move southward. But the men insisted on finding their womenfolk, the women on finding their children. A few families, together again, were starting to move south, but too late and too slowly.

Then, like a blood-red, flaming comet, Pyros soared from the fortress of Pax Tharkas, his wings sleek, held close to his sides. His huge tail trailed behind him. His taloned forefeet were curled close to his body as he gained speed in the air. Upon his back rode the Dragon Highlord, the gilded horns of the hideous dragonmask glinting in the morning sun. Verminaard held onto the dragon's spiny mane with both hands as they flared into the sunlit sky, bringing night's shadows to the courtyard below.

The dragonfear spread over the people. Unable to scream or run, they could only cower before the fearful apparition, arms around each other, knowing death was inevitable.

At Verminaard's command, Pyros settled on one of the fortress towers. Verminaard stared out from behind the horned dragonmask, silent, furious.

Tanis, watching in helpless frustration, felt Sturm grip his arm. "Look!" The knight pointed north, toward the gates.

Tanis reluctantly lowered his gaze from the Dragon Highlord and saw two figures running toward the gates of the fortress.

"Eben!" he cried in disbelief. "But who's that with him?"

"He won't escape!" Sturm shouted. Before Tanis could stop him, the knight ran after the two. As Tanis followed, he saw a flash of red out of the corner of his eye—Raistlin and his twin.

"I, too, have a score to settle with this man," the mage hissed. The three caught up with Sturm just as the knight gripped Eben by the collar and hurled him to the ground.

"Traitor!" Sturm yelled loudly. "Though I die this day, I'll send you to the Abyss first!" He drew his sword and jerked Eben's head back. Suddenly Eben's companion whirled around, came back, and caught hold of Sturm's sword-arm.

Sturm gasped. His hand loosened its grip on Eben as the knight stared, amazed at the sight before him.

The man's shirt had been torn open in his wild flight from the mines. Impaled in the man's flesh, in the center of his chest, was a brilliant green jewel! Sunlight flashed on the gem that was as big around as a man's fist, causing it to gleam with a bright and terrible light—an unholy light.

"I have never seen nor heard of magic like this!" Raistlin whispered in awe as he and the others stopped, stunned, beside Sturm.

Seeing their wide eyes focused on his body, Berem instinctively pulled his shirt over his chest. Then, loosening his hold on Sturm's arm, he turned and ran for the gates. Eben scrambled to his feet and stumbled after him.

Sturm leaped forward, but Tanis stopped him.

"No," he said. "It's too late. We have others to think of."

"Tanis, look!" Caramon shouted, pointing above the huge gates.

A section of the stone wall of the fortress above the massive front gates began to open, forming a huge, widening crack. Slowly at first, then with increasing speed, the massive granite boulders began to fall from the crack, smashing to the ground with such force that the flagstone cracked and great clouds of dust rose into the air. Above the roar could be dimly heard the sound of the massive chains releasing the mechanism.

The boulders began to fall just as Eben and Berem arrived at the gates. Eben shrieked in terror, instinctively and pitifully raised his arm to shield his head. The man next to him glanced up and—it seemed—gave a small sigh. Then both were buried under tons of cascading rock as the ancient defense mechanism sealed shut the gates of Pax Tharkas.

"This is your final act of defiance!" Verminaard roared. His speech had been interrupted by the fall of the rocks, an act that only enraged him more. "I offered you a chance to work to further the glory of my Queen. I cared for you and your families. But you are stubborn and foolish. You will pay with your lives!" The Dragon Highlord raised Nightbringer high in the air. "I will destroy the men. I will destroy the women! I will destroy the children!"

At a touch of the Dragon Highlord's hand, Pyros spread his huge wings and leaped high into the air. The dragon drew in a deep breath, preparing to swoop down upon the mass of people who wailed in terror in the wide-open courtyard and incinerate them with his fiery breath.

But the dragon's deadly dive was stopped.

Sweeping up into the sky from the pile of rubble made when she crashed out of the fortress, Matafleur flew straight at Pyros.

The ancient dragon had sunk deeper into her madness. Once more she relived the nightmare of losing her children. She could see the knights upon the silver and golden dragons, the wicked dragonlances gleaming in the sunshine. In vain she pleaded with her children not to join the hopeless fight, in vain she sought to convince them the war was at an end. They were young and would not listen. They flew off, leaving her weeping in her lair. As she watched in her mind's eye the bloody, final battle, as she saw her children die upon the dragonlances, she heard Verminaard's voice.

"I will destroy the children!"

And, as she had done so many centuries before, Matafleur flew out to defend them.

Pyros, stunned by the unexpected attack, swerved just in time to avoid the broken, yet still lethal teeth of the old dragon aiming for his unprotected flanks. Matafleur hit him a glancing blow, tearing painfully into one of the heavy muscles that drove the giant wings. Rolling in the air, Pyros lashed out at the passing Matafleur with a wicked, taloned forefoot, tearing a gash in the female dragon's soft underbelly.

In her madness, Matafleur did not even feel the pain, but the force of the larger and younger male dragon's blow knocked her backwards in the air.

The rollover maneuver had been an instinctive defensive action on the part of the male dragon. He had been able to gain both altitude and time to plan his attack. He had, however, forgotten his rider. Verminaard—riding without the dragon saddle he used in battle—lost his grip on the dragon's neck and fell to the courtyard below. It was not a long drop and he landed uninjured, only bruised and momentarily shaken.

Most of the people around him fled in terror when they saw him rise to his feet, but—glancing around swiftly—he noticed that there were four, near the northern end of the courtyard, who did not flee. He turned to face those four.

The appearance of Matafleur and her sudden attack on Pyros jolted the captive people out of their state of panic. This, combined with the fall of Verminaard into their midst, like the fall of some horrifying god, accomplished what Elistan and the others had not. The people were shaken out of their fear, sense returned, and they began fleeing south, toward the safety of the mountains. At this sight, the draconian captain sent his forces pouring into the crowd. He detailed another messenger, a wyvern, to fly from the fortress to recall the army.

The draconians surged into the refugees, but, if they hoped to cause a panic, they failed. The people had suffered enough. They had allowed their freedom to be taken away once, in return for the promise of peace and safety. Now they understood that there could be no peace as long as these monsters roamed Krynn. The people of Solace and Gateway—men, women, and children—fought back using every pitiful weapon they could grab, rocks, stones, their own bare hands, teeth, and nails.

The companions became separated in the crowd. Laurana was cut off from everyone. Gilthanas had tried to stay near her, but he was carried off in the mob. The elfmaiden, more frightened than she believed possible and longing to hide, fell back against the wall of the fortress, her sword in her hand. As she watched the raging battle in horror, a man fell to the ground in front her, clutching his stomach, his fingers red with his own blood. His eyes fixed in death, seeming to stare at her, as his blood formed a pool at her feet. Laurana stared at the blood in horrid fascination, then she heard a sound in front of her. Shaking, she looked up—directly into the hideous, reptilian face of the man's killer.

The draconian, seeing an apparently terror-stricken elven female before him, figured on an easy kill. Licking its blood-stained sword with its long tongue, the creature jumped over the body of his victim and lunged for Laurana.

Clutching her sword, her throat aching with terror, Laurana reacted out of sheer defensive instinct. She stabbed blindly, jabbing upward. The draconian was caught totally off guard. Laurana plunged her weapon into the draconian's body, feeling the sharp elven blade penetrate both armor and flesh, hearing bone splinter and the creature's last gurgling scream. It turned to stone, yanking the sword from her hand. But Laurana, thinking with a cold detachment that amazed her, knew from hearing the warriors talk that if she waited a moment, the stone body would turn to dust, releasing her weapon.

The sounds of battle raged around her, the screams, the death cries, the thuds and groans, the clash of steel—but she heard none of it.

She waited calmly until she saw the body crumble. Then she reached down and, sifting the dust aside with her hand, she grasped the hilt of her sword and lifted it into the air. Sunlight flashed on the blood-stained blade, her enemy lay dead at her feet. She looked around but could not see Tanis. She could not see any of the others. For all she knew, they might be dead. For all she knew, she might herself be dead within the next moment.

Laurana lifted her eyes to the sun-drenched blue sky. The world she might soon be leaving seemed newly made—every object, every stone, every leaf stood out in painful clarity. A warm fragrant southern breeze sprang up, driving back the storm clouds that hung over her homeland to the north. Laurana's spirit, released from its prison of fear, soared higher than the clouds, and her sword flashed in the morning sun.

15

The Dragon Highlord.
Mataflour's children.

Verminaard studied the four men as they approached him. These were not slaves, he realized. Then he recognized them as the ones who traveled with the golden-haired cleric. These, then, were the ones who had defeated Onyx in Xak Tsaroth, escaped the slave caravan, and broken into Pax Tharkas. He felt as if he knew them—the knight from that broken land of past glories; a half-elf trying to pass himself off as human; a deformed, sickly magician; and the mage's twin—a human giant whose brain was probably as thick as his arms.

It will be an interesting fight, he thought. He almost welcomed hand-to-hand combat—it had been a long time. He was growing bored with commanding armies from the back of a dragon. Thinking of Ember, he glanced into the sky, wondering if he might be able to summon aid.

But it appeared that the red dragon was having his own problems. Matafleur had been fighting battles when Pyros was still in the egg; what she lacked in strength, she made up for in guile and cunning. The air crackled with flames, dragon blood dropped down like red rain.

Shrugging, Verminaard looked back at the four approaching him warily. He could hear the magic-user reminding his companions that Verminaard was a cleric of the Queen of Darkness and—as such—could call upon her aid. Verminaard knew from his spies that this magic-user, though young, was imbued with a strange power and considered very dangerous.

The four did not speak. There was no need for talk among these men, nor was there need for talk between enemies. Respect, grudging as it may be, was apparent on both sides. As for the battle rage, that was unnecessary. This would be fought coolly. The major victor would be death.

And so the four came forward, spreading to outflank him since he had nothing to set his back against. Crouching low, Verminaard swung Nightbringer in an arc, keeping them back, forming his plans. He must even the odds quickly. Gripping Nightbringer in his right hand, the evil cleric sprang forward from his crouched stance with all the strength in his powerful legs. His sudden move took his opponents by surprise. He did not raise his mace. All he needed now was his deadly touch. Landing on his feet in front of Raistlin, he reached out and grasped the magic-user by the shoulder, whispering a swift prayer to his Dark Queen.

Raistlin screamed. His body pierced by unseen, unholy weapons, he sank to the ground in agony. Caramon gave a great, bellowing roar and sprang at Verminaard, but the cleric was prepared. He swung the mace, Nightbringer, and struck the warrior a glancing blow. "Midnight," Verminaard whispered, and Caramon's bellow changed to a shout of panic as the spellbound mace blinded him.

"I can't see! Tanis, help me!" the big warrior cried, stumbling about. Verminaard, laughing grimly, struck him a solid blow to the head. Caramon went down like a felled ox.

Out of the corner of his eye, Verminaard saw the half-elf leap for him, a two-handed sword of ancient elvish design in his hands. Verminaard whirled, blocking Tanis's sword with

Nightbringer's massive, oaken handle. For a moment, the two combatants were locked together, but Verminaard's greater strength won out and he hurled Tanis to the ground.

The Solamnic knight raised his sword in salute—a costly mistake. It gave Verminaard time to remove a small iron needle from a hidden pocket. Raising it, he called once more upon the Queen of Darkness to defend her cleric. Sturm, striding forward, suddenly felt his body grow heavier and heavier until he could walk no more.

Tanis, lying on the ground, felt an unseen hand press down on him. He couldn't move. He couldn't turn his head. His tongue was too thick to speak. He could hear Raistlin's screams choke off in pain. He could hear Verminaard laugh and shout a hymn of praise to the Dark Queen. Tanis could only watch in despair as the Dragon Highlord, mace raised, walked toward Sturm, preparing to end the knight's life.

"*Baravais, Kharas!*" Verminaard said in Solamnic. He lifted the mace in a gruesome mockery of the knight's salute, then aimed for the knight's head, knowing that this death would be the most torturous possible for a knight—dying at the mercy of the enemy.

Suddenly a hand caught Verminaard's wrist. In astonishment, he stared at the hand, the hand of a female. He felt a power to match his own, a holiness to match his unholiness. At her touch, Verminaard's concentration wavered, his prayers to his Dark Queen faltered.

And then it was that the Dark Queen herself looked up to find a radiant god, dressed in white and shining armor, appear on the horizon of her plans. She was not ready to fight this god, she had not expected his return, and so she fled to rethink her options and restructure her battle, seeing—for the first time—the possibility of defeat. The Queen of Darkness withdrew and left her cleric to his fate.

Sturm felt the spell leave his body, his muscles his own to command once more. He saw Verminaard turn his fury on Goldmoon, striking at her savagely. The knight lunged forward, seeing Tanis rise, the elven sword flashing in the sunlight.

Both men ran toward Goldmoon, but Riverwind was there before them. Thrusting her out of the way, the Plainsman received on his sword arm the blow of the cleric's mace that had been intended to crush Goldmoon's head. Riverwind heard the cleric shout "Midnight!" and his vision was obscured by the same unholy darkness that had overtaken Caramon.

But the Que-shu warrior, expecting this, did not panic. Riverwind could still hear his enemy. Resolutely ignoring the pain of his injury, he transferred the sword to his left hand and stabbed in the direction of his enemy's harsh breathing. The blade, turned aside by the Dragon Highlord's powerful armor, was jarred from Riverwind's hand. Riverwind fumbled for his dagger, though he knew it was hopeless, that death was certain.

At that moment, Verminaard realized he was alone, bereft of spiritual help. He felt the cold, skeletal hand of despair clutch at him and he called to his Dark Queen. But she had turned away, absorbed in her own struggle.

Verminaard began to sweat beneath the dragonmask. He cursed it as the helm seemed to stifle him; he couldn't catch his breath. Too late he realized its unsuitableness for hand-to-hand combat—the mask blocked his peripheral vision. He saw the tall Plainsman, blind and wounded, before him—he could kill him at his leisure. But there were two other fighters near. The knight and the half-elf had been freed of the unholy spell he had cast on them and they were coming closer. He could hear them. Catching a glimpse of movement, he turned quickly and saw the half-elf running toward him, the elvish blade glistening. But where was the knight? Verminaard turned and backed up, swinging his mace to keep them at bay, while with his free hand, he struggled to rip the dragonhelm from his head.

Too late. Just as Verminaard's hand closed over the visor, the magic blade of Kith-Kanan pierced his armor and slid into his back. The Dragon Highlord screamed and whirled in rage, only to see the Solamnic knight appear in his blood-dimmed vision. The ancient blade of Sturm's fathers plunged into his bowels. Verminaard fell to his knees. Still he struggled to remove the helm—he couldn't breathe, he couldn't see. He felt another sword thrust, then darkness overtook him.

High overhead, a dying Matafleur—weakened by loss of blood and many wounds—heard the voices of her children crying to her. She was confused and disoriented: Pyros seemed to be attacking from every direction at once. Then the big red dragon was before her, against the wall of the mountain. Matafleur saw her chance. She would save her children.

Pyros breathed a great blast of flame directly into the face of the ancient red dragon. He watched in satisfaction as the head withered, the eyes melted.

But Matafleur ignored the flames that seared her eyes, forever ending her vision, and flew straight at Pyros.

The big male dragon, his mind clouded by fury and pain and thinking he had finished his enemy, was taken by surprise. Even as he breathed again his deadly fire, he realized with horror the position he was in—he had allowed Matafleur to maneuver him between herself and the sheer face of the mountain. He had nowhere to go, no room to turn.

Matafleur soared into him with all the force of her once-powerful body, striking him like a spear hurled by the gods. Both dragons slammed against the mountain. The peak trembled and split apart as the face of the mountain exploded in flames.

In later years when the Death of Flamestrike was legend, there were those who claimed to have heard a dragon's voice fade away like smoke on an autumn wind, whispering:

"My children . . . "

The Wedding

he last day of autumn dawned clear and bright. The air was warm—touched by the fragrant wind from the south, which had blown steadily ever since the refugees fled Pax Tharkas, taking with them only what they could scrounge from the fortress as they fled the wrath of the dragonarmies.

It had taken long days for the draconian army to scale the walls of Pax Tharkas, its gates blocked by boulders, its towers defended by gully dwarves. Led by Sestun, the gully dwarves stood on top of the walls throwing rocks, dead rats, and occasionally each other down on the frustrated draconians. This allowed the refugees time to escape into the mountains where, although they skirmished with small forces of draconians, they were not seriously threatened.

Flint volunteered to lead a party of men through the mountains, searching for a place where the people could spend the winter. These mountains were familiar to Flint since the hill dwarves' homeland was not far to the south. Flint's party discovered a valley nestled between vast, craggy peaks whose treacherous passes were choked with snow in the winter. The passes could be easily held against the might of the dragonarmies and there were caves where they could hide from the fury of the dragons.

Following a dangerous path, the refugees fled into the mountains and entered the valley. An avalanche soon blocked the route behind them and destroyed all trace of their passing. It would be months before the draconians discovered them.

The valley, far below the mountain peaks, was warm and sheltered from the harsh winter winds and snows. The woods were filled with game. Clear streams flowed from the mountains. The people mourned their dead, rejoiced in their deliverance, built shelters, and celebrated a wedding.

On the last day of autumn, as the sun set behind the mountains, kindling their snow-capped peaks with flame the color of dying dragons, Riverwind and Goldmoon were married.

When the two came to Elistan to ask him to preside over their exchange of vows, he had been deeply honored and had asked them to explain the ways of their people to him. Both of them replied steadily that their people were dead. The Que-shu were gone, their ways were no more.

"This will be *our* ceremony," Riverwind said. "The beginning of something new, not the continuation of that which has passed away."

"Though we will honor the memory of our people in our hearts," Goldmoon added softly, "we must look forward, not behind. We will honor the past by taking from it the good and the sorrowful that have made us what we are. But the past shall rule us no longer."

Elistan, therefore, studied the Disks of Mishakal to find what the ancient gods taught about marriage. He asked Goldmoon and Riverwind to write their own vows, searching their hearts for the true meaning of their love—for these vows would be spoken before the gods and last beyond death.

One custom of the Que-shu the couple kept. This was that the bridegift and the groomgift could not be purchased. This symbol of love must be made by the hand of the beloved. The gifts would be exchanged with the saying of the vows.

As the sun's rays spread across the sky, Elistan took his place on the top of a gentle rise. The people gathered in silence at the foot of the hill. From the east came Tika and Laurana, bearing torches. Behind them walked Goldmoon, Chieftain's Daughter. Her hair fell down around her shoulders in streams of molten gold, mingled with silver. Her head was crowned with autumn leaves. She wore the simple fringed doeskin tunic she had worn through their adventures. The medallion of Mishakal glittered at her throat. She carried her bridegift wrapped in a cloth as fine as cobweb, for the beloved one's eyes must be the first to see it.

Tika walked before her in solemn, misty-eyed wonder, the young girl's heart filled with dreams of her own, beginning to think that this great mystery shared by men and women might not be the terrifying experience she had feared, but something sweet and beautiful.

Laurana, next to Tika, held her torch high, brightening the day's dying light. The people murmured at Goldmoon's beauty; they fell silent when Laurana passed. Goldmoon was human, her beauty the beauty of the trees and mountains and

432

skies. Laurana's beauty was elvish, otherworldly, mysterious.

The two women brought the bride to Elistan, then they turned, looking to the west, waiting for the groom.

A blaze of torches lit Riverwind's way. Tanis and Sturm, their solemn faces wistful and gentle, led. Riverwind came behind, towering over the others, his face stern as always. But a radiant joy, brighter than the torches, lit his eyes. His black hair was crowned with autumn leaves, his groomgift covered by one of Tasslehoff's handkerchiefs. Behind him walked Flint and the kender. Caramon and Raistlin came last, the mage bearing the lighted-crystal Staff of Magius instead of a torch.

The men brought the groom to Elistan, then stepped back to join the women. Tika found herself standing next to Caramon. Reaching out timidly, she touched his hand. Smiling down at her gently, he clasped her little hand in his big one.

As Elistan looked at Riverwind and Goldmoon, he thought of the terrible grief and fear and danger they had faced, the harshness of their lives. Did their future hold anything different? For a moment he was overcome and could not speak. The two, seeing Elistan's emotion and, perhaps, understanding his sorrow, reached out to him reassuringly. Elistan drew them close to him, whispering words for them alone.

"It was your love and your faith in each other that brought hope to the world. Each of you was willing to sacrifice your life for this promise of hope, each has saved the life of the other. The sun shines now, but already its rays are dimming and night is ahead. It is the same for you, my friends. You will walk through much darkness before morning. But your love will be as a torch to light the way."

Elistan then stepped back and began to speak to all assembled. His voice, husky to begin with, grew stronger and stronger as he felt the peace of the gods surround him and confirm their blessings on this couple.

"The left hand is the hand of the heart," he said, placing Goldmoon's left hand in Riverwind's left hand and holding his own left hand over them. "We join left hands that the love in the hearts of this man and this woman may combine to form something greater as two streams join together to form a mighty river. The river flows through the land, branching off into tributaries, exploring new ways, yet ever drawn to the eternal sea. Receive their love, Paladine—greatest of the gods; bless it and grant them peace at least in the hearts, if there is no peace in this shattered land."

In the blessed silence, husbands and wives put their arms around each other. Friends drew close, children quieted and crept near their parents. Hearts filled with mourning were comforted. Peace was granted.

"Pledge your vows, one to another," Elistan said, "and exchange the gifts of your hands and hearts."

Goldmoon looked into Riverwind's eyes and began to speak softly.

> Wars have settled on the North
> and dragons ride the skies,
> "Now is the time for wisdom,"
> say the wise and the nearly wise.
> "Here in the heart of battle,
> the time to be brave is at hand.
> Now most things are larger than
> the promise of woman to man."

> But you and I, through burning plains,
> through darkness of the earth,
> affirm this world, its people,
> the heavens that gave them birth,
> the breath that passes between us,
> this altar where we stand,
> and all those things made larger by
> the promise of woman to man.

Then Riverwind spoke:

> Now in the belly of winter,
> when ground and sky are gray,
> here in the heart of sleeping snow,
> now is the time to say
> yes to the sprouting vallenwood
> in the green countryside,
> for these things are far larger than
> a man's word to his bride.

Through these promises we keep,
forged in the yawning night,
proved in the presence of heroes
and the prospect of spring light,
the children will see moons and stars
where now the dragons ride,
and humble things made large by
a man's word to his bride.

When the vows were spoken, they exchanged gifts. Goldmoon shyly handed her present to Riverwind. He unwrapped it with hands that trembled. It was a ring plaited of her own hair, bound with bands of silver and of gold as fine as the hair they surrounded. Goldmoon had given Flint her mother's jewelry; the dwarf's old hands had not lost their touch.

In the wreckage of Solace, Riverwind had found a vallenwood branch spared by the dragon's fire and had carried it in his pack. Now that branch made Riverwind's gift to Goldmoon—a ring, perfectly smooth and plain. When polished, the wood of the tree was a rich gold color, marked by streaks and whorls of softest brown. Goldmoon, holding it, remembered the first night she had seen the great vallenwoods, the night they had stumbled—weary and frightened—into Solace, bearing the blue crystal staff. She began to cry softly and wiped her eyes with Tas's handkerchief.

"Bless the gifts, Paladine," Elistan said, "these symbols of love and sacrifice. Grant that during times of deepest darkness, these two may look upon these gifts and see their path lighted by love. Great and shining god, god of human and elf, god of kender and dwarf, give your blessing to these, your children. May the love they plant in their hearts today be nourished by their souls and grow into a tree of life, providing shelter and protection to all who seek refuge beneath its spreading boughs. With the joining of hands, the exchanging of vows, the giving of gifts, you two, Riverwind, grandson of Wanderer, and Goldmoon, Chieftain's Daughter—become one—in your hearts, in the sight of men, in the eyes of the gods."

Riverwind took his ring from Goldmoon and placed it upon her slender finger. Goldmoon took her ring from Riverwind.

He knelt before her—as would have been the custom of the Que-shu. But Goldmoon shook her head.

"Rise, warrior," she said, smiling through her tears.

"Is that a command?" he asked softly.

"It is the last command of Chieftain's Daughter," she whispered.

Riverwind stood up. Goldmoon placed the golden ring on his finger. Then Riverwind took her in his arms. She put her arms around him. Their lips met, their bodies melded together, their spirits joined. The people gave a great shout and torches flared. The sun sank behind the mountains, leaving the sky bathed in a pearl-like hue of purples and soft reds, which soon deepened into the sapphire of night.

The bride and groom were carried down the hill by the cheering throng and feasting and merriment began. Huge tables, carved from the pine trees of the forest, were set up on the grass. The children, freed at last from the awe of the ceremony, ran and shouted, playing at dragon slaying. Tonight care and worry were far from their minds. Men broached the huge casks of ale and wine they had salvaged in Pax Tharkas and began drinking salutes to the bride and groom. Women brought in huge plates of food—game and fruits and vegetables gathered in the forest and taken from the stores in Pax Tharkas.

"Get out of my way, don't crowd me," Caramon grumbled as he sat down at the table. The companions, laughing, moved over to give the big man room. Maritta and two other women came forward and placed a huge platter of deer meat before the big warrior.

"Real food," sighed the warrior.

"Hey," roared Flint, stabbing at a piece of sizzling meat on Caramon's plate with his fork, "you gonna eat that?"

Caramon promptly and silently—without missing a bite—emptied a flagon of ale over the dwarf's head.

Tanis and Sturm sat side by side, talking quietly. Tanis's eyes strayed to Laurana occasionally. She sat at a different table talking animatedly with Elistan. Tanis, thinking how lovely she looked tonight, realized how changed she was from the willful, lovesick girl who had followed him from Qualinesti. He told himself he liked the change in her. But he caught himself wondering just what she and Elistan found so interesting.

Sturm touched his arm. Tanis started. He had lost track of the conversation. Flushing, he began to apologize when he saw the look on Sturm's face.

"What is it?" Tanis said in alarm, half-rising.

"Hush, don't move!" Sturm ordered. "Just look—over there—sitting off to himself."

Tanis looked where Sturm gestured, puzzled, then he saw the man—sitting alone, hunched over his food, eating it absently as if he didn't really taste it. Whenever anyone approached, the man shrank back, eyeing him nervously until he passed. Suddenly, perhaps sensing Tanis's eyes on him, he raised his head and stared directly at them. The half-elf gasped and dropped his fork.

"But that's impossible!" he said in a strangled voice. "We saw him die! With Eben! No one could have survived—"

"Then I was right," Sturm said grimly. "You recognize him, too. I thought I was going mad. Let's go talk to him."

But when they looked again, he was gone. Swiftly, they searched the crowd, but it was impossible to find him now.

As the silver moon and the red rose in the sky, the married couples formed a ring around the bride and groom and began singing wedding songs. Unmarried couples danced in pairs outside the circle while the children leaped and shouted and reveled in staying up past their bedtime. Bonfires burned brightly, voices and music filled the night air, the silver moon and the red rose to light the sky. Goldmoon and Riverwind stood, their arms around each other, their eyes shining brighter than the moons or the blazing fire.

Tanis lingered on the outskirts, watching his friends. Laurana and Gilthanas performed an ancient elvish dance of grace and beauty, singing together a hymn of joy. Sturm and Elistan fell into conversation about their plans to travel south in search of the legendary seaport city of Tarsis the Beautiful, where they hoped to find ships to carry the people from this war-torn land. Tika, tired of watching Caramon eat, teased Flint until the dwarf finally agreed to dance with her, blushing bright red beneath his beard.

Where was Raistlin? Tanis wondered. The half-elf recalled seeing him at the banquet. The mage ate little and drank his herbal mixture. He had seemed unusually pale and quiet.

Tanis decided to go in search of him. The company of the dark-souled, cynical mage seemed more suited to him tonight than music and laughter.

Tanis wandered into the moonlit darkness, knowing somehow he was headed in the right direction. He found Raistlin sitting on the stump of an old tree whose lightning-shattered, blackened remains lay scattered over the ground. The half-elf sat down next to the silent mage.

A small shadow settled among the trees behind the half-elf. Finally, Tas would hear what these two discussed!

Raistlin's strange eyes stared into the southlands, barely visible between a gap in the tall mountains. The wind still blew from the south, but it was beginning to veer again. The temperature was falling. Tanis felt Raistlin's frail body shiver. Looking at him in the moonlight, Tanis was startled to see the mage's resemblance to his half-sister, Kitiara. It was a fleeting impression and gone almost as soon as it came, but it brought the woman to Tanis's mind, adding to his feelings of unrest and disquiet. He restlessly tossed a piece of bark back and forth, from hand to hand.

"What do you see to the south?" Tanis asked abruptly.

Raistlin glanced at him. "What do I ever see with these eyes of mine, Half-Elf?" the mage whispered bitterly. "I see death, death and destruction. I see war." He gestured up above. "The constellations have not returned. The Queen of Darkness is not defeated."

"We may not have won the war," Tanis began, "but surely we have won a major battle—"

Raistlin coughed and shook his head sadly.

"Do you see no hope?"

"Hope is the denial of reality. It is the carrot dangled before the draft horse to keep him plodding along in a vain attempt to reach it."

"Are you saying we should just give up?" Tanis asked, irritably tossing the bark away.

"I'm saying we should remove the carrot and walk forward with our eyes open," Raistlin answered. Coughing, he drew his robes more closely around him. "How will you fight the dragons, Tanis? For there will be more! More than you can imagine! And where now is Huma? Where now is the Dragonlance? No,

Half-Elf. Do not talk to me of hope."

Tanis did not answer, nor did the mage speak again. Both sat silently, one continuing to stare south, the other glancing up into the great voids in the glittering, starlit sky.

Tasslehoff sank back into the soft grass beneath the pine trees. "No hope!" the kender repeated bleakly, sorry he had followed the half-elf. "I don't believe it," he said, but his eyes went to Tanis, staring at the stars. Tanis believes it, the kender realized, and the thought filled him with dread.

Ever since the death of the old magician, an unnoticed change had come over the kender. Tasslehoff began to consider that this adventure was in earnest, that it had a purpose for which people gave their lives. He wondered why he was involved and thought perhaps he had given the answer to Fizban—the small things he was meant to do were important, somehow, in the big scheme of things.

But until now it had never occurred to the kender that all this might be for nothing, that it might not make any difference, that they might suffer and lose people they loved like Fizban, and the dragons would still win in the end.

"Still," the kender said softly, "we have to keep trying and hoping. That's what's important, the trying and the hoping. Maybe that's most important of all."

Something floated gently down from the sky, brushing past the kender's nose. Tas reached out and caught it in his hand.

It was a small, white chicken feather.

The "Song of Huma" was the last, and many consider the greatest, work of the elven bard, Quivalen Soth. Only fragments of the work remained following the Cataclysm. It is said that those who study it diligently will find hints to the future of the turning world.

SONG OF HUMA

Out of the village, out of the thatched and clutching shires,
Out of the grave and furrow, furrow and grave,
Where his sword first tried
The last cruel dances of childhood, and awoke to the shires
Forever retreating, his greatness a marshfire,
The banked flight of the Kingfisher always above him,
Now Huma walked upon Roses,
In the level Light of the Rose.
And troubled by Dragons, he turned to the end of the land,
To the fringe of all sense and senses,
To the Wilderness, where Paladine bade him to turn,
And there in the loud tunnel of knives
He grew in unblemished violence, in yearning,
Stunned into himself by a deafening gauntlet of voices.

It was there and then that the White Stag found him,
At the end of a journey planned from the shores of Creation,
And all time staggered at the forest edge
Where Huma, haunted and starving,
Drew his bow, thanking the gods for their bounty
and keeping,
Then saw, in the ranged wood,
In the first silence, the dazed heart's symbol,
The rack of antlers resplendent.
He lowered the bow and the world resumed.
Then Huma followed the Stag, its tangle of antlers receding
As a memory of young light, as the talons of birds ascending.

The Mountains crouched before them. Nothing would
change now,
The three moons stopped in the sky,
And the long night tumbled in shadows.

It was morning when they reached the grove,
The lap of the mountain, where the Stag departed,
Nor did Huma follow, knowing the end of this journey
Was nothing but green and the promise of green
that endured
In the eyes of the woman before him.
And holy the days he drew near her, holy the air
That carried his words of endearment, his forgotten songs,
And the rapt moons knelt on the Great Mountain.
Still, she eluded him, bright and retreating as marshfire,
Nameless and lovely, more lovely because she was nameless,
As they learned that the world, the dazzling shelves
of the air,
The Wilderness itself
Were plain and diminished things to the heart's thicket.
At the end of the days, she told him her secret.

For she was not of woman, nor was she mortal,
But the daughter and heiress from a line of Dragons.
For Huma the sky turned indifferent, cluttered by moons,
The brief life of the grass mocked him, mocked his fathers,
And the thorned light bristled on the gliding Mountain.
But nameless she tendered a hope not in her keeping,
That Paladine only might answer, that through his
enduring wisdom
She might step from forever, and there in her silver arms
The promise of the grove might rise and flourish.
For that wisdom Huma prayed, and the Stag returned,
And east, through the desolate fields, through ash,
Through cinders and blood, the harvest of dragons,
Traveled Huma, cradled by dreams of the Silver Dragon,
The Stag perpetual, a signal before him.

At last the eventual harbor, a temple so far to the east
That it lay where the east was ending.

There Paladine appeared
In a pool of stars and glory, announcing
That of all choices, one most terrible had fallen to Huma.
For Paladine knew that the heart is a nest of yearnings,
That we can travel forever toward light, becoming
What we can never be.
For the bride of Huma could step into the devouring sun,
Together they would return to the thatched shires
And leave behind the secret of the Lance, the world
Unpeopled in darkness, wed to the dragons.
Or Huma could take on the Dragonlance, cleansing
all Krynn
Of death and invasion, of the green paths of his love.

The hardest of choices, and Huma remembered
How the Wilderness cloistered and baptized his first
thoughts
Beneath the sheltering sun, and now
As the black moon wheeled and pivoted, drawing the air
And the substance from Krynn, from the things of Krynn,
From the grove, from the Mountain, from the abandoned
shires,
He would sleep, he would send it all away,
For the choosing was all of the pain, and the choices
Were heat on the hand when the arm has been severed.
But she came to him, weeping and luminous,
In a landscape of dreams, where he saw
The world collapse and renew on the glint of the Lance.
In her farewell lay collapse and renewal.
Through his doomed veins the horizon burst.

He took up the Dragonlance, he took up the story,
The pale heat rushed through his rising arm
And the sun and the three moons, waiting for wonders,
Hung in the sky together.
To the West Huma rode, to the High Clerist's Tower
On the back of the Silver Dragon,
And the path of their flight crossed over a desolate country
Where the dead walked only, mouthing the names
of dragons.

And the men in the Tower, surrounded and riddled
by dragons,
By the cries of the dying, the roar in the ravenous air,
Awaited the unspeakable silence,
Awaited far worse, in fear that the crash of the senses
Would end in a moment of nothing
Where the mind lies down with its losses and darkness.

But the winding of Huma's horn in the distance
Danced on the battlements. All of Solamnia lifted
Its face to the eastern sky, and the dragons
Wheeled to the highest air, believing
Some terrible change had come.
From out of their tumult of wings, out of the chaos
of dragons,
Out of the heart of nothing, the Mother of Night,
Aswirl in a blankness of colors,
Swooped to the East, into the stare of the sun
And the sky collapsed into silver and blankness.
On the ground Huma lay, at his side a woman,
Her silver skin broken, the promise of green
Released from the gifts of her eyes. She whispered her name
As the Queen of Darkness banked in the sky above Huma.
She descended, the Mother of Night,
And from the loft of the battlements, men saw shadows
Boil on the colorless dive of her wings:
A hovel of thatch and rushes, the heart of a Wilderness,
A lost silver light spattered in terrible crimson,
And then from the center of shadows
Came a depth in which darkness itself was aglimmer,
Denying all air, all light, all shadows.
And thrusting his lance into emptiness,
Huma fell to the sweetness of death, into abiding sunlight.
Through the Lance, through the dear might and
brotherhood
Of those who must walk to the end of the breath
and the senses,
He banished the dragons back to the core of nothing,
And the long lands blossomed in balance and music.

443

Stunned in new freedom, stunned by the brightness
and colors,
By the harped blessing of the holy winds,
The Knights carried Huma, they carried the Dragonlance
To the grove in the lap of the Mountain.
When they returned to the grove in pilgrimage, in homage,
The Lance, the armor, the Dragonbane himself
Had vanished to the day's eye.
But the night of the full moons red and silver
Shines down on the hills, on the forms of a man
and a woman
Shimmering steel and silver, silver and steel,
Above the village, over the thatched and nurturing shires.